**Praise for the Novels of
Diana Pharaoh Francis**

The Cipher

"Francis has crafted an original world, real people, and high-stakes intrigue and adventure. Great fun."
—Patricia Briggs, *New York Times* bestselling author

"Lucy is as engaging a character as I've met in a long time." —Lynn Flewelling

"The first in a fascinating new series by Diana Pharaoh Francis, and so far, it's shaping up to be a remarkably intriguing twist on the usual fantasy setting.... It's a refreshing change of pace, and a setting that seems ripe for exploration.... This is definitely a fantasy to look out for." —The Green Man Review

"So well described that readers will believe that they're in the midst of the storm that opens the book.... Intrigue, action, and a bit of romance make for a highly satisfying story." —*Romantic Times*

"Intriguing fantasy ... a delightful read.... Genre fans will enjoy Diana Pharaoh Francis's fine character-driven saga." —Baryon Magazine

continued ...

Path of Blood

"Excellent characterizations, intriguing political maneuvering, and some fascinating battle scenes, both mundane and magical, make this sword and sorcery tale a must-read for fans of Katherine Kurtz's Deryni Chronicles." —*Midwest Book Review*

"A glorious conclusion ... many surprises and plot twists ... some so delightfully shocking and incredible that they will stun the reader as they are cleverly worked into the book and provide the unexpected." —*SFRevu*

Path of Honor

"A stubborn, likable heroine." —Kristen Britain

"Well plotted and exhibiting superior characterization, [*Path of Honor*] is definitely a worthy sequel." —*Booklist*

Path of Fate

"Plausible, engrossing characters, a well-designed world, and a well-realized plot." —*Booklist*

"This is an entertaining book—at times compelling—from one of fantasy's promising new voices." —David B. Coe, award-winning author of *Seeds of Betrayal*

Other Novels
by Diana Pharaoh Francis

Novels of Crosspointe
The Cipher
The Black Ship

The Path Novels
Path of Blood
Path of Honor
Path of Fate

THE
TURNING TIDE

A NOVEL OF CROSSPOINTE

Diana Pharaoh Francis

A ROC BOOK

ROC

Published by New American Library, a division of
Penguin Group (USA) Inc., 375 Hudson Street,
New York, New York 10014, USA
Penguin Group (Canada), 90 Eglinton Avenue East, Suite 700, Toronto,
Ontario M4P 2Y3, Canada (a division of Pearson Penguin Canada Inc.)
Penguin Books Ltd., 80 Strand, London WC2R 0RL, England
Penguin Ireland, 25 St. Stephen's Green, Dublin 2,
Ireland (a division of Penguin Books Ltd.)
Penguin Group (Australia), 250 Camberwell Road, Camberwell, Victoria 3124,
Australia (a division of Pearson Australia Group Pty. Ltd.)
Penguin Books India Pvt. Ltd., 11 Community Centre, Panchsheel Park,
New Delhi - 110 017, India
Penguin Group (NZ), 67 Apollo Drive, Rosedale, North Shore 0632,
New Zealand (a division of Pearson New Zealand Ltd.)
Penguin Books (South Africa) (Pty.) Ltd., 24 Sturdee Avenue,
Rosebank, Johannesburg 2196, South Africa

Penguin Books Ltd., Registered Offices:
80 Strand, London WC2R 0RL, England

First published by Roc, an imprint of New American Library,
a division of Penguin Group (USA) Inc.

First Printing, May 2009
10 9 8 7 6 5 4 3 2 1

For Tony, Q-ball, and Princess Caesar

Acknowledgments

Welcome, my friends, to this glorious realm where I get to romp merrily across the pages, telling lies and truths and wallowing in wonder and magic. Thank you—*thank you!*—to all of you who read my books and keep coming back.

Thanks also go to Lucienne Diver, Jessica Wade, Paul Youll, Cortney Skinner, and all the rare and wondrous folks at Roc who magically turn my words into a lovely book and then put them into readers' hands.

Thanks to Melissa Sawmiller, Christy Keyes, and Kenna and Megan Glasscock for being my guinea pig readers as I draft books. They read the dreck and help me polish it into gold. They also cheer me on and make me laugh and generally do not allow me to take myself too seriously.

Thanks to my LiveJournal buds who visit my blog and remind me that I don't write in a vacuum. (Come hang out with me yourself! http://difrancis.livejournal.com.)

For lots more about Crosspointe and my other books, come visit my Web site at www.dianapfrancis.com.

And lastly, I wouldn't be able to write books without the patience and support of my family.

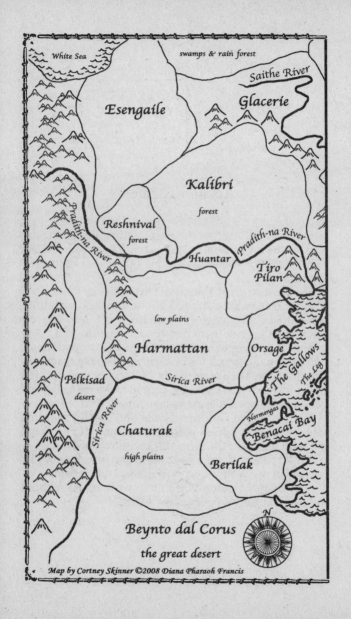

White Sea

swamps & rain forest

Saithe River

Esengaile

Glacerie

Kalibri

forest

Reshnival

forest

Pradith-na River

Huantar

Pradith-na River

Tiro Pilan

low plains

Harmattan

Orsage

The Gallows

The Leg

Pelkisad

desert

Sirica River

Sirica River

Chaturak

high plains

Normengas

Benacai Bay

Berilak

Beynto dal Corus

the great desert

N

Map by Cortney Skinner ©2008 Diana Pharaoh Francis

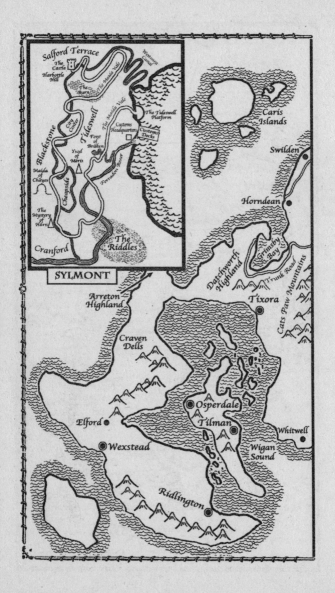

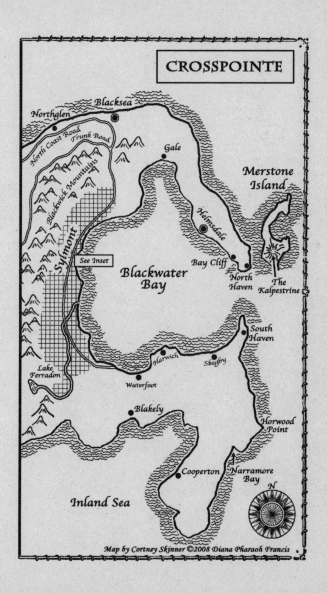

CROSSPOINTE

Northglen
Blacksea
North Coast Road
Trunk Road
Blackwick Mountains
Gale
Sylmont
Halmsdale
Merstone Island
See Inset
Blackwater Bay
Bay Cliff
North Haven
The Kalpestrine
South Haven
Lake Ferradon
Harwich
Skegby
Waterfoot
Blakely
Horwood Point
Cooperton
Narramore Bay
N
Inland Sea

Map by Cortney Skinner ©2008 Diana Pharaoh Francis

Chapter 1

"You'll chew your fingers off if you keep gnawing at them like that," Shaye said laconically to Fairlie. "I'm guessing," he continued from where he leaned against a tall cabinet, his arms crossed over his chest, "that you may want the use of them in the future. It would be difficult to do your work without them."

Fairlie gave him a baleful look. "It's not like I have anything better to do."

She thrust suddenly to her feet with a sound of frustration, knocking her stool over with a clatter. "They've been knackering in there more than a glass. What can they possibly have to talk about? Yes or no—perfectly simple," she said, stomping down a crooked aisle inside her cramped workroom, her heavy boots thumping on the slate floor. It hardly seemed possible that this crammed-to-the-rafters room was fully as large as her forge on the other side of the obstinately closed doors.

The outer workroom contained an array of tables, workbenches, shelves, and cupboards, most of which were heaped with the detritus of her trade: tools, wire, metal scraps, rags, buckets, boxes, casks, ropes, chains, leather aprons and gloves, shards of glass, *sylveth* and precious stones, and a thousand other little bits and oddments that Fairlie had collected in the expectation that someday they would be useful. She never threw anything away.

There was an unusual chill in the air. Outdoors, the

winter held on with a desperate grasp, and she'd not yet been allowed into her forge to stir the coals today. Her fingers flexed. She felt invaded, even though she'd invited the guild to evaluate her work. She was nearly ready to toss them all out on their asses.

"What is taking so cracking long?" she grumbled again when Shaye remained silent. She dug her hands deep in her pockets and balled them into fists.

"They have to make a good show of it," he said with aggravating equanimity. "Wouldn't do to pronounce you master metalsmith without deep ruminations and end-less blatherings to prove that they took your applica-tion seriously enough. They at least have to pretend to consider, though clearly the sculpture is unequivocally without compare."

Fairlie narrowed her eyes at Shaye, suspecting that he was mocking her. He was one of her two best friends, and yet it wasn't often easy to tell when he was being serious or sardonic. Usually he didn't turn the sharp end of his wit against her, since as a result she was just as likely as not to dribble molten metal on his foot, and he disliked it when she resorted to such defenses. Of course, since that first time, he'd taken care to always wear majicked boots when in her workroom. Now he held up his hands as if in surrender, his sleepy brows rising in innocence, though whether real or feigned, Fairlie couldn't decide.

"It is absolutely the truth," he said. "Your work is superlative—no sane person could possibly argue other-wise. Of all the living masters, you are certainly the finest, and in time you will outshine everyone who came before you. That much is obvious. But they have the politics of the guild to consider. Making you a master so young is nearly unheard of in any crafts guild, and add in the fact that your sponsor is the crown—the politics are a quag-mire. They don't want to gain a reputation of peddling favors to the crown. They must appear like they've been exceedingly stringent. But even if they err on the side of raising the criteria only for you, still they cannot set any standard so high that they can refuse your petition."

"You aren't usually so forgiving of politics and maneuverings," Fairlie said, warmth for his words steadying her nerves. Even so, she could not believe him. She knew the sculpture was good—but she could see its flaws as clearly as if they were lighthouse beacons. The guildmasters would surely see them as well. "In fact, you downright despise them. So why are you being so patient with them?"

"Perhaps I'm turning over a new leaf."

Fairlie snorted. "I'll believe that when the sea turns pink." She waved away the digression and returned to the subject foremost on her mind. "But say that you're right. They could just as well refuse me the badge and tell me to try again later."

"No. They cannot." He rubbed a finger over his *illidre*. It was flame-colored, with brilliant flickers of orange, red, yellow, and edged with hints of blue and purple. Made from worked *sylveth*, it was fashioned in an elegant swirl, like living fire. It was a focus for majick, allowing him to perform higher majicks than he could without it. Slowly he said, "If they did refuse you, they would not like what I would do in return."

Fairlie stared. There wasn't the slightest hint of a smile on his thin face, and his gaze was smoldering and implacable. She shook her head. Why was she surprised? He was a majicar and a Weverton and between the two, more powerful than any one man ought to be. And he wasn't afraid to use his power to his own ends. But not this time. She wagged a blunt, scarred finger at him.

"No. No matter what happens, don't even think it. I want to earn this on my own. You tormenting them with majick isn't going to help."

He shrugged, one shoulder lifting and falling. "Possibly. Possibly not. But they will learn the cost of letting politics interfere with what's right."

Fairlie rolled her eyes. "Now that's the Shaye I know. So much for a new leaf. But this isn't about right and wrong. This is a guild matter and it isn't any of your business."

She came to stand in front of him, putting her hands on her hips. He was about six feet tall, and she barely came to his chin. She looked up at him, annoyed at him for being so large.

"I'm telling you, Shaye. I want you to stay out of it. I'm not a child needing a rescue. I can take care of myself."

He made another little shrug, his mouth compressing into a thin line, his dark eyes gleaming hard and bright.

"I mean it, Shaye . . . ," Fairlie said as warning.

"Do not ask me to do nothing," he said, straightening with violent energy, his long, bony fingers flexing. "I do not have so many friends that I'm willing to sit by and watch while one is wronged. Not when I can do something about it."

"This is my battle," she said softly. She'd leaned on his strength since she'd first come to Sylmont as a child—she'd leaned on him and Ryland. But since Ryland had begun traveling the Inland Sea on diplomatic missions for his father, the king, Shaye had adopted the role of Fairlie's protector. She'd never had to stand on her own two feet. Of late, that had been bothering her, especially as she got closer to achieving her master's badge and Shaye made no progress toward his. That was her fault. She'd taken all his time and attention, bullying him into helping her in the forge. But that was about to end.

"That reminds me," she said, broaching the subject she'd been hesitating to raise for several sennights. She looked down, twisting her fingers together. They were hashed with scars and speckled with splinters of steel and *sylveth*. The latter sent a chill trickling down her spine. She quelled it. Everyone knew that worked *sylveth* was safe. She dropped her hands to her sides, flattening her palms against her thighs. "Whether or not they award me a master's badge, I've decided to go home."

"Home?" he repeated, his dark brows winging downward ominously. "This is your home."

"It's time I went back to Stanton. I haven't been back since Toff first brought me here. My mother's last letter said she was growing more feeble. She wants to see me."

"How long do you plan to stay there?"

Fairlie looked away. This was harder than she'd thought. She didn't really want to leave. She would miss him and Ryland unbearably, not to mention the bustling, cosmopolitan Sylmont and her forge. But she did need to go home and see her mother, and Shaye needed time to work on his master's badge. "I thought perhaps until next spring."

"Next spring? But that's more than a year," he said incredulously.

"And Ryland says that you never learned anything from your tutors," Fairlie taunted with a sharp smile.

"You can't be serious about this. What could you possibly find to do in that backwater town for that long? You'll be Pale-blasted within a month."

"I am serious. My mother wants to see me."

"She sure as the black depths was in a hurry to get rid of you when Toff came around," he snarled.

It was true. Fairlie had been a wild, undisciplined child. Very difficult to manage. Her mother had told her so frequently, as had most everyone in Stanton. She was always running off to the smithy or dangling about a tinker's cart or climbing up on rooftops or playing in a fire. It was an accepted fact that she *would* burn down her mother's house and likely half the village before she was ten. In fact she had come fairly close, lighting her mother's chimney aflame. Luckily, it was easily doused before much damage could be done.

So it was little surprise that when Toff arrived and offered to take Fairlie as his apprentice with no expectations of a fee, Fairlie's mother happily sent her nine-seasons-old daughter packing with hardly even a kiss. Fairlie could not forget that last expression on her mother's face as she drove away with Toff—it had been relief. Fairlie soon forgot it in her delight at learning what Toff had to teach her. He was gruff and hearty and boisterous in nearly all that he did. He did not remonstrate

against her instincts for fire and danger. He laughed
and encouraged her, no matter how underfoot she was,
no matter how risky the enterprises she decided to un-
dertake. He had been her father and mother both, and
Ryland and Shaye her brothers. It had been all the family Fairlie needed. Between them and her work, she was
supremely happy.

And then Toff had died, nine months since. For the
first time, she was truly on her own. And despite her
grief, she'd found she liked making her own choices. But
her mother's letter had reminded her of what she'd left
behind. She *did* want to go home again. A more than
small part of Fairlie wanted to show off what she'd become. Another part of her wanted to go back and look
again on where she'd come from. Now was an ideal time
to go.

She met Shaye's gaze squarely. "If your family cut you
off for every poor decision you made, you would be a
penniless orphan. She's my mother, and she wants to see
me. I want to see her as well. Sending me with Toff was
a priceless gift."

"She didn't know that," Shaye growled.

"No, but it was the result. I have always believed she
wanted the best for me, and sending me with the crown's
metalsmith was an opportunity she could never have
dreamed of." She hesitated. "While I'm gone, you won't
have me bothering you all the time. You can work on
getting your master's badge."

He stiffened, his chin lifting, his nostrils flaring haugh-
tily. "What makes you think I have not time to do both?"

Fairlie gave a little shrug and looked pointedly at his
illidre. As beautiful as it was, Shaye had not made it for
himself. He couldn't. He either didn't know how to or
else he didn't have the strength to shape raw *sylveth*.

A quaking shudder ran down Fairlie's spine all the
way to her heels. *Sylveth* was a majickal substance that
ran through the Inland Sea in rich, silvery ribbons. It was
a gift and a curse from the Moonsinger Meris. It was
the source of all majick in Crosspointe. But it was also

extremely dangerous. Whatever it touched transformed, usually into spawn—dreadful, ravenous monsters straight out of the minds of the maniacal and deranged. Legend said that a lucky few walked away from an encounter with *sylveth* with some positive gift, though Fairlie had never heard of any such thing happening. Crosspointe was protected by the Pale, a fence of tide and storm wards that kept raw *sylveth* out. Worked *sylveth*—shaped and hardened by a master majicar—could be transported across. It was inert—no danger to anyone. Fairlie didn't quite believe it. She worked with it—chiseling and sculpting it for whatever she needed it to be, from jewelry to sculptures. But she never trusted it.

Shaye followed her glance, his angular face hardening into glacial ice. "Do not tell me that you are making this stupid journey on my account."

"What journey?"

Fairlie turned, a grin already spreading across her face. "Ryland!" She reached out and hugged him tightly, then stood back to look him over. "You look wonderful."

He appeared every inch the prince that he was. He had the family physique—a square jaw, broad shoulders, and long golden hair that he wore loose around his shoulders. He was dressed in green silk and velvet. His trousers were closely fitted in the current fashion, with a long vest to the middle of his thighs, and topped with a sleeveless surcoat, the shoulders rolled. His blouse was heavily embroidered and glinted with beads of citrine *sylveth*. He wore an exotic perfume—musky and spicy. It made Fairlie want to sneeze.

"You're late," Shaye said, stepping forward to pull Ryland into a stiff hug.

Fairlie smiled at them. Shaye was not the sort who was comfortable with such gestures, but he made allowances for her and for Ryland. It was amazing that the two were friends at all. The Majicars' Guild and the Merchants' Commission hated the king and Rampling rule. Shaye's uncle Nicholas Weverton was a loud voice condemning the crown.

"What, have they made you a mastersmith already?" Ryland demanded, turning to Fairlie.

She shook her head. "They have not, and as long as they are taking to deliberate, I think they may very well refuse me."

"They'd better not," he said, his eyes flashing. "Not if they don't want their shipments ending up in the customs warehouses for months. They might even see a sudden surcharge on exports and imports heading from and to metalsmith forges."

Fairlie stared. From Shaye she expected this sort of thing. But Ryland? He had to think about his family and the crown, and he always acted decorously and carefully.

"You wouldn't," she said.

"Wouldn't I?"

"Shaye, tell him he can't." Fairlie made the appeal, knowing it was useless.

Shaye's only response was to sling his arm across Ryland's shoulders and smile fiercely. "Whyever would I want to do that?"

"Crack it! Can't either of you two mind your own business for once?"

"But, Fairlie, you *are* our business," Ryland said seriously, his eyes glinting with wicked humor. "You are our family. And if there's one thing true about both Shaye and I, it's that we don't let anyone persecute our families."

"Sweet Chayos! Persecute? You can't be serious. These are the masters of my guild."

Ryland shrugged. "That doesn't rule out that they are bastards. If they refuse you, it cannot be for the quality of your work, and you are incapable of making enemies. That leaves only your relationship to me and my father, or to Shaye. Either way, we won't stand for it."

Both of them were perfectly serious. Fairlie's fingers tapped restlessly against her thighs. She was not going to win this one. Not that she ever won when they decided to throw in together against her. She shook her head, emitting an exasperated sigh. "This is why I have to leave. I think I might kill you both if I don't."

"Leave?" Ryland asked, glancing askance at Shaye.

"She wants to go to Stanton to visit her mother."

Ryland looked at Fairlie. "What for?"

She glared. "You two are exactly alike—do you know that?" In fact they were completely unalike, except when it came to needling Fairlie. Then they might as well be twins. She drew a breath and blew it out. "Why do you think I want to go? I want to visit her."

"Really it's because she thinks I'll never get my master's badge if she doesn't run off to the hinterlands and leave me alone to work," Shaye confided to Ryland with a curl of his lip.

"It is not," Fairlie protested. "Weren't you paying attention? I want to go. And maybe I'm sick of the two of you."

"Me? I've not been back for hardly a sennight and I've hardly had a chance to see you. It must be Shaye's fault," Ryland objected.

"Or maybe she's offended that you cannot make a moment in your schedule to visit her," Shaye retorted. "You are more than two glasses late today, and about to run off again, unless I misunderstand the meaning of that collection of papers." He nodded at the stack of papers and slender ledgers that Ryland had set down when he entered.

"As it happens, I do need to get back. But that can be blamed on you," Ryland said with a sour look at his friend.

Shaye turned to face him. His lips were curled in a faint smile. Fairlie shook her head. Shaye enjoyed sparring with Ryland far too much.

"I beg your pardon. *I* am responsible for your tardiness and sudden quick departure? I am not aware that ever in our friendship have I been able to make you sit down, much less come and go at my whim. Unless you are suggesting I am using majick against you?"

"I wish it were majick," Ryland said. "No, it's your fam-

ily. Your uncle, to be exact. He's brought a stack of petitions and a dozen toadies with him and has demanded
an audience with my father. And so I am summoned to
aid in the discussions. Damn Vaughn to the depths anyhow! If he hadn't turned his back on his responsibilities,
I'd still be in Normengas tying up the trade treaty. Instead I've been dragged home to listen to more of your
uncle's attempts to undermine the crown."

"You have my sympathies, of course," Shaye said in-
sincerely. "But surely I am not to blame for my uncle?"

"You're a Weverton," Ryland said. "You're root and
branch of the same tree."

"As are you a Rampling. However, my uncle does exactly as he wishes without consulting me. I expect your
father does much the same."

"He listened to Vaughn," Ryland said in a bitter voice.

Fairlie reached out and gripped his arm. Vaughn
was Ryland's elder brother, whom he idolized. A few
months before, in a scandal that had shaken the castle
to its foundations and resulted in the king's summoning
Ryland home, Vaughn had publicly broken ties with his
father and his family. For the first time in Crosspointe
history, a Rampling had turned against the crown. It was
worse than if he had died. Ryland could hardly speak of
him, and when he did, it was with a venomous anger that
wrapped a terrible, bloody hurt. Fairlie's throat ached
for him—ached for them both. Vaughn had always been
one of her favorite people in the castle. He had a quick
wit and a generous smile. He'd always let her win at
cards, and he kept her favorite candies handy for whenever he happened to see her.

Ryland pressed a hand over hers, then shook himself
visibly. Fairlie let her hand fall. He straightened his collar, brushing the wrinkles from his sleeves. He glanced
apologetically at her, his expression pained.

"Nevertheless, it is true. I am late already and I must be
off. I am sorry to leave you dangling without news. Send
word as soon as you hear anything." His gaze flicked
meaningfully to Shaye. "Whatever the outcome."

"You may hear for yourself, Prince Ryland."

Fairlie spun around. She'd not heard the pocket doors to her forge slide open. Now the delegation of master metalsmiths filled the doorway. Her stomach twisted. All five of them looked stern, eyes opaque and shuttered. Master Lowe, the Dean of the Metalsguild, stood in the middle. His arms were folded, his hands tucked inside his voluminous sleeves. He wore a high-necked robe of black dosken, the arms cut out in a filigree lined with yellow silk. His shirtsleeves showed a rich emerald from within. Like most metalsmiths, he was a bulky man. His hair skirted his skull in a thick fringe of shaggy brown, his jaw was covered in a close-cropped beard, and his nose was large and unformed. The round dome of his bald head was hashed with scars and flecks of red where he'd been burned. On his chest was pinned a badge. It was two crossed hammers made of silver on a bed of *sylveth* flames. Behind the flames was a gold anvil. Dangling from the bottom and attached by two gold chains was a thirty-two-rayed compass, the symbol of Crosspointe and of Master Lowe's position as Dean of the Metalsguild.

Fairlie clenched her hands, hiding them in her pockets with a jerky thrust. Her mouth was tight and dry, and her heart galloped in her chest. Whatever she'd said to Shaye and Ryland, this meant more to her than she could begin to say. She was good. She knew it. But was she good enough?

All the craft guilds liked to be selective, even punitive, when it came to the master ranks. Too many masters made for too much market competition and lowered prices on everybody's work. No matter how good her work was, they could not allow too many journeymen to advance. And she didn't have the friends or connections in the guild to smooth the way. There had been only Toff, and Toff was dead.

"After some consideration," Master Lowe began in slow, measured speech, "and with much discussion and careful examination, we have concluded that you, Fairlie Norwich, are a master of your craft. Congratulations."

Fairlie could only stare. She had been certain they would refuse. Her mind seemed frozen, unable to turn in another direction.

"Well? Have you nothing to say?" Master Lowe demanded, his large knotted hands slipping from his sleeves to perch on his hips.

"I . . . thank you," Fairlie said lamely.

Suddenly she was enveloped in a bony hug. "I knew you could not fail," Shaye said into her ear, then brushed a kiss against her forehead.

A moment later Ryland pulled her free, then snugged her tight and kissed her cheek. "Father will be pleased. This will only be the icing on the cake of the gala."

Fairlie stiffened, leaning back to look at him. "Gala?" she asked suspiciously.

"He's planning one for just over a sennight from now. Didn't I mention it? It will be a tribute to those who died during the Jutras attack. Your master work will be unveiled for all of Sylmont to see. So don't plan on going off on your journey until after."

A mixture of pleasure and complete horror raced through Fairlie. She pushed back, flicking a helpless look at Shaye, who was grinning maliciously, as if he'd read her mind. She glared. But before she could say anything, Master Lowe intervened.

"If I may?" he asked, reaching out a hand behind him.

Master Dorset passed him a polished ebony box, her pocked face looking severe. Master Lowe thumbed open the latch and slowly lifted the lid. Inside, on a blue silk pillow, was a master metalsmith badge. He took it out and stepped forward.

Fairlie's breath caught. She couldn't look away from the heavy jewelry as he pinned it to her wool vest. His thick, scarred hands fastened it with unexpected deftness, then settled heavily on her shoulders. She looked up, meeting his solemn gaze, her heart pounding with elation. *She'd done it!*

"You have been measured and found worthy to wear

this badge. Know that this honor is a heavy one. It comes with a great deal of responsibility to your craft and to your guild. You must always allow only the finest of your work to survive. You must pass your knowledge to others. You must serve your guild with all the strength in your body, the talent in your heart, and the skill in your hands. Always recall that as a master, you are bound to give the guild the best of yourself."

Fairlie licked her lips as he fell silent, knowing that she must reply. "I understand. I will not disappoint you."

He smiled, a kind expression. "I know you won't. My good friend Toff did as well. I think he would want you to have this."

He reached inside his robe and withdrew a crisply folded linen paper. It had been sealed, a trace of the blue wax still smudging its edges. Fairlie took it and turned it over in her hands. It was addressed to Master Lowe in the bold, scrawled hand of Toff. She pressed her hand to her mouth to cover the crumbling weakness of her chin. Her eyes burned with tears. She blinked them away.

"Thank you," she mumbled.

"We must be away," he said in a cheerful voice. "We shall have a celebration at the Guildhouse in your honor, though am I to understand you will soon be leaving Sylmont?"

"To visit my family," Fairlie said softly, still looking at Toff's letter.

"Well, then we will have the celebration upon your return, and you will have the opportunity to meet those journeymen and apprentices who wish to learn from you. Also, you will need to make arrangements for your guild fees. Will the king continue to serve as your patron?"

"Of course he will," Ryland said stoutly. "If Fairlie desires it."

A frown creased Master Lowe's forehead. "Perhaps it is something to discuss later," he said quietly. "Congratulations, Fairlie. Toff always said you were an extraordinary talent. None here would argue that."

The expressions on the faces of his fellow master met-alsmiths were dour, but each nodded and murmured congratulations, shaking Fairlie's hand as they filed out.

When the door shut behind them, Ryland seized Fairlie again and hugged her hard. He let her go and reached for his papers. "I apologize, but I must dash. Shall we plan a late supper to celebrate?"

Fairlie and Shaye both nodded, she still clutching the parchment bemusedly in one hand and stroking her fingers over her badge with the other.

"I had better go as well," Shaye said. He gave Fairlie a dark look. "But do not think I am done discussing your trip back to Stanton."

She flashed him a defiant grin. "Talk all you want, but I am going."

"We'll see," he said, and then stomped out.

Ryland rolled his eyes and fluttered his fingers at Fairlie, then followed after the glowering Shaye.

Fairlie fastened the door behind them and went to sit on a stool. She felt strangely numb. For several minutes she stared into space, absently crinkling the parchment between her fingers. At last she unfolded it. It contained only a few scrawled lines. She frowned at them. She wasn't a good reader, and Toff's hand was bold but poor. Slowly she made the words out.

Dear Cameron, my old friend—
It has been far too long, and I fear that we will not see each other again this side of Chayos's Altar. I expect to cross the Veil very soon. There is nothing the majicars can do for me. As I put my affairs in order, I wish to recommend my apprentice, Fairlie Norwich, to the rank of Master. Her talent outstrips even mine, and you know that I have never been ac-cused of being humble. I must ask you, my friend, to see that she achieves Master. She is ready, as you will see for yourself. Do not let politics interfere.
I know that I can count on you in this matter.

The boldly flourished signature that followed took up fully a quarter of the page.

Fairlie traced a finger over the lines, reading them again. Tears slid down her cheeks, and her heart felt squeezed. She remembered how he'd written a stack of letters just before his death. He'd refused to give in to the pain of his illness and had forced his body to carry him about the business of his dwindling life. She was certain that this missive had been in that last stack, that she had posted them for him just the day before his death. That was nine months ago, and Master Lowe had waited for her to apply for mastership. Would he have sought her out if she had not? He seemed very kind at the end—perhaps it had been the politics. So many rivers of intrigue ran through Crosspointe, it was impossible not to get caught up in a current—or several.

She swiped at her tears, folding the letter and pressing it against her knotted stomach, painful happiness blooming inside her. She touched the badge, heavy against her chest, a slow smile bending her stiff lips. Toff had believed she was a master metalsmith. That was a treasure beyond all counting.

She stood and put the letter away in the drawer of her nightstand. Then she changed clothes and headed for her forge. It was time to get back to work.

Chapter 2

Shaye strode violently down the corridor. Fury rode him, grappling him close with steel claws. He was nearly mindless with it. Behind him he heard the door of Fairlie's workshop close and Ryland's quick footsteps. Shaye stopped and spun around.

"What in the black depths is she thinking? And you! You didn't say a word about it. Are you just going to let her run off into the hinterlands for Meris knows how long?"

Ryland shrugged infuriatingly. "There's little either of us can do if she wants to go."

"That's shit. I'll stop her."

"Then there is no problem, is there?" Ryland said dismissively, starting to walk again.

Shaye followed reluctantly. How could he be so cavalier? But then, Ryland was used to being without Fairlie. Shaye could not imagine it; or rather, imagining it nearly gutted him with pain. If she actually went away, he didn't know if he'd survive. Not that he could tell her so. She didn't want to know.

"Can you tell me just what your uncle is cooking up with the lord chancellor?"

Shaye's brow creased. "Nothing that I'm aware of. The lord chancellor is a crown man, isn't he?"

"He's a coldhearted bastard, and that wife of his is vicious. I wouldn't trust them if they said the sea was black."

"Strange. Your father appointed him. Surely he must have some faith in his own man?"

Ryland cast him a sidelong glance, his brows rising. "You know better. The lord chancellor wormed his way into the office, and he keeps it by doing an impeccable job. He follows the law with exactness. But he is starving for power. He plays quiet games, moving in the darkness and shadows. He's never been caught breaking any laws, and believe me, we've tried. I'd rather have your uncle coming at us; he's more honest about it."

Shaye snorted. "My uncle is as devious and twisted in his dealings as a ball of knotted string."

"Exactly. But the lord chancellor is far worse. He's unwilling to commit himself until he knows he can win. I worry about the game. I can't imagine that your uncle trusts him any more than Father does. And yet they are working together."

Shaye smiled maliciously. "It will no doubt be interesting to find out what they are plotting," he said.

"Like finding out what it'll be like when Fairlie goes off to Stanton?" Ryland riposted without missing a beat.

"She's not going," Shaye growled.

"Maybe. But you know our Fairlie. Once she decides on something, she doesn't easily change her mind, and neither of us have ever been able to control her.

"There's always a first time."

Ryland was silent a moment, then spoke in a quiet, sober voice. "Just be careful. Think about what you're willing to risk with her. You don't really want to be on the opposite side in a battle, do you?"

The idea made Shaye reel. The muscles of his entire body knotted. Days without Fairlie gaped empty, but he could easily push her too far so that she felt she had to leave and never come back. Or if she *did* come back, she might not welcome him in her life. That he could not risk.

"I've got to go," he said abruptly, and then turned away from Ryland, striding up a corridor without knowing where he was going. He'd not gone more than five steps when something hit his mind.

He staggered, feeling wild majick sweeping through him. It seared him, boiling up in white and blue flames. He lurched against the wall, bracing his hands wide, his fingers curling hard against the stone.

He tasted smoke and felt the ethereal caress of the minor elements he could command: *Breath* and *Shadow* and *Dance*. *Forewarning*. He forced himself to relax into the majick, to let it tell him what it wanted. He lifted one hand to his *illidre*, trying to bring the majick into focus. But the message was as nebulous as mist. *Danger*. It whispered in his blood and rippled through his heart. *Breathtaking, heartbreaking danger. Soon.*

Suddenly the majick unraveled. It flailed apart, whipping through him with fire-edged wildness. Shaye snatched at it, wrapping his *illidre* in his hands. He felt the majick crackle on his skin, unformed and violent. He reached deep into the *illidre*, triggering a spell within. It was designed just for this, to capture the collapsed majick of a forewarning. It sent out hundreds of sticky, tangled threads. They looped and corkscrewed outward, circling and clinging to the wild majick, drawing it back inside the *illidre*. It would stay there, ready to be turned into something useful. Freed, Shaye slumped to the floor. He sucked in a deep breath.

"Are you all right? Should I call for a healer?"

Shaye looked up at Ryland, who crouched beside him. His friend recoiled as their gazes met. Instantly Shaye covered his eyes with his hand, even as he pieced back together the illusion spell that made them appear ordinary brown instead of majicar silver and crimson. When it was in place, he dropped his hand again.

"What is it?"

Shaye shook his head. "I suppose the wine, women, and late nights are catching up with me," he said lightly. His head throbbed and his entire body felt parched.

"Right," Ryland said disbelievingly, offering his hand to pull Shaye erect. "And I'm Chayos's daughter."

Shaye smiled. "Maybe you should buy some dresses for yourself. Frilly, with ribbons and bows."

Ryland didn't return the smile or engage in the banter. "What happened?"

"Nothing."

"Didn't look like nothing; it looked like a foreboding. If something's wrong, I need to know. Father needs to know. It wasn't . . . Jutras, was it?"

"Don't you think I'd tell you?"

"I hope so. Would you?"

"I'd tell you if I knew—if I thought—anything was threatening Crosspointe," Shaye said flatly.

Ryland stared at him a moment, then nodded. "Good. I've got to go. I'll see you later?" He didn't wait for a reply but strode away, leaving Shaye alone.

The young majicar leaned against the wall, his head tipping back as his eyes closed. They'd been coming regularly recently. Forebodings full of unease. But this . . . this was much stronger than any that had come before. But like all of them, it was too murky to actually be helpful. His second affinity was stone. Had it been water or wind, his ability to forecast would be much stronger. As it was, this amorphously ominous feeling was next to useless. Enough to make him worry and nothing to tell him why. Worry. As hard as that foreboding had hit, he should be walking the line of panic. Something very bad was going to happen to him, and soon. He did not think it was about Fairlie's going home to visit her mother. No, this was worse. Much worse. But what it was, he did not know.

He'd have to see his uncle and warn him, have him warn the family to be careful. Shaye's mouth twisted and he levered himself away from the wall, striding along the corridor as though he had somewhere to go. The trouble was, the foreboding could mean almost anything. There was no way to predict. He considered asking for a reading from a wind or water majicar. But dreams and scrying were unreliable and difficult to interpret. He doubted he'd get any solid answers from one of them. He rubbed his chest, feeling an ache deep inside. Still, it was better than doing nothing. He would see about consulting someone—and soon.

Chapter 3

All of Ryland's attention was wrapped up in whatever had happened to Shaye. He'd never before seen the majicar lose control of his majick. He'd never before seen Shaye's eyes without the covering illusion that all majicars used. The secret to becoming a majicar was closely guarded. If the people of Crosspointe ever learned that majicars were really spawn, that they became majicars by touching *sylveth*, there would be riots. The country would tear itself apart. And it wasn't just majicars; it was Pilots too. Crosspointe could not survive without either, and yet the people would be terrified to know that spawn lived among them.

He sighed, running his fingers through his hair. Shaye was only a journeyman majicar, but he was powerful. The only thing that kept him from becoming a master was the fact that he was too distracted by Fairlie to do it. Ryland wondered, not for the first time, if Shaye even knew he was in love with her. If he did, he was careful to keep it hidden from her, but Ryland could see it like a lighthouse beacon. Still, the fact that Shaye *could* be a master if he chose made the episode in the corridor all the more worrisome. He'd been known to get forebodings— hints of the future. Shaye didn't have the affinities to do a full forecasting, but his forebodings had been accurate so far. What did this one mean?

He had little time to consider. He was late. He hurried along. Fairlie's workshop attached to the castle, beyond the remote guest wings that went largely unused except during major celebrations when visitors came from all over the Inland Sea.

Ryland crossed into the more frequently used sections, nodding polite hellos to those he passed, but not slowing. At last he reached the main hall and the public rooms. He went to the throne room and strode up the center. The thrones were empty, though Crown Shields lined the walls. They were well armed, and shields had been added to their equipment. Ryland's gaze settled broodingly on the left throne. He wasn't sure that an army of Crown Shields would have saved his mother when the Jutras sorcerers had invaded months ago. He shied away from the thought.

Swallowing a hard lump, he skirted the dais and went through a door in the far wall. It led into a long passage with maple paneling and thick rugs running the length of it. The walls were heavily decorated with paintings, tapestries, sculptures, and an assortment of other oddments from all around the world. More Crown Shields stood guard, four at each end of the passage and two patrolling in between.

At the end of the passage, Ryland passed into an office occupied by several scribes and a senior clerk, who was scribbling furiously in a book. He nodded at her as he crossed the room and entered a small, circular foyer. Half a dozen Crown Shields stood hard-eyed and watchful inside, tensing as the door opened and Ryland stepped in. He moved slowly, letting them see him. They were forbidden from physically searching him—he was a crown prince, after all.

A hard-eyed captain examined Ryland from head to foot, then gave a slight nod. Ryland crossed to the door, entering a spacious sitting room. It was like stepping into summer. The room was decorated in warm yellows. A fire crackled in the enormous hearth, and thickly cushioned chairs and chaises were set in a cozy semicircle around its warmth. Orange blossoms from the hothouses filled vases on the tables in the corners, perfuming the air with their bright, clean scent.

But the atmosphere of the room was as cold and sharp as a sword of ice. Ryland's father sat in an armchair. His face could have been carved from the side of a mountain. Across from him was Nicholas Weverton, Shaye's uncle. He did not look like a powerful man, nor a dangerous one. He was a slight man, with shaggy brown hair that was clipped short over his collar. He was dressed expensively and conservatively in gray. There was little about his appearance to say what he was. Except his eyes. Dark eyebrows hooked over polished green stones that seemed to see everything. They hid a brilliant, calculating mind. Ryland suppressed a grimace. What an ally he would have made. But he was the enemy. He hated the crown, and he was determined to reform Crosspointe, starting with eradicating the monarchy.

Between the two men and off to Ryland's right sat Lord Chancellor Geoffrey Robert Hazelton Truehelm. He was a pale man, with dark curly hair fastened sharply at the nape of his neck. His face was shaved, his hawk nose and thin mouth like sculpted alabaster. He was dressed in a brilliant blue waistcoat and a darker blue suit, his legs encased in the close-fitting trousers that had become so popular of late. He wore several rings on each hand, and his heavy chain of office lay flat around his neck, the square links glittering with *sylveth* and gold. The turned-back cuffs of his sleeves and the wide collar of his coat sparkled with yellow *sylveth* beads. As usual, there was a subtle sneering, smug cast to his expression, as though he were superior to everyone else and was quite certain of it.

Standing behind Ryland's father was Niall, his steward, his thin face looking bland. No one else was present. Ryland frowned. This was not an ordinary meeting.

"Good afternoon, Father," Ryland said, making a low, formal bow. "I apologize for my tardiness."

"Quite all right. We were just having some refreshment before getting to business," his father said, gesturing at the sideboard. "Join us."

Ryland gave a shallow bow to the two guests, then took a seat on the chaise beside the lord chancellor. His father's voice and countenance were genial, but there was a stiffness to his shoulders and a hard glitter in his eyes that told an angrier truth.

"Now let us get to it," his father said crisply, looking at Weverton and Truehelm. "I can give you a quarter of a glass. I suggest that you be brief."

Ryland hid a small smile as he accepted a cup of tea from Niall. Given the opportunity, Weverton and Truehelm would batter his father with a tornado of petitions. The time limit guaranteed that they would focus on their highest priorities, which would reveal a lot about whatever intrigues they were currently fomenting. Of course, they wouldn't hesitate to use their allies to push other important petitions. It was a very good thing that his father had a strong network of spies and informants throughout Crosspointe.

Nicholas Weverton slipped his pocket watch from his waistcoat. He opened it, then nodded and tucked it away. "Something needs to be done about the Burn. It's been months and the majick hasn't diminished, nor has the heat. It must be cleaned and rebuilding must begin. Too many lost their houses and their businesses—most were not sufficiently insured. The crown needs to take up the burden of repairing the damage." He paused, his gaze not wavering. "After all, a Rampling caused the damage, did she not?"

A ripple of anger ran through Ryland. Several decades ago a chancery suit had been brought against the Ramplings. It was an endless morass of legal maneuverings that tied up all of the Rampling funds, except what swiftly drained away in a tide of legal fees. It meant that all of the family had to earn their own money. That in itself was no terrible thing. In fact, it served to justify family members' spreading out through Crosspointe and working in nearly every possible trade. It had the unforeseen benefit of lending the crown eyes and ears where it had had none before. But it also meant that his father didn't have any personal funds to cover the cost of fixing the Burn.

Shortly before Chance, before the Jutras had killed Ryland's mother, Lucy Trenton—a cousin—had become attached to a cipher. The majickal artifact had somehow caused her to start the fire that had destroyed a huge swath of Salford Terrace, where the wealthy kept homes and businesses. The majick-born flames had been nearly impossible to put out and had burned stone and wood alike. Nothing had been spared. Now there was nothing left but a black wasteland that spread from the base of Harbottle Hill nearly to the harbor. The remaining dirt was still hot to the touch, and the Majicars' Guild warned that it needed an expensive majickal healing. The price was more than Crosspointe's annual income. Ryland didn't know if they merely wanted to gouge his father for every last copper they could get, or if they simply didn't have the skill or knowledge to accomplish it and were charging so much to guarantee that the crown would not hire them.

Ryland didn't let his sudden anger over Weverton's none-too-subtle accusation show on his face. Instead, he looked to see how his father would respond.

Before Chance, before the death of his wife and Ryland's mother, William Rampling had been a hale, ruddy-faced man. But he had aged since then. Now he was pallid, and much of his sturdy bulk had melted away. His skin hung loosely on his face, and his hands sometimes trembled. His hair had already been going to gray, but now it was dull white. His voice remained strong and determined, though, and his eyes flashed with the fire of a vigorous and agile mind.

"Ah, the Burn. Ryland, perhaps you might like to address this."

Weverton's mouth flattened for a moment, then carefully relaxed. He turned his sharp stare on Ryland. "Please, Prince Ryland. You have my undivided attention."

The lord chancellor gave no reaction at all to the king's seeming disinterest. He only continued nonchalantly sipping his steaming tea.

"I'm afraid there's little to be done about the Burn at this time, Mr. Weverton," Ryland said. "The problem is with the majicars. They can give no assurances of their ability to rehabilitate the Burn, despite what they've told the papers. And if they could, their fees are exorbitant. It would more than bankrupt the treasury, which means a broad-based raising of tariffs, taxes, and fees, as well as increasing majicar service requirements. Obviously this could seriously undermine our economy and increase friction with our trading partners. Before making such a move, it is important to establish the certitude of a positive benefit.

"Of course, insurance has paid many for their homes and businesses, and the crown has begun subsidizing the purchase of other properties throughout Sylmont to further help those who have been displaced. Such a strategy will stimulate our city's sagging economy, supplement tax revenues, and stabilize employment without creating an undue financial burden on the people."

"On the crown, you mean," Weverton said sardonically.

Ryland didn't let himself frown, but his gaze sharpened. This didn't matter to Weverton. At least not today. It was a pretext of some sort. He could feel it in his bones. He had on more than one occasion sat in on discussions with the man, and in negotiations Weverton was as tenacious and voracious as ravening spawn. He didn't let anyone get in his way. But today he seemed as soft as holiday pudding. What was he up to?

Ryland spared a glance for the lord chancellor. When he caught Ryland looking at him, the other man's lips formed a smirk. He said nothing.

Fuming, Ryland turned back to Weverton, infusing his voice with warmth, despite the insult. "Indeed, it would be a severe burden on the crown. The Chance storms this year were worse than anyone predicted. Many towns and villages were flooded or suffered slides. There are food shortages and more spawn incursions than usual. Roads and bridges washed out. The additional expenses combined with the loss of so much business in Sylmont has left the treasury straitened."

Weverton nodded as if agreeing. He didn't, of course, if only because he generally sided opposite the crown. But he wasn't interested in pushing the issue at the moment. Ryland looked at his father, one brow raised. The king tapped his forefingers lightly together, watching Weverton. He too recognized that this was a feint. It was as if, Ryland thought suddenly, the two petitioners were waiting for something, and wasting time until whatever it was happened.

As if on cue, the opposite door, the one through which Weverton and the lord chancellor had entered, was thrust open without any ceremony. Before Ryland could do more than leap to his feet, a woman stepped in and Ryland gaped like an idiot.

It was the Naladei, the bright priestess of Chayos. Her clothing was a green-gray color. Her hair hung long around her hips, the color of the morning sun gilding the frost. Her face was rosy and tanned, her lips full and sensual. Her eyes were the rich green of summer leaves, and her apricot skin was soft as velvet. Despite the lusciousness of her beauty that begged to be caressed and possessed, the cold predatory ambition glinting in the depths of her eyes turned any desire Ryland might have felt to stone.

He bowed low. Beside him, the lord chancellor did the same. He straightened as the Naladei brushed past him to halt before his father. The king bowed low as well. She brushed her fingers over the back of his head, then gestured for him to rise. Ryland didn't miss her swift glance at Weverton. Shock jolted through him, though he kept his face carefully expressionless. This was what those two bastards had been waiting for? It was a rare day that either of Chayos's priestesses left the Maida. Once a year she and her dark sibling, the Kalimei, ventured down to the harbor to bless the ships before the vessels sailed out again after Chance. Even his father attended the priestesses inside the Maida. To have the Naladei come here was nearly inconceivable. And yet here she was, clearly in the service of Nicholas Weverton and the lord chancellor.

Cold slithered into Ryland's stomach. Braken's balls. What was going on?

"Naladei, you honor me beyond dreams. How may I serve you?" his father asked deferentially.

"You have always recognized my Lady's authority," she mused in a slow, sultry voice that should have raised shivers of desire on Ryland's skin. But the shivers were chills of foreboding. Something was *very* wrong.

"I have come here so that you know you have my Lady's benediction."

"I thank you," Ryland's father said humbly, but his mouth was tense, his eyes narrowed, whether in suspicion or fury there was no way to tell.

"You and I have oft spoken of the future of Crosspointe," she said.

She did not sit, nor did anyone else.

"We have. Your counsel has been an enormous benefit to me."

"You have always looked after the best interests of this land and people." She stroked her hand down his arm.

Ryland scowled. She was not declaring herself against his father or crown rule; in fact she was reaffirming her support. But Weverton's faintly pleased expression never wavered, and the lord chancellor remained comfortably smug. This scene was following a script that they had already learned. The cold in Ryland's stomach hardened into glacial ice.

"But the dangers have changed and Crosspointe must also change. I come to you here so that you know how strongly my Lady feels about what must be done."

"What must be done? About what?" Ryland's father asked.

"It is time to name a regent in the event that you—or some future king or queen—is incapacitated."

"A regent?" The king was nonplussed, as was Ryland.

"In past times, such was not necessary. Crosspointe did not face certain attack from beyond the sea. We had the luxury of peace; there was time to wait until a new Rampling was elected. But now, with the threat of the Jutras and unrest from within Crosspointe, it is vital that a strong hand remain at the helm until a new Rampling sits upon the throne. I think you will agree."

Ryland's father went very still. It was a trap. Ryland could sense it, though he couldn't see its teeth.

"What are you proposing?" the king asked.

"I believe it is time to name a regent," the Naladei said softly. It was not a suggestion.

She looked so young—barely a woman—yet she was more than two hundred seasons old. She was every bit as powerful as a master majicar—even more so—though her majick came from Chayos rather than Meris. Her expression was unrelenting and disapproving, as if Ryland's father had disappointed her. But she was going to correct that. She was going to bring him to heel. All this Ryland could read in the set of her shoulders and the hard gleam of her eyes. He was good at reading people, an invaluable skill for a prince and a diplomat. She was determined, and she would win her way. His father would never oppose a priestess of Chayos.

He bit the insides of his cheeks until he tasted blood. There was nothing he could do. He glanced again at Weverton and the lord chancellor. Somehow they had engineered this scene. That in itself was dreadfully worrisome. The Naladei and the Kalimei had always supported Rampling rule. Was that about to change? And if it did, his father would lose the support of the people entirely. No one would give fealty to a king who'd lost Chayos's blessing.

"Who do you have in mind?" his father asked.

"The lord chancellor would make an admirable choice."

"The lord chancellor?" Ryland couldn't help repeating it.

"He is your man, is he not?" the Naladei said to the king, ignoring Ryland. "His office is to protect and uphold the laws of Crosspointe. Is there anyone more suitable? I expect Lord Chancellor Truehelm is willing," she said, slightly sardonically.

"I expect so," the king said, equally dryly.

"Crosspointe needs to feel safe," she said, settling one hand on his arm. "The people need to know that there is a firm hand on the helm if something should happen to you, or whoever sits next on the throne. The sea no longer protects us as it once did, and the attempts on your life have not escaped my knowing. The Charter must be changed to authorize a regent should the crown become incapacitated or killed, until a new king or queen can be elected from the eligible Rampling line."

It was a good trap—sensible, reasonable, unavoidable . . . dreadful. Ryland could see that his father knew it too.

"It shall be done," the king said finally with a slight bow to the Naladei.

"By the end of the sennight," she pressed.

"As you say," he agreed.

She bent, cupping his face in her hands and pressing her lips to his forehead. "I knew you would not fail to see reason," she murmured.

She withdrew as quickly as she'd come. Both Weverton and the lord chancellor rose to follow, having obtained what they'd come for. The lord chancellor bowed.

"Your servant, as always, Your Majesty. I hope that I will always deserve your trust and that of the Naladei," he said smoothly.

His barely suppressed glee set Ryland's teeth on edge. Everything he'd told Shaye was true. The man was a snake, though he did his best to appear upright and innocuous. His position was a lifetime appointment, and the lord chancellor was far too careful to give legal cause for removal. And now he was about to be in line to rule, if only temporarily, and clearly he was in Weverton's pocket.

Weverton also bowed. In contrast to the lord chancellor, there was no smugness in his expression, despite the fact that he'd won a major victory in his crusade against the crown. Instead he smiled with a faintly rueful curl of his lip. Clearly he was aware of what the lord chancellor was.

"It is a wise thing that you do, Your Majesty."

Ryland's father's mouth tightened. "Perhaps." His gaze flicked to the lord chancellor. "For Crosspointe's sake, I hope your services never become necessary in such a capacity," he said.

If the lord chancellor recognized the insult in the king's comment, he did not reveal it.

"I couldn't agree more, Your Highness," he said with oily grace.

"You are busy," Weverton said. "We will take no more of your time. Thank you for giving us an audience."

With that, he and the lord chancellor departed.

"Did you know what they were up to?" Ryland asked his father, who shook his head.

"No. How they managed to rope the Naladei into their scheme I don't know. But it must be done now." He rubbed his hand over his face, pinching his lower lip thoughtfully. "It is a good idea—at least in principle. But Truehelm would make a dangerous regent." He dropped his hand, meeting Ryland's gaze with a cold, determined look. "We'll need to remove him from office and soon."

"What can I do?" Ryland asked.

His father smiled, the chill never leaving his eyes. "If I need you, I will let you know. In the meantime, I need you to attend the ambassador of Reshnival at tonight's banquet. She has brought her daughter with her, and intends that the two of you should meet." At Ryland's pained look, his father added, "She is a comely enough girl, if a bit silly. It should not be a hardship to entertain her. The ambassador is here to negotiate a new trade treaty. I should like her to feel welcome. It would not go amiss for her to hope for a stronger alliance between our two countries, though, Ryland, I should not wish her hopes to have any real foundation," he added warningly.

"I understand, Father. I shall be witty and charming and willfully blind to all blandishments."

He began to leave, but stopped when his father spoke again. "I know I do not need to tell you that what passed here should not be discussed with anyone."

"No, Father. You do not." Ryland gave a small bow, feeling stung. He wasn't stupid, nor loose-lipped.

"And Vaughn? What have you heard?"

Ryland felt his face harden, his teeth gritting, the muscles of his jaw knotting. "Rumor has it that he's being cultivated. Not many Ramplings have turned against the crown, and the king's own son—he's being swarmed like flies on rotted fruit."

The king nodded without expression. "Rotted fruit, indeed," he murmured, rubbing a hand over his mouth. He turned away. "Enjoy your dinner tonight."

Ryland stood a moment, then strode out, shutting the door more firmly than necessary. His father had a lot on his mind, and this regency thing was a blow. Worse, his father had relied heavily on Vaughn for many tasks, but did not yet trust Ryland to carry those burdens. Instead he had to do them himself. Somehow he would prove himself, Ryland vowed silently. Whatever it took, he would do it.

Chapter 4

She glided along on padded feet, claws clicking where the floor was bare of rugs. She went wherever she wished and no one stopped her—no one even knew she was there.

She sniffed. Tasting. Seeking. The people moved away from her, instinct guiding them, though they could not see what lifted the hair of their scalps and made their stomachs clench with fear.

She stopped at the top of an empty stairway and lifted her head. The air was rich with the scent of her kind. They did not suspect her presence either. They also hid what they were.

She reached out to listen, to pluck the meaning of their language from their minds. She did not care about them. They were not hers, though they were Kin, and because they were, their minds were open to her.

She slid between their thoughts, as invisible inside their minds as her body was outside. She took what she wanted and skipped to another mind and then another. She was searching, both for what she'd promised to find and for that which she would be allowed after.

A mind grated against hers. Her lips curled. He could not reach into her thoughts as she could his, but he could touch, poking at her like a randy goat. She did not respond to his call; she listened silent in his mind.

Want. Throbbing. Determination. Iron. Certainty. Cloudless. Worry. Would she break? Would she do what was needed? Would she come to him at last? Could he make her?

She growled low in her chest. A man climbing the stairs hesitated. He smelled of sex and onions. She padded downward, passing him by.

Elusive scents caught her in nets of hope and pulled her along. She wandered, unwilling to give up, unwilling to return to his demands, unwilling to go back and do what must be done.

Not yet.

Chapter 5

"If it would help, I could light Ryland's coattails on fire and you could make your escape in the uproar of smothering the flames from his dainty royal ass."

Fairlie eyed Shaye sideways. His eyes were shadowy, as if he hadn't been sleeping, and his usual thinness now looked gaunt. She frowned concern. He was still angry with her. She'd hardly seen him the sennight since she'd been named master, except when he'd appeared in her workshop to badger her about her journey to Stanton. He had not changed her mind; she would leave the day after tomorrow. But for the moment, it seemed he'd made an effort to set aside his ire to keep from ruining the night. She was grateful. She smiled. "What makes you think I want to escape?"

He turned to look fully at her. "Perhaps because it would prove that you still cling to some small vestige of sanity."

The smile faded. "But haven't you told me all week that I'm completely bent? Pale-blasted. Maggot-headed. Cinders for brains. Not a drop of sanity left, I'm afraid."

Shaye crossed his arms, his chin lifting in unconscious arrogance. "You must have some small fragment remaining to you. Otherwise, how else would you have had the sense to retreat into hiding from all that?" he asked, waving a white-fingered hand at the crowded ballroom. It was full of glittering men and women dressed in their finest gowns and waistcoats. Jewels of light twinkled down from the *sylveth* chandeliers. An army of liveried servants offered champagne and wine from delicate crystal goblets and silver platters of sweet and savory morsels—the best the royal kitchens could create. At the far end of the ballroom was a low dais. On it was a large, bulky object swathed in gold silk. It stood twenty-five feet tall and about the same wide. In front of it stood King William with Ryland, his younger brother and two older sisters, and a handful of advisers and dignitaries. In a few minutes, Fairlie would be called to the dais to stand with them. Shaye was right. She did want to hide.

She pushed a strand of hair off her forehead, wishing for a glass of plain water. Her head ached. Her borrowed lady's maid had tortured her hair into a complex coif, stabbing it through with combs and pins. The result had been passable, though not particularly beautiful. Not that Fairlie had expected it to be. She didn't have much to work with. At least she hadn't been forced to wear a corset. She'd flat out refused and declared she would not attend the fete if a corset was required. On that, at least, she'd won the day.

"I was overheated," she said, wincing immediately, knowing Shaye would not let that pass. And he didn't.

"Of course. It is so much hotter here than beside your forge," he said sardonically. He fanned himself with little flips of his hand. "I am beginning to feel faint myself."

"You're an ass."

"Oh, dear me. Did I say something wrong? I apologize most heartily."

Fairlie gritted her teeth. She didn't really want to leave Sylmont without resolving things with Shaye, but she didn't know how to break through his anger and her sympathy for whatever hurt he felt was getting thin.

"I didn't expect so many people," she said, hoping the new subject would not inspire more barbs from him. Her fingers nervously smoothed her skirt, the roughness of her calloused hands catching on the fine fabric and snagging the intricate embroidery. She knotted her hands together over her stomach to keep herself from destroying it altogether.

Shaye caught her movement. "Nice dress," he said, standing back to eye her from head to toe.

She gave him a suspicious look. Finally she said tartly, "Of course it is. Ryland sent a swarm of seamstresses to my quarters, and they held me prisoner at needlepoint while they measured and pinned and measured again and hemmed and stitched and turned me round and round like a top."

He chuckled, sounding almost friendly. "I'm surprised you didn't sneak away to your workshop."

"I tried. But Ryland actually put Crown Shields at the door to keep me from escaping. And then I wasn't about to cross Mistress Ula. Have you met her?" She shook her head. "I'm not entirely sure, but I think she would have broken bones to make me cooperate. Not to mention to fit me into the dress."

"Ah. The lady Koreion. But she is the best. And you do look lovely."

Fairlie glared at him, her hands settling on her hips. "I've had about enough of this from you. You can be as mad at me as you want, but you do not need to be mean."

His brows rose. "Am I being mean?"

She gripped her skirt in her fists, crushing the silk. "I expected laughter from you, not false compliments."

He frowned. He looked quite elegant in severely cut black trousers, with a black cravat, black waistcoat, black shirt, and black boots. The only color he wore was a dangling drop of red *sylveth* in one ear, a matching pin in the middle of his cravat, and his flame-colored *illidre*, which hung just above the top button of his waistcoat. Fairlie had made the earring and pin for him as a thank-you for his help with her work. She'd given them to him two days ago after they'd had yet another battle over her going to Stanton. He'd pocketed the gifts and left her without a word. She was pleasantly surprised to see him wearing them tonight.

"What makes you think it is a false compliment?"

"Because I've looked in a mirror and I am not blind. I'm well aware that I look perfectly ridiculous. Look at my hands." She held them up. "Are these the hands of a woman who should be prancing about in silks and satins with her face painted?"

The anatomy in question was hashed and blotched with old and new burn scars and cuts. Her fingers were blunt, with the nails cut short where they weren't torn. And nothing could get rid of the black wedged beneath her nails and speckling her skin. Her palms were wide and thick with muscle. She had been supposed to wear gloves this evening, but she had spilled tea on one and had stained the other with kohl, resulting in the necessity of making repairs to her face and attending the gala bare-handed. The lacy sleeve of her dress fell over her hands like a shroud, and an aggravated Mistress Ula declared that if Fairlie was careful, she could keep the ugliness hidden. Just as the puffed and slashed sleeves disguised her powerful chest, shoulders, and arms, not to mention covering the splinters of steel and *sylveth* that had sheathed themselves in her flesh over the years, making ugly patterns on her arms.

"Do you know that the lady's maid Ryland sent me suggested a wig since my hair is so frowzy? She said frowzy. And she was right. I am a metalsmith, after all. My hair gets burned all the time. She clucked and *tsk*ed like it was a personal insult, and then she put all this stuff in it to make it soft and shiny. I bet if I got anywhere near a spark or a candle my head would go up like a torch."

"It's no wonder then that you picked this alcove to hide out in rather than skitter back to your workshop," Shaye observed.

"I would have, too," she muttered, her arms crossing over her chest. It's not that she didn't have a decent enough figure. Her borrowed lady's maid—Angela—had returned to that over and over again, as if she needed to say *something* positive about her charge's appearance and could think of little else. Fairlie had enough of a chest for it to get in her way far too often when she was working. Her waist was thin—too thin, Shaye complained constantly. She was always forgetting to eat. When she was working, she didn't think about anything else.

"You'll have to get used to it, you know. After tonight you'll be invited everywhere," Shaye said.

Fairlie gaped. This had been a special night, one of a kind. She had put up with the primping and yanking and greasing and poking, deciding that she could tolerate it just once. But more than that? It didn't bear thinking about. It was enough to make a person puke.

"I don't have to accept," she said, scowling at Shaye, who was now laughing.

"You can try to refuse," he said, "but I'm afraid this is the end of your life as a hermit. If nothing else, you will have to obey the king's invitations. Such are not to be refused."

"Maybe I'll stop bathing," she muttered.

Before Shaye could answer, a sudden brassy flourish from the orchestra made Fairlie start. It felt like her stomach was full of wriggling snakes. She drew a deep breath and blew it out. "I guess it's time," she said.

"Hold on. I have something for you," Shaye said, fumbling in an inside breast pocket of his coat.

He pulled out a small suede pouch and handed it to Fairlie. "It's not much."

She eyed him warily. "What is it?"

"Look inside."

"It's not a trick, is it? A face full of pepper powder, maybe?"

"I would not do that to you."

"Yes, you would," she said, but began loosening the leather ties with no little eagerness. She wiggled her fingers into the top of the pouch and pulled out a pendant. It hung on a silver chain. She turned it in her fingers, her mouth dropping open. It was made of worked *sylveth*, full of the colors of the setting sun—purple, indigo, orange, pink, and black. Shaped like a Lius tree, it faded to green at the spreading tangle of roots. A twisted circle of silver and black surrounded the tree, and in the heart of its trunk was an orange flame. It looked nearly alive.

It was utterly breathtaking.

"Did you make this?" she asked softly.

"Yes."

She glanced at him. He scowled as he watched the pendant twisting. Fairlie turned it in her hands, her fingers careful. The craftsmanship was nearly perfect. "It's brilliant. More than that. It's . . . perfect."

"Really? You like it?"

Shaye's voice was eager, with a cutting edge almost like anger. Or nervousness. It was hard to tell, and she didn't know if she wanted to find out. For the moment, he was in charity with her, and she didn't want to shatter his mood. She nodded.

"I love it."

"Let me put it on you."

He took it, putting it around her neck. He fumbled with the clasp. Fairlie lifted the pendant so she could see it again.

"When did you learn how to do this? I thought you couldn't work *sylveth*." Instantly she wanted to bite her tongue. Shaye's face darkened. By the depths, why did she always have to put her foot in her mouth? Just when she'd managed to soften his mood, she went and reminded him of the very thing that made him so angry.

"You are leaving because of me," he said. "Well, as you can see, your concerns are unfounded." He touched the pendant with one finger, then jerked it back, curling his fingers into a fist. His chin lifted and he looked down his nose at Fairlie. "I am able to adequately perform master tasks."

"Sorry," she mumbled, though she wasn't quite sure what she was apologizing for.

Again the fanfare sounded and the crowd looked expectantly at the dais. The king had stepped forward. In the group of dignitaries that made a semicircle behind him, there was a tall, mysterious figure wearing a heavy veil that covered him—or her—from head to foot. Beside the person was a striking man. He was tall, with broad shoulders. He stooped slightly. His dark hair hung long and loose to his elbows. His skin was tanned and his eyes were piercing. There was something about him that, even from across the room, made Fairlie uneasy. He seemed to be looking right at her.

"Who is that?" she asked, glad for any diversion that might distract Shaye from his anger.

He followed her gaze. "I don't know."

"Really?"

He shook his head. "I may be a Weverton, albeit the unsavory reprobate of the family, but that does not mean I know all who visit the king." He scanned her expression. "Why?"

She shrugged, giving a little shake of her head. "There's just something. . . . It's nothing. I'm just feeling a little out of sorts tonight. We'd better go join the festivities."

She started to walk away and then stopped, turning to face him.

"Thank you. The pendant. I won't ever take it off."

She leaned close and kissed his cheek. Just as her lips brushed his skin, he flinched. She pulled back in surprise, then grinned. "You're right."

She took his handkerchief from his pocket and rubbed the smudge of lip color off his cheek. She put the cloth in his hand, but before she could turn away again, he gripped her arm tightly.

"It wasn't a false compliment. You look beautiful."

Fairlie stared, then flushed and looked away. He reached out and straightened her collar and smoothed the front of her skirt where she'd clutched it.

"There. Now you are perfect."

"I should have had you for a lady's maid." She eyed him thoughtfully. "Now there's an idea. What are you doing after this is all over? Care to save me from the ministrations of Angela?"

Red flooded Shaye's cheeks. "I think not."

Fairlie stared and then a slow grin broke across her mouth. "Oh, dear Chayos, you're not embarrassed? How is that even possible?"

Shaye straightened. She had to tip her head back to look at him.

"I have manners enough to realize that it is not appropriate for me to be undressing you," he said loftily.

She chortled, making nearby heads turn curiously. She bit her lip and lowered her voice.

"First, you *don't* have any such manners. And second, I recall you undressing me on at least one occasion. Do you remember the night that you and Ryland introduced me to Pelkisad candy-wine?"

"*Both* of us undressed you, and you were three sheets to the wind at the time. You couldn't even stand up. We were merely trying to save you from ruining your last clean and holeless shirt by puking your guts onto it."

"So what you're saying is all I have to do is get cross-eyed drunk and you'll help me?" She tapped her fingers thoughtfully against her lips. "It's an interesting idea."

Shaye was shaking his head before she finished. He folded his arms over his chest, his bony chin jutting. "Do not even think about it. I will make you regret it."

She shrugged. "Might be worth it. Come on now. Stop dawdling."

With that, she exited the alcove, skirting the crush as she made her way up to the dais, leaving Shaye to trail behind.

Chapter 6

Shaye followed swiftly after Fairlie, settling a guiding hand on the small of her back. She glanced back at him.

"Do you think I'll get lost?" she whispered.

The crowd had hushed, all eyes on King William.

"Not after they see what you've done," Shaye said, his voice dropping low. "After this, you'll be as recognizable as the king."

A pleased flush colored her cheeks, and her fingers fluttered over her master's badge. She wore it pinned above her heart. "Flattery? That must have hurt. Did you break anything?"

Shaye didn't let his smile show. Nor did he allow his unending anger and hurt that she was leaving Sylmont rise up again. He'd lost a sennight of her company to his own bitterness already, and he'd started the night no better. If he was to salvage it, he had to keep himself reined. Besides, he'd made up his mind. He would let her go off on her journey, but he would not be far behind. If he had to settle in the miserable backwater Stanton until she was ready to go, he would.

"It's not flattery," he told her. "It's fact. You're about to be the most famous and sought-out metalsmith in Crosspointe. By tomorrow morning there will be a dozen merchants banging down your door for the exclusive right to sell your work. Every one will already have a list of a hundred or more orders for custom commissions, each paying more than the last."

A horrified expression suffused Fairlie's face. "Good thing I'm leaving then, isn't it?" she said weakly.

Shaye's anger surged and he snatched it back. "They'll find you. In fact, it will make them want you more."

Now she rolled her eyes at him. "In Stanton?"

"Maybe I'll tell them where to look," he said, the bite returning to his voice despite himself.

She shook her head, but only changed the subject. "I want to go to the Maida of Chayos tomorrow morning. I want to take her an offering before—" She broke off with a small wince. "Anyhow, I have some bags of trinkets I've made. I don't suppose you'd be willing to help me?" she asked doubtfully. "I plan to go early."

"Of course. I shall be there first thing."

There was no time to say more. They'd arrived at the foot of the dais. Fairlie stopped and Shaye could feel the shiver that ran down her back to her heels. He bent close to her ear, grasping her cold hand and squeezing.

"I could still light up Ryland's coattails."

She gave a faint shake of her head, staring straight ahead and taking a deep breath. She let go of his hand and straightened her shoulders. Shaye curled his fingers into his palm and shoved his hand into his pocket. Fairlie never leaned on anyone for anything unless she absolutely did *not* need to.

King William nodded to Fairlie and then lifted his chin to speak. "Welcome to all of you," he began, smiling as he opened his arms expansively. "I am pleased that you came, despite the weather."

It had been raining for three days straight and the wind had been gusting sideways. Water ran in creeks down the streets of Sylmont. Only people who couldn't avoid to ventured out. That most every member of Crosspointe's elite had answered the crown's invitation was worthy of note, a sign that the crown was not nearly as weak as Shaye's Uncle Nicholas would like it to be.

"You have been invited here to celebrate the emergence of a truly unique and wonderful talent. As you all know, nearly five months ago, Queen Naren was killed by Jutras invaders," the king said, his voice thickening. He swallowed, looking down for a moment. Slowly he lifted his head again. "We suffered an inconceivable loss that day. Not only did we lose a devoted, beloved, and brilliant queen, but we lost our innocence. We learned that day that we are not safe from the Jutras."

The king scanned the room, his gaze blistering. "But my friends, my courageous subjects, tonight is not a night for mourning. It is a night for remembering. I have asked you here to remember the sacrifice of my queen and those who died that day. It is because of the sacrifices of those men and women in the throne room that night that we can still gather in fellowship and joy. They must never be forgotten, and Crosspointe must learn the hard lessons of their deaths. We can no longer go on as we have. Our world is changing and we must change with it or we will surely be overrun."

Shaye snorted softly. Not that he too had not been deeply saddened by Naren's death, but the king was plastering it on thick. Just then, King William's gaze settled on him. It was heavy and full of reprimand. Shaye glared back. He did not cow so easily, and he was no sheep to be manipulated by pretty words. Nor was he impressed by the crown. His family was nearly as powerful, and wealthier.

The king looked out over the hushed assembly again. "Tonight I also want to introduce you to a woman of extraordinary talent. She is a brilliant star, outshining every other. You will shortly see the proof of my extravagant claims," the king said. "She was the last pupil of one of the finest master metalsmiths who has ever lived. Perhaps you've heard of him; perhaps you are lucky enough to have one of his works. His name was Toff Durkin."

A ripple of whispers spread over the room. Toff's works were highly prized all over Crosspointe and in faraway cities all around the Inland Sea. Now that he was dead, their value had increased dramatically.

"Toff told me that he knew from the moment he met Fairlie as a young girl that she would far outstrip his own talents. That was thirteen seasons ago, and before he died, he declared her a master of her craft."

Shaye felt Fairlie rock back on her heels. Tears slipped from the corners of her eyes, trailing black kohl behind them. Shaye nudged her with his elbow and handed her his handkerchief.

"Do you want to scare everyone?"

She sniffed and rubbed at her face, making more of a mess. He took the handkerchief and deftly wiped her face. The king, who'd been watching their interaction, chose that moment to intervene.

"Ladies and gentlemen, let me present Fairlie Norwich, master metalsmith."

Fairlie looked stricken as she stepped up onto the dais. She shook off Shaye's steadying hand on her elbow. She went to stand beside the king, her chin raised. The king turned and embraced her, whispering against her ear. She flushed, then straightened and nodded. He brushed his knuckles over her master's badge and murmured something else. Fairlie murmured back at him, and then the king turned back to his audience.

"When I first saw Miss Norwich's masterpiece, I was deeply moved . . . and grateful. It will be hung in the throne room as a tribute to Queen Naren and those who died that dreadful day." His voice had gone gruff and there were white dents on his nostrils, as if he grappled hard with his emotions. Though Shaye suspected there was more to the speech, the king stepped back and gestured. "Now, without further ado . . ."

Liveried footmen stepped forward, grasping the gold silk and pulling it away with a flourish.

Silence.

Not a single word broke the sudden quiet. Shaye wasn't certain anyone was even breathing.

Fairlie had created a wondrous sculpture. At its heart was the face of Queen Naren in silver. The contours were smooth and the likeness was true. The light of the chandeliers rippled over the delicate shades of pink and red that brushed her smiling lips and cheeks. Her eyes, made of inlaid diamond, sapphire, and obsidian, looked upward in delight. All around her spun an invisible wind. On it floated leaves and flower petals made of brightly colored *sylveth*. Shaye had helped her shape the *sylveth* chips using majick and chisels. They were attached to fine wires of a black metal that Shaye had not recognized, and Fairlie refused to tell him what it was.

"It's rare," she said with a flirt of her eyebrows. "And a guild secret."

The metal came in ingots. The making of the wire alone was a master-level skill. Its black coloring made it nearly impossible to see the wires, enhancing the impression of a whirling wind.

Also riding the frozen swirl of wind were *sylveth* seeds of every sort—acorns, chestnuts, sunflowers, peppers, melons, berries, and many more. Each was etched with the name of someone who had died when the Jutras had attacked.

A slow clap began somewhere in the crowd. Then another pair of hands joined. The applause spread, a solemn swell growing into a thunderous roar. Fairlie went pale and then red. Her hands shook and her fingers twisted together.

"Are you well?" Ryland said, coming to stand beside Shaye.

The prince was taller and heavier than Shaye. Dimples cut deep into his cheeks as he smiled and nodded to a fat matron with pink feathers in her hair.

"Shouldn't I be?" Shaye growled, unaccountably annoyed at the prince. It was because Ryland had witnessed the foreboding. He didn't like questions without answers, and a foreboding, by its nature, was a riddle until it was answered by time.

"Did you have another ... episode?" Ryland asked, confirming Shaye's suspicion.

"No."

"And no better understanding of it?"

"Only that it certainly can't refer to you choking on your dinner, as that would certainly be a joyous occasion."

Ryland snorted softly, one hand covering his mouth. "You are certainly in a sharp mood. Still chafing over Fairlie's trip home?"

"Just tired of the ill-bred company I'm keeping," Shaye drawled.

"Ah, but my breeding is impeccable. I am, after all, a prince."

"You're a rash on my ass."

"And I thought that was just your charming personality."

Shaye smiled, his mood lightened for the moment.

"Fairlie looks like she's about to throw up," Ryland observed, crossing his arms over his chest. "I do hope she keeps her skirts out of the way. She looks good in the gown."

"Thanks to you, I hear," Shaye said, a slight edge sharpening his voice again. He grimaced. Something about Ryland grated on him. It hadn't always been that way. But now . . . something had changed. He wasn't sure when it began, but he found himself irritated and on edge in his friend's company.

"Thanks to my father," Ryland corrected. "He wanted her to shine as bright as her sculpture." Ryland looked up at the face of his mother, a shadow sliding over his features. "She deserves that much and so much more."

Shaye put a hand on Ryland's shoulder, squeezing. "It's a worthy tribute. Your mother was kind to Fairlie. Do you remember when she tore a strip off Toff for letting Fairlie burn herself? As if Toff could have stopped her from trying to grab that piece when she dropped it in the forge. Your mother in a temper was truly magnificent. A good match for your father. I never saw him get the last word in on her."

Ryland smiled crookedly, wiping surreptitiously at the corners of his eyes. He cleared his throat. "She was fierce. You always knew what mood she was in—she could never mask herself the way my father does."

"He does do that, doesn't he? It's lucky gambling is

illegal or there are a lot of pockets that would be considerably lighter."

"Now that Fairlie has her master's badge and is determined to visit her mother, are you going to stop dangling about her forge and earn yours?" Ryland asked, changing the subject.

The corners of Shaye's mouth pulled down. "That's her plan, isn't it?"

"She's going to push you right out of the nest and make you fly, whether you like it or not."

"She'll hate Stanton. And her mother."

"Maybe. But how fast she comes back is up to you. How fast can you get your master's badge?"

"Go to the depths," Shaye growled.

"At any rate, I will not be leaving. Father is keeping me here for a while."

"Oh?" Shaye turned, frowning. "Because of Vaughn?"

"That, and I'm sure he has other reasons. I'm not privy to his plans. I know very little about the inner workings of court business."

"But then again, your answer would be the same if you were in the thick of things, wouldn't it?"

"I expect so." Ryland shrugged, tugging his waistcoat down and adjusting his watch chain. Unlike Shaye, his clothing was ornate and extremely fashionable. Though he wore only two pieces of jewelry—a gold ring with the royal family crest inlaid in indigo *sylveth* on his right forefinger and a cravat pin—his pale blue waistcoat and turned-back cuffs were embroidered with silver thread that followed a marvelously intricate pattern. Lace frothed along the cuffs of his shirt and fountained from beneath his chin. His shoes gleamed, and his collar was so high and stiff that it looked as if it might choke him at any moment. Shaye's gaze settled broodingly on the cravat pin before he looked away. A gift from Fairlie. His fingers found his own pin and he twisted it absently.

"Better say nothing than unwittingly betray a state secret, eh?"

"So I've heard. Sensible too."

"You should really look into finding honest work."

Ryland smiled, the shadows sliding away from his face. "So should you, majicar. Watch now. I think the spectacle is nearly over."

The king raised his hands and the noise died down. "Thank you all for coming and sharing this wondrous work and remembering your valiant queen and those who died during the Jutras invasion. Now I invite you to come up closer and view the work, then step into the banquet hall for supper. Enjoy yourselves. And you can all accost Master Norwich to get on her list for a commission."

He stepped down, a thin applause following him. He was flanked by half a dozen Crown Shields and accompanied by the knot of advisers and dignitaries who'd been on the dais with him, each stopping to congratulate Fairlie. The last to step off the dais was the veiled stranger and her companion. "You are Chayos-blessed," she said to Fairlie, bowing slightly inside her draperies. Her voice was rich and deep, like the low sound of a temple bell. "May she hold you close and keep you safe." Her accent was strange; Shaye couldn't place it.

There was something in the way she said the words that made Shaye's hackles rise. As if she was warning Fairlie. He started to step up on the dais. Ryland caught his arm.

"Wait."

"Why?"

"My father would prefer they were not offended."

"What makes you think I'll do any such thing?"

"Because you think you're Fairlie's watchdog and because giving offense is what you do best. Let it go. They are important, Shaye. This is their first visit to Crosspointe, the first time their country has met with us."

"And you know this, even though you are not privy to the inner workings of the court," Shaye noted sardonically.

Ryland's smile was thin. "That's right. You don't have to worry. They aren't hurting Fairlie."

The veiled woman's companion had taken Fairlie's hand in his. He bent and kissed it, his long brown hair falling in a curtain around his face, his mouth lingering. Shaye stiffened, pulling against Ryland's grip. The ambassador from the nameless country straightened, but did not let go of Fairlie's hand.

"Your talent is extraordinary," he said, his thumb stroking her skin. "You will do great things. Greater even than this marvelous sculpture."

His lips were red and shaped the words stiffly. His accent was different from his companion's, and somehow familiar. There was a predatory look in the ambassador's eyes that sent another jolt of unease through Shaye.

He jerked away from Ryland and stepped up on the dais just as the foreign ambassador dropped Fairlie's hand and collected his veiled companion. They stepped down, following the king. Fairlie stared after them, rubbing her hands together.

"What's wrong?"

She shook her head, her brow crimping. "His touch is very . . . powerful."

"Powerful?" Ryland asked with arched brows as he gave her a hug. He stepped back, holding her at arm's length as he eyed her. "I can arrange a quiet assignation for the two of you."

Fairlie rolled her eyes. "Why are you always after me to find a lover? I don't even know him."

"But you said his touch was powerful. Perhaps your body knows something your mind is slow to understand. What do you think, Shaye?"

The look he turned on his friend was too innocent.

"I say that just because you're a rutting prick, it doesn't mean Fairlie has to join your adventures. If she wants a lover, she's perfectly capable of taking the matter into her own hands. But clearly she is not interested, and you baiting her now when everyone in this room is here to celebrate her talent is unforgivable." The words rolled off his tongue with feverish heat. A foreboding was coming. He could feel the majick starting to curl in tight around him. Not here. He couldn't let it happen here.

Ryland sobered. "You're right. I apologize, Fairlie." He offered her his arm. "Would you care to walk with me?"

"You're incorrigible," she said, hugging him close against her for a moment, then pinching him so hard that he yelped. "Between you and Shaye, I'm glad I didn't have actual big brothers or I never would have survived. You two are bad enough."

"I am not your brother," Shaye said, a little too loudly.

Ryland looked back. "Then what are you?"

Shaye did not answer. He had to get out of there. He veered off into the crowd, shoving through until he reached an exit. A few minutes later he staggered into a small, unlit library. He shut the door and collapsed back against it, letting the majick swallow him.

This time the foreboding struck like a hammer. It was the price for staving it off long enough to get out of the crush. Flames consumed him, searing the marrow of his bones. Majick tore through him in a tornado. He slid down to sit on the floor, his leg muscles spasming. His stomach lurched and he gritted his teeth hard.

The urgency of the foreboding swept him up, spinning him inside a maelstrom. He caught glimpses of trees and curved teeth and heard the flutter of a terrified heart and the beat of wings. It seemed for a moment that the foreboding would coalesce into something more tangible, but then it shattered apart and the wild majick went careening off in every direction. Swiftly Shaye clutched his *illidre* and invoked the capture spell.

Moments later the light of his *illidre* faded and he was left alone in the dark room. His breath sounded ragged and loud, and his limbs sprawled limply. The sour smell of sweat filled his nose. He sat there for some time, hardly aware of the time passing. The fear didn't let go of him. Something dreadful was coming and he could do nothing about it. He could feel that he was running out of time. He needed to consult a majicar with more experience, and he had to do it soon. *Tomorrow*, he promised himself. After he accompanied Fairlie to the Maida of Chayos.

It was a while later that he was able to stand. He straightened his clothing, feeling the pulse of power inside his *illidre*. It was like a second heartbeat reverberating through his body.

He opened the door and let himself out. The crowd had spilled from the main ballroom into the constellation of smaller receiving rooms. Shaye found himself pausing in the doorway of the ballroom, surrounded by heavy waves of noxious perfume and a cacophony of idiotic chatter. He eyed the crowd inside. There was no sign of Fairlie or Ryland. He spun around and strode away, shoving through until he reached the exit. A few minutes later he was striding out of the castle walls. He didn't feel the chill wind or the driving rain, intent as he was on getting to his favorite tavern as quickly as possible, where he could find a bottle of good brandy and a limber whore.

Chapter 7

The swarming crowd descended on Fairlie like mag-
pies on a pile of jewels. She smiled uneasily at the people gushing praise at her, asking her when they could
drop in on her, whether she was available for afternoon tea or supper, whether she could make jewelry,
or shoe buckles, forks, swords, and an endless list of
other items.

"I am certain that Miss Norwich will be glad to entertain any projects. However, you will need to see her
secretary for an appointment," Ryland said firmly, and
then repeated it again and again as he guided Fairlie
through the crowd.

They took refuge in a small salon that was empty of
revelers for the moment. Fairlie collapsed onto a chaise,
rubbing her temples and heaving a deep sigh. She looked
at Ryland.

"You do realize I don't *have* a secretary, don't you?"

"You will tomorrow," he assured her. "I'll arrange it.
Congratulations. I believe you are a sensation." He went
to stand in front of the fire, his hands caught behind
his back. "You'll have to think about an apprentice or
several and a journeyman to help you. You should also
consider what you want to charge for your work. I can
help you with that. I suspect you will sell yourself far too
cheaply. You'll need to charge an enormous fee if you
want to whittle down your orders to something man-
ageable. You'll also want to consider limiting how many

projects you take on at any given time to make sure you allow yourself adequate time for your own works."

Fairlie's hands had dropped to her lap as she stared at him. She shook her head. "This is a nightmare."

Ryland grinned. Only Fairlie would consider such a spectacular success a nightmare. "I should have such bad dreams. Let's see. You have become a master metalsmith, and you are only twenty-two seasons old. The king has thrown an elegant party with you as guest of honor, and all of Crosspointe's elite are groveling at your feet for the chance to pay you ridiculously exorbitant sums for your work. You're going to be very wealthy, very soon."

"Thank the gods I'm going to Stanton in two days," Fairlie said, looking as though someone had struck her on the head.

"Oh, come now. It isn't that bad. What did you think you were working so hard for?"

"To be a master! To be the best at working metal."

"And you are. And these are your wages, so enjoy them," he said dismissively. "Would you like something to eat? I'll fetch you something and you can stay here and rest. Or would you like to come out and visit your adoring public again?"

"Dear Chayos, no!" Fairlie shivered exaggeratedly. She looked at the door. "Where is Shaye?"

"Probably holed up in the Emerald Eye by now," Ryland said.

"He left?"

Her disappointment was palpable. Ryland hid a smile. Shaye would give his right hand to know she was bothered by his disappearance. The idiot was totally besotted with Fairlie and refused to admit it to himself or to her. He loitered endlessly around her, like a stray dog begging for table scraps. Meanwhile, Fairlie was oblivious to Shaye's attachment. Her whole life was wrapped up in metalcraft, and a mere flesh-and-bone man had a difficult task in tearing her attention away from her anvil. But her disappointment proved she was not as indifferent to him as she seemed.

"You know Shaye. He doesn't go in much for these sorts of crushes." He tipped his head. "You look beautiful, if I hadn't mentioned it yet."

Fairlie looked startled. "Don't be an ass. My dress is beautiful. I'm . . . adequate."

"You really ought to learn how to accept a compliment gracefully."

"I know how. But *you* are always supposed to tell me the truth. Remember? At least what you are free to tell."

"And what if the truth is that I think you *are* beautiful?" Ryland crossed his arms, leaning against the wall and watching her sideways.

"Then either you've been drinking or you need spectacles."

"No. The dress is pretty, but it's the woman inside it tonight who draws every eye like moths to a flame."

She rolled her eyes and slumped back against the chaise, regarding him balefully. Ryland straightened and came to crouch in front of her.

"You have no idea what you are, do you?"

"Tired, annoyed, and a little bit murderous?"

Ryland chuckled, shaking his head. "You're a force. Like fire, wind, and wave. Inside you is something that makes everyone look twice, and they don't even know why. But when they look in your eyes, they know. It's like looking into the heart of your forge. They want to be near and bathe in your heat."

Fairlie stared at him a moment, her eyes narrowed. She pulled her hands from his grip and set them on his shoulders. She smiled and Ryland smiled back.

"You *are* an ass."

She shoved. Ryland tumbled over backward, landing flat on his back. Fairlie chortled. He sat up.

"Am I interrupting?"

The man who slouched casually into the room was shorter than Ryland by an inch or two. He had one hand in his pants pocket; the other held a glass of wine. His brown hair was cut short. His eyes were blue, his face tanned—it was thinner than Ryland's, with angled cheekbones and a sharp chin. But the family resemblance was obvious.

Ryland scowled at his brother. He shouldn't be here. Vaughn ignored Ryland, drinking the rest of his wine and setting the glass down with a hard click.

"Vaughn! I didn't think to see you tonight!" Fairlie tumbled across the room, pulling him into a hug.

He hugged her back, finally looking at Ryland over her head. His eyes were stony.

As Fairlie laughed again, Vaughn broke the glance, pushing her to arm's length and examining her from head to foot. "How could I miss your triumph? I am humbled by your talent. And I have to thank you. My mother would have been amazed and pleased at the way you captured her. My heartiest congratulations to you, Master Norwich."

He glanced at Ryland again, his expression austere. "But it appears I've interrupted something. What did my little brother do? Should I punish him for you?"

"Do you think I can't do it myself?" Fairlie asked, putting her hands on her hips. "He was teasing me."

"Really? Brother, where are your manners?"

Ryland climbed to his feet. He tipped his head, his brows rising in a silent question. His expression twisted into a scowl when Fairlie turned to look for his reply.

"I thought you swore not to set foot in the castle anymore," he said, cold hardening his voice. He was certain that anyone lingering outside the door would hear the antagonism and believe it. Fairlie did. She stepped back from between them, her expression tense.

"And I wouldn't have had to, if you had returned any of my messages," Vaughn said.

"I've been busy."

"I'll remind you we have a business together. Though I will gladly buy you out anytime you wish."

"I don't think so. I have worked hard to make Fathom Enterprises profitable. I am not going to give it up just because my partner is intent on undermining the crown at every turn, not to mention getting into bed with every unsavory character he can find. Father should disown you," Ryland said venomously.

"If you want to keep our business making money, then you should make yourself more available. Something pressing has come up. Are you able to tear yourself away from the festivities?"

Ryland curled his lip, his heart thudding. "If it will get rid of you, then certainly. Shall we?"

He stalked to the doorway and stopped as Vaughn took Fairlie's hand again and smiled, his mouth stiff.

"My apologies. We have forgotten civility, my brother and I. Congratulations again. I'll be one of those lining up for a Fairlie Norwich original work. Forgive me for abandoning you so suddenly. Ryland will no doubt return quickly."

He kissed her hand. Ryland followed him out into the gallery. Vaughn swung around.

"Your offices?" He gave a minuscule tip of his head toward the ballroom.

Ryland barely twitched his head in a nod. Anyone watching them would have seen only a bitter standoff between the two brothers, once close, now at odds. And they *were* being watched. Always and inevitably.

"After you," Ryland said, gesturing.

Vaughn walked in front of him. They did not speak as they wound a serpentine path through the crowd. As people started to notice them, there were first startled looks and then a rippling of quiet followed by behind-the-hand whispering. No one had expected to see Vaughn here tonight. This was the first time the elder prince had returned since his very public break with his father. There was no one who had not heard the story, and there was no one who wasn't watching avidly as the brothers approached their father. A hush fell over the assembly.

"I do not recall seeing your name on the guest list," the king said coldly, his eyes glittering.

"Apparently I was overlooked. But I came to visit my

brother on a matter of business. Unless you object ...
Your Majesty?"

The last was said with a sneer. Their father flashed a
blistering look at Ryland, who glanced down at his feet,
appropriately cowed.

"My apologies, Father," he muttered. "I did not expect
him."

"See that you don't linger longer than necessary," King
William said to Vaughn, ignoring Ryland's apology.

"Unfortunately this business is of a complicated sort.
It may take a while. Possibly another visit or two. Your
Majesty." Vaughn tacked on the last, drawling it dispar-
agingly.

The king stared murder at his elder son. "If you have
business to conduct with Ryland, do so in his offices.
You are not welcome elsewhere." He started to turn and
then stopped, looking back. "Be sure to use the servants'
entrance, won't you?"

Their father turned his back. Ryland led the way through
the whispering quiet out of the gala. He strode quickly, not
bothering to look to see if Vaughn was keeping up.

The castle was a spreading maze covering more than
fifty acres. That didn't include any of the outer buildings,
mews, kennels, gardens, or any of the parks and forests.
More than four hundred seasons old, it had been added
to and remodeled and rebuilt more than a hundred
times. As children, Ryland and Shaye had explored every nook and cranny of it. Not even the seneschal was
more familiar with the castle. Now Ryland turned off
into an unused corridor, ducking in and out of rooms.
Sheets gray with dust covered the furniture and puffs
rose around his shoes as he walked. He heard the thud
of Vaughn's boots behind him, and strained to hear the
footfalls of anyone following them. He heard nothing,
but that didn't mean someone wasn't using majick to
conceal himself.

They went down stairs and then up, through unused
suites of rooms, galleries full of moldering portraits,

musty hangings, and yellowing marble sculptures. It took them out of the way of watching eyes, the dust on the floor proving no one else had passed through recently.

Ryland led them back into the occupied sections of the castle near his offices. They were located in the northwest wing on the third floor of Torquist Tower. It was hexagonal in shape and filled with broad windows, the ceilings ribbed with heavy timbers. Each floor was divided into four spacious interconnected rooms.

Ryland's touch unlocked the wards on the door and he swung it open.

"Make this quick. I've no stomach for your company," he said, motioning for Vaughn to enter first.

"Ah, such mewling. And here I thought it took a strong stomach to live in this pile of stone and mortar, licking our father's boots."

Ryland shut the door behind them, touching the wards on the inside of the door to lock it again. Protected by majick, in this room they were safe from spying eyes, even with the windows wide-open.

Ryland rubbed his hands over his face and turned to his brother. He reached out, grabbing Vaughn and pulling him into a back-thumping hug.

"By the gods, I've missed you. Mewling? Boot licking? Should I be giving you a bruise or two to prove my wrath and hatred to the world?"

Vaughn returned the hug with equal fervor. "You could try, little brother." He dropped one arm, leaving the other about Ryland's shoulders and looked around hopefully. "Do you have anything to drink in here?"

"In the main office."

Ryland led his brother through another room into a third. Sitting in front of the broad windows was an enormous desk littered with papers and ledgers. On the inner walls were floor-to-ceiling bookcases holding a mishmash of books, rolled parchments and maps, more ledgers, and an assortment of bric-a-brac. The floor was covered with a thick black and maroon patterned rug from Tiro Pilan. Facing the desk was a cushioned leather couch and two wingback armchairs. Between the windows and the first of the bookshelves on the right was a sideboard made of teak with grotesque feet carved like spawn.

Ryland crossed to it and pulled open the doors. He glanced at Vaughn, who'd stretched out on the couch.

"What's your pleasure?"

"I don't suppose you have any of that Kalibrian Pervach?"

"I do."

Ryland took out a decanter three-quarters full of the spicy red liquor. It had a slightly bitter flavor, stinging the tongue and burning the gut. Vaughn had introduced him to it many seasons ago, and it remained a favorite, particularly on cold, blustery nights.

He poured two glasses and handed one to his brother before sitting in one of the wingback chairs. He lifted his glass in a silent toast and took a large swallow. The resultant fire in his belly felt good.

"So, big brother of mine, what really brings you to the castle?"

Vaughn rubbed one hand over his eyes, yawning. "Trouble. What else?"

"Anything in particular?"

His brother shook his head, his lips tightening. He swirled the liquor in his glass and then took a deep swig.

"No. And yes."

"Very cryptic."

Vaughn smiled. He looked thinner than he had, and worn. Or rather, Ryland thought, studying his brother, any softness had been stripped away and what was left was the basalt core. Their father had been right to choose him for this hunt.

Vaughn's job was to ferret out information about potential attacks on the crown—political or physical. Publicly, he'd put himself at violent odds with his father in order to turn himself into a tempting prize for the powerful coterie who wanted to be rid of the king and Rampling rule altogether. Vaughn could be the key to mounting a successful rebellion. But to preserve his story and his mission, he could not openly meet with their father to report his findings—it would be too suspicious. On the other hand, visiting with Ryland was perfectly natural since they shared ownership of Fathom Enterprises.

But playing the part of the traitor prince was a strain. People had to believe that he despised his family and that the split between him and his father was too vast and acrimonious to ever be repaired, and painful enough to merit breaking ranks and turning traitor.

"This business with raising taxes and the rumors of increasing majicar service has stirred the hornets' nest," Vaughn said. "It was supposed to draw out conspirators, but it's made things tumultuous, so much that I can't tell who's merely angry and resentful and who is plotting against the crown." He took another drink, sipping this time. "Any other assassination attempts?"

Ryland shook his head. "Not that I know of. I'm not sure Father would tell me."

Vaughn nodded. "Keep your eyes open all the same. That last attempt was sloppy—poison with a majicar healer standing nearby. There was never a chance it would work. Yet they got that close. I keep thinking about it—what if it was a feint? They make him look one way for trouble and then attack from the unexpected corner."

Worry coiled in Ryland's gut. He sat forward, his elbows on his knees. "What sort of thing are you thinking of?"

Vaughn shook his head in frustration, emptying his glass. "I don't know. But either that assassination attempt didn't have anything to do with the people involved in bringing the Jutras here or it was a decoy for something else. Something feels wrong."

He stood, pacing restlessly.

"The hate for the crown is thicker and deeper than I ever imagined. They've been laying the foundation for years—the chancery suit was the first salvo. Father may have let it go too long. This is not going to go away before there is bloodshed. Tell him that. The tension is growing—it's a boiling volcano and soon it's going to blow."

"Surely he knows that. Isn't that why he's planted you among them?"

"I don't think he knows how bad it is. And another thing: there's been a push among the merchants to strike against the new taxes. Just the threat of a disruption in the food supply would lead to hoarding and riots. It would tear the country apart, and it's Father who would be blamed. He needs to head it off somehow."

"Is that the worst of it?"

Vaughn shook his head. "I don't know. There's something afoot. But not everyone is convinced I'm not playacting. It may take a little more to get them to believe I've really turned on Father and will do anything to bring him down. But I do know that something big is in the works, and I have to tell you, Ryland, I'm worried."

"I'll let Father know. I doubt he'll be surprised. His plans are like onions—endlessly layered. We don't know a speck of what he's got his fingers into."

"Make sure he knows how hard the sentiment is against him. From wealthy to poor—the lies, the rumors; they are working. Father may have plans, but if he doesn't win back the hearts of his people soon, he'll lose everything. We all will. Starting with our heads."

"A future to look forward to. You headless and incapable of speaking," Ryland said.

Vaughn laughed, a harsh sound. "You'd better get going before anyone starts to wonder if I've killed you."

"Or if we're conspiring. All right."

"I'll send you a suitably rude message demanding your presence as soon as Father lets me know what he wants you to do."

"Tell him I'll need something to feed back to them. Something I've wormed out of you that you didn't mean to tell me."

"Ah, so I play idiot to your brilliant mind," Ryland said, draining his drink. "You'll destroy my reputation."

"Your reputation, dear brother, is with the ladies. Something about your limp wick and the speed at which your candle gutters."

Ryland shook his head, then stood. "And now I'll be stupid to boot."

"Call it too trusting."

"Stupid."

"Maggot-headed," Vaughn agreed. "Give me another drink before I go, won't you? I need a little more fortification."

Ryland poured them both another glass of Pervach. They drank quickly, neither speaking again. With silent accord they returned to the door.

"Ready?" Vaughn asked.

Ryland drew a breath, then keyed the wards. He thrust the door open violently and stomped out into the corridor.

"I'm not approving any contract without seeing it first. I don't trust you. So messenger it up here. When I'm ready to discuss changes, I'll send for you."

Vaughn leaned in, his nose nearly touching Ryland's. "Be careful, little brother. You never know when something might happen to you. Remember the survivorship clause. You choke on your breakfast bacon and Fathom Enterprises belongs entirely to me. Don't for a single moment think that I'll let you yank me hither and yon like a dog on a chain. I'll not sit idly for it. The next thing you know you'll be tits up and feeding the sea."

Ryland thrust his hands out in a stiff shove, sending his brother staggering backward to the wall.

"Don't threaten me. I'll have your kidneys on a spit if you even think of coming after me. Now be a good old dog and go fetch me those contracts. And, Vaughn, don't forget to use the servants' entrance."

Chapter 8

Found.

He told her so, gloating and triumphant. His talent to find, hers to hold.

His mind groped hers. She did not turn him away; she did not invite him in. He put a hand on her back, pushing harder through the connection of touch. His mind nuzzled and bumped like a hungry child—a violent, demanding child. *Elation. Determination. Want. Need. Hunger* bled through the connection.

She could not shut him out. He was hers and that was a tie that could not be cut. She snarled. A razor claw of thought raked along his exposed mindscape. He shuddered and made a sound of pain. His hand dropped. Triumph blazed. *She* controlled the tie between them, not him. She would do what was needful, but she would not allow him to encroach. *She* was Warden; *she* was Speaker.

Chapter 9

Ryland did not want to return to the gala. He would much rather have trotted off after Shaye to the Emerald Eye.

His head throbbed, and the Pervach only made it worse, as well as making his knees a little wobbly. But there was no choice. Everyone would be waiting for his return, watching to see his reaction. He had to play the night's game out to the end. He checked his pocket watch. He'd been gone less than a glass.

If anything, there were more people packed into the vast ballroom than when he'd left. He circled around the edges, squeezing through the thicket of bodies. He could not avoid getting waylaid by officious parents looking for husbands for their darling mule-faced daughters. He pulled himself away, offering noncommittal smiles and promises that as soon as he could, he would return for a glass of wine or a dance.

He went to the salon where he'd left Fairlie. She was gone. The room was full of giggling young men and women playing a game of knucklebones. Losers were required to perform some silly chore, or consume something inedible, or engage in any number of more salacious activities. Ryland glanced in and then left them to it.

He returned to the main hall. He finally found Fairlie in a corner surrounded by a dozen women, each talking and waving to demand her undivided attention. They were his mother's orphaned ladies-in-waiting. They had all been devastated by her death. Fairlie looked wan and stiff and patient, as if she was willing herself to stand there until they stopped or she fainted. The latter of which might occur very soon. She'd not eaten; Ryland was sure of it. His fault. He grimaced. Duty sometimes was a pain in the ass.

He pushed through the middle of the room, sliding in behind her and gripping her elbow.

"Ladies, please excuse us. I've promised the ambassador to have a moment with Fairlie. Won't you excuse us?"

He didn't wait for an answer to his vague request but steered his charge through the crowd toward the dining hall.

"What ambassador?" Fairlie asked, her voice sharp and energetic, belying her appearance.

"The one to put you back into a good mood. Specifically, a plate of food and some wine." He eyed her. "Maybe a bottle or two. Didn't I tell you to eat?"

"Actually you offered to fetch me something and let me rest. And then you ran off to have your little pissing match with Vaughn," she said sourly.

Ryland felt the smile slide from his face. It sounded so mild, so reversible. If only she knew. Brothers they remained in the heart, but for everyone else, the break was permanent. And in this case, appearances might as well be real. "My apologies," he said.

She covered his hand with hers, saying no more. In the dining room, they loaded plates with the delectable dishes presented on a long buffet. Ryland pocketed two glasses and took a bottle of a dry red wine from Esengaile. They perched in the window seat of an alcove that was lent some small measure of privacy by draperies caught up in drooping bunches on the sides.

Ryland poured out some wine and drank deeply, then attacked his food ferociously.

"That lamb is already dead, you know," Fairlie pointed out. "You don't have to kill it twice."

Ryland flicked her a black look. She finished eating and set aside her plate, watching him as she sipped her wine.

"Is it completely broken, then?" she asked. "You and Vaughn?"

Ryland swallowed, glancing about. The illusion of privacy was only that. All around them people listened, faceless behind the sheltering curtains. More performance. He shook his head, letting the bitterness and regret for the necessity of this role fill his face. As expected, Fairlie misread it as he meant her to.

"I can't forgive what he's done. He ought be up in front of the lord chancellor for treason."

"Vaughn loves Crosspointe," Fairlie objected. "He would do nothing to harm it."

Ryland couldn't take it anymore. He felt like he was being torn in half. "Enough about my lunatic brother," he said gruffly. "Let us take a stroll. You are the one everyone wants to talk to, after all."

He kept her with him for the next few glasses, introducing her to everyone he could, making small talk and keeping a carefully pleasant smile pasted on his lips.

"Good evening, Prince Ryland." Nicholas Weverton stepped in front of them. His clothes were perfectly cut. The creases in his trousers were crisp and straight, and his cravat was a delicate and subdued froth of blue lace at his throat. He bowed to Fairlie, taking her hand and kissing it. "Your work is lovely, my dear. I congratulate you on attaining master, and I hope you will allow me to purchase a commission very soon."

Ryland stiffened, trying hard not to show his antagonism. "Fairlie, this is Nicholas Weverton."

"Thank you," Fairlie said warmly to Weverton. "You're Shaye's uncle, aren't you?" She sounded more than a little surprised.

Weverton smiled. "His mother was quite a bit older than my father, and my father had his children much later. Thus Shaye is only a few seasons younger than I. Most people are startled to see how close in age we are."

He leaned forward conspiratorially. "Though I am far more handsome."

Fairlie grinned. "That isn't difficult to accomplish."

He laughed. "Now I know why he likes you."

She shook her head. "He doesn't like me. He pities me. Says I'm an infant and cannot take care of myself." She rolled her eyes. "How often do I have to eat and bathe anyhow?"

She stopped suddenly and flushed. Then quickly, "Oh dear. I'm sorry. I really shouldn't have said that, should I? I'm afraid I'm not very good at this." She waved her fingers at the rest of the crowd. "It's why I keep hidden in my workshop. I know how to talk to metal, and it never thinks I'm silly or impertinent. Unfortunately, Shaye has deserted his post and left me to say whatever pops into my head, so really it's all his fault."

Weverton took her hand again and squeezed it. "My nephew can hardly judge you on that front. He's notorious for letting his mouth get away from him. It is why he has so very few friends. But I find you to be absolutely perfect. I am delighted to be in your company. Would you care to walk with me? If Prince Ryland will relinquish you, of course."

He nodded at Ryland and led Fairlie away, not waiting for permission. Ryland watched them uneasily. Fairlie was safe enough in Weverton's company. Shaye would make sure his uncle did not take advantage of her in any way. He snorted softly to himself. *Fairlie* would make sure of it. If Weverton tried anything, she'd break his arm for him.

He waited to retire until after his father had abandoned the festivities, and then he returned to his own quarters. He removed his coat and shirt and washed the stink of the night off himself in the cold water of his basin. He shivered as he put on his nightshirt and fell into bed. Exhausted as he was, he couldn't help but go over the events of the night.

Their father had always meant for Vaughn to be the next king, and he still did. Except that with so much anger stirring against King William and his rule, any approbation on his part would guarantee that Vaughn would never be elected. Ryland rubbed his eyes. There was no specific and decided heir to the throne in Crosspointe. Any and all legitimately born Ramplings were eligible to be elected, once the current king or queen died. It was a strange mix of democracy and monarchy, driven by the noble purpose of binding together the people and the monarchy and choosing the best mind and soul to lead the people.

But people could be stupid. And they might not know what was best. So sometimes they needed a little help to find the right path. In this case, it involved tricking them into thinking that their king hated his elder son and that Vaughn would do anything to undermine and destroy his father.

Ryland punched his pillows, wriggling onto his side in an effort to get comfortable. He'd done his best to help solidify that notion tonight. He hoped he'd been convincing. He wasn't sure he was that good an actor.

It wasn't yet dawn when a hand on his shoulder woke Ryland. He snapped awake, lunging up, the dagger he kept under his pillow clutched in his hand.

"Your father wishes you to join him for breakfast."

Niall Strong was his father's steward and closest friend. He was thin and dapper, with a pencil mustache and a neatly trimmed goatee, the top of his head bald. He pushed the dagger to the side with a disdainful finger.

"He would like you to attend him as soon as you are able. Shall I tell him a quarter of a glass?"

Ryland yawned and nodded, setting the dagger on the nightstand and shoving aside the bedclothes. He stumbled out of bed. His eyes were gritty and his mouth tasted like bilge. "Make sure there's plenty of tea. *Strong* tea," he said.

"Of course, Prince Ryland. It will be my pleasure."

He walked to the closet and disappeared inside, shutting the door behind himself.

Ryland used the garderobe and then dressed quickly, not calling his valet. That was the point of having the secret passage in his closet. There were occasions his father didn't care to advertise whom he met with or when. This was one of those times. As far as Ryland's valet was concerned, his master was slothfully asleep and would remain so until well into the afternoon.

Ryland glanced at his watch and groaned. He'd been in bed for no more than three hours. He hoped to the gods that his father didn't keep him long.

He buttoned his shirt to his neck and went to his washbasin to splash his face, the cold water slapping him alert. He wet his comb and ran it through his hair, gathering it into a silver clip at his nape. He poured himself a cup of water and sloshed it around his mouth before spitting it into an ivy plant on the windowsill. Then he slid on his shoes, pulled on his coat, and opened his closet. *Sylveth* lights jumped to life.

The small room was filled with tall drawers and racks of hanging clothing and shelves for shoes and toiletries. In the rear was a full-length mirror. Ryland knelt, feeling along the bottom edge. A *zing* went through his fingers as they brushed across the locking ward. The door hidden behind the mirror sprang open. More lights blossomed in the darkness of the corridor beyond. Ryland stepped inside, pulling the door firmly shut behind him.

He walked along, his footsteps muted by the thick carpet lining the floor. The walls were polished wood, unrelieved by anything but the dim *sylveth* sconces every dozen feet. At the end of the passage was a set of stairs leading upward. He climbed them and turned down the left branch beyond the landing. He made a series of turns, climbing and descending several flights of stairs before arriving at the doorway of his father's private chambers. He did not knock, but touched the door and pushed inside. He made no sound. He opened the closet door a crack. There was no one in the chamber beyond. It was not his father's bedroom, but an unused salon.

Ryland crossed it and made his way into his father's favorite sitting room, where breakfast was arranged on a round table covered with a lacy tablecloth. His father was waiting, looking somber and worn.

"Prompt as usual," he said, lifting his orange juice glass in greeting. "Sit and eat. We've much to discuss."

Ryland did as he was told, sitting down and spooning onto his plate eggs, potatoes, bacon, and fresh berries from the greenhouses, covering the last with clotted cream. He poured himself tea and began to eat. He was uneasy. Niall was nowhere to be seen, and this invitation had come too early and too secretly to be merely social.

"What did Vaughn tell you?" his father asked.

The tension in Ryland's chest loosened. Of course. Vaughn. He was stupid to imagine something more dire. His father would want to hear the report as quickly as possible.

"He wanted me to warn you of two things. The current of hatred for the crown is much deeper than he expected. He doesn't know if you are aware of its full magnitude. A spark could set the people off. He says the merchants are considering a strike against the new taxes, and that would lead to food riots."

Ryland waited for a response, but his father only nodded for him to continue as he scraped soft cheese onto his toast.

"The second thing is more nebulous. He says there is something in the works, but he's not gained enough trust to get inside and find out what exactly is going on. All he knows is that it is something big, and it worries him. He also thinks it might require something more . . . dramatic . . . to convince everyone that he really has broken with you and the family."

His father tapped his fingers, chewing thoughtfully as

he stared off into the middle space above the table. Finally he nodded. "Very well."

Though he'd expected something cryptic and unrevealing, Ryland had to swallow hard to keep his frustration from clawing its way out. He shoved a forkful of potatoes into his mouth, staring down at his plate while he settled himself.

"There is a great deal I haven't told you."

Ryland lifted his head, his eyes narrowing. "About?"

"About the running of this country. About the games of leadership. About what it will take to ensure Crosspointe's safety and survival for the next four hundred seasons."

His father was sitting back, his elbows resting on the arms of his chair, watching his son.

"The question is, are you ready to hear these things? I need your help. I need your heart and your mind and your strength. I need every part of you. If I open the door on the truth of what it takes to rule this realm, you can never close it again." He paused, his blue gaze fixing Ryland like arrows.

"I will do anything Crosspointe needs, whatever you need," Ryland said, his chest clutching tight again. Though whether with fear or excitement, he wasn't sure.

His father smiled, but the expression didn't reach his eyes. They remained relentless and—faintly—sad.

"Consider well. Understand what I am asking. Rule is tricky and requires doing things that are unpalatable at best. If you step into my Chosen Circle of trusted advisers, you will most certainly be asked to do things that you may consider dishonorable, unethical, and immoral. You may be asked to do things you would rather die than do. The only thing that will keep you sane, the only thing that will keep you from suicide, is knowing that everything you do is designed to keep Crosspointe safe. This is the sworn duty of the crown and every Rampling, and sometimes it requires dreadful measures."

Ryland didn't hesitate. He could not imagine anything he wouldn't do for Crosspointe.

"Anything you require of me, I will do. Anything you need me for, I am always at your service, Father." He pushed back from the table and dropped to one knee, bowing his head. "I serve you and Crosspointe with my whole heart, my soul, my body, and my mind. There is nothing you can ask of me that I will not do."

He spoke fervently, the truth of his words resonating through his body. This had been the entire purpose of his life. Everything he'd done, everything he'd learned, had been for the sole purpose of answering the call of his king if and when it came. Tears burned his eyes. Thank the gods it had come and he was prepared.

His father's hand settled heavily on his head and stroked gently. "I wish it could be different," he murmured, so softly that Ryland wasn't sure he'd even heard the words. Then, crisply, "Finish your breakfast. We have some things to go over before the others arrive."

Ryland sat back in his chair, not asking who the others were. His father smiled tiredly.

"My Chosen Circle has the right and duty to challenge me, to make me think carefully about the decisions that I make. You must unleash your tongue. It is important that you question everything, just as it is important that once my decision is made, you obey immediately and without defiance."

Ryland nodded, his stomach churning. He would not fail. He pushed his food around his plate, unable to eat anything else. Finally his father set aside his napkin and rose.

"Come on, then. Let us go sit more comfortably."

They sat by the fire in thickly cushioned leather chairs, brass tacks pocking the leather and indenting the cushions.

"Before we meet with the others, I want to explain what I need of you."

"Anything."

"Hmmm," his father said thoughtfully. He shook his head as if to be rid of a fly. "With the creation of a regent, I have decided to create another post of equal power and equal weight—a prelate. The prelacy will be a lifetime post, and the holder will not be eligible to rule. The crown shall choose the designee. You will be the first. You are clever, with a head for strategy and tactics. You read people well. There is no better choice. If assassins succeed in their business with me, I want someone in place who will know the plans I've made and what's been done to further their success so that the new king or queen can be properly advised. You will also have to curb the lord chancellor. He will not easily give up the regency once he has it."

Ryland nodded slowly, his mouth dry. Having the prelacy meant he'd be privy to all his father's plans. It was an exhilarating, daunting thought. "You can depend on me."

"I would not have chosen you if I could not. I plan to sign the amendment to the Charter this afternoon and post the broadsides by morning announcing what I've done."

He paused, the lines of his face seeming to deepen. "But that brings me to the second thing. Two days ago the month of Tragedy began, and it is equally fitting that what I ask next will be as dreadful to you as any tragedy you can imagine. It will be only the first of many terrible trials to come. But this is what being the crown's prelate requires."

Ryland stiffened and straightened, nervousness making his hands tremble. He braced himself, curling his fingers into his palms, holding his fists tightly as he waited. He didn't let himself look away from his father's steady gaze.

"Do you know how ships' compasses are made?"

Ryland stared, thrown by the complete shift of subject. "Ships' compasses?" he repeated stupidly. Then, collecting himself, "The majicars make them, don't they?"

"They do. But not just any majicar can do it. It requires a very special kind of majick, a very special kind of skill. There is only one still able to make them right now, the second having died last year."

Ryland sat forward, his eyes wide. "Only one? By the gods!" The Inland Sea was a dangerous, fickle thing. One moment it was shallow, the next it was deeper than imagining. Knucklebones—reedlike stalks that looked like skeletal fingers—appeared out of nowhere. Hard and sharp as swords, they could tear out the bottom of a ship in moments. Mountainous rocks sprang up like teeth and disappeared as quickly. Vicious predators prowled hungrily for ships, and *sylveth* ran in rivers through the black waters. Only the majickal compasses allowed Pilots to guide ships around the hazards of the sea. Without them, Crosspointe would wither and die. Ryland's breakfast lurched in his stomach. He swallowed hard.

"Frightening, isn't it? But making compasses requires a talent that cannot be learned. A majicar must be ... *born* ... with it." There was an odd emphasis on the word *born*.

Ryland gaped. "Are there no apprentices? Journeymen?"

His father shook his head. "No. No one at all. Before I go further, I want to remind you that anything you learn here is not to be discussed outside of these walls. Do you understand?"

"Of course."

"As you can see, with only one compass-majicar, we are in dire straits."

Ryland nodded when his father did not immediately continue.

His father pinched his lower lip, considering. At last he spoke, the words coming slowly. "Complicating matters, several months ago I began selling compasses to Glacerie."

Ryland stared, thinking he had not heard correctly. "Selling ships' compasses?"

"Exactly so. They were salvaged for me from wrecks, and only a small handful of them."

"But— I— That's—," Ryland sputtered. He was going to say treason. Finally he said, "Why would you do that?"

"After the Jutras attack, I realized that being the only ones capable of navigating the Inland Sea was not going to protect us for much longer. We need allies, and we need them on the sea. Certainly, in time, the Jutras will obtain compasses, but only we will have the knowledge and power to make them, and we have far better ships. If we help outfit our allies, we will outnumber them. The funds from the compasses will allow me to establish other security measures on Crosspointe.

"But as you might imagine, the Majicars' Guild is not simply going to make me compasses to sell—even if they had the compass-majicars to make extras. Nor do I wish them to discover my plans yet. They would interfere, and there is a great deal left to be done before my plans can come to fruition. This is only the first small step. All of which means that I must have a compass-majicar of my own, one who answers only to me."

"That's a needle in a strawstack," Ryland said. He was one of the few who knew how majicars were made—that they were really the rare and beneficent result of *sylveth* transformation. Pilots were created the same way, the compasses enhancing their ability to read and predict the chaotic Inland Sea.

"Yes, under ordinary circumstances, finding someone with the potential to become a compass-majicar would be nearly impossible."

"But these are not ordinary circumstances?" Ryland felt almost feverish. His head spun. He'd worked all his life to earn his father's trust, but now . . . He never imagined what he'd learn. He felt shaken to the soles of his feet.

"No, they are not," his father said. "We have one possible solution to the compass problem, something that is unexpected but hopeful. I would not try it if the circumstances were not so dire, nor so opportune." He paused, then spoke slowly. "I have the means to predict who, when exposed to raw *sylveth*, will have the ability."

"That's . . ." Horrifying. Brilliant. Terrible beyond all understanding. Ryland just sat there, trying to assimilate it.

"The difficulty is this. The talent is predictable—the extent of the change to the person is not." He paused again, waiting.

Ryland scrabbled to put the pieces together. "You mean that once exposed, he could become mindless, ravening spawn, unable or unwilling to tap his majicar abilities."

"Exactly so." His father nodded approvingly.

Ryland's chest swelled and his nerves steadied. His father was placing a lot of trust in him, and he didn't know if he had the strength to bear that trust without faltering. But he would, he told himself. He could and would, no matter what it took.

"There is a way to help ensure that the transformation is less drastic," his father went on, steepling his hands. "The person exposed to *sylveth* can be reminded of himself; he can hold on to himself and keep the change from going too far. It is likely he will still appear . . . inhuman . . . but he would retain his mind—and the ability to create ships' compasses."

Bile burned in Ryland's throat. He swallowed hard, but bitterness flooded his mouth. "What if the person doesn't want to be changed?" he asked, his voice hoarse.

"Being king requires hard decisions. For the good of Crosspointe, I would turn him anyway."

"He could refuse to make the compasses for you. What then?"

"There is always leverage; there are always ways to get what you want. If you are willing and you have the stomach for it. I have the stomach." He leveled a hard look at his son. "The question is, do you?"

Ryland frowned, sensing something else looming. It was big and it was dreadful. Fear streaked through him, shriveling his balls. He wanted to run. Instead he settled himself into his seat, forcing his fingers to relax. "What do you mean?"

"I have found my compass-majicar. We will make the transformation tonight. I wish you to be there, to be an anchor that helps her retain her mind. We are going to turn Fairlie."

Chapter 10

William watched his son, not allowing pity to color his expression. He'd saddled the boy with a heavy load, and this last was the sort of thing that could break him. His chest ached to see first the horror and then the fierce struggle that Ryland sought to hide. He had become an extraordinary diplomat, careful, thoughtful and well-spoken. He was the absolute best choice to serve as prelate. But asking his help to turn Fairlie . . . it was more than any man should have to bear. It was more than any father who loved his son should ask.

William wanted to offer comfort, but he had none. There was nothing that could make this any less foul than it was. Ryland had to choose between destroying his best friend and serving Crosspointe.

"It is necessary. With your help or no, I *will* do this. Your presence there may make the transition easier for Fairlie." He didn't say again that it was just the first of many tests, many terrible choices. Ryland had declared his loyalty, but now he had to prove it; now he had to understand just what it meant to be a confidant and adviser to the crown.

"There's no more time to consider, Ryland. I did not want to ask you this in front of the others, but they are assembling now and I need your answer." He allowed his voice to soften.

Ryland turned. He looked as though he'd aged years.

William felt the hurt of it, was glad Naren was not alive to witness her son's devastation.

"It might not work. It might be for nothing," he rasped.

William nodded. "It is a risk. But the future of all Crosspointe is at stake. She will only be the first. Once I have my own compass-majicar, I will have to rebuild the ranks inside the Majicars' Guild."

"I have no choice?" Ryland asked, stalking around the room. "You'll do this to her whether I help or not?"

"That is the sum of it. I am told it will be easier for her if someone she cares about helps anchor her to herself. If Shaye wasn't a Weverton and a majicar, I'd have him there too."

Ryland's bark of laughter was harsh. "Shaye would burn everyone in the room alive if anyone threatened Fairlie in front of him."

"We can deal with that. But his loyalties are not the same as yours."

That caught Ryland up short. He stared, his eyes hot. Finally he turned, his shoulders squaring.

"I will do it."

William nodded. He waited a moment, but Ryland said nothing more. His jaws looked fused together. Ever since he'd taken his first steps, Ryland had always looked at William with adoration and trust. It had only grown with age. But now it was all gone, snuffed like a candle. Instead his eyes were full of hatred and fury and hurt. William had expected no less, though it did not ease the ache in his heart. He'd gained a loyal adviser, but he'd lost his son. Forever. For a single instant he let himself feel the ripping pain of it. Then he hauled it in, crushing it down inside the armored box deep within him where he kept every emotional distraction no king could afford.

"Why are you doing it? For me or for Fairlie?"

Ryland licked his lips, rubbing his chin with a hard thrust of his fingers. "Both. Is that good enough for you?"

William smiled. If nothing else, Ryland's anger and hurt were lending him the strength to challenge his king. "Well enough. Then let us go in and introduce you to the rest of my Chosen Circle."

He gestured for Ryland to precede him. His son stalked stiffly past, jerking away when William reached out to touch his shoulder. He let his hand fall. He ought to be used to this sick feeling of being struck in the gut. Over the years he'd learned to hide it, but he'd never learned to keep himself from feeling it. It felt like death.

They went to a large meeting room attached to his apartments. There were three entrances hidden along the walls—one behind a bookcase, another behind an ornate cabinet full of books and art, and one behind a dramatic painting of the first ship's arrival at Crosspointe. A fourth provided the ordinary entry that William and those not arriving under a veil of secrecy used. Niall was serving tea to the handful of people gathered around the teardrop-shaped table made of curly maple wood. William went to his seat at the head of the table, noticing that Ryland chose a chair as far from his as possible. His expression was shuttered.

William glanced around the table. On his left was Keros, a renegade majicar with no ties at all to the guild. William wasn't entirely certain how loyal Keros was to him, but the majicar was capable of master-level majick, and he was one of only two majicars that William knew of who were not bound to the guild. At the moment, he didn't entirely trust any guild majicars to sit at this table, not even those of royal blood.

One seat over was his daughter Margaret. She'd been a member of this circle for eight seasons. She looked a lot like her mother, with the same reddish brown hair and delicate bones. To all appearances she was as fragile as porcelain. But looks were deceiving. She had a steel backbone and ice-water blood. She never lost her composure, and she could slit a man's throat without blinking an eye. But most people never saw through the guise of sweet graciousness that she habitually wore.

She was watching her younger brother with hooded eyes. When Ryland met her gaze, she nodded but did not smile. An offer to join the king's Chosen Circle was an honor, but it was not a particularly welcome one. It came with a lot of pain, as both had already learned too well.

On the other side of Margaret was George Plentop, a third cousin. He was almost as old as William, with narrow shoulders and a paunch around his midsection. His legs were bandy and he dressed in an eye-scarring pastiche of colors and patterns that made him look like a street performer. An appropriate disguise for his master of spies. George had a brilliantly cunning mind and a knack for worming information out of nearly anyone. He was an affable rogue with a good head for business. He was head of accounting at Mason and Moran, a provider of cargo and ship insurance. He was welcome at every party and every dinner table in Sylmont, his quick humor making him much in demand.

At the foot of the table was Ryland, and on the right side were the king's two foreign guests of honor. The first was draped in a heavy veil as usual. The second appeared quite average—taller than George and slightly stooped. His hair was the color of bitter tea and hung to his lower back. His face had blunt, strong features and his eyes were a dark pewter. Everywhere they touched, power pulled like a heavy, aching current. The others could feel it. It made them uneasy.

"I'll not keep you long," William began abruptly. "It wouldn't do for anyone to notice you've all gone missing at the same time. First, let me inform you that Ryland has agreed to the post of prelate."

"Very good," George said, with an approving nod to Ryland. "I have great hopes for you, my boy."

Margaret shook her head. "You and the lord chancellor—not a bed I'd like to lie in. You're welcome to him."

Ryland's lips stretched into a smile that looked nearly natural. "Please Chayos, I'll never have to."

"I couldn't agree more," William said dryly. Then, "Ryland, you know George and Margaret, of course. This is Keros," he said, gesturing to the majicar. His curly brown hair hung around his shoulders and looked like it hadn't seen a comb in several days. His clothes were wrinkled and stained and his boots muddy. Unlike Ryland, he didn't—or couldn't—mask his feelings. And he was damned unhappy to be here this morning. He was going to hate it more when he found out why.

"Keros is an unregistered majicar of some talent," William explained.

The man in question winced and ducked his head, his unruly hair shadowing his face. Since becoming a majicar, he'd spent his life hiding what he was. Unregistered majicars were illegal. Having the king announce it in front of strangers always made him squirm. But soon his discomfort would turn to anger. He was going to like what was coming less than Ryland did.

"I want to present Fallon and Nya to the four of you. They are ambassadors from . . . the Root."

That made them all sit up. Even Keros was now staring across the table, his brow furrowed. Then his eyes widened, and his head jerked slightly as if he'd seen something no one else had. Fallon nodded once at the majicar, his mouth smiling, though the rest of his expression remained austere.

The Root was a tangle of twisted, spiny ridges that sprawled out into the Inland Sea like the roots of an ancient tree. It was a wasteland. No country claimed it. They couldn't. The currents running through the narrow channels burrowing in and out of the Root were very dangerous. Passage for ships was nearly impossible through most of it. Add in *sylveth* tides and Chance storms—the Root was a spectacularly unsafe place. But it had its treasures. Nya and Fallon were two of them.

"They have come offering an alliance, and I have agreed to certain terms in exchange for their services," William said in answer to the flabbergasted astonishment that had met his introduction.

"Services?" Margaret asked in her low, desultory way, her fingers tracing the grain of the table.

"Yes. But before I elucidate what those services entail, let me put Ryland on the same page."

Ryland visibly braced himself. William's chest tightened again. This was going to be the longest and worst day of his son's life. He wished, not for the first time, that there was any other way to do this, without destroying his children. He glanced at Margaret. Once that sweet mask had been her real face. Then she learned how cold and bleak the world could be; she learned just what it took to keep Crosspointe safe. The knowledge was no gift.

"Several months ago, I had a new Pale established on the Root."

William marveled that he could say it so matter-of-factly. It shouldn't have been possible. Up until a few months ago, not even every majicar alive and working together could create a Pale. But then the gods had given him a gift beyond imagining: Lucy Trenton. The very same woman who had ignited the Burn had also become the most powerful majicar William had ever seen. She was powerful enough to create a Pale by herself. She was also a Rampling, loyal to the crown. But with all her power, she could not make a ship's compass.

"This new Pale will provide a refuge should the Jutras gain a foothold here. It will also be a base for a fleet of warships I am building."

When Ryland opened his mouth to ask a question, William gave a firm shake of his head. Not now. There were things he didn't want the ambassadors to know. Ryland subsided.

"The Root has always been a haven for spawn. That fact, plus the treacherous currents through many of the bays and passages, makes the Root ideal for building a safe base."

"So long as you aren't just making a feast for spawn," Keros drawled.

William nodded. "We have some majickal protections

to help us keep spawn at bay, and Nya and Fallon will help as well."

"How will they manage that?" Keros pushed.

William bared his teeth in an approximation of a smile. Keros didn't hesitate to speak his mind, which was one of the reasons William had come to value him as highly as he did. But that didn't change the fact that the majicar was as difficult and irritating as a bed full of fleas. Keros had almost no tact and no interest in using what little he had. It made him dangerous.

"Not all ... spawn ... are made of mindless hunger," Nya said. Her veil fluttered where her mouth was. It was made of layers of sheer black material that together made it impossible to see her.

"Aren't they?" Keros said dryly.

"I do not speak of majicars or Pilots," she corrected in a gentle voice.

To listen to her, one would imagine a dewy face, sloe eyes, and rose petal lips. One would be very wrong, William thought.

He glanced around the table, gauging reactions. None of the others gave any hint that they were surprised that she knew how majicars and Pilots were made. That majicars and Pilots were actually *sylveth* spawn was a closely guarded secret. If the ordinary populace discovered it, the knowledge could crack the country in half. Very few people who were transformed were lucky enough to become Pilots or majicars. Most became bizarrely formed monsters, voracious for flesh. Early in Crosspointe's history, before the Pale, before there had been enough majicars to protect the island, and before there had been knacker gear to protect those who hunted spawn, entire villages had been wiped out by ravening swarms of the creatures. The gruesome memories of those tragedies remained as fresh in the minds of William's people as if they'd happened yesterday.

"It is true: Many that you call spawn are born mindless," Nya continued. "Such are made when *sylveth* kisses dead things—things that do not already have minds of their own. A new mind is made, but it is very young, seeking only to eat and survive. These are most dangerous. They cannot be reasoned with and they run wild in hunger."

"Reasoned with?" Margaret repeated in disbelief.

She was not alone in her incredulity. Everyone but William stared with undisguised shock. Nya continued, unhurried.

"When *sylveth* kisses what is living, it happens that they may survive with their minds unbroken. Those with the strongest sense of themselves change least. Those who are afraid, who forget themselves, whose minds scatter—they suffer deeper changes. Sometimes they go mad, and these also cannot be reasoned with. But those who hold even a few fragments of what they were can learn to have reason. Some may change and keep their minds whole, though at first they are frightened and may do themselves and others harm before they settle into what they have become. After a short time, they mostly accept what has happened to them and know not to come hunting their human brothers and sisters."

"Wait," Keros said, laying his hands flat on the table and leaning forward, his eyes unblinking. "You're saying that there are differences in the kinds of spawn?"

"We call them Kin, and yes, it is so."

The majicar sat back. He speared his fingers through his hair and then let his hands fall into his lap, grasping them tightly together. "How do you know?" he demanded, his mouth pulled tight. "How can you possibly *know*?"

Again Nya bowed, and then she stood up. Her veil bunched and she pushed it off with a dramatic sweep, letting it fall to her feet in a pool of black fabric.

"I know," she said, meeting Keros's gaze squarely.

To his credit, he neither flinched nor blanched. William was impressed. He had not been in such good control of himself the first time he'd seen Nya without her shrouding veils.

George had come to his feet, his chair tumbling backward onto the carpet. Margaret was standing behind her chair, and Ryland was gripping the arms of his with white-knuckled fingers. Fallon merely smiled, saying nothing.

Nya stood stood just over six feet tall, though somehow she seemed much bigger. She had a human shape insofar as she had a head, legs, and arms. But she was also clearly not human anymore. Her body was feminine, though her arms seemed a little too long. She wore a leather vest laced up the front and leather pants, with no shirt or coat. Her skin was covered in velvety fur striped sand and black, like the hunting dogs of Chaturak. The fur along her neck and belly was a pale buff color. Black talons curved from the tips of her fingers in wicked spikes. Her hands were covered in fingerless gloves that laced up to her elbows. Hard muscles rolled along her shoulders, back, and legs. She wore no shoes, and the talons on her feet were as lethal as those on her fingers.

Striking as her body was, her face was even more riveting. It was shaped like an upside-down triangle. The black stripes faded along her cheeks and forehead and jaw, leaving her face the same buff color as her neck and stomach. Her nose and jaw protruded slightly, like a cat's muzzle, and her teeth were pointed, with long, thin canines that looked as though they could tear flesh. Her hair was jet-black and fell down her back to her buttocks like a coarse mane. Her ears pricked up from her head and swiveled. Her eyes slanted in a long teardrop shape and were a dark orange verging on blood red. Around the outer edge was a thin line of black. Perhaps the most unnerving thing about her was her ability to turn her head nearly all the way around, like an owl.

William frowned as his gaze ran over her. There was something about her that tugged at him and stirred his loins. Each time he saw her, he felt it more. Guilt prodded him. He'd lost Naren only a few months ago. But Nya was beautiful in an exotic fashion, and she radiated wild femininity. Ruthlessly, he tamped down his stirring lust.

"I am a Warden and Speaker for my people," she said to Keros. "That is how I know."

The majicar rubbed a shaking hand over his mouth. "What is that: Warden and Speaker?"

Her head tipped sideways and then she scanned everyone else, smiling slightly, her gaze coming back to settle on Keros. "Warden is guardian. Wardens protect the Kin from harm. Speakers may talk to the minds of Kin, if there is something inside that can hear." She tapped a finger against her head. "I reach through the fear and madness to help the mind accept. If the transformation is not complete, I can help the mind focus and control the change."

"Control the change?" Margaret's voice was slightly strangled.

"As much as can be. It requires that the new Kin have some ability for majick. Even very small."

"Which is why I have called everyone here this morning," William inserted smoothly. "Fallon also has a significant ability. He is able to determine what talent someone might have once exposed to *sylveth*, and with Nya's help, it's possible to control the transformation sufficiently to prevent insanity. We must have a compass-majicar for my plans or everything I've done so far will fall apart."

Keros stared. "You plan to transform someone with *sylveth*," he rasped. "Someone who hasn't felt the draw of majick pulling him to the sea and a *sylveth* tide."

It wasn't a question. William answered anyway. "I do. It's not unprecedented. The Majicar Guild has used forecasting to help identify potential majicars as children. They are often successful."

Keros's lip curled. "And wrong just as often, no doubt. If they are so good, then why haven't they turned up more compass-majicars? They ought to have a stableful."

William smoothed his fingers over the tabletop. "They cannot. For whatever reason, they are unable to find compass-majicars. But Fallon can. And he will."

"It's—," Margaret began, but she did not finish.

"It's necessary," William declared firmly. "And it is decided. In return for their services, Nya's and Fallon's people will be given a Pale of their own on the Root, and they will be treated as favored allies."

"You've found someone," Keros grated. "Who?"

"Fairlie Norwich."

Keros's head twisted and he stared down the table at Ryland. William wasn't surprised that Keros knew of Ryland and Fairlie's close friendship. The majicar would have made an excellent spy. "You know about this? You're going along with it?"

Ryland's mouth tightened, but he only nodded, revealing nothing of his own turmoil and disgust. "Yes."

Keros's attention returned to William. "Lucy would not allow this. She'd stop you."

"Perhaps. But she is not here. This will be done before sunrise tomorrow."

"Why should they help us? Why should you trust them? What makes you think they are telling the truth?" Keros demanded.

"I'd like to know as well," George said, the first words he'd uttered since greeting Ryland.

"In answer to your first question," Fallon interjected, "when Nya arrived among us, it was a blessing. She spoke to us, reached deep into our hidden selves. She woke our minds from foggy sleep to bright awareness. Since she came to us, we have come to understand how much like animals we have lived. We wish to live better. To become what we are meant to be." He slid a possessive look at Nya.

"What is that?" George asked, slow and measured.

"Civilized."

"You are spawn also?"

Fallon went still, then slowly he dissolved. Or rather, his outward seeming dissolved. He was far different from Nya. He was taller than the disguise he'd worn, with thin shoulders, the bones ridging through his shirt. His skin was stretched tightly over the sharp edges of his frame. His scalp was covered in white hair the color of old ivory, exposing a wide expanse of forehead that sprouted two ivory horns. They curved up and back and then down and up in a lazy S shape along the side of his head. His ears were two holes set low below his horns. His skin was dark brown the texture of polished leather. He had two pairs of arms, one set high, the other along his ribs. Ivory bone ruffs rose around his neck and flared along the outside of each of his forearms. His hands had three fingers, each having a flexible, tentacle quality to them. They were slightly webbed and tipped with chips of flat oval bone. His face was long and flat, his nose thrusting sharply like a knife blade. His mouth was lipless and wide, his teeth filling his jaws in short, serrated points. His eyes were turned vertical and slanted slightly inward, blinking from side to side. They were as yellow as egg yolks, with a black line slicing downward through each.

"I am Kin," he said to George. "And I am a majicar. I can sense what talents—if any—Kin will have once kissed by *sylveth*."

"But you can't predict the extent of the physical transformation," Keros said accusingly.

"No. Much depends on the person's mind. But understand, I do not consider the change to be something to dread. It is merely . . . change."

"Change she would refuse if she had the choice," Keros said, his hands clenching into fists.

"Perhaps. Perhaps not."

"But you won't ask, because you don't care what the answer is, do you?" he said to William.

"I do," he said bleakly. "But the king cannot. This is for Crosspointe."

"And you?" Keros turned furiously on Nya and Fallon. "How can you do this? Do you want her to turn out like you?"

"And what is wrong with us?" Fallon demanded, the black lines of his eyes seeming to harden. "Is it that we are vermin to you? You who are also one of us, maji-car?" The last word he drew out, baring his teeth.

"What is wrong with *us*," Keros said flatly, "is that *we* are spawn and *she* is not, and this will ruin her life. The people she cares about will be terrified of her; she'll lose her home and all that she's worked for; and she'll be turned into a slave in service to building compasses." He skewered Nya on a gaze of steel. "You are disgusting."

Her head tilted, her liquid eyes unreadable. "Am I? Do *I* hate those you call spawn? Do *I* hunt them? Do *I* pluck them from the tree of their lives and turn them into *monsters* because I need them to make compasses? Who exactly is disgusting here?"

"But you'll do it. And you want to be civilized." Keros sneered. "It's barbaric. And after? Will you be her Warden? Guard her? She wouldn't need guarding if you left her alone."

That seemed to catch Nya up. William watched her. This was where things were going to get chancy. Nya was bound to Kin, as she called spawn. She was bound to protect them. Once Fairlie was changed, if she asked for Nya's help, there would be trouble. He would just have to keep Fairlie from asking.

"I will ward her, as I ward all Kin," Nya said to Keros. "She is not mine to worry about now. That belongs to you—" She glanced around the table. "You are her king and her countrymen. Do *you* not protect her?"

Silence answered her. Keros's mouth worked, but he only clenched his hands tightly, his mouth clamping shut in a white line. She nodded.

"It is necessary for you that this girl be made Kin, and it is necessary for the Kin on the Root to have a Pale. We cannot build homes, we cannot have crops or possessions—the Chance storms transform all. With a Pale we will have safety—permanence. We will thrive." Her gaze settled on Keros, her voice softening. "I do not care to make this choice. *Sylveth* made me Warden; *syl-*

veth made me Speaker. I do as majick demands. If Kin tell me they need help, or if I become aware of it, I must. So, yes, I will help to make her Kin because it helps those I serve, and then I will help her to escape from you if that is her desire, because I will serve her also."

The last was directed to William. He rubbed a hand over his face. Nya and Fallon were extraordinary treasures. If they could do as promised, then he could create all the compass-majicars Crosspointe needed, as well as finding enough Pilots and majicars to create an undefeatable army, and all of that without creating any unnecessary spawn. But their bargain was only to find one compass-majicar and then Fallon and Nya would return to the Root. If he let them. But that was a concern for later.

He nodded at Nya. "As I said before, I understand, and should it come to that, our bargain will still stand."

"Why her?" Keros demanded suddenly. "What makes her so special?"

Fallon gave a shrug that rolled through his entire body. "I do not know. I examined many in the palace and city this last sennight. But when I met her last evening, I knew she was what we were looking for."

"How can you be sure?"

Again the shrug. "I just am."

"That's not cracking much."

"We tested him," William said. "He is capable. I am satisfied."

"How?"

William gave Keros a quelling look. "It is enough that I am satisfied. It will be done," he said with finality.

The majicar glared, his face twisting, his jaw quivering. Then he looked down at his hands and said nothing more. William breathed out silently. He couldn't afford to have Keros revolt. The man was too valuable.

William turned to address the rest of the table briskly. "Now, the reason I have asked you all to be here is because you each have a role to play. George, I want you to retrieve Fairlie and bring her to her workshop. The place itself will help anchor her, and it is far enough away from the main buildings to provide some secrecy. The attached wing is empty, since Toff hadn't taken on any other apprentices or staff in some time. Set up a discreet perimeter of guards to keep anyone from intruding.

"Margaret, you will divert any castle staff, as well as merchants and clients eager for a Fairlie Norwich original work. Ryland, I have already explained what I wish you to do. If you have no further questions, that will be all. Keros, I would like you to stay a moment."

William nodded dismissal at the others, and Niall appeared in the doorway to lead them out. Nya donned her veil again, and Fallon's appearance shimmered and once again he appeared to be a normal man. They followed Niall, leaving just Keros.

William looked at the majicar. He'd not known him long, less than half a season. Keros served because he was Lucy's friend and because William had given him little choice. Keros was honorable to a fault, generous, kind, and he looked after the weak and the poor. He was, in a nutshell, a very good man and, at the moment, an inconvenient one.

"I wanted to ask you to be there in case anything went wrong," William began. He held up his hand when Keros started to speak hotly. "I have changed my mind. I would rather not lose you, and I think I will if I force you to help with this. Instead, I want you to go out of the city for a while. I have had word that Elford, a small village north of Wexstead on the west coast, has been struck with mudslides. They need help, and I know I can trust you to give them all they need without stinting. See Niall about the necessary supplies." He paused. "Will that do?"

Keros stared back, a look of naked anger and disgust on his face. He shook his head, looking away. His jaw flexed.

"I'll go," he said, thrusting to his feet and shoving the chair back so hard that it tipped over. He strode to the door without another word.

"Keros?"

The majicar stopped, turning his head impatiently. "What?"

"Will you be coming back?"

Keros's mouth worked. "I don't know." He stalked out, slamming the door.

William dropped into his chair, his legs feeling suddenly weak. He braced his elbows on the table and pressed his face into his palms. His stomach churned and his throat burned with bile. By the gods, was this the right path?

He was sacrificing honor, his children, the respect of men like Keros, not to mention a sweet and talented girl, all for the hope of making Crosspointe strong enough to defend against the Jutras when they came. For come they would, sooner or later. Of that, William had no doubts. And while Lucy Trenton was strong enough to hold them off now, she could not live forever, and the Jutras had majick of their own. If they sent an army, even Lucy might not prevail.

Crosspointe needed allies; it needed to strengthen itself with warships and weaponry. But change was a slow thing and he had little time. People were going to start to notice that there were ships on the Inland Sea without guild compasses and without guild Pilots. When they did, there would be an uproar, if not a flat-out revolt. Before then, he had to have more compasses. And majicars. Fairlie would not be the last innocent transformed in the name of Crosspointe. Fallon and Nya had just begun, whether they knew it or not.

William took a breath and sat back in his chair, staring sightlessly into the middle space above the table. Transformation was only the first step. After that, he had to convince the newly turned spawn to serve Crosspointe. That was going to be quite a trick. He didn't doubt it would require him to do more things that he found sickening. But it didn't matter. He was committed to this path. He had no other choices. He had known from the first that it was going to be a difficult journey and that there would be hard sacrifices for a lot of people. Now that things were getting ugly, he could not let himself weaken and retreat.

He took a deep breath and stood, leaning on the table and staring at his reflection in the polished wood. He straightened. It was getting harder to look at himself, much less his children. He wondered when he would do something so dreadful that it would become impossible.

He thought of Fairlie, her gurgling laugh that invited everyone to laugh with her, her vibrant energy, her easy trust.

Perhaps tonight would be the point of no return.

Chapter 11

It had been a very late night. Fairlie had fallen into bed only a few hours before dawn. She was still wearing her ridiculously expensive gown—she was unable to remove it without help and she refused to call for her borrowed maid. Yet despite her late bedtime, her body would not let her sleep past the start of day. Her eyes popped open just as the sun was rising over the horizon in a glory of gold and pink. The storm of the night before had passed, leaving behind only a light breeze and a panorama of shining puddles.

Fairlie groaned, knuckling the grit from her eyes. Smudges of black blotched her fingers and she made a face. She hadn't washed off the thick layer of makeup before collapsing into bed either.

Feeling a sudden desperate urge to be clean, she rolled off her bed and landed on the floor, her legs tangled in her crinoline and skirts. She growled and scissored her legs furiously, finally grappling with the dress's hem and hiking it up so that she could stand up and walk. She went to the washstand and splashed her face with the frigid water in the basin. She rubbed a generous dollop of soap on a washrag and scrubbed her face hard, then rinsed the rag and repeated the scrubbing until the water was gray and her skin was raw and red. Some kohl remained around her eyes, giving them a dramatic look. Fairlie stuck her tongue out at herself for liking the effect.

Dealing with her hair was more difficult. She'd managed to pull out all the pins and combs before falling into bed, but now it was a tortured mess, poufed up on one side and matted to the side of her head on the other. She grabbed a comb and dragged it through her hair, yelping when she yanked on a tangle. She dampened her hair with her hands and combed it back, using a twist of copper wire to fix it in a stumpy tail at the nape of her neck. She promised herself a proper bath and wash that evening.

Getting the dress off turned out to be easy enough, since she didn't care if she tore the fabric. She slid a knife down the front panel's laces, slicing them through, then pushed the sleeves off and twisted the dress back to front until she could get at the rear lacing of the skirt. She cut through it, slid the dress to the ground, and kicked it aside. The underskirts and crinoline followed quickly, and then she stripped off the chemise and undertrousers.

The *sylveth* pendant Shaye had given her the night before hung between her breasts. She lifted it, tracing the delicate work with her forefinger. It was lovely. And while *sylveth* made her nervous in general, this felt right and safe, as if it was imbued with the spirit of Chayos. Fairlie smiled. It was perfect. Shaye had clearly spent a lot of time on it. She would treasure it for that, if nothing else. But it told her more than anything else that her decision to return to Stanton was the right one. If he was this close to becoming a master majicar, she needed to get out of his way so he could devote himself to it.

Naked, she shivered in the chill air of the morning. She hurriedly dumped the gray wash water into the drain in her garderobe and filled the basin again with clean water and poured a mug for herself, guzzling it down. The cold made her throat and head ache. She gave herself a quick rag-bath before using the garderobe.

She dressed herself in a clean pair of tightly woven woolen trousers, the insides lined with soft flannel, the tops of the thighs paneled with thick leather. She then pulled on a wool sweater over a long-sleeved cotton chemise. A pair of socks followed and then her heavy work boots, designed to protect her feet from the dangers of her forge. They were also majicked against heat so that when she managed to dribble molten metal on them, she wasn't burned. It was a circumstance that happened more frequently than she cared to admit. She had to put a belt around her pants to keep them from falling down. When she worked, she forgot to eat, and in finishing the sculpture of Queen Naren, she'd lost a lot of weight.

Her stomach growled and she looked around for a snack. Her quarters were spare. She had a bedstead made of wrought iron, decorated with the shapes of vines and flowers—one of her first successful projects. There was also a nightstand, a wardrobe, a washstand and mirror, the door to the garderobe, a window looking out on a small flower garden, and a large wooden chest filled with an assortment of keepsakes. Another trunk sat open on the floor, not yet packed for her journey. There would be time for that later in the day. *Sylveth* sconces along the wall provided light when touched. But nowhere was there even the smallest scrap of food.

She sighed and walked through the door from her bedroom into her workshop. She picked her way through the maze to the other side. From there she went into her forge. For once it was cold inside; she hadn't lit the forge in days, having been hounded into dress fittings and preparations for the trip to Stanton. She itched to stoke it and start something new. A pang struck her as she realized it would be months and months before she would be able to do that.

The forge itself was on the far wall. The massive stone hearth formed a semicircle, with a copper hood hanging low above it. An enormous bellows was fixed into a heavy wood frame on the left side, with an overhead arm fastened to the rear that allowed Fairlie to pump air while she stood in front of the hearth. Various hammers, tongs, and pliers hung along the rails in front, and cooling troughs and casks were pushed into a corner on the right side. There were half a dozen anvils besieging the forge, each varying in shape and size. Piled on a bench behind were several dozen swage blocks. Another bench held rasps, hammers, wire brushes, and an assortment of shaping tools. A coal bin took up most of the right wall. It was divided into sections for hard, soft, and charcoal. On the left side of the building were piled ingots of all sorts of metals and sacks of plaster-casting materials. On the near wall were bins of beads, ceramic decorations, chunks of wax, chisels, scrapers, buttons, and more. Beside them were hooks holding several leather aprons, round leather caps, and above them on a shelf, an assortment of gauntleted leather gloves. In the center was a broad clear space where Queen Naren's sculpture had stood as Fairlie worked on it.

Fairlie drew a deep breath, filling her lungs with the smell of charcoal, burnt wood, and metal. Contentment stole over her. Then her stomach growled again. She looked around. Still nothing to eat.

She wandered back into the other room, standing in the middle and considering. She didn't want to go into the royal kitchens or send for something. She didn't like the idea of facing any more congratulations. She glanced at the pile of fat leather sacks sitting on a table in the corner. She wanted to go to the Maida of Chayos anyway. She'd stop and buy breakfast on the way.

She went to fetch her coat, then stopped. Shaye. He had said he'd be here first thing. She went into her bedroom and found the battered watch she kept in her nightstand. It was sitting next to her master's badge. She looked at the two together, her throat hurting, tears burning in her eyes. The watch had been Toff's. He should have been there to see her make master. She swallowed and pressed the stem, popping it open. It was only half past the seventh glass. First thing for Shaye meant midday.

She closed the watch and put it back beside the badge and slid the drawer shut. Annoyance tightened in her stomach. Why should it bother her that Shaye had left so early last night? He was always going off on his own without a word. It was nothing new. But still, it hurt that he hadn't stayed—that he'd left her in that sea of strangers. *Not alone*, she told herself firmly. *Ryland was there*. She sighed, touching the *sylveth* tree pendant. Shaye was Shaye. She shouldn't expect more of him than he was. Her lips pressed together. Crack him. He couldn't expect her to wait if he was going to kite off without a word. Besides, he didn't want to go to the Maida of Chayos anyway. He'd only badger her the entire way about her trip to Stanton, and she wasn't sure she wouldn't give in. It was hard to leave him and Ryland and her forge. But she did need to see her mother and make peace with her childhood.

Fairlie snatched her coat from behind the door and tossed it down beside the fat leather bags in the other room. There were sixteen bags all told, each weighing about fifteen pounds. They were stuffed with most of the bits of jewelry Fairlie had made over the last few years. She was always restless, always needing her hands busy. She crafted them late at night and when her larger projects needed to rest and she couldn't.

She began pairing the bags and tying the strings together to make them easier to carry. They were going to be heavy. She'd have to use a handcart to get them to the gates of the castle, then hire a cart to get them all the way to the Maida, though she hated to be inside. It was a beautiful day and she didn't want to miss the sun or the bustle and chatter of the streets. She *did* spend too much time locked up in her workshop, much as she hated to admit it. Her stomach growled again. She rolled her eyes. She had better get going or her stomach was going to claw its way out and get its own breakfast.

She put on her coat and then patted her trouser pockets. Grumbling, she returned to her bedroom and dug for some money in her nightstand. She found a pouch and opened it, checking the contents. Inside were two silver glyphs, six crescents, and a couple of dozen coppers. She pulled the drawstrings shut and shoved the pouch into her left pocket before going to fetch the bags.

Fairlie stopped short, astonished to find Shaye just closing the door.

"What are you doing here?"

"Aren't we taking your offerings to Chayos today?" he asked.

His cheeks were flushed from the brisk morning, and shadows underscored his hooded eyes like he'd been up all night. *With who?* The question whispered through Fairlie's mind and she found her annoyance growing a harder bite. He eyed her from head to foot. His mouth curved down, his eyes narrowing. "You weren't leaving without me, were you?"

Fairlie shrugged. "I didn't expect you."

His brow furrowed. "Didn't I say I'd help you?"

"I thought you might have forgotten. It looks like you had a late night."

He sniffed and went to the table where the sacks were piled. He started digging at the top of one to pull it open. "I always remember you," he said as he tipped the bag, spilling a tangle of jewelry onto the table. He sifted his fingers through it. "You should keep some of these to sell," he said, hooking a bracelet on one finger and holding it up. It was a series of round disks with delicate raised roses on them. The petals were silver limned in copper to match the links holding them together.

She shook her head and went to stand beside him, pulling the bracelet away and stuffing the spilled jewelry back in the sack.

"I can make more. These go to Chayos for thanks."

"You're wearing that to the Maida of Chayos?" he asked, scorn dripping from the words.

She looked at herself. "Why not?"

"You look like a pauper. You're a master metalsmith now. You need to think of your reputation and not go wandering about in rags. And besides that, what will Chayos think of you? I thought you wanted to show her respect."

Unfamiliar anger began a slow uncurling in Fairlie's stomach. "There's nothing disrespectful about my clothes. What would you have me wear? My ball gown from last night?"

"You must have *something* less shabby."

Fairlie met his gaze, heat filling her cheeks. "No. I don't. I didn't know you were so ashamed of me."

He had the grace to look abashed, his gaze dropping. "I'm not ashamed of you. I just want you to get the respect and courtesy you deserve. If you're dressed like that, everyone will think you're just another dirt-grubber."

"I *am* a dirt-grubber," she said, only slightly mollified.

"You're an artist," he corrected. "An extraordinarily talented one. Though you look like you've not eaten in days."

Just then her stomach growled. Instead of smiling, Shaye scowled harder.

Before he could chastise her, Fairlie said, "I was going to get some breakfast on the way to the Maida of Chayos."

"You should have sent for something while you waited for me," he said, crossing his arms.

Fairlie shook her head and turned back to the sacks on the table. She checked the knots to make sure the strings wouldn't separate. Shaye was in one of his difficult moods this morning. It was catching. She retied a knot, trying not to ask the question that prodded at her lips. But the words escaped. "Where did you disappear to last night?"

"Did you miss me?" He propped his hip against the table, looking down at her.

"I don't know why I did. Are you going to keep sniping at me the entire day? Because I can go by myself."

"Carrying all this? You'd be dragged into an alley and knifed."

Fairlie shrugged dismissively. Shaye was such a mother hen, always pecking and pecking. "Chayos will look after me. You missed Vaughn. He came to the reception," she said, changing the subject.

Shaye raised his brows. "Did he? Were there fireworks?"

"Ryland dragged him out. Vaughn wanted to talk to him about Fathom Enterprises. He didn't come back after that. I wish they could get along better. I miss Vaughn."

"You're not a prisoner. You can go visit him."

"I know. But Ryland would get all ruffled about it."

"Is he a child that needs mothering?"

"No, and neither am I, for that matter. Yet you insist on treating me like one," Fairlie retorted.

"You act like one more often than not."

Fairlie put her hands on her hips and glared at him. "I'm sick of this," she said, her anger surging. "What are you doing here anyway? Shouldn't you be sleeping off last night? Or working on your master's project? You can't spend all your time in my forge nipping at my heels."

Shaye's eyes widened, clearly taken aback. Fairlie was a little shocked at herself. Usually she didn't mind his teasing and sniping. He rarely aimed his darts at her. So long as he directed them elsewhere, they didn't draw blood—at least not hers—and she was content to let him be himself without chiding him. But she was feeling bruised and bloodied this morning, and she remained unaccountably nettled that he'd disappeared the night before.

"I have a mother, and while she is leagues away I am also of legal age. I am a master metalsmith, and I do not need you hovering over me and spoon-feeding me. If that's what you want to be, then you can leave now."

He gawped at her a moment, then smiled slowly, his eyes glittering, reminding Fairlie of a snake about to strike. His arms dropped to his sides. Fairlie felt ice slide down her spine. Oh. Dear. What sort of trouble had she just stirred up? She knew better than anyone how foolish it was to antagonize Shaye, especially when he was in the mood he was in now.

"And what would you have me be instead?" he drawled.

She swallowed, sticking to her purpose. "My friend."

Something tightened in his expression. It wasn't pleasant. She didn't understand it.

"Is that all?"

"What else?"

"Maybe—" He broke off sharply, his lips clamping together in a white line.

Fairlie watched him uneasily. There was something going on. Something was under his skin, irritating him. He was angry and clearly wanted to strike out. More so than usual. But why?

"Maybe what?" she asked carefully. She wasn't afraid of him, but if he went into one of his rare harangues at her, it would mean she wouldn't see him for days, maybe weeks, until he showed up again as if nothing had happened. She always missed him when that happened, and this time she'd be on her way to Stanton before he recovered. Her stomach twisted into a knot—though he'd never failed to come back, she always wondered if this time might be it. Shaye was volatile. Who knew what could drive him off permanently?

"Maybe you want someone to help you haul all this scrap to the Maida of Chayos," he snarled, and picked up eight of the heavy sacks, slinging them over his shoulders. Fairlie followed suit, watching him warily.

"What crawled up your stovepipe and died?" she asked finally. "You were pleasant enough last night. Did something happen after you left?"

An unexpected stillness swept his face. "Possibly."

"Are you going to tell me about it?"

He lifted one shoulder, the bags clanking. "Maybe. One of these days."

Fairlie sighed. Pushing Shaye would get her nowhere. He was stubborn, and when someone poked at him, he just dug in harder. She knew better than to back him into a corner.

"All right. Let's get going. It's already late."

"After that party, I expected I'd be hauling you out of bed."

"Because you virtuously had an early night?" She said it more sharply than she had intended.

His jaw flexed. "No. I had company. I was awake quite late."

Fairlie couldn't help the hurt that hit her stomach like the kick of a mule. Shaye had left the reception last night to bed one of his women. She looked away, her eyes hot and gritty with indignation and resentment. "Maybe you should go back home and rest then. I can manage without you." She reached out to snatch Shaye's bags off his shoulders.

He gripped her forearm in his long white fingers. "Don't."

He was strong, but she was stronger. She was a metalsmith after all. She twisted her arm away, but didn't step back. She stared into his chest, furious that he was so much taller than she. Her foot rocked back slightly as she considered kicking him.

Shaye read her intention and settled his hands on her shoulders, pushing down. "I came to help," his voice mollifying as if he recognized he was antagonizing her.

"I don't need you." Fairlie's anger swelled, prodding at her. She clenched her fists, wanting to hit him. The feeling was unfamiliar. Usually her temper was a quiet thing, too lazy to rouse. She couldn't remember the last time she'd been this angry, and she did not know why. She jerked beneath the weight of his hands, but he only gripped tighter. She stilled.

"You needed me to shape the *sylveth* for your sculpture and help you with the fire," he said softly, his eyes glittering.

"I would have managed."

His lip curled, his nostrils flaring white. "So nice to be appreciated."

"I can pay you for your time, majicar, if it will make you feel better."

His fingers contracted, digging into the muscle of her shoulder painfully. "I don't want your money. Buy some damned decent clothes with it."

The last was enough to unleash Fairlie's fury altogether. "Then why bother?" She spat at him. "Why did you even come last night if you would rather be between the legs of one of your whores?"

Shaye went still, then let go, thrusting himself away and striding toward the door. "Let's go."

Fairlie didn't move. "Why did you leave? One minute you're there, the next you're gone without even a single word."

He turned, leaning a shoulder against the door, not looking at her. "You seemed in good hands."

"What in the holy black depths is that supposed to mean?"

Shaye grimaced. Then he straightened, rubbing his eyes with the heel of his hand. "Look. I was an ass. I am an ass. I just needed to get out of there. I apologize. Are you happy now?"

Fairlie stared, then shook her head, scowling. The flames of her anger weren't so easily tamed, once roused. "No. What's all this business about my clothes? Isn't the old me good enough for you anymore? Or are you more attached to the Weverton status than you've always said? You don't want to be seen with a poor village metalsmith? Which is what I am and always have been."

He bit his lower lip, making white dents in his flesh. "I never said you weren't good enough for me," he gritted in a harsh voice. "I just—"

"Just?" Fairlie prompted.

"Just drop it. You really don't want to know."

"Yes, I do."

He stared at her. Something moved in his eyes, and he looked more angry than she'd ever seen him. Something inside her quailed. She held herself steady. Suddenly he shoved himself away from the door, letting the bags on his shoulders fall to the floor. He strode across the room, stopping only inches from her. His fury rolled off him in palpable waves. Fairlie stiffened, not giving ground.

"Fine. But remember, you asked. I tried to keep it from coming to this."

Then he grabbed her arms and pulled her close, his lips crushing her mouth.

Fairlie stood rigid, her eyes wide. His lips moved on hers as he stared fiercely at her. It was shockingly intimate. Not that she hadn't ever been kissed, but *looking* at him, so close, his mouth so hot and wet and urgent. And to have it be Shaye—it was hardly conceivable.

But then she came aware that her lips had opened and she'd slanted her head, her tongue slipping out to taste his. She felt his body spasm like he'd been jabbed with a knife. He yanked back, breathing hard.

"What are you doing?" he demanded hoarsely.

Fairlie touched her lips. They felt hot and tingly. She felt out of breath. "Kissing you, I thought."

"Why?"

Her brow furrowed. "Because you were kissing me?"

He nodded, looking down between them. He drew a ragged breath. "All right."

"Wasn't I doing it right?"

"What?" His head jerked up.

"I don't have the kind of experience you do. And you stopped. Was I doing it wrong?"

He looked like he'd been struck in the head with a hammer. "No. You were fine."

"Oh." She licked her suddenly dry lips, embarrassed heat dripping over her face and neck onto her chest. *Fine.* Not a compliment. "Oh," she said again, dropping her eyes and staring straight at his neck. She watched him swallow. She didn't know what to say. She didn't know what to think. Except . . . the tingling now filled her body down to her toes, and the flames of her anger had turned to something else. Something unexpected and yet . . . *right.*

"Are you going to do it again?" she asked, her lips stiff as wood.

His fingers tightened on her arms. His breath whispered across her forehead and his voice was thick. "I want to. Very much."

He didn't move. Fairlie caught her upper lip in her

teeth and slowly lifted her chin until she was looking at him again. He looked terrified. She'd never seen him afraid of anything. She didn't know he was capable of it.

"All right."

"All right?" he repeated incredulously.

She nodded. He didn't ask again. His hands slid slowly up her arms to her neck, his fingers slipping around to cup the back of her head. Then his mouth came down on hers again, this time more gently. Fairlie leaned into him, opening her lips. He tasted of tea and stale whiskey. He lifted his head.

"Still all right?"

"Yes."

Then he kissed her again, pulling her close, his arms wrapping around her and the bags dangling from her shoulders. His gentleness turned hungry. Fairlie didn't know how long they stood there, the kiss deepening. She found herself pushing up on tiptoe and shaking the bags off her shoulders so that she could get closer to him. He made a sound deep in his throat, and his arms tightened so that she could hardly breathe. She didn't think. She couldn't think. All she could do was feel. And it was glorious. Like flying. Like the bliss of losing herself in her work. She'd never felt like that apart from the forge before. She hadn't known it was possible.

At last his arms loosened and Shaye lifted his head. He looked at her, as if waiting for something. Fairlie reached up, brushing a loose strand of hair from his cheek.

"What exactly is going on?"

"You just found out my deepest, darkest secret," he said sardonically.

"And that is what?"

"I love you." The words wanted to choke him, coming out with sharp, jagged edges. His face reddened, but he didn't stop. "I have for"—he looked over her head, taking a deep breath and letting it out with a gust—"for a long time." He looked down at her, wary.

"I—" Fairlie didn't know what to say.

"It's all right. At least you didn't hit me. I'm encouraged."

She smiled uneasily. "I'm not sure—" She broke off, licking her lips, tasting him again. It was good. "I never thought of you like this before."

"Of course not. You think only of metal and fire." There was only affectionate tolerance in the words.

"You didn't want me to know," she said, her brain starting to work again.

He shook his head. "I was afraid you'd be uncomfortable around me." He paused, his brow furrowing, his body going rigid. "Are you?"

She laughed, a pitiful sound. "Yes. But I think—"

"What?"

"I think I like it."

"You don't want me to go away—and stay away?"

She gave a faint shake of her head. "No. I don't want you to do that. But I need to let it sink in a little. Think about it. Is that . . . all right?"

He rested his forehead against hers, his eyes closing. "It's more than I hoped."

Her stomach growled again, loud in the quiet. She giggled nervously, her blood jumping. Her heart was racing and her hands were shaking. She felt brilliant, like the morning sun, full of colors and heat.

"We should go," she said reluctantly, liking the pressure of his arms around her too much to step away.

"You need to eat," he agreed. He didn't move either.

"There's time," she pointed out, as much for herself as for him. "Plenty of time. We can . . . talk . . . alone together . . . later." Fleetingly she thought of her trip home to Stanton. It could be postponed for a while.

He nodded, then brushed his lips against hers as if he couldn't help it. "Very well. We will talk later."

He pushed away and bent to pick up her bags, helping her to sling them over her shoulders. Then he picked up his. He started for the door, then stopped, turning and reaching out his hand to her. Fairlie took it, smiling bemusedly. Shaye smiled back, looking almost astounded when she slipped her hand in his.

His fingers curled around the door handle and he stopped again, looking down at her. "You won't change your mind?"

Her smile was starting to hurt her cheeks. "I don't think so."

His eyes darkened, his expression going taut. "You don't *think*?"

If anything, his uncertainty made her want to smile more. This was not a side of Shaye he'd ever shown her before. "I won't."

His hand tightened on hers. "Then let us get you fed and pay your respects to Chayos."

He opened the door, letting her pass through first. "For the record, I did not spend my evening with any other woman, whore or otherwise," he said.

She looked at him sharply. He flushed.

"I confess I meant to, but I didn't have the stomach for it. Instead I spent most of the night with Randall Turvey, a merchant who had just had the misfortune to let his mistress meet his wife. A most unsavory situation. He was deep in his cups and bent my ear until quite late." He paused. "I am sorry I didn't stay with you. I should have."

"But then where would that have left poor Randall Turvey?"

"Drunk and in a cold bed, same as if I hadn't met him."

"And you? Where would it have left you?"

He shrugged. "Exactly where I was."

"That would be better?"

"It would be safer."

"I never thought you would prefer safety," Fairlie said, tipping her head to the side.

"I have a lot to lose."

She nodded. "Yes. We do."

Chapter 12

Fairlie thought she'd remember every single moment of that day for the rest of her life. They left the castle grounds and wandered out into the city. They walked down Harbottle Hill to Glamley Street. Just below was the massive Burn. Usually when Fairlie left the castle, she stopped at a bench set on a rise just above the vast field of ashen devastation. She would sit and marvel at the power of the fire and wonder at its power to turn even metal to ash. But today she could think only of Shaye's hand wrapped around hers.

He loved her.

The idea of it seemed absolutely preposterous. If he hadn't been so adamant and nervous, she'd have thought he was gaming her. How had it happened? And when?

She didn't know what to think or how to feel. She had always loved Shaye. He and Ryland were her best friends. They knew everything there was to know about her. She told them all her secrets. The three of them were partners in crime, always getting in and out of trouble together. Of course she loved him. But *how* did she love him?

She had never had a lover. In the last few years she'd had a couple of romances here and there with boys from the castle, but they only went as far as a few kisses and hand holding and then she'd forgotten about them as she returned to her forge and lost herself in the hot metal. Her heart had never become tangled up in anyone else. But now—

Something inside her was swelling. Her throat hurt with it. Her legs shook and her mind spun. It was terrifying.

Shaye glanced down at her and stopped in the middle of the street.

"What's the matter? You look like you're going to puke."

Fairlie couldn't find a smile. Her stomach was knotted and she tasted bitter bile on the back of her tongue. Her stomach lurched. She yanked out of his grasp and ran to the side of the road, dropping her sacks as she did. She bent and puked into the dried grass. Little came up. Acid filled her nose and mouth and she spat, rubbing her mouth.

Shaye stood next to her, saying nothing. Her stomach twisted again and she bent double. Over and over again she heaved, though she had nothing left to throw up. She rested her hands on her knees and panted.

Finally, when she thought she had control again, she stood. She made a face at the taste in her mouth. She didn't meet Shaye's eyes.

"Changed your mind?" he asked, sounding very much like his usual acidic self.

If Fairlie didn't know him so well, she would not have heard the fear underneath his mocking tone. She felt paralyzed with it. Shaye wasn't the kind of man to love easily. He didn't open himself up that way. She could hurt him terribly just by not returning his feelings. It would shatter their friendship. He'd known that and he hadn't wanted to risk it. That's why he'd kept it hidden. The sickening terror of that realization struck like a blow. Her lungs constricted and she could hardly get her breath. She pressed her hands against her chest, trying to quiet herself.

But he was waiting for an answer, and every passing grain convinced him she didn't care.

Except . . . she did. Didn't she? Yes. It was an attraction she'd never permitted herself; a hunger that she had never been able to fill except with her work, and it was always better when he was there helping her, keeping her company. The joy was similar, but not the same. She'd always had a *want* that she couldn't satisfy.

Until now. She searched inside herself. It was ... gone.

Her lungs slowly relaxed. She breathed deeply, the air bright and cold. She looked up at Shaye, her eyes wide. She shook her head.

"No. I haven't changed my mind. It just ... hit me, is all."

"What hit you?" The words were icy.

Fairlie chose her words carefully. "I don't want to hurt you—to hurt *us*. I suddenly thought, what if I couldn't feel as much as you feel?"

He looked away, his jaw flexing, his expression austere. He didn't say anything. He wouldn't ask, Fairlie knew. He wouldn't force a confession he didn't want to hear. She reached up, touching her fingers to his cheek. He flinched and looked down at her, his gaze dragging unwillingly. He had the powerless look of a drowning man who didn't expect a lifeline.

"I don't know what I am feeling," she said, wanting to give him all of the truth.

"Don't you? You just lost your guts. Surely that tells you something," he said harshly.

"Yes. It does. I am scared," she said. "I do not want to lose you. You are too important to me."

He nodded and smiled without humor, and started to turn away.

"No. Let me finish," she said, gripping his chin tightly. "That isn't all."

He went still.

"I don't know what I am feeling," she repeated. "But I want you to know now, so that you don't eat yourself up all day, that I do feel more than friendship. I didn't realize it," she said, her brow furrowing at the lack of self-awareness. "I feel ... I want you," she confessed, unsure what she meant, but knowing it was as close to the truth as she knew how to get. She felt her cheeks flood with color at the admission, but she looked at him steadily so that he'd know she meant it.

He jerked as if struck. Then his hand caught hers, pulling it from his chin. His eyes were blistering, boiling with a mixture of emotions.

"Don't— You don't have to. I understand. I should never have said anything."

He didn't believe her. It meant too much. He wanted to protect himself and her, protect their friendship. Soon he'd be telling her he didn't really love her. It had been a bad joke. But how to convince him?

"Don't be more of an ass than you have to be," she found herself saying sharply. "If there is one thing you ought to know about me is I don't lie to you. Not ever. I am not starting now."

She didn't know if it was her words or the acerbic tone of her voice that caught him up.

"You want me?"

The flush in her cheeks burned hotter and she gave an exasperated sigh. She dropped her gaze, embarrassment making her cringe. She again contemplated kicking him in the shins, if only to make him stop looking at her. It was his turn to grip her chin, lifting it until she looked at him again. His brows were arched nearly up to his hairline, his sleepy eyes alert.

"You *want* me?"

"Have you gone deaf?"

"I'm not sure. I'd like to hear it again."

"Fine," she snapped, embarrassment making her irritable. "Yes. That's what I said. I want you."

A thin smile broke over his mouth, then faded. His thumb stroked her lips. "If you change your mind, if you are wrong, I can take it. Don't be afraid for me. I want you however I can get you. Friendship is enough."

She snorted, twisting away and reaching for the sacks she'd dropped. She swallowed, her lip curling at the foul stickiness on her tongue.

"Just so I understand—you are giving me permission to stick a knife in your chest and you won't bother screaming?"

"I would rather you didn't."

She slung the bags over her shoulders. "All right."

She started walking again. He didn't follow. She turned. "You promised me breakfast."

He still didn't move. "What does 'all right' mean?"

"It means I understand. I agree."

"To what, exactly?"

She sighed. "I agree to your terms."

Surprise. "My terms?"

"That I can walk away and we'll be friends and you won't mind in the least." She smiled wickedly. "A hard bargain, I'm sure. Now, I'm hungry."

This time when she walked away, she didn't stop and eventually he overtook her, falling in beside her. For a while he was silent. They turned right onto the Maida Vale—a wide avenue winding in a desultory way from the castle, through the sprawling city and past the Maida of Chayos, ending at the harbor. Finally Shaye spoke again.

"I am an unmitigated ass."

"Can that condition be cured? It seems to cause you no end of trouble."

He chuckled. "I have high hopes."

"On the other hand, if you weren't an ass, I might still not know how you feel."

"And that would bother you?"

"Would you believe it if I said yes? You seem to find me uncertain of myself."

"I believe you."

"Good."

His hand found hers again and his fingers laced tightly through hers.

They ate a breakfast of sausages, eggs, fresh rolls, and black tea at a cozy teahouse in the corner of a bakery near the corner of the Maida Vale and Haygate Street.

Shaye steered the conversation into safe waters, talking about Vaughn and Ryland.

"I never thought I'd see them so hateful to each other," Fairlie said. "They didn't even seem like brothers. It affected Ryland deeply. When he came back to the party, he was almost shaking with anger. I've never seen him that way."

"Not even when I locked him in the garderobe during the ambassadorial visit from Normengas? The king was furious with him."

"And he tried to knock out your teeth," Fairlie said, laughing. "It was a mean trick."

"He earned it."

"What did he do to you?"

Shaye looked at her steadily. "Nothing."

Fairlie frowned in confusion. "But—" Realization seeped in. "Me? You did that because he did something to me? He didn't—"

She broke off when he gave a sharp, adamant shake of his head.

"All right. Tell me. What did he do?"

Shaye hesitated, then shrugged. "You were sixteen seasons old. You'd just made journeyman and he took you to celebrate. Do you remember? I couldn't come because my sister was ill and asking for me."

She nodded. "He dressed me up the way he did last night"—her nose wrinkled—"and then took me to the theater at Hewick and after to Petrie's for a spectacular dinner. And then we went to some place in the Riddles. I had never been to the Riddles before."

The Riddles was a lawless maze inside Sylmont. The original city had been built there before the settlers had realized no one could follow them across the Inland Sea. To protect themselves from invasion, they'd built a city without any rhyme or reason. Streets corkscrewed and ended nowhere. Doors opened up onto brick walls. Underground tunnels tangled beneath and without a map or a guide, most people would get lost in a matter of grains. An invading army would have been confounded.

Nowadays it was easy to hide inside the Riddles and never be found; the Crown Shields and government officials never went there. It was a crumbling, broken place, littered with debris from collapsing buildings and buckling streets.

There was one small part of the Riddles that had been made civilized and habitable by powerful consortiums that hired private police forces to protect their interests. These resided along Ashford Avenue, a well-maintained street that matched the elegance and style of the affluent Salford Terrace. Hiding here were a number of highly illegal gambling dens secreted inside various lawful houses of entertainment catering to every taste, from the highest brow to the most degrading. In the Riddles anything was possible, for a price.

"Ryland took you to a place called Brick Lane, which can't afford to be on Ashford Avenue. It hosts a less affluent clientele." His lip curled. "The two of you took a hack without any guards, without telling anyone where you were going. That's because he wasn't there just to celebrate. He had an appointment to keep with someone who needed the anonymity of the Riddles."

Fairlie set her cup down, her brows arching. "Really? I don't remember that."

"You never knew. He took you to Brick Lane and excused himself. He left you in the main room and paid one of the house guards to keep an eye on you. Which he did. In fact, he kept such a good eye on you that he got you drunk, and Ryland returned barely in time to prevent you from being dragged upstairs to one of the rutting rooms." Shaye gritted his teeth, his hands clenching.

Fairlie stared at him in shock, trying to remember. She'd had such fun that night. The musical play they'd watched had made her laugh so hard her ribs had hurt. The dinner had been course after course of delicacies from all the countries surrounding the Inland Sea. Then Ryland had suggested the Riddles with a kind of flourish, knowing she'd always wanted to visit. They'd taken a hack to Ashford Avenue, then walked up the street. Fairlie remembered how excited she'd been, how amazed at the unending stream of private coaches filled with a glittering array of wealthy men and women.

Ryland had led her into a dark, winding alley, turning corner after corner until they'd finally arrived at Brick Lane. It was dilapidated, its clientele rough and loud. He'd led her into the taproom. *I'll order for us. I'll be right back.* But instead of Ryland, a gregarious man had brought her a cup of potent wine. He wore what passed for livery in the place—a blue shirt with stains down the front, a monkey jacket, and a tarnished badge shaped like a brick with two hammers crossed on the front it. It was the hammers on the badge that made her trust him.

They'd talked. He'd been joking and funny and brought her cup after cup of wine. She frowned, rubbing her forehead. She couldn't remember after that. She looked at Shaye.

"I can't remember."

"I know. You drank a lot that night."

She nodded with a pained look. "*That* I remember. I was really sick the next day."

"You've never been drunk again."

"I didn't like it much," she admitted. Fairlie's brows drew together. She looked at Shaye through the steam of her cup as she held it to her lips. "But how do you know all this? You weren't even there."

"You told me some. Ryland told me the rest," he said, a grim look chilling his expression. "I asked Ryland about it when I realized something had happened. I didn't think you'd be able to tell me."

"What do you mean—something happened?"

Shaye's lips twisted. The words sounded like they tore his throat. "The knobbing bastard left marks on you."

Fairlie looked down herself as if they'd still be there. She couldn't even imagine them. "What marks?"

"You must have realized where he was trying to take you. When he didn't let you say no to him, you fought him. Hard. He hit you. Here—" He brushed a finger just above her left cheekbone. "And here." He touched the corner of her mouth. His murderous expression cleared when a gloating smile turned his lips. "You paid him back and more. He didn't expect any woman could have fists of iron. By the time Ryland got back, you'd bloodied and bruised him. He was on his knees."

The fog in Fairlie's mind clouding the incident wouldn't clear. She scrunched her forehead, concentrating, trying to push through. To no avail. She shook her head, touching her fingers to her mouth and sliding them up her cheek.

"Why don't I remember?"

"That much drink erases the memory. When Ryland brought you back, I sent for a healer. A cousin of mine. You'd passed out by then. When you woke up and didn't remember—" He shrugged. "It seemed better to let you forget."

"And that's why you locked Ryland in his garderobe?"

Shaye nodded. "He deserved worse. But I expect it pained him more to lose stature in his father's eyes than to break his legs as I wanted to."

"But it wasn't his fault. Not really. I'm the one that was fool enough to drink so much."

"Ryland knew better than to take you there at all, much less leave you there," Shaye said, his jaw set stubbornly. "Do you understand what that cracking bastard was going to do to you?"

"I've a fair idea," Fairlie said dryly. The thought of being attacked somehow didn't frighten her; it didn't feel like it had happened to her at all. Mostly it made her angry that he would even try it. And it made her feel more than a little stupid for having let herself get so drunk and having to be rescued.

Anger surged inside her. It wasn't so much for herself as for other unsuspecting women who might have fallen prey to him. "I hope I hurt the bastard. I hope I hurt him a lot."

Shaye's smile turned malevolent. "Enough so that he did not want to lie with another woman for some time. And then he developed a mysterious festering illness. Weeping sores. Rather disturbing to look at and painful as well. Especially for his prick and balls. Last time I checked, he couldn't bed a woman if he wanted to."

Fairlie cocked her head. "You did that?" He nodded. "Good." She squeezed his hand. "I'm fine though. Nothing happened."

"It nearly did. Ryland shouldn't have taken you there."

"Maybe not. But he has a lot of responsibility as the king's son. His father asks a lot of him, and Ryland has always been scared to death of coming up short in his father's eyes. He probably didn't even think about what could happen. He just had to get something done and . . . it was a mistake. He would never hurt me on purpose."

"He didn't think about you because you didn't matter nearly as much as whoever he needed to meet there." Shaye held up his hand to forestall her next argument. "We will not agree on this one. But it is in the past. Ryland and I have settled our differences over it."

The flash in his eyes told Fairlie that he was no less angry about it, though. They may have settled things, but Shaye had certainly not forgotten or forgiven. Her stomach squirmed with an unfamiliar sense of pleasure—that she was so special to him, that he would get so angry on her behalf. She smiled inwardly. To think that last night she'd thought he'd left because he cared too little! But at the same time, it was hard for her to fault Ryland. She knew the pressures he was under and how hard he struggled to measure up to his father's expectations. And she was perfectly capable of taking care of herself. She was far more to blame than Ryland. But Shaye wasn't going to listen to that. She decided to change the subject.

"I met your uncle last night," Fairlie said.

He raised a brow, sitting back, his fingers turning his teacup in its saucer. His expression softened slightly. "How did you like him?"

"He's charming. I thought he would be older."

Shaye lifted a shoulder. "He was born old."

"He was very kind to me. Squired me about for at least a glass. Told me stories about nearly everyone we saw. Does he know everybody's secrets?"

"Nearly. It helps him run the business."

"He seems very fond of you," Fairlie said.

"So long as I don't get underfoot and in the way, he is."

"You? Underfoot and in the way? Hard to imagine," she said.

He smiled. "Nicholas has a sense of humor. But it has its limits. He was pleased enough to send me to Merstone Island to let the Majicars' Guild have the care of me. But he has always been someone I can rely on when I have need."

"When have you ever needed anything?"

"Right now. Come on. Let's go deliver all of this so we can spend the rest of the day together. I'll take you to the Riddles if you want."

"I thought it was too dangerous for me."

He shook his head. "Not with me around. I won't let anything happen to you, if I have to burn the place to the ground."

Fairlie wrinkled her nose. "I don't think King William will like having two Burns in the city."

He shrugged deliberately, bending to help her with her sacks. "I don't much care. You are all that's important to me. Everyone else be damned to the depths, for all I care."

That took Fairlie aback. She frowned at him. "That's too much. You can't—" She didn't know what. He couldn't depend that much on her?

"I can. You wanted to know. You wanted the whole truth. That's it then. You are my entire world. If anything ever happened to you—" He broke off, shaking his head. "I wouldn't be responsible for what I would do."

She licked her lips. They were dry as straw. "I don't know what to say." She didn't know what to feel. Her insides were at war. Fear, wonder, amazement, shock, horror—it all pulled into a maelstrom in her stomach. Her breakfast churned and she fought the urge to puke again. She didn't like to waste perfectly good food and she really needed to stop acting like such a child. Nor did she want to scare Shaye again.

"Let's go," she said instead, and hurried out onto the sidewalk.

Fairlie walked quickly, staring at the ground in front of her. Shaye made no effort to overtake her.

The Maida of Chayos was on the other side of Blackstone and west of Cheapside. Traffic and bustle made it a slow trek. The Maida backed up against the foothills, and a greensward aproned out behind it for several square leagues. Behind it, the heavily wooded Cat's Paw Mountains rose in dull, green-gray undulations.

The Maida itself was an astonishing place. It looked like a great hill. It bulged up from the ground in a broad hump, fully a thousand paces in diameter. The sides were gentle swells that steepened into a towering dome. From it grew all manner of things—trees, bushes, flowering plants, vegetables, grains. Grazing among them were cows, sheep, goats, pigs, rabbits, deer, chickens, ducks, and geese. The vines were heavy with grapes, the bushes loaded with ripe berries. Everything was ripe and ready. Delats—those called to serve Chayos—picked food, putting it in baskets. They handed it out to any with need who asked. The Maida of Chayos was ever-fruiting, ever green, ever full of life and hope.

More Delats wearing simple green or brown robes were already handing out food to a waiting line of people that coiled through the broad cobbled plaza fronting the Maida. It was filled with small copses of grass and trees with benches and burbling fountains fed by springs. The entrance itself was a simple arched doorway with no door. It had been cut directly into the earth. It was bracketed by two tall cast-iron urns. The metalwork was crude and rough. The shapes of the wild world cavorted across the urns in bas-relief. From the top of each rose flames. They were eternal fires fueled by Chayos herself.

Fairlie stopped beside one of the verdant islands in the plaza, turning around to face Shaye at last. His face was quiet, washed clean of all emotion. He lifted his sacks down and settled them on a bench. She didn't know what to say to him. She didn't know what she *wanted* to say. A large part of her wanted to go back before the morning so that she wouldn't have to know. Another part of her mocked herself for being a coward.

"Are you coming in?" she asked.

He gave a faint shake of his head. "I don't belong in there."

"Why not?"

"I'm a majicar. *Sylveth* is the source of our strength— the blood of Meris, the Moonsinger. Chayos is not for us."

Fairlie nodded, not having expected anything different, and picked up the sacks from the bench. She lifted them over her shoulders with a grunt. Luckily she didn't have to take them far.

"Are you going to wait?" she asked, though she already knew his answer.

"I'll wait."

She couldn't read his mood now. He had completely masked himself. She found she didn't like it any better than finding out how much he cared. *Loved her*, she told herself. Loved. Not merely cared—that was too weak a word for the way he felt. She couldn't pretend otherwise. It wasn't fair to him. He'd risked a lot; she had to honor that. But she needed to adjust to it first. She took a breath and then turned away, not knowing what else to say.

The doorway into the Maida of Chayos was unguarded. Anyone was free to enter. Fairlie hitched the bags on her shoulders and passed inside the entrance and stopped. As usual, chills ran down her neck all the way to her heels.

The inside of the Maida resonated with a deep, pulsing

power. It vibrated through Fairlie like someone else's heartbeat. Before her was a simple shrine made of a massive circle of undressed upright stones with a rough slab stone table in the middle. Each of the outer stones was at least three times as tall as Fairlie. The altar table was large enough to seat two dozen people. On it were offerings of all sorts—cloth, money, liquor, bread, candies, porcelain, clay pots, blankets, twists of hair, scraps of paper, bits of rag—whatever a person had to offer, no matter how small.

Fairlie walked between two of the upright stones and lifted the heavy bags from her shoulders, piling them on a brightly dyed wool blanket. There was a dirt path that led around the shrine. Fairlie followed it. She wanted to go into the vale itself, the center of the Maida, where she could be closer to Chayos. It was not an easy journey to make and few felt the need to do so. But Fairlie wanted to make sure that Chayos knew how grateful she was for the gift of her talent with metal and fire.

She paused on a patch of grass, gazing out over the Maida. A dense forest grew inside. The trees were ancient, with enormous gnarled boles and stretching limbs. Some were tall and majestic, others withered and small. Brilliant sunlight shone on half of the Maida. The other side was swathed in total darkness. Fairlie could see where a curtain of rain fell, and a brush of icy wind caressed her face. She shivered, turning her face up to the heat overhead. Both night and day and all the seasons turned inside the Maida of Chayos at once. To get to the vale at the center, you had to walk through all four seasons and whatever weather dominated each. Once you set out on the spiraling path, there was no turning back and no stopping to rest.

She looked down. The path led away from the grass patch underneath a low-hanging limb of an ancient oak. Its leaves were dusky green, the edges pointed. Acorns and spiky leafmeal littered the ground beneath. Fairlie took a breath and stepped onto the path.

Instantly she felt power surge around her. It was not

entirely uncomfortable. It was like a hand gripped her from head to foot, holding her firmly, though not crushingly. It made her feel a little claustrophobic, but she didn't fight it.

Sweat soon dampened her scalp and trickled down her forehead and neck. The air was humid and sticky, and her winter clothing was too heavy. But she kept moving. The trees grew more dense, and she was forced to climb over mossy logs and slog through muddy puddles. A storm had passed through this quadrant recently, and the air smelled of rain and rich, wet dirt.

She came to an area where it appeared a tornado had come through. The path was made nearly impassable by fallen trees. But Fairlie had no choice. There was no going back, and leaving the trail was not permitted.

She scrabbled over and under and through, scratching her face and hands and tearing her clothes. She reached the other side on her hands and knees. She stood slowly. Her boots were clumped with thick red mud and matted with leaves. Her trouser legs hung heavy with the wet and dirt. She dusted away the bits of leaves and twigs embedded in her hands, and then winced. There was a sliver of wood buried deep in the heel of her palm. Before she could work it out, there was a hard shove in her back. She stumbled forward, looking back. There was nothing there. Again a shove.

"All right. I'm going." She started walking, shuffling a little, her boots clumsy. She stamped her feet, but the mud was tenacious.

She was still working on removing the splinter when she walked from summer into spring. The temperature cooled and the path was dry. Birds twittered merrily and flew overhead in colorful streaks of scarlet, blue, yellow, and brown. It was easier going here, and almost before she knew it, Fairlie crossed the line between spring and winter.

It was frigid. Instantly she began to shiver as the mud caking her legs began to freeze. She stamped her feet, and thick chunks of mud cracked away. Up ahead was night. There would be no moon to help her see. The moon was the dominion of Meris.

She stepped into night and into a blizzard. Snow piled in deep drifts. Fear jolted through her. She lost the path. She went still, snow choking her when she tried to draw a steadying breath. She coughed, wrapping her arms around herself for warmth.

Only a few grains had passed when she felt the familiar shove against her back. She took a careful step forward. Another shove. And another. Another. Each one angled, forcing her along the path like a surly guide. Fairlie whispered a prayer of gratitude.

She had no idea how long she remained in winter. The cold reached frigid fingers into her insides, and she shivered so hard that she was forced to clench her teeth to keep them from cracking apart. She slid and fell, swallowed by drifts of snow or tangled in fallen limbs. Each time she levered herself up blindly and waited for the next shove to set her on her way.

She fell again when she crossed from winter into fall. Leaves crackled beneath her as she lay on the ground, panting, her entire body shaking with the cold. The shove pushed against her feet and she obeyed it, getting to her knees and then to her feet. She staggered forward. It was still too dark to see the path. The thickly woven tree canopy blocked most of the starlight, and Fairlie was forced to rely again on the invisible guidance of the shove.

The temperature was crisp, the ground white with frost. Her breath plumed in the air. Still, it was warmer than winter and much more dry. She kept going. Soon she would find the center of the Maida.

A chill wind blew up, and before long she was shivering just as hard as she had been in winter. She hunched into her coat, tucking her hands beneath her armpits. She hated the cold. It gave her aches and made her mind sluggish. She reveled in the volcanic heat of the forge when it was stoked high, its coals gleaming brilliant orange and red, yellow and blue.

The wind seared her face and ears. She pulled her collar up and waited for the next shove. Then suddenly a dazzling light bloomed. Fairlie blinked and squinted, lifting her hands to shade her eyes as she stepped out onto a flat dirt circle. At the center were two ancient trees. The first was a hazel, its trunk splitting into a dozen thick stems. From its foot sprang a gurgling stream. The other was a Lius tree. The bark of its trunk was smooth gray, as were its thick, heavy branches. The younger growth was fiery orange. Flames crackled beneath it in a tight circle. Both trees were sacred to Chayos, but the Lius was the one Shaye had sculpted into Fairlie's pendant. It was the tree of metal and flame.

"Welcome, my daughter," a voice said. It was feminine, deep and rich like new-turned dirt.

The light flared and then subsided into a soft yellow glow. Fairlie lowered her hands. Her gaze swept the clearing. A ring of white salt circled the outer edge, and inside was a ring of black coal. The interior was bare dirt but for the two trees. Fairlie's gaze followed the spreading trunks of the hazel tree upward. On one broad curving branch a woman sat. She wore green and gray, making her nearly indistinguishable from the tree itself. Her blond hair was long and loose, her face and body rounded and lush. Her eyes were green.

Fairlie stared and then dropped to her knees, bowing her head. The woman chuckled.

"I am the Naladei of Chayos. Her Voice. Her Eyes. Her Hands. What has brought you to me?"

"And I am the Kalimei," another voice interjected with velvet darkness. "I am also the Voice of Chayos, Her Eyes, Her Hands ... Her Heart."

Fairlie's head jerked to face the other priestess. The Kalimei stood inside the flames, one arm wrapped around the trunk of the Lius. Her long hair fell to the sides in a shining curtain, as dark as the black waters of the Inland Sea. Her eyes were the same brilliant green as those of her sister priestess, her skin the rich brown of newly turned soil. She wore a black robe, the inside lined with orange. Her fingers stroked the bark of her tree.

"Ah, sister. I did not expect you," the Naladei said, with noticeable irritation

"Or perhaps you hoped I would not attend our daughter's arrival." She didn't allow the other woman to answer. Instead she turned to Fairlie with a small but genuine smile. "Welcome, child. What has brought you on the difficult journey to meet us here, in the heart of the Maida?"

"I wanted—" Fairlie's voice cracked and she swallowed, beginning again. "I wanted to give my thanks," she said clumsily and flushed with embarrassment.

"Yes, so I see," the Naladei responded. "You are generous."

Fairlie glanced up. At the foot of the hazel tree lay her pile of stuffed bags. "Chayos is generous. I could not have made those without her blessings. She has given me everything."

"You walked the path here to tell her this?"

Fairlie nodded. "It seemed disrespectful not to."

The Naladei nodded. "I see."

She slid from her seat in the tree in a graceful, flowing movement. She crossed the dirt, her feet seeming to float. She stopped in front of Fairlie, putting her fingers under Fairlie's chin and tipping her head up. Her fingers were surprisingly coarse and rough, much like Fairlie's.

"Chayos is pleased with you."

Fairlie heard a sudden sound of hundreds of wings flapping overhead, then a cloud of ravens swept through the clearing, alighting on the ground in a shifting, restless blanket. They made no sound other than the soft flutter of feathers. Fairlie felt a chill run over her skin. Then one strode to the edge of the Kalimei's fire. It stared at her, giving a loud, rasping squawk, its beak snapping loudly shut at the end of it.

"It appears you are needed," the Naladei said to her sister priestess with a pleased expression.

"It seems so."

There was something angry and bitter in the way the Kalimei said it. The hairs on the back of Fairlie's neck rose. Then suddenly the air was again full of flapping wings. The ravens swirled around the Lius tree, then flowed away in a liquid cloud, out into the Maida. Fairlie looked for the Kalimei; she was gone.

"That leaves just you and I," the Naladei said.

Fairlie lowered her eyes.

"No, child. Look at me."

She did as bade. The Naladei stroked a hand over Fairlie's hair, much as a mother might soothe her child.

"You are truly Chayos's daughter," she mused. "Completely untainted . . ."

Fairlie frowned. *Untainted?* But then the Naladei stepped back. Her eyes closed and it seemed a cloak of shadow closed around her. Then suddenly her eyes opened. Light spilled from them, running like liquid gold over her skin. Fairlie could only stare, her mouth falling open. The Naladei's head tilted and she frowned. It was a shockingly sinister look and Fairlie felt herself recoil.

"Do you carry *sylveth* on you?" Her lip curled in repugnance.

"I—" Fairlie cleared the sudden dryness from her throat. "I do." She fished the pendant Shaye had made her out of the collar of her shirt, her fingers trembling. "I did not mean to offend."

The priestess took the pendant between two fingers as if it was excrement. She examined it.

"It was a gift," Fairlie said, her stomach twisting. She'd brought *sylveth* to the heart of the Maida. The blood of the Moonsinger was not welcome here. But she would not have taken it off. She'd promised Shaye. *No*, she chastised herself. *That's not why*. He'd made it for her and she liked it next to her skin; she liked knowing how much thought and effort went into the design and making of it. Quiet realization stunned her. She did love him. She had for a long time. She just never thought he would look at her that way.

"My sister's Lius tree. It is beautiful," the Naladei

said, letting go of the pendant. "It will serve you well," she added cryptically.

"Serve me?" Fairlie repeated. Surprise struck her. She frowned. "You don't mind that it's *sylveth*? And here in the Maida?"

"*Sylveth* is not a threat to Chayos," the priestess replied tartly, as if insulted. "Nor is Meris. She is less than nothing."

"But majicars are not allowed in the Maida."

A low chuckle. It was not pleasant. "And what would they want here? They are creatures of Meris, no matter that they tread Chayos's soil. She suffers them because they are necessary, but they do not belong here."

Without warning, between one grain and the next, something changed in the quality of the light from her eyes. The hue of the gold darkened and somehow hardened. It seemed almost brittle, like the light on a cold winter morning.

"Chayos takes pride in you, child. She ever will. But you are on a road that has no fork. There is no way to avoid the difficulties ahead. She cannot interfere. I offer you three things to aid you. *The first*— The path is you. Know yourself and you will know your path. *The second*— Always you will belong to Chayos; always will you be welcome in Her Maida, and here in its heart. *And finally*— I give you this."

She reached for Fairlie's hand, turning it palm upward. She laid a hazel leaf on it, the soft oval roughly edged.

"When you need it, crush this leaf. It will stop time for the space of three heartbeats only. You will need to remember all of you in that time."

Fairlie stared up at the Naladei, bewildered. "I don't understand."

"You will. Life is lived in every season. Spring is lovely, but winter is no less so. The tree loses its leaves and it appears entirely different, but it is always the same. Do not forget."

The priestess stepped back. "All life is change," she said. "This is the one truth."

Light flared white. Fairlie turned her head, squeezing her eyes closed. She could see the pink of her eyelids and the red seam sealing them shut. Slowly the brilliance faded to what it had been when she first stumbled into the circle. She turned back, blinking. Black blotches danced across her vision. When it cleared, she saw that the Naladei was once again perched in the tree.

"I don't understand," Fairlie said again. She still had her hand outstretched, the leaf soft on her palm.

The Naladei smiled, her teeth white and sharp. "It is hoped that you will before time runs out." She pointed to a spot behind Fairlie. "Go now. The way will be smooth."

Then the air around her softened and fluttered. Fairlie blinked, but air continued to shift like rippling water. Slowly it settled again. The Naladei was gone.

Fairlie stood, staring down at the leaf. She closed her hand gently and slid it into her coat pocket. Then she turned. A path had opened, straight as an arrow, leading away through the ancient grove. It bored through the darkness in a glowing streak. Fairlie stepped jerkily over the ring of salt and coal and stumbled away.

Her mind tumbled over itself. Her thoughts scattered. She snatched at them, but nothing fit together. She knew only that she'd been warned. *Of what?* Smoke in the darkness. Weeds in the wheat. Fox in the henhouse. Knucklebones rising. *Change.*

Change didn't frighten Fairlie. It was the heart of her craft. She turned ore to molten metal to jewelry and sculpture. It was the nature of things. From birth through life to death. Change ruled all.

Was that it? Was she going to die? Her first thought was *not now*. Not now when she'd just started with Shaye.

The instant and visceral quality of her reaction shocked her. Her heart knocked hard against her ribs, making her breathless. How was it possible that she could feel so much for him and never know it before? But she did. If she was truthful, she'd always quietly thought of Shaye

as belonging to her. He was always there, always understanding, teasing, helping, comforting, laughing. More so
even than Ryland. Shaye was her constant, her anvil. He
loved her. She loved him.

All of which mattered very little if she was to die.

But now she had been warned. She could avoid it. Was
that not the purpose?

She frowned, trying to remember what the Naladei
had told her. She was the path. *To what?* Her fingers
caressed the leaf in her pocket. Three heartbeats to remember herself. It did not sound like a fatal warning.
She dragged her hands through her hair, pulling it from
its wire twist. Her fingers tightened into fists and she
pulled sharply. The pain did nothing to clear her thinking. Remember herself? How could she forget? What
did it all mean?

A frisson of unease spiraled down her spine. Her stomach felt hollow. She stopped, unable to keep herself from
looking back. The path behind was gone, swallowed by
the trees and grass and night. She turned around again,
striding forward with a purposeful confidence she did
not feel.

Before time runs out.

And just when would that be? she wondered. Her
mouth went dry. *And what would happen when it did?*

Chapter 13

Do not.

Fallon's touch receded, but he hovered behind, his thoughts like groping fingers, trapping Nya inside a bristling circle of speaking silence.

"It is necessary. It is the only way to protect Kin."

"She will be Kin. Should I not protect her?" Nya said bitterly, knowing he was right, knowing she could not change her mind, knowing that the guilt and horror of transforming the innocent girl would never let her out of its jaws.

"She will be Kin; she is not now. You have no cause to worry for her now."

Nya snarled. "That is the logic of *them*." The word was laced with disgust and loathing. "Just as once she is Kin, they need not worry what she wants. They will make her Kin and they will hate her for it." She drew a harsh breath, her claws curving. She wanted to carve out someone's entrails. "Who cares for her now? Who protects her if not me?"

"It is not for you to do. She has family. She has friends. It is not your fault that they use her this way."

Fallon raised his hand to lay it on her shoulder. Nya twitched away. His arm fell, his face revealing nothing. But his mind battered at her like a raging bull. *She was his; she would be his. His. His. His.*

Never. Nya strode across the room, putting distance between them. "Stop. I belong to another."

"One of *them*," he derided. "What would he think of you now?"

The fear of it rippled over her. What *would* he think, her beloved? Would she be spawn to him? Evil? Monstrous? Vermin? She was nothing like she had been when they wed, though her heart remained his.

"You dare not go to him. It is better that way." *Mine. Mine. Mine.*

Nya spun and glared, one clawed hand raised between them. "I *will* go to him. When this is done. I will find him."

Fallon only laughed. *Mine. Mine. Mine.*

Chapter 14

Shaye paced. As soon as Fairlie disappeared inside the Maida, he retreated away from the plaza to the Maida Vale, where he strode up and down. He ignored the annoyance of other pedestrians. Nor did he pay any attention to the footspiders in their green and white uniforms hauling their passengers in handcarts, who were forced to suddenly veer aside as Shaye made an about-face and strode back over the ground he'd just covered.

He shouldn't have told her. He never meant to.

She'd kissed him back.

And then puked, he reminded himself sourly. She'd had a chance to consider things and she'd become terrified. Or simply disgusted. "Maggot-headed fool," he muttered.

An elderly woman with a patched dress and a ragged canvas sack on her arm started and stared at him. He scowled back without apology, and she paled and hurried across the plaza to the food line. Shaye rolled his eyes at himself. Now he was terrorizing old women. Brilliant.

He went back to pacing and stewing.

She had kissed him back.

He touched his lips in wonder. She'd said she *wanted* him. He dropped his hand. His entire body pulled taut. He wanted to hope, wanted *so much* to believe she meant it. . . .

But she was unsure of him and what she felt. She would

try to make him happy because she *did* love him—at least as a friend and brother. The question was whether she would try to convince herself to feel what she didn't feel so that she didn't hurt him. The thought of her twisting herself inside out to soothe him was enough to make him want to puke. He shouldn't have said anything. Why had he?

"Because you're cracked," he muttered. "A damned maggot-headed, Pale-blasted fool."

Again his outburst provoked askance looks from people walking past. He glared and pinched his lips together.

Why had he told her? He'd known it was a bad idea. Worse than bad. Disastrous. He'd known he shouldn't say anything since he first realized how much she meant to him. Ryland thought he didn't recognize his own feelings. He snorted. And Prince Diplomat thought himself so observant. Shaye had realized within a few months of meeting her. She'd only been nine seasons old and he thirteen. He remembered thinking how ridiculous he was. He'd scoffed and promised himself the feelings would pass, that he'd grow out of it. But the feelings had only strengthened over the seasons, becoming more and more undeniable.

Then this morning he'd broken the first of the two rules he'd given himself when it came to Fairlie. The second was to protect her, and he may have broken that rule too, in shattering the first.

It was the foreboding. He rubbed his chest, feeling an ache deep inside. It had set him on edge last night. It hadn't been just the foreboding, though. It was what followed after and the gnawing sense of Fairlie's upcoming departure. All together, they'd conspired to make him lose his reason.

He speared his fingers through his hair, thinking of the conversations he'd had the previous night at the Emerald Eye. Before he'd been cornered by Randall Turvey and his maunderings of woe about his wife and mistress, Shaye had been waylaid by two of his fellow majicars.

They had approached him as he sat in a corner steadily putting away a bottle of whiskey. It was Weverton stock, distilled on the highlands of northeastern Crosspointe, past Grimsby Bay. It had a smoky flavor with a lot of oak, and it was easy to drink. Last night he'd felt driven to the brink by Fairlie and by the unidentified threat. And though his majick burned the whiskey nearly as fast as he drank it, he was determined to outstrip it and get drunk.

Brithe and Maesonril slid into the seats on either side of him. Brithe was a tall, lanky majicar with dry yellow hair, white skin, and an aloof disposition. He was older than Shaye by ten seasons or more. Maesonril was his lover and partner in majick. She was a pert, startled-looking woman with short, glossy black hair threaded with white at the temples.

"May we join you?" Maesonril said to Shaye, clearly not caring whether he said yes or no.

He sat back in his chair, wondering what this was about. He was neither friends nor foes with either. He walked that line with most majicars. It came from being a Weverton—he had long ago learned the knack for keeping people at arm's length without making enemies of them. Though, admittedly, more often than not he didn't care whether they were enemies.

"I didn't expect to see you here," Shaye said, pouring himself another drink and draining it down. In fact the Emerald Eye was his favorite tavern because so few majicars every crossed its threshold.

"I expected you'd be at the castle for the fete," Brithe said, waving at a serving boy.

"I was."

"You left early."

"Did I? It seemed late," Shaye said sardonically. "But what brings you here tonight?"

"A drink on a cold night seemed like a very good idea," Maesonril said, tapping her fingers.

"It is, indeed. The Emerald Eye is a little out of the way for you," Shaye observed, drinking another whiskey. He refilled his glass without offering the others anything from his bottle.

"You're right," Brithe agreed, accepting his drink from the serving boy.

"So you came looking for me?"

"We did."

"Though you thought I wouldn't be here."

"You usually turn up, sooner or later," Maesonril replied with a sharp smile.

That was true. But how did she know that? Shaye didn't ask. He didn't say anything at all, merely swallowing the contents of his glass. The silence stretched.

"There's some trouble brewing," Brithe said finally, leaning in and dropping his voice.

"Isn't there always?" Shaye replied with a quirk of his brows.

"There is word that the crown intends to increase the service duty for majicars," Maesonril said. "It is said that it will be temporary—in order to facilitate the repairs on the Burn. But it will take years to mend the Burn, if we can at all. And even if we succeed, these things are never really temporary."

"Seems like an issue for the Sennet to deal with."

Brithe nodded. "It will, once the crown makes its decree."

"So why are you talking to me?"

"We want to know what you know about it. And where you and your family stand."

"Is that all?"

"For now. What do you know?"

Shaye shook his head. "Nothing."

"That's difficult to believe. You are in Prince Ryland's confidence and you are a Weverton."

"If Ryland knows anything, he certainly did not share it with me," Shaye said, draining his glass and reaching for the bottle.

"Would you tell us if he did?" Maesonril asked.

Shaye tipped his head, eyeing her balefully. "Probably not."

"You took an oath to the guild!" she exclaimed.

"But not to you."

"So if the Sennet asked you," Brithe said, "you would tell what you know?"

The urge to tell them both to go crack themselves was nearly overwhelming. Shaye resisted. "Of course."

"And what about the information your family contacts have given you?"

Shaye's knuckles went white on his glass. He drained it again, setting it down with a hard click. "My loyalty is pledged first to the guild. Are you saying you doubt it?"

Brithe shrugged. "It is well known how close to the prince you are. And Wevertons generally put blood before anything else."

"So does the royal family. Have you asked these same questions of the majicars with royal blood?"

"We are asking everybody."

"Then you must have balls of brass," Shaye said. He looked at Maesonril. "Tits of brass?"

She grinned, holding up her glass in a toast. "Coming from you, that's a compliment."

"The Merchants' Commission is considering taking action to protest the new taxes," Brithe said in a low voice. "If they do, there will be food riots. The crown will have its hands full. It will be our opportunity to become independent."

"Independent?"

Brithe gave Shaye a knowing look. "Don't play coy."

Shaye smiled thinly. "Habit."

It was no real secret the Majicar Guild wanted to be free of crown rule. The question was always whether the royal blood majicars would give their support. The Sennet didn't want a guild civil war.

"A good habit for outsiders," Maesonril said. "We will leave now. It is good to know your first loyalty is with us."

They left and Shaye continued to drink, soon joined by Randall Turvey, who was bewailing the accidental meeting between his wife and mistress. Shaye was hardly aware of him. It was true that his first loyalty was to the guild, if it came down to a choice between family, crown, and guild. But if Fairlie was added to the mix, she knocked everything else off the list. Luckily no one had figured that out, or they might have made a pawn of her.

He drank to get drunk that night, putting away two full bottles. But he never succeeded. Instead he stayed up listening to Randall Turvey's lamentations, and when he at last fell in bed, he didn't sleep. Which is why he was early enough to Fairlie's workshop to catch her before she left for the Maida of Chayos, and why he had been enough on edge to stupidly confess his true feelings to her.

Please Meris it hadn't been the biggest mistake of his life.

The sun rose high overhead and had begun sliding down toward sunset before Fairlie emerged from the Maida. She stumbled out, her arms wrapped tightly around herself. Shaye strode quickly to meet her, worry making his words sound harsh.

"What's wrong? What happened?"

She looked up at him, her eyes looking bruised. Then without a word she slid her arms around his waist, burying her face in his chest. Shock froze Shaye for several grains; then he clasped her tight against him.

He could feel her breath, short and quick, her heartbeats thundering. "What's wrong?" he asked harshly.

"I want to go home," she said, still clinging to him.

"All right. I'll take you."

He loosened his arms and she slowly followed suit. The memory of the foreboding filled him. That sense of *something coming* twisted in his gut. He would not let it hurt Fairlie. He took her hand and started to lead her away. She stopped him.

"Wait."

He turned back. "What is it?" He sounded more brusque than he meant to.

She stared at him. "I want to tell you that I—" She

broke off, biting her lips. She tried again. "I wanted to tell you before it's too late, that—"

"Too late?" he demanded. "What do you mean?"

Before she could say anything, someone stopped beside them.

"Fairlie? Is that you?"

Shaye turned in sharp annoyance. But after a moment's surprise, Fairlie smiled wide welcome, stopping his cutting remonstrance.

"Captain Plusby? I am so pleased to see you. You look very well."

There was a question in her words that Captain Plusby met with a pained grin.

"I'm well enough. Better than I was." He sobered. "I'm sorry I wasn't there when Toff returned to Chayos."

"It was a grand ceremony and he would have hated it all," Fairlie declared.

As she spoke, the color seeped back into her cheeks and the tense set of her face relaxed. It pleased Shaye to no end that she kept a firm hold of his hand. He eyed the interloper suspiciously. Captain Plusby was a slight man, just an inch or so taller than Fairlie. Typical of most captains, his blond hair was cut short on the sides, the long top lengths pulled back in a tail behind his head. His face was tanned and he wore a close-cropped beard and no uniform. He glanced at Shaye curiously.

"Forgive me," Fairlie said, seeing the look. "Shaye Weverton, this is Captain Leighton Plusby."

The two men shook hands. The captain's name itched in Shaye's mind. He knew it from somewhere, but couldn't place it.

"What are you doing here?" Fairlie asked.

Plusby smiled, and again it was pained. "Paying my respects to Chayos. It has been far too long. She may not forgive me."

"You had cause," Fairlie said quickly, then flushed. "I am sorry. I don't mean to remind you of—" She broke off.

Plusby shook his head. "No need for apologies. She's never out of mind."

Then it clicked. Leighton Plusby had lost his lover when her ship wrecked. He'd become crazed, refusing to accept her death or the possibility that she'd been turned to spawn. He'd taken his ships and scoured the Root for her, endangering his crews, his Pilots, and his cargoes. Eventually the Water Guild had stripped his ticket so that he could no longer captain a ship. How did Fairlie know him?

As if reading his mind, Plusby answered Shaye's unspoken question. "Toff was a good friend of my father's and then mine."

"Are you . . . sailing again?" Fairlie asked.

Plusby's expression tightened and shadows flickered in his eyes. He shook his head. "No." Shaye was sure he was hiding something. Then woodenly, "I've been out on a ketch here and there. Just to feel the deck. It isn't the same." He looked away, his jaw working, and then looked back. "I had better go inside. I am leaving the city today to accompany someone overland to Wexstead. I don't wish to be late."

Fairlie reached for his hand. "I'm glad to see you better."

His mouth tightened and he bent and kissed her cheek. "I'll stop in and see you when I return."

"I'd like that."

He nodded to Shaye and then crossed the plaza to disappear inside the Maida.

Without a word, Fairlie began to walk away. Shaye went with her. He said nothing. She was struggling with something. He didn't want to push her; she might choose not to speak at all. Sometimes she could be as unyielding as steel. Something had happened to her inside Chayos's Maida, something that connected with the wrongness and foreboding he'd been sensing. He had to go carefully if he didn't want her to shut him out.

They'd left Cheapside and were following the Maida Vale through the upper reaches of Tideswell when she finally spoke. She did not address what had happened inside the Maida. Shaye swallowed his impatience.

"Do you know Captain Plusby's story?"

"I've heard a few things." He repeated what he knew.

She nodded. "That's mostly right. Except that it was his wife who disappeared at sea, not his lover. They'd been married in Tapisriya, before it fell to the Jutras." She paused. "He went mad. I knew him before it happened. He came and visited Toff often during Chance and whenever he was in port. After.... He lost his reason. He has a bracelet—did you see it?"

Shaye shook his head.

"It's a marriage bracelet. It's made of woven wire—gold, silver, copper, and yeboron."

"Yeboron?"

A smile flickered over her lips. "The black metal I used in the queen's sculpture. It's only mined in Tapisriya—what used to be Tapisriya. Captain Plusby brought it back for Toff. Anyhow, the bracelet is beautiful work. I can't begin to describe how very fine it is—it's like patterned cloth. The weaving is part of the Tapisriyan wedding ceremony. It's majickal. I don't know what it does exactly, but the patterns on it change. Even after Captain Plusby's wife—her name was Sherenya—vanished into the sea, the patterns kept changing. He was certain it meant she was still alive, though she might have been spawn."

She stumbled on the last word and Shaye felt a chill. Like nearly everyone in Crosspointe, Fairlie was terrified of spawn. What would she think if she found out he was spawn? That all majicars and all Pilots were? Would she fear him? Would she shun him? The idea that she might was a pain that never stopped clawing at his insides.

Fairly didn't notice his distress. "He completely lost himself when she disappeared. He lost his mind, his captain's ticket—everything that made him who and what he was."

She looked up at him, that bruised look back. "I don't want to lose you."

"You can't," he said. "Nothing will change that," he said flatly. "We will be friends no matter what happens."

"You don't know that."

"I do."

She smiled, a pained expression. "No. You don't. The Naladei spoke to me in the Maida. She warned me."

"She warned you? What about?" The sense of uneasiness curled tighter around Shaye, prodding at him to take her somewhere safe and hide. He unconsciously pulled his majick into him, feeling it waiting for him to direct it. It did not warm the ice that froze him. Deep down he felt a stirring. A foreboding was coming again. The timing was no coincidence. Somehow the warnings were about Fairlie. He glanced about, looking for a place to let it hit where he would not draw undue attention to himself. He found it in the shape of a small courtyard dining area attached to a tavern. It was empty, the tables and chairs stored for winter. Leafmeal and puddles dotted the red tile patio, and skeletal black stems twined the pillar walls.

Shaye drew Fairlie inside, settling her on a stone bench. Within the tavern he could hear the rise and fall of voices. The scent of roasting meats and root vegetables floated through the afternoon air.

"Tell me what she said," he urged, holding both Fairlie's hands in his.

She looked down, her thumb rubbing absently across his fingers. "She said that I am on a road with no fork. There is no way to avoid the difficulties ahead. She said she could not interfere to change things. I don't know what she means."

"That's all she said? Nothing more definite?"

Fairlie shrugged. She pulled her hands from his and

wrapped her arms around her stomach, hunching into herself. Shaye resisted the urge to snatch her back.

"Nothing that made sense. She said that the path is me, that if I know myself, I will know my path. She said that I will always be hers, I'll always be welcome in the Maida, and then she gave me a leaf from her sacred hazel tree. She said I should crush it and it will stop time for the space of three heartbeats. I have to remember all of me in that time."

Shaye stopped dead in the street. *No. It could not be.* But echoes stirred, memories that somehow matched the words she'd spoken.

You must remember yourself. Do not panic. Do not fear. You will be a majicar. We know. We have foreseen it.

Then they'd put his hand in *sylveth*.

He'd been only five seasons old and hardly knew what was happening. But he'd always heard the *sylveth* calling, a song in his dreams, a drumbeat beneath the thud of his heart during his days. He never remembered not hearing it. An aunt had heard him mention it and brought him to the guild where it was predicted he would be a majicar and so he was made one.

But Fairlie was afraid of *sylveth*. She'd never heard its song. She was a child of Chayos. Who would do this and why? But no. Surely he was misinterpreting the message. It could be something else.

But nothing else made sense, not the way that this did.

Then, without warning, the foreboding struck him. It smashed through him. His body spasmed, his head wrenching backward. Stars and suns spun through his head and he felt an image coalescing. He reached for it eagerly—too eagerly. It evaporated beneath his touch, leaving only a fleeting impression of stone walls and bloodred eyes.

The wild majick began to spin in a whirlwind, and almost by rote he activated the capture spell to gather it up.

"What's wrong? Shaye?"

He became aware of Fairlie's voice, her hands firm on his arms. He sat up, closing his open mouth and shaking off the clinging dregs of the foreboding. "We have to get you somewhere safe," he told her gruffly.

"Where? Whatever is going to happen will happen. The Naledei said there was no way to avoid it."

"The Naladei is just a woman, and an ambitious one at that," Shaye said.

Fairlie stared, eyes wide. "She's the bright priestess of Chayos. She is Her Voice, Her Hands, Her Heart."

"So is the Kalimei and where was she in all this?"

"She was called away."

"I wonder what she'd have to say about all this," he muttered. Fairlie was naive. She would never believe the priestesses had motivations beyond serving Chayos. But he knew enough to know that the Naladei in particular was ambitious enough to ally herself with his uncle, at least on certain issues. She had no compunction about dabbling in mortal politics.

Fairlie was looking at him, her eyes narrowed. "You know something, don't you? You had a foreboding just now. Was it about me?"

Shaye licked his lips, then glanced out at the street. People were hurrying past, and two footspiders nearly collided as someone crossed the road unheedingly in front of them. It was all so ordinary, so safe. And yet he could feel the danger rising. His heart pounded with the need to run, to get Fairlie to safety. He grasped her hand.

"I've been having forebodings. I think it's something to do with you, but they don't tell me what is coming. It sounds like—" He caught himself. He didn't give a damn about his oath to the guild to never tell anyone what he was or what majicars were. When it came to Fairlie, nothing else mattered. But how could he tell her he was spawn? The words stuck in his throat.

"Let's get out of here," he grated at last. "Your workshop is inside the castle. No one can get you there. I'll set wards to make sure."

He stood, pulling her up with him.

Fairlie hesitated, then nodded. "All right. But just one thing first."

"What?" he said sharply.

She shook her head, rolling her eyes. "You don't make any of this easy, do you? I'm not sure how much time I have before—" She stopped, smiling tightly with gallows humor. "Before whatever is going to happens happens. So I want to tell you that I discovered something else inside the Maida." She flushed, tucking a wisp of hair behind her ears, her eyes dropping. "I realized how much I . . . love . . . you," she said, the words sounding like they cut her tongue in the speaking of them.

Shaye couldn't move. He didn't believe her. Couldn't believe. When he didn't speak, she lifted her eyes and met his burning gaze.

"I'm afraid it's true. Like it or not." She locked her hands together in front of her. "Aren't you going to say something?"

His throat worked, but nothing came out. He didn't know what he wanted to say. He cupped her face between his palms, bending so that his forehead touched hers.

"Be certain," he said tensely. "Because nothing now that happens to you will ever separate us. Do you understand? Nothing."

She laughed shakily. "You can't promise that."

"Yes, I can. I do." He would make sure of it. "Now let's get you back where you'll be safe."

And they were safe. All the way up to the castle and threading through the courtyards and twiggy gardens that were waiting for spring—no one stopped them, no one noticed them. Down the castle corridors and through the deserted wing to her workshop they went unmolested. Fairlie opened the door and went inside.

"Ryland!" she said in glad surprise.

Shaye looked past her to see the prince waiting. He

had been pacing. He turned to face them, looking wasted and gaunt.

Fear curdled Shaye's blood, and he reached for his majick, hardly knowing what he wanted to do. Then a heavy blow slammed him on the back of the head and he knew no more.

Chapter 15

The timetable for transforming Fairlie had been moved up. Ryland wasn't entirely surprised. The quicker it was done, the less chance he would back out. His father was not a stupid man.

Ryland had spent the morning after his meeting with his father planning his betrayal of Fairlie, punctuating his efforts with shouted invectives at himself and his father and punching his fists into walls and furniture. He'd torn apart his sitting room, throwing books and kicking the furniture like an enraged child. The furniture refused to break, but his knuckles were shattered and his hands were swollen and bruised. They ached and throbbed. The pain wasn't nearly enough.

Then Niall had emerged from the secret passage with a note from his father. The steward eyed the wreckage with lifted eyebrows but made no comment, merely handing Ryland the parchment.

He fumbled at the letter, smearing blood on the outside before cracking open the seal.

Do not wait for tonight. Go now .

The message was unsigned. Ryland swallowed, his body shaking. This was wrong. Beyond wrong. And he was going to do it anyway. He reached for a candle, sliding it close and lighting the parchment aflame before tossing it on the cold grate. He watched the flames turn it to ash, then turned back to Niall.

"Will you fetch Nya and Fallon to the solar in the

forge wing?" he asked crisply. "I will meet them there shortly. Use the secret passages if you would. I will also need two guards—I assume Father has his own cadre of trusted men in the Crown Shields?"

"Will two be sufficient?" Niall asked, his hands folded in front of him.

"More will attract undue attention. Tell Margaret to clear the wing. Go now."

He waited until Niall departed and then righted a chair and slumped into it, pressing his hands against his face.

"Dear Chayos forgive me," he whispered. "Mother Moonsinger be kind to Fairlie."

He sat up, going over the plan in his head. It was simple enough. They would go to Fairlie's workshop under the pretense of showing the ambassadors where she created her sculpture. The guards would remain outside and Fallon would set wards to seal the doors and keep noise from escaping. Then her transformation would be done, quickly and without any fuss. If she wasn't there when they arrived, they'd go inside and lie in wait.

The problem was going to be if Shaye turned up in the middle of it. Ryland doubted Margaret would be able to divert him, and he didn't know if his friend was powerful enough to destroy Fallon's wards, but assuming he was, it could be a disaster.

He went into his library and sat at his kneehole desk. He took a parchment from a drawer. Gripping the pen was difficult. His throbbing hands were clumsy. He reveled in the pain—he needed it. It was a tangible punishment for what he was about to do. He scribbled a hasty note requesting that Shaye meet him at the Emerald Eye as soon as possible.

He thrust the pen away. It trailed a line of ink across the wood of the desk. He stared at the scrawled words on the page. The writing was nothing like his usual precise penmanship. It looked desperate, thanks to his battered hands. Blood smeared the document in several places.

He rubbed a hand over his mouth and pain spurted up his arms. He deserved it.

He really was going to do this.

He folded the parchment awkwardly, using a lit candle to melt the wax for his seal. He pressed his signet into the blue puddle. He would give the letter to Niall and hopefully it would deflect Shaye. Otherwise he'd need a knacker box large enough to contain him. Getting one before they started on Fairlie would be impossible, not without potentially alerting the guild to what they were about. No, he had to hope that if Shaye turned up, the transformation would already be completed. Though he couldn't help but wonder, for Fairlie's sake and for the success of this venture, if Shaye's presence wouldn't be beneficial. He loved her deeply and he wouldn't be the one doing this to her like Ryland was. Shaye would be by far the better choice to anchor her to herself.

Ryland stood, went to the fireplace, and spat into it. All his life he'd dreamed of serving Crosspointe, of earning his father's trust and pride. He never imagined he'd be asked to do anything this heinous. It was criminal. And if he believed his father, it was necessary for Crosspointe's survival.

He believed. He didn't have a choice. He had to trust his father; he had to serve his king.

But Shaye was going to kill him when he found out. He might level the entire castle. Ryland imagined his father was taking precautions, though he didn't dare think what they might entail. He didn't want to know. He might be losing two friends today. No, he *was* losing them; there was no doubt of that. The question was, would either Fairlie or Shaye still be breathing tomorrow?

He took a deep breath that did nothing to loosen the tight bands constricting his lungs. He went to his closet and slipped on his coat and adjusted his cravat, leaving behind smears of blood on the crisp green material. He paused, then reached for his sword belt and buckled it on. It took a while, his hands fumbling like they weren't really his. But they were. These hands would betray his friend.

He tucked a stiletto in his boot. He looked at himself in his mirror. His hair was a rat's nest and made him look mad. He groped his brush, pulling it through his hair until the worst of it was smooth. He let it hang around his face, unable to fasten it back. His eyes still had that haunted, hollow look, and his hands trembled. He tried to curl them into fists. His fingers twitched but hardly bent. He returned to his desk and managed to pick up the letter and tuck it into his coat pocket. More blood smears patterned the parchment. He shook his head. Those alone would be enough to bring Shaye running to help him.

Their friendship was a stiff, uncomfortable one, but it was true. Or had been. Today it would be shattered.

When he could find no other reason to dither, Ryland opened the secret passage and stepped inside. He arrived in the solar a few minutes before Nya, Fallon, and Niall. He wandered aimlessly, staring out the window at the garden. A few shoots were starting to push up, and the bushes and trees had swellings where leaves and flowers were readying themselves for spring. The sun was brilliant and the sky was a cerulean blue. Ryland scowled at it.

Behind him there was a quiet *snick* and a tall bookshelf moved silently away from the wall.

Nya stepped through first, shrouded in her black floor-length veils. Next was Fallon, looking entirely human, though there was a fluidity to his movements that was more—or less—than human. Niall was last, followed by two burly men. They wore the black and red uniform of the Crown Shields. Grim-faced, they went to stand by the door.

"See that Shaye gets this," Ryland told Niall, fumbling at his pocket for the note he'd written.

"But what has happened? This will not do. Allow me," Fallon said.

Before Ryland could say or do anything, the spawn

majicar clasped his hands over Ryland's. There was heat
and warmth and then a savage biting sensation. Ryland
gasped and jerked back. The sensation continued, chewing up his wrists. He looked down at his hands. The swollen knuckles shrank back into proper shape, the bruises
faded, and the cuts closed. He flexed his fingers. The pain
was gone. He looked at Fallon.

"Keep your damned majick to yourself," he gritted
through clenched teeth.

Fallon's brows rose. "You prefer yourself crippled?"

"As a matter of fact, yes."

"My apologies then," Fallon said with a flourishing
bow. "Pardon my rudeness."

There was a note of ridicule in his voice and Ryland
flushed at his own ingratitude.

"Thank you," he said curtly.

"My pleasure," Fallon said mockingly.

Ryland took the note from his pocket and handed it
to Niall, then waited for him to depart through the secret door. When he was gone, Ryland cleared his throat
and addressed his four companions.

"It is my hope that we will find Fairlie alone. In such
a case, you two"—he motioned at the Crown Shields—
"you two will remain outside and prevent anyone from
intruding. If she is not there, we will wait for her inside.
If she is not alone, we will tell her that our dignitaries
wish to tour her workshop. The two Crown Shields will
position themselves so they can quickly take control of
her guest." He looked at them. "He will be a majicar.
You must move quickly and decidedly or he will certainly protect himself and you will die. Try not to harm
him unduly."

"Why don't I control him?" Fallon asked.

"Can you?"

"I am quite powerful." It sounded just slightly defen-
sive.

"So is he. The question is which one of you is more so?"

Fallon's expression did not falter, but neither did he
answer.

Ryland nodded. "My way then."

"This man—is he important to Miss Norwich?" Nya asked in her deep, musical voice.

Ryland hesitated. It felt too much like betrayal to speak of what was private. He jeered at his sentimentalism. Was it worse than turning Fairlie into spawn? He couldn't just dip a toe in these waters; he had to jump all the way in.

"They've been friends a long time. He's in love with her," Ryland said shortly.

"And she does not return his love?"

"She is very fond of him. If he is with her, he must be constrained, but not harmed unduly. It would shatter her."

"It will frighten her, this hurting of him."

"You mean more than turning her into spawn?" Ryland said bitterly.

"Yes. More than that," she answered without any emotion.

Fury and guilt converged in Ryland. He forgot about discretion and the guards and what they might not already know.

"How can you do this to her?" he demanded. "You know what will happen. You'll turn her into a monster, just like you. She'll be hated and feared. She'll lose everything. Everything."

Fallon laughed harshly. "It is us you blame, but it is you who make this choice for her. Are you not the real monster? Besides, the change is not so terrible. There is much to be desired in it."

Before Ryland could retort, there was an abrupt movement beneath the veils as if Nya had thrust out a warning hand at Fallon. She stepped in front of Ryland.

"This act does not please me. But it is necessary, yes? We are bound to serve our peoples, and Miss Norwich is a treasure for us both. I deeply wish that she had chosen this path herself. But we knew when we set out to make this alliance that it might not be so. Now the choice is made—it must be done to help both our peoples."

She sounded both sad and determined. That, more than her words, recalled Ryland to himself and what he needed to do. He gathered himself.

"Let's get this over with," he said quietly.

Fairlie was not in her workshop. The five intruders slipped inside, the two Crown Shields taking up a ready post just inside the door. Nya wandered about, aimlessly picking up tools and half-finished work and examining them through the veils. Fallon sat on the edge of a table, as still as if he'd turned to stone. Ryland wasn't even sure he was breathing.

The silence was smothering. Ryland found himself pacing as, one after another, the glasses turned and still Fairlie did not return. Where was she?

At long last he heard footsteps and voices outside. He froze, staring as the door handle turned. The two Crown Shields stood ready, each prepared with a bar of iron. Fairlie entered first. She didn't see the two men hiding beside the door. Neither did Shaye, who followed on her heels.

"Ryland!" Fairlie called, even as one of the Crown Shields clumped Shaye on the head. He fell to the floor in a boneless heap.

Fairlie spun. "Shaye!"

She dropped to her knees. "What have you done? Ryland! Help us! Is he breathing? What have you done?"

Ryland couldn't move. The second Crown Shield reached down and grabbed Fairlie, pulling her away. She struggled. She was strong. Her body was heavily muscled from her work, and the guard quickly lost his grip. The other came to his rescue, and the two of them wrestled her to the floor, kneeling on her shoulder and legs and twisting her arms above her head.

"What now, Highness?" one of them asked Ryland.

"It would be better if she could be calmed," Nya said, entering from the forge.

It wouldn't happen. He didn't say it. "Secure her to a chair."

The two Crown Shields lifted Fairlie into an armless

straight-backed chair, tying her hands behind her back with lengths of heavy twine. She kicked and struggled, landing several thumping blows with her heavy boots. Her two captors swore and grappled her ankles against the legs of the chair, then wrapped her from foot to ankle. She wrenched against her bonds, all the while staring wildly at Ryland.

"Ryland? What's going on? Why are you just standing there? Help me! Get these knobbing brutes off me! Ryland!"

He couldn't speak; he couldn't look at her. He fixed his gaze on the wall beyond her, his teeth fused together. Every word she spoke ripped at his insides. He was bleeding to death. He snarled at himself. He was a cracking bastard! He had no right to feel anything when he was the goat-cracking mother-clutcher who was doing this to her.

The Crown Shields finished and turned to look at Ryland.

"What about him?" one of them asked, jerking his head at the still unconscious Shaye.

"Ryland—what is going on? What are you doing here?" Fairlie asked in a small, cold voice.

He didn't acknowledge her. "Tie him up as well," he ordered. "Then wait outside."

"Ryland—I don't understand. What are you doing?" Fairlie's voice dropped and she began to struggle again. "Answer me, damn you! Leave him alone! You're going to kill him!" This aimed at the Crown Shields as they flopped Shaye over to deftly bind his hands and feet.

They finished and stepped over his body and out of the room, shutting the door firmly behind them. The workshop pooled with silence punctuated only by the scrape and click of the chair's feet as Fairlie rocked back and forth.

Ryland was aware of Nya's and Fallon's patient regard. They waited for him to orchestrate the rest of this evil.

"Set the wards," he said to Fallon.

He then went to kneel in front of Fairlie while the spawn majicar went silently about his task.

"What are you doing, Ryland? What is going on?"

Her voice was careful and even, as if she did not want to judge too quickly, as if she was still clinging to her trust in him. He winced against the fierce pain twisting his gut. He couldn't do this to her. He couldn't.

"I'm sorry, Fairlie. I do not wish to upset you. Shaye will be well enough, I'm sure. After—"

"After?" she prompted when he did not go on.

"After the Jutras attack, my father devised a risky plan to protect Crosspointe against future invasion. It revolves around establishing firm alliances with other countries and allowing them free access to the Inland Sea."

He paused, thinking she would ask what that meant or what it had to do with her and Shaye, but she only stared at him, her lips pressed hard together, her eyes devouring. It left him nothing but to continue.

"He has sold them ships' compasses. But he needs more. And he cannot get them from the Majicars' Guild. Did you know they have only one compass-majicar left? No, of course not." He was rambling. He forced himself back on track. "It is a rare skill. But Fallon can sense what majick—if any—someone will have if cursed by *sylveth*. That is how majicars are made. They are all really spawn. Shaye too."

He was beginning to babble as he tried to put off the dire moment. Fairlie was still watching him with no sign of comprehension or even shock, only wariness. He blundered on. "Fallon says that you will be a compass-majicar when—"

He couldn't say it. He saw comprehension strike her. Shock now. Her eyes widened and she drew away from him, as far as her bindings would let her.

"What are you saying?"

Still that disbelief, that faith that he would not harm her, though she was tied to a chair. He couldn't take it. He thrust to his feet, stalking away, his back to her.

"Fallon, Nya—do what you have to do."

"You cannot even look at her. How will you make an anchor for her?" Fallon asked.

Ryland's mouth twisted. The memory of Fallon's and Nya's true appearances rose in his mind's eye. Animals. *Monsters*. His eyes burned with tears and his vision blurred. They slipped down his cheeks and he did not rub them away.

"Use Shaye. He'll work better for her."

"He is a majicar. He will fight this. It could be . . . unpleasant," Fallon pointed out.

"We'll have to chance it. I'll not see this fail because I—" Fail. "He'll anchor her better. Can't you do something to keep him from using his majick?" he asked Fallon.

The spawn majicar shook his head. "What can be done is done. Awake, he will be able to use his power. Though complex spells require much focus and concentration, he will have power enough to smash and pound."

"Then do you have suggestions? We need him awake."

Fallon hesitated. Then, "I have a poison made from a plant that grows on the Root. The majick that flows through a majicar usually destroys the Loviena before it kills him. Until then, he is made helpless, unable to move more than to breathe or speak. We often use it on wild majicar Kin to keep them from hurting anyone when Nya first speaks to them."

"How long until it takes effect?"

"Poison?" Fairlie demanded in the same moment that Ryland asked his question.

Fallon answered the prince. "The count of ten at most."

That could be forever, if Shaye managed to gather his power. He could kill them all. Ryland was willing to risk it. He deserved it. They all did. He almost wished for it. "How long before it wears off?"

"Depending on his strength, a few minutes only. Perhaps as many as five. Or he will die. It will require a strong dose."

"Do you have it with you?"

"I do."

Fallon fished it out of his illusionary robes. The bottle was made of gold filigree and red glass. Ryland didn't ask why Fallon had it with him. It didn't really matter.

"Then wake him and whenever you're ready."

"As you wish," Fallon said with a short bow, his voice as dry as autumn leaves.

"No, Ryland! Shaye could die."

Now Fairlie's control broke. She sounded panicked. Ryland didn't answer or turn around.

"Ryland—this is Shaye. He's our friend. You *can't* poison him." Her voice went high and cracked.

He whirled on her. "*You're* my friend and I'm about to curse you with *sylveth*. If I can do that, I can poison him to try to keep you from going too far in your transformation," he said brutally.

She only stared. "You're going to . . ." She swallowed like there were rocks in her throat. "You're going to curse me?"

"Yes. Aren't you paying attention? You'll be a compass-majicar." He spoke roughly. He needed to gain distance from her. How? She was as close to him as a sister. A voice inside laughed at him. And Vaughn was his brother. He'd learned to fake that hatred. He'd have to fake indifference now.

She was silent, staring at him as if from very far away, as if she didn't recognize him. "You could kill Shaye."

She surprised him. She ought to be worried for herself. *Sylveth* terrified her. He told her so, watching her blanch as if the words were blows. Self-disgust churned in his stomach and he turned away again, only to find Nya standing in front of him.

"She should not be bound. Her mind will panic more."

"Should we poison her, too, so she can't move?" Ryland asked bitterly.

"No," Nya said with gentle seriousness. "It will kill her."

Ryland's gorge rose and his mouth filled with burning

bile. He swallowed hard. "She isn't going to sit still for this."

"You must cut her bonds at the very moment Fallon releases the *sylveth* inside her."

He couldn't answer. He nodded.

"Ryland, stop him!" Fairlie's voice sliced through the air, raw and agonized.

He spun around. Shaye was sitting up against the door, blinking groggily. Fallon held Shaye's head back, opening his mouth and tilting his open bottle. A viscous yellow liquid dribbled out in a slow stream.

"No!"

Fairlie struggled, her chair rocking until she tipped it over with an echoing crash. Ryland looked down at her in dawning understanding. Shaye had finally realized what he felt for Fairlie; he'd finally told her. And from the shattered look on her face, she returned his love. Ryland rubbed his hands over his face, feeling a thousand seasons old. But there was no turning back now.

He lifted the still-thrashing Fairlie upright. "It's done. All we can do is wait. Calm yourself." He sounded strange, even to himself.

"You poisoned your best friend," she said hoarsely, staring at Shaye, who was beginning to twitch and suddenly started to convulse. "Shaye!" she screamed.

Ryland went to stand over the spasming man, watching the waves of convulsions grow more violent. He felt distant, as if he were looking at a stranger through a faraway lens. He wanted to feel that way. And he was repulsed at himself for clinging to such a shield.

Shaye's eyes rolled up in his head and his skin sparked with majick. The sparks smoked on his clothing, and Ryland squatted down and patted them out with his bare hand. The sting of the burns felt good and right.

Shaye gasped, his tongue thrusting from his mouth. It was a dark gray. His eyes were wide and staring. They were also gray and circled with red. The eyes of all Crosspointe majicars were this color. They kept them hidden with illusion. But all of Shaye's power and energy were going into this fight against the poison.

Minutes ticked past. Fairlie was silent. Ryland couldn't look at her. Everything inside him was searing to ash. He felt brutal and inhuman—more monstrous than Fallon and Nya. Suddenly Shaye went still. He sucked in a long, deep breath and blinked. Awareness came back to him. Ryland grabbed his friend and hauled him up to sit against the wall. He caught Shaye's face between his palms, angling his head until he could meet his furious gray eyes.

"No time to kill me now, my friend," Ryland said. "In a few grains, Fallon is going to turn the *sylveth* splinters in Fairlie's arms to raw form. There's nothing you can do to stop it. Father wants a compass-majicar, and Fairlie will be one. The only question is how much of Fairlie will survive. You can help to anchor her mind and keep the transformation from going too far."

"I'll . . . kill . . . you," Shaye whispered through lips that hardly moved.

"Not before Fairlie is cursed. Up now, let's go."

He and Fallon hooked Shaye beneath his arms and lifted him, dragging him over in front of Fairlie and settling him in a chair opposite hers. His body slumped and his arms dangled lifelessly. But his fingers twitched. Ryland pushed Shaye's head back so that he could look at Fairlie.

"Ready?" he asked Fallon and Nya, going to stand behind Fairlie. He pulled out his stiletto, ready to cut her bonds as soon as Fallon liquefied the *sylveth* splinters in Fairlie's arms and hands.

"One moment."

Nya pulled her veil away. Fairlie gasped, staring at the other woman's strangeness. She shrank back in her chair, her face turning to chalk. Nya rested her hand on Fairlie's head, her fingers splaying wide, the black talons curving over Fairlie's skull. She closed her eyes, her mouth moving, though no sounds issued forth.

"You should hurry. Shaye will not long be incapacitated," Ryland warned.

Nya's eyes opened. She looked at Shaye, ignoring Ryland. "I can help her hear you. I can help her fight through the confusion and the fury when her Kindred soul is released. But I do not know her. You will need to remind her of who she has been; you will need to call her back. I will make your voice louder—" She glanced at Ryland. "Both your voices."

Shaye did not look at her. His attention was locked on Fairlie. He could lift his head now. "Fairlie. Look at me," he rasped.

Her gaze slid reluctantly away from Nya. Her eyes were hollow and sere, a wasteland of ash and darkness. "I wanted more than just one day," she said to Shaye, her voice brittle.

"There will be more than one day," Shaye said urgently. "Look at my eyes, Fairlie. I am spawn. I. Am. Spawn. I love you. I will love you no matter what happens. You can trust *me*. Do you hear? Now and forever."

She made no answer and Ryland couldn't stand to wait any longer. "Do it," he whispered to Fallon.

The spawn majicar laid a gentle hand on Fairlie's shoulder. At the same moment, Shaye made a grating, animal sound deep in his throat. His body twitched and his hands swung up into his lap to lie like dead things.

Fairlie went suddenly rigid.

"Free her! Quickly!" Nya said, her taloned fingers closing more tightly on Fairlie's head.

Ryland slashed through the bonds on her wrists and sliced desperately at those on her legs. But it made little difference. Her body had gone soft like smoke. It wriggled, snakelike. Her feet slid out of her boots and from under the twine. But they were feet no longer. Ryland couldn't say what they were or would be. There was a flash like sunshine on a knife blade and a brilliant flickering orange like flames. The rest was shrouded in dense gray smoke.

Through it all, Fairlie made no sound.

"Stay. You can stay. Hear me, hear my words." Nya said it like a command.

"Fairlie!" Shaye shouted in an agonized voice. Then nonsensically, "The leaf! The leaf!"

He lunged from the chair and slid to the floor. His hands groped clumsily at Fairlie's coat pocket. It had crumpled, no longer supported by her smoky body. He got his fingers inside. He pulled out a jagged-edged green leaf. He flung himself across Fairlie's disintegrating lap, holding it to her now featureless face. He crushed the leaf in his fingers. Instantly the pungent smell of hazel filled the room. Mixed in with it was the scent of rain and green meadows, freshly turned earth and wood smoke.

"Remember yourself, Fairlie. Remember you and remember me," Shaye grated desperately. "Remember!"

Chapter 16

Fear held Fairlie in a crushing grip. She could hardly breathe. The woman—Nya—was no woman at all. She was spawn. Beautiful, horrible spawn.

Ryland wanted to make her into that. Wanted to make her into his father's pet compass-majicar. More than wanted to. He was doing it.

She felt gutted. The air pressed at her, crushing her.

They were going to make her into spawn.

It took everything she had not to scream.

At least Shaye was all right. He was stronger than the poison they'd given him. He wasn't going to die. The relief made her chest ache with a deep and abiding pain.

She would miss him. Small words for her sudden anguish. They should have had longer together. "I wanted more than just one day," she said to him, trying to tell him how much she really did love him. But her voice was thready and repulsively weak. The crushing fear was grinding her down to nothing. She welcomed oblivion. She didn't want to feel the change and the loss of herself. She didn't want to know she'd become a mindless, ravenous beast.

Shaye's voice snagged her, pulling her back to the room, to herself. She reluctantly let herself focus on him.

"There will be more than one day," he said forcefully. He was unable to move yet. He was helpless if the spawn she became attacked him. She shuddered. No. If there was one thing she wouldn't do, it was hurt Shaye. Somehow—she didn't know how—she would stop herself. The other three, however, and especially Ryland—she'd rip them to shreds. They'd never do this to another soul.

"Look at my eyes, Fairlie," Shaye said. She did. Gone were the polished brown orbs. Now they were a tarnished silver ringed with crimson. The pupil was also crimson. Not human. But still Shaye. Always Shaye. "I am spawn," he said. "I. Am. Spawn. I love you. I will love you no matter what happens. You can trust *me*. Do you hear? Now and forever."

She had no time to digest his words. A grain later, Ryland said, "Do it."

Warmth streamed into her from the hand Fallon rested on her shoulder. In her arms, there was a flickering of energy, like fragments of lightning caught in her skin. They burned with infinite heat and blistering cold. She felt her body lock. Her vision faded.

She tasted.

Sour. Cream butter and burnt sawdust. Rotten meat. Sweet, sweet blood. Salt. Pungent rosemary. Vinegar and limes. Sugar and mold.

Hunger bloomed.

Rage.

She heard a voice. Inside her skull. She crouched and raked iron claws at the intruder. A woman. Firm and demanding. The intruder didn't give ground when the newborn creature that had been Fairlie circled her, baring her teeth. Hungry. Thirsty. Brutal.

"Fairlie. You must hear. You must remember yourself. You can temper the transformation. You do not have much time."

The hungry newborn slashed again, this time with claws of shining *sylveth*. There was a gasp and whimpering and a satisfying thud. The spawn licked its claws, tasting pain and death. They rolled sweet across her tongue, filling her body with throbbing lust.

There was another voice. She snarled. This one ribboned through her like liquid gold. The newborn licked it. Fire. Delicious fire full of orange, green, blue, and yellow. Heat roared in her, clean and fierce. She clutched at the voice, wrapping it around herself.

Then suddenly a new smell. Crisp and green and mellow: wind and forest and farm. She felt her body—as insubstantial as the thick smoke that billowed off her forge and as powerful as the fire burning inside. She heard a thudding sound. A heartbeat. Her heartbeat.

Remember.

Fairlie.

The name slid along the river of gold. A caress. A need.

Shaye.

A flood of images rolled through her. Snippets of memory from a life well lived and too short.

Too short.

But it was over. She was spawn. Shaye was spawn. She loved Shaye. Not all spawn was evil.

Thud.

Another heartbeat.

For the space of three heartbeats. She *remembered.*

You will need to remember all of you. Life is lived in every season. Spring is lovely, but winter is no less so. The tree loses its leaves and it appears entirely different, but it is always the same.

Change.

Ore to molten metal to jewelry, swords, sculpture—anything she could imagine. She was a master metalsmith. She could make anything.

She was ore. She was molten metal. Alloyed now, with *sylveth.* What would she be? *What would she make of herself now?*

She was no coward.

Change was simply change.

She would be . . .

Thud.

The gift of Chayos faded. But Fairlie remembered.

She felt the potential in her body, and she felt the changes that could not be reversed. There were always limits to forging.

She concentrated, swimming in the golden river of Shaye's voice. She felt herself solidify.

She opened her eyes. Shaye lay across her lap, clutching her . . . hands. She didn't let herself look at them. Not yet. On the floor before her was Nya. She was curled into a ball and whimpering. Fallon knelt beside her. He appeared stricken, though it was difficult to read the expression on his face. His real face, no longer hidden by illusion. He lifted Nya in his four arms, stroking her hair. Her head fell back, exposing the buff fur of her throat. There was no blood. He looked at Fairlie.

"Look what you've done!" he said ferociously, baring his pointed teeth.

Fairlie only glared at him, anger flaring inside her. She turned her head, looking for Ryland. He sat behind Shaye, slumped and staring. His face was ravaged, like he was a hundred seasons old. The anger turned to fury and roared into rage.

"Get. Out."

He flinched. "You have to understand," he said softly, tears streaming down his cheeks.

Her lip curled. "No. Go. We are done." Her voice was the grumble of rocks in an avalanche, the low mournful song of a cello.

Still he didn't move. "This was done for a reason. Crosspointe needs you. Needs your skills."

She laughed. The sound was hoarse and deep. "Surely neither you nor your father is insane enough to expect me to help you."

She jerked forward, her jaw jutting. Ryland flinched. She was frightening to look at, then. Good.

"I said get out of my forge. Go before I rip out your throat."

It wasn't an idle threat. Her mouth watered as she looked at him. Her stomach turned at the sudden hunger for flesh. Dear Chayos—what was she? Ryland blanched, scrabbling backward. Then he stood and went to Fallon, pulling him up. Fallon lifted Nya easily, his strength far beyond that of a normal man. They went together toward the door. Ryland never took his eyes off Fairlie. Fallon keyed the wards and they left. Fairlie continued to watch the door. She didn't trust that the guards wouldn't come rushing through brandishing swords, followed by majicars in knacker gear. But grains passed and there was only silence.

She didn't dare look at Shaye. She didn't want to see what he thought of her now. The glimpse of her hands told her she was no longer human. Not even a little. As if the cannibalistic hunger hadn't already told her.

But she could not avoid this forever. She gently pushed him away from her and stood. She went into her room. There was a mirror on the inside of her wardrobe door. She reached for the handle and paused.

Her hands were almost delicate, long-fingered with too many joints. She counted. Five knuckles. She flexed. There was a fluidity to them, and strength. Her skin was smooth as polished steel. The tips of her fingers were black, with short, oval nails. The color faded to lighter and lighter grays, turning to silver on her forearms. Twists of delicate gold filigree vined over her arms and the backs of her hands.

Fairlie marveled at herself. She'd done this. She'd crafted herself as she would craft any metal.

She touched her arm. Warm, soft flesh. Sensitive. A tingle of sensation crept up to her shoulder. But she could feel the metal in her flesh. She would not damage easily. That pleased her. She smiled. It felt the same as before. She opened the wardrobe door and looked at herself in the mirror.

She was completely naked. She was lovely in a strange, unnatural way. The silver on her arms swept up her shoulders, fading to green. It graduated to indigo blue between her breasts—they were smaller now and more stiffly conical, the nipples a burnished copper color. From them looped copper filaments in a lacy pattern that traveled around their outer curves and up over her shoulders. Another set twined together in the center of her stomach and stopped at the apex of her thighs, disappearing beneath a patch of silky black wire. The blue of her stomach turned plum at her hips and then lightened into red and orange. At her knees the color darkened. Her feet were coal black. More copper tracery wound around from her backside, overlaying her skin from mid-thigh to her toes.

Her feet were wider now and narrow at the heel. Her toes were long, with extra knuckles, just like her hands. There were six toes. Fairlie looked at her hands. Five fingers and a thumb on each. Finally she raised her gaze to her face.

It was the same and different. The skin was silvery, the shape oval, but there was a slope to it now. Her nose was longer and broader, her eyes farther apart. They were bigger, and inside them—smoke and flame. There was no pupil. A memory caught her, making her gasp with fury and pain. The gala, Ryland on his knees, holding her hands. He was talking about her eyes. *They are like looking into the heart of your forge.* Now they blazed, fiery reds and oranges eating away the charcoal mist. It was as if Ryland had predicted what they would look like.

She clenched her hands, pushing him out of her mind. In a moment she calmed, the fires in her eyes dimming. She continued her inventory.

Her lashes were long and spikey and looked like delicate shards of red *sylveth*. Her cheeks were high and hollowed beneath, her chin thrusting in a sharp curve. Her charcoal lips were full and wide. Her hair was a mane of silky wire that made a metallic sound when she shook it. But each strand was as fine as gossamer. It hung down to her buttocks and shone silver, gold, copper, and black. Her ears were flat against her head.

Her hearing was better than before. She heard Shaye rising off the floor and stop in the doorway, heard his breath catch. Her nose was more sensitive too. She smelled the salt of his sweat and the sour tang of his fear. She didn't look at him.

Instead she turned to the side and glanced at her backside. The lacy trails of copper converged between her shoulders and dropped down her spine, separating at the top of her buttocks, sweeping down to twine her legs. Her spine was ridged and flexible. Along her heels and halfway up her calves were short, wicked spikes of black edged in gold.

She turned to face herself again. Her shoulders and arms had lost the bulky muscles of her trade. She opened her mouth; its interior flesh and her tongue were black except for the shine of her opalescent teeth. They were nearly transcluscent, each one a thin, pointed spike curving slightly inward. She shut her mouth, noticing now that there was a line of knobby black protuberances running down the outsides of her forearms. She touched them. They were hard and silky, like polished onyx.

She felt Shaye watching her. Oddly, she felt no embarrassment at her nudity. But she wasn't sure what she did feel. She considered. Rage continued to flow through her in a volcanic river. And hurt. A vast deep ocean of pain—that Ryland could do this to her. The rest of her felt cold and numb. She didn't know if this was what she was now, or if soon the numbness would wear off. She clenched her strange hands again, feeling the strength in them. Muscle she might not have, but she was not a weakling.

At last she turned to meet Shaye's gaze. He leaned weakly in the doorway, his face ravaged by hatred and fear.

"You're beautiful," he rasped.

"Yes," she agreed. She *was* beautiful, like an exotic work of art. Men didn't want to kiss works of art. "But I am spawn."

What did that mean? She remembered Fairlie. She remembered her life. Her body was different, but wasn't she still herself inside?

She did not know.

"I don't care. You are still Fairlie."

She tipped her head. Her long hair fell to the side with a metallic swish. It was heavy, she realized. And—

She concentrated. Locks of her hair twisted together,

braiding and curling. She watched the movement from the corner of her eye. She was doing this. Her hair was responding to her wants. She straightened it in a flat, shining curtain, compressing it until it seemed like a single sheet of metal. Her eyes found Shaye again.

"Am I still Fairlie? Or am I someone else? Some*thing* else? If the outside of me has changed this much, what has happened to the inside?"

She asked in the same way she might ask a merchant about the price of fabric or ask a friend to borrow a book. Shaye frowned, clearly uncertain how to read her. Fairlie made no effort to clarify for him. She didn't know how to explain what she didn't know herself. Instead she waited for his reply. As if he had an answer.

He surprised her.

"The real truth is that only time will tell you what you've lost and what you've gained." He took several shaky steps into the room, stopping a few feet away and swaying, his face sallow. He was sweating. The lingering effect of the poison. "I look at you and I still see Fairlie in your eyes and in the way you hold your head. I see her in your body—so much like the rest of your sculptures. I hear her in your words. Whatever else has changed, you are still her and I still love you."

"How can you be sure?" Something was pressing against the inside of her chest. A lump of emotion that swelled like a cancer. It was full of sharp things and corrosive lye. She fought it, trying to keep the bubble from rupturing. It threatened unimaginable pain.

He shook his head. "I just am."

Fairlie opened her mouth. What she meant to say, she didn't know. Instead she screamed.

Chapter 17

Fairlie's scream dropped Shaye to his knees.

The sound ripped through him. His vision blurred. In a moment his head would crack to pieces.

He crawled toward Fairlie. If he was going to die, he was going to do it wrapped around her.

The floor beneath him trembled, and he could hear the grumble of stones and mortar under pressure. An ache ran down the roots of his teeth and up his jaw to spread spiny fingers through his skull. Dust rose in a fog from the walls, floors, and ceiling, and chips of stone clicked against the floor, stinging his face and hands.

Shaye kept crawling until he reached Fairlie's side. She had collapsed to the floor on her knees. Her head was caught between her hands, and her eyes glowed with all the rich colors of sunset. The tears that rolled down her cheeks were molten gold. One fell on the back of his hand as he reached for her. It sizzled on his skin. He shook it off, but a milky blister rose instantly where it had fallen.

He pulled Fairlie into his lap. She was hot, like the hearthstones in front of a crackling fire. Her body was stiff as she resisted him, and her scream went on. She did not seem to need air. Shaye stroked her cheeks and arms, pulling her closer against him. He rubbed his hands in slow circles over her back, whispering soothing nonsense. Scalding tears continued to drip onto him, falling on his arms and legs. He didn't care.

The floor bucked and the ceiling timbers groaned. More dust filled the air. A thundering crash sounded in the workshop. Shaye coughed and sneezed, but he didn't let go of Fairlie. Then suddenly she went silent. Her body softened against his, curling into him like a child desperate for comfort. Shaye tightened his arms.

For a long time neither spoke. Shaye took in the scent of her. It had not changed—earthy, with a tang of metal and the mellow smoke of fire and a hint of green, like the first blades of grass after winter.

When at last she shifted so that she could look at him, it was all he could do to loosen his arms. He didn't want to let her go. He was afraid she'd leap to her feet and run. Not that she had anywhere to go. His heart hurt for her.

Her eyes turned darker, more smoky. "I don't understand how he could do it."

Shaye bared his teeth. "I will kill him." The words were clipped, precise, and cold. If it didn't mean leaving her, he'd be on his way right this minute.

She stared at him. He couldn't read what she thought. It would take time to learn her expressions, the reasons for the churn in her eyes. Would she give him the time? Or would she push him away? But it was a different fear that thrust a sword of ice through his gut. She couldn't stay here; he had to get her out of Sylmont and away from people. He had to disable whatever guards surrounded the workshop, then find a way to smuggle her out. If anyone saw her, they'd panic and call out the knackers to capture her. She'd be taken to Merstone Island.

Shaye's face hardened. Majicars knew that some spawn were gibbering pits of hunger and fury, while others retained the ability to think and know themselves. But all the creatures that went to Merstone were prisoners or worse—things to be used in spells and ritual, or cut apart to look inside, or be bombarded with majick to find out what majickal abilities they might have, if any. Any of those might be Fairlie's fate. Unless Ryland was right. If she could make ships' compasses, she'd be forced to do so. His mouth twisted, his nostrils flaring. No one forced Fairlie to do anything. If they tried, she'd fight. And die.

She looked away from whatever she saw in his face.

"You don't want me to kill Ryland?"

She shook her head. Her wire hair brushed his cheek. The touch was softer than he expected, and slightly cooler than her body. He leaned into her, breathing deeply of her scent. He could not lose her. This day had taught him how much it would cost him. The price was his soul.

"I—" She stopped. "Is it unnatural that I want him to die?"

There was a wealth of pain and fear in her voice. Shaye gripped her arms, turning her to face him.

"No. It's normal."

"But . . . he's meant so much to me."

"Which is why the betrayal is so much worse," Shaye snarled.

"How can I hate him so much?"

Shaye heard the question beneath her words. The old Fairlie hadn't been capable of the hatred and loathing that now swam in her eyes.

"He raped you," Shaye said. "Maybe didn't use his prick, but it's rape all the same. He didn't care about how you felt or what would happen to you—at least not enough to stop. He did it knowing what would happen and how much he was hurting you. And he'd do it again. You have every right to hate him."

Every word he spoke fueled Shaye's own fury. He *would* see Ryland dead. But first he had to figure out how to make Fairlie safe.

"I . . . I need to be alone. I need to think," she said.

It was all Shaye could do to release her and get to his feet. "You can't stay here. The king has gone to the trouble of turning you. He'll come for you soon. And you can't go wandering about or the Majicars' Guild will capture you. We must leave Sylmont as quickly as possible. My family has many properties. It will be easy enough to take refuge in one, maybe at Rudlington or Whitwell, at least until we can figure out where to go next."

She didn't answer.

"Fairlie?"

"I'll see what clothes will fit," she said.

"Pack anything you value."

Her shoulders stiffened and her head bowed lower. Shaye could have kicked himself. She couldn't take her home or her forge, and she valued little else. Except for her friends. But all she had left was him. Not exactly a bargain.

He reached out and touched her head and then left, his throat tight. He stopped dead as he stepped into the workshop. Spiderweb cracks crawled over the floor and up the walls to the ceiling. A pile of wood and stone from high up had fallen, smashing several tables. A good wind and the rest of the place would come down.

He looked at the overturned chair where she'd been tied. Her clothes lay like rags. He caught a glimpse of color. Slowly he bent and picked up the pendant he'd made for her. Pain clutched him again. No *sylveth* could hurt her again, but he doubted she'd ever be willing to wear it. He tipped the chair up and set the pendant on the seat.

He went to the door and leaned his head against it, considering what must be done. Getting Fairlie out of the castle would require illusion. So long as he stayed in physical contact with her, he could mask her real appearance. He didn't have time to work a cipher to create an illusion to cover her. Nor any handy veils like the spawn-bitch wore. It would be better if he could get a hack. But where from there? The Trunk Road was the main artery that went north through the eastern spur of the Blackwick Mountains and then turned west, following the foothills to Grimsby Bay. It would be too obvious to take that route. They had to choose something less traveled. He could borrow a Weverton vessel, but it would be difficult to maintain her disguise aboard ship, and too many people would know where they'd gone. There was no safe place in Sylmont, but perhaps he could find a cottage up in the mountains, or down in Waterfoot or Blackley. If they could find a place to hide until he could create a cipher to disguise Fairlie, they could go almost anywhere. It would buy them some time.

He pushed himself upright and wrenched open the door. There were no guards. That surprised him, but he didn't have time to worry about it. He was to the end of the corridor where it crossed into another before he came to his senses. He stopped. No guards? That was ridiculous. And what was he doing leaving her alone? She was defenseless. He swung around. It was too late.

A black hood dropped over his head and his arms were grasped roughly and pinned to his sides. His captors made no sounds. Shaye struggled and reached for his majick. It bounced harmlessly off the material now pulled down to his thighs. He was shoved over onto the floor. He kicked and yelled, hoping Fairlie would hear and know to escape. The knacker sack was drawn tightly shut over his feet. In a matter of a few grains he'd been entirely subdued. He swore furiously at himself. What kind of maggot-headed fool was he? What kind of majicar?

He continued to thrash and yell until a boot slammed hard into his stomach and another into his head. He slumped, dizzy and breathless. A white-hot pain sliced into his chest. His ribs bellowed as he fought for air. Pain turned his ragged breathing to a whine.

Still no one spoke, nor did anyone touch him again. A door opened. Footsteps.

"Take him to a smother cell. I'll deal with him later," King William said quietly.

"Yes, sire."

Shaye was lifted again. Despite the pain in his head and side, he began to struggle again. But there were at least four men carrying him. They merely gripped him harder and ignored his feeble movements, tipping his head downward so that the blood filled it, making it throb. He lost consciousness.

He woke still encased in the knacker sack and lying on a cold stone floor. He was stiff and it hurt to breathe. He began to wriggle and kick until the drawstring closing the bottom of the sack loosened. He lay still until he caught his breath again and then began working himself free. He twisted and bent until he could get his fingers under the lip of the sack. His ribs hurt unbearably, and every minute or so he had to rest, gasping for air.

But at last he was free. He kicked aside the knacker sack and gazed around his cell. It looked very much like a workroom on Merstone Island. It was square and lined with shiny black knackerstone. Silver wires were inlaid in the stone in complex containment spells. It was a cell designed to hold spawn, or more specifically, a majicar. There was no furniture, not even a slop jar. Shaye pushed himself upright and staggered to the door. It had no interior handle. He pushed against it. It did not give.

He returned to the center of the room, his hands curling into fists. There was no way out. He wanted to curse and kick at the door. He wanted to blast someone with raw majick.

He had to think. He rubbed his face and shook his head to clear it. What could he do? He didn't dare think of Fairlie. She was a hurt inside him that ached so deep he could never assuage it. He had to keep his head now, not batter himself helplessly against the walls. Sooner or later someone would come back for him. He had to be ready.

He turned in a circle, staring at the scrolling pattern of the spells written in silver on the black walls. Knackerstone was made of a mixture of obsidian and *sylveth*. The making of it in itself was a monumental task—blending the two without allowing the obsidian to transform into spawn took years of study and control.

Shaye stepped close to a wall, tracing his fingers over the silver. It was a powerful spell—complex and careful. He could see no weakness in it. If he hit it with majick, he would only feed its strength while making himself weaker. Knackerstone could not be breached by a majicar liquefying the *sylveth*, as Fallon had done to the splinters in Fairlie's hands and arms. Nor could knackerstone take a spell. That was what the silver was for. The knackerstone simply absorbed majick and amplified the spells etched into it.

Shaye leaned both hands flat against the wall, his head dangling as he glared at the floor. He had to do something. Fairlie needed his help.

And then—

He had an astonishing idea. He straightened, his fingers caressing his *illidre*. He sank to the ground, hardly noticing the burst of pain in his chest. He stared at the wall before him. Could he? Was he capable of such a thing, if such a thing was even possible? It was true that he was no master majicar, but it was not for lack of natural ability. He had merely not applied himself to his studies as he ought to have. The time had been better spent with Fairlie. But he had time now, and need. He could not imagine a more difficult task to test himself. Nor one less likely to succeed.

If not for his work with Fairlie, he'd never have thought of it. But because of her, he knew more about the properties of metal and stone than he had ever dreamed possible. His cardinal affinities were stone and fire, which improved his odds. He smirked at himself. It might be the merest ghost of a chance, but he had to try.

Shaye rubbed the contours of his *illidre*. King William should have taken it from him. But why would he? The smother cell should contain any majicar, since what Shaye wanted to try wasn't supposed to be possible. He pulled the *illidre* from his neck. It was shaped and colored like living flame, the edges rounded and elegant. It served as his focus and as a foundation for his spells. But it needed to be more powerful.

Spells were constructed by aligning some or all of the thirty-six majickal elements. Mixing antagonistic elements from opposite alignments of the majickal com-

pass rose was both difficult and dangerous. The larger
the spell, the more complex the construction. Spells
were often physically created out of whatever materials
made best sense: cloth, wood, metal, stone, earth, water,
ice, blood, bone.... Anything at all might be used to call
the majick and bind it into a casting. Such grand spells
could take months or even seasons to build properly. It
was said that the first majicar, Errol Cipher, didn't need
physical patterns for his spells. He had so much power
at his beck and call that he only had to imagine what he
wanted and call it into being. But there had never been
another to match him. Ordinary majicars used physical
constructs to bend, twist, and bind the majick to their
purpose. The constructs also allowed for crescendo effects, the power echoing and building until it was more
than its beginnings.

But for a majicar to have to construct a spell every
time he wished to use majick was inconvenient and even
dangerous. *Illidren* were impregnated with a number of
half-formed spells, like building blocks or puzzle pieces,
allowing a majicar to piece together a formal spell on
the fly. To do what he wanted now, Shaye had to begin
by making his *illidre* truly his own, by reforming it and
investing it with his own majick. He needed more-complex
spells than those provided by the master who had created it for him.

This alone could kill him.

He folded his legs and took a breath, ignoring the
aches in his body and the piercing pain in his side from
his damaged ribs. He pushed away all thoughts of Fairlie and what might now be happening to her. He could
afford no distractions. He didn't think about how abys-
mally this experiment could fail, or how long it had been
since he'd eaten or drunk anything, or how little sleep
he'd had the night before.

He called up his majick. The feeling of it was dimmed
inside the Pale, but still it rolled through with slow, curling waves full of steel spikes and jagged stone. It hurt.
Dear Meris how it hurt. But it was an agony of delight. It

filled him intimately, pushing into every hidden part of himself. He let it build, the pressure swelling in him until it felt like his skin might split. Was it enough? He waited, sweat running down his forehead and sides. When it seemed as if his eyes would boil from his head, he began the dismantling of his *illidre*.

As Shaye released the majick that kept the *sylveth* hard, it softened eagerly. He held it back, unraveling the half-spells inside. Each one let out a blistering surge of majick that he had to collect and hold. It became even more difficult to breathe. His body trembled with a palsy. The *sylveth* pooled in his hands, rooting against his skin like a baby kitten searching for milk. He held it carefully, not letting it escape inside him; nor could he let it fall. If that happened, the knackerstone would absorb it. He had to have every drop to create the *illidre* he needed.

Time passed. It might have been grains, it might have been glasses, or even days. He had no sense of it; he couldn't afford to think about anything but what he was attempting to do. He had to create and hold the spells in his mind, then push them inside the *sylveth* while shaping and hardening it with majick. It was like juggling knives with a blindfold. If he lost focus or control for even a single grain, the spells would shatter and rip him apart.

A fragment of his mind halted. He followed it. Had he forgotten something? Yes. "Meris help me and bless this endeavor." A weak prayer. Nothing to raise him in the goddess's estimation. So be it.

He returned his attention to his task, then pulled up short again as an idea burrowed into his head. He shouldn't. It wasn't right. Not for him. *Fairlie*. Very well. "Chayos, I ask your blessing and aid as you can give it." Terse. Even curt. Fearful.

He pulled all his attention back to his task. Fear could only destroy him. There were no gods in this room; it was all up to him.

He began crafting.

The majick pulled at him. It wrung his mind like a rag,

turning his body to taffy. He clung with all his might to the spells, setting them into the waiting *sylveth*.

He couldn't do it; he wasn't strong enough

He threw his head back and screamed defiance of his weakness.

Liquid heat stroked his forehead. Glacial cold brushed his lips. He smelled brine and wind mixed with earth and . . . smoke.

His mouth snapped shut. He was not alone. He would not give up.

He poured all of himself into completing the *illidre*.

It was like crawling up a mountain of broken glass. The pain was overwhelming; it was inconsequential. He could not fail this first step. Nor the next. He could not and he would not.

He had no idea how much later it was when he woke on the floor. His mouth was parched and blood crusted his beard from where it had run from his nose. Cramps in his legs and arms made him groan. He stretched out his limbs and the spasms clenched harder. His clothing was stiff from dried sweat, and the stink of himself was overpowering. He pushed himself upright, becoming aware at last of something clutched in his hand.

He looked at it. It was a tree of flame against the backdrop of a full moon. Green tinged the leaves of the tree. It was a partner for the pendant he'd made for Fairlie. He reached into it. It was perfect. The ten partial spells had taken, floating inside, ready to be made into something else. He closed his eyes and blew out a shaky breath. *He'd done it.* He pressed it against his forehead. But his relief was short-lived. There was no time for celebration. He had made only part of the journey. He had a long steep climb to go yet.

But he was tired. He had to let himself rest. He lay back down on the floor, curling into himself. He let himself think of Fairlie. Not as she had been. He thought of her as she was now. Despite all the changes, the woman he loved had still looked out at him through those strange eyes and she'd spoken to him from that alien mouth. But oddly, he found little comfort in the thought of her. His soaring hopes of the morning—was it only this morning when he'd kissed her?—all those effervescent hopes now teetered on the brink of a vast chasm of dread and dead dreams. He loved her yet, but she hadn't been sure she wanted him before her transformation. And now—

Now she knew he'd lied to her about what he was. And even if she forgave him that, she was different now. She might not want anything to do with him.

He startled away from the fear like a deer from the lonely howl of a wolf. It didn't bear thinking about.

The clenching ache of hunger woke him. He sat up stiffly, rubbing the grit from his eyes. He felt somewhat rested, but his thirst was dreadful. He swallowed, his throat feeling thick and dry. Then he looked again at his prison. No one had brought food or water—how long had he been here? Surely sooner or later they would bring something. But by then it could be far too late for Fairlie. He could wait no longer.

The smother spell in the walls had not been activated by his work with his *illidre* because he'd directed no majick at attack or escape. That was about to change. Coming now was the real test of his determination and stamina. And he'd come so close to failing already. . . .

The thing he was about to try was simple, really. Just separate the silver from the walls while carefully unwinding the smothering spells. At the same time, he had to dissolve the knackerstone and keep the released *sylveth* from turning everything it touched to spawn. Then, when he was finished, he could blast open the door.

A simple plan, as easy as plucking the moon from the sky.

The symphonic weaving that created a smother cell was done simultaneously with at least five master majicars of carefully balanced cardinal strengths and minor affinities. Such teams practiced together for seasons on end. The resulting spellwork was astoundingly powerful. No one had ever successfully escaped a smother room, nor had any collapsed majickal experiments cracked its shields.

Exhilaration unexpectedly thrilled through him, melting away his exhaustion. His heart pounded and he wanted to throw back his head and laugh. It was the alluring dance of majick and knowing he was going to push himself to the limits, all in an effort to do something truly extraordinary. And though he could very well die, he might also succeed. Buoyed by the sudden sweep of feeling, Shaye forgot everything but the majick as he turned his attention entirely to his task.

He gathered himself, holding his *illidre* firmly between his palms. Then he thought of stone. He reached for the minor affinities that he needed to create this spell: *Stillness, Pain, Flesh, Light, Dance, Name, Hate*. This time he envisioned them each as threads: *Stillness* was black, *Pain* was orange, *Flesh* was blue, *Dance* was green, *Name* was gold, *Hate* was crimson. He twisted them together, anchoring them to his core. Then he coiled them around himself, building a cocoon of majick. When he was completely enclosed, he put one hand on the floor and tried to push it down into the knackerstone.

The stone depressed beneath his touch, then deadening majick looped around the tips of his fingers. It pulled apart the edges of his spell. Shaye withdrew and came at it from another tack.

He thought of stone. Of fire and smoke and stillness. This time he wove the majick differently, remembering the heat of the forge and the way fire melted even stone if it was hot enough. He called the heat. He was in the middle of an oven. His lungs tightened, his breathing shallow under the sharp bite of his hurt ribs. *He thought of fire and stone*. He thought of the forge, of the crucibles filled with molten ore. Molten stone. Hotter.

He rested his fingertips on the knackerstone beside his thigh. He held his majick inside a glove of pulsing heat. His hand pushed through. He curled his fingers, hooking them.

What melts stone melts silver.

He splayed his hand, pushing the heat out and his majick inside it. Lava flowed through him. *Sylveth* and obsidian separated. He captured the *sylveth*, pulling it into him. He couldn't let it loose. It filled him. His body strained to hold it. His bones cracked. He heard them snap, felt himself collapsing. The *sylveth* healed him, and then broke him again. He endured it, concentrating on clutching his *illidre* in his right hand and keeping contact with the knackerstone with his left. The pain of his body was too great to feel and still let him stay sane. In defense, his mind walled itself away. It was alone, separate. Free. The body was dying. He had to hurry.

The smother cell walls started to dissolve.

Droplets of silver sweated from the spell inlaid in the wall. The swirling lines blurred and ran like wax. Majick erupted wildly. The whirlwhind caught Shaye, spinning and twisting him. He opened his mouth to scream, but no sound emerged. The majick dashed him against the walls. Instantly the *sylveth* he'd taken inside himself healed him again. He clutched his *illidre* in desperation, grappling with the majick. It ripped away from him. He clutched it again, dragging it inside him in an agonizing harvest.

It sank inside him like boiling oil. It seared his insides, simultaneously tearing him apart and cauterizing the wounds. He tried to wall off the pain as he had before, but he couldn't. He focused his shattering mind as best he could. It wasn't too late. He *could* do this. Pain was a tool, a key affinity between stone and fire.

Blood. Pain. Stillness. Flesh. Light. Dance. Name. Hate.

His eight chosen elements. Now he must make something of them.

Raggedly he scrabbled at his wits, trying to collect himself. *Blood* he had aplenty. He was covered with it. And *pain. Stillness* was much, much harder. But necessary to pull all the rest together. *Stillness* was the foundation of it all.

He reached for it deep inside his mind—it was an elusive island of total calm and quiet. He'd learned to find it as an apprentice, and it had become second nature as a journeyman. Tortured as he was now, it took a dozen tries before he found his way back. On this island, he could feel no pain. But he knew very well that his body was nearly used up. He had to hurry.

Now, a *Name*—Fairlie. Next, *Hate*—Ryland. *Flesh*—his own. *Dance*—flame and intrigue. Those defined his life and his path to this place on this day. *Light*—firelight, moonshine, love.

He began to push them together, bending them to his purpose. But at the last moment he realized these weren't going to be enough. He needed something more—one more affinity. He knew instantly what it had to be. *Bliss*. It was an affinity opposite to those he'd chosen and not his to claim. He reached for it anyway, stretching across the majickal compass rose into the domain of water and wind.

It didn't want to answer. What did a foul-tempered bastard like him know of *Bliss*? What did stone and fire know of the elements of water and wind?

He thought of kissing Fairlie and her hand warm in his. He thought of the way majick filled him like a second heart. Those two things gave him a joy like nothing else. Was that bliss? He didn't know. It had seemed like it. It was all he had.

He used this last chosen element to form the warp of his weaving. He threaded it through with the ready forms he'd impressed into his *illidre*. The majick resisted him, uncoiling and unwinding. He twisted and pushed and knotted, coaxing and forcing the spell shapes into the pattern.

He'd known it was going to be hard; but it was so much worse than he'd expected. Before he was half done, the weaving began to loosen and unravel. He grabbed at the unwinding threads, stitching them to the minor affinities he'd chosen. It wasn't good enough. The patterns contorted into a shapeless mass.

Shaye could have wept. Instead he began again. He had to try a new shape—something more solid. He'd have to rely more on his own dwindling strength and brute force, losing the layering and crescendo effects. But there was no other choice and no time to lose. An idea flickered to life—a four-sided pyramid. It could work.

He threw himself into building the spell. It was an intricate puzzle, one that did not want to be put together. The affinities pushed against one another here and drew together there—exactly where he did not want them to be. He fought them, coerced them, stroked them, and shoved them. He assembled each side of the pyramid in a careful lattice, then bound them together one by one. Far off he could feel his body faltering, his heart slowing. He had to hurry. He washed the outside in *sylveth* and hardened it before setting the final spell inside the center, where flame burned and obsidian swirled hot as the sun.

Even as he finished, Shaye knew it wasn't going to work. The spell was brittle and delicate. The slightest blow would crack it apart. To do what he needed, it had to be much, *much* stronger. A noise escaped his throat, deep and desperate. The edges of his mind swirled away, the island of *Stillness* beginning to sink into a sea of molten lava. *No! Not yet!* He scrabbled for his wits. Could he strengthen it? He examined his spell, turning it to look at every angle. What was missing?

The answer danced across his consciousness. One more affinity. It belonged to stone and water. He was nearly out of strength. Could he claim it? He could bind the pyramid to the puddle of silver on the floor and wrap it around the pyramid. It was simple enough, but it might be more than he had left.

The decision was made even as the idea flashed through his mind. He let go of the stillness, leaping into the lava. He sank under. Convulsions racked his body. Agony streaked through him. He didn't know his name. He knew only his purpose, but that was swiftly dissolving, seeping away like water through a sieve.

Want.

He clung to it. He could not fail. He fed all his need into the silver. He layered it around the pyramid like a shield. It smoothed around the walls of the spell, lending it strength. *Want* for success, *want* for revenge, *want* for Fairlie, *want* for survival.

Then everything went black.

Chapter 18

Fairlie waited for Shaye to return. It had been more than three glasses since his departure. She'd told him she wanted to be alone, she reminded herself. Still, she couldn't help but feel something was wrong. He'd told her to pack; he'd told her they needed to leave soon. He would not have stayed away so long if something had not kept him.

The certainty grew as another glass passed, and then another. It was nearly dark outside. Fairlie was getting ready to go look for him. She wore woolen trousers and a loose smock cinched tight with a wide leather belt. Over it she pulled a long leather vest that no longer quite closed. Her shoes didn't fit and her hair had woven itself into braid when she thought about it. She'd stuffed a few clothes into a bag along with some spools of wire, a pouch of jewels and money, her mastersmith badge, and Toff's watch. She found the pendant Shaye had made for her, and with some reluctance she put it back around her neck, though it no longer sparked the same joy it had. Now it felt tainted, or maybe she felt tainted. She wasn't sure.

As the glasses dribbled past, she walked through her workroom and forge, bidding farewell. Not just to the place, but to her childhood there and to her memories of Toff and. . . Ryland.

She couldn't think his name without a thrust of mad fury, the like of which she'd never felt before. She wanted to *hurt* him. Her fingers curled into claws. She looked at them. She could easily tear out his throat with them, just as she'd threatened.

What had she become that she could even think of doing such harm to another soul? And enjoy it. The thought of his warm blood gave her a craving that revolted her. What kind of monster was she?

Her thoughts twisted around each other, full of horror and self-loathing, even as she admired the beauty of her new skin and the graceful strength of her body. And there was more.

She could feel the metal around her as she never had before. She could feel the variations and flaws in the stones beneath her feet and everywhere she touched. And *sylveth* ... every little shard and fragment in her studio sang to her. It ached for her, wanting her caress, wanting her to release it from the bounds of the majick that hardened it into stone. Far off she could feel the deeper song from the *sylveth* out in the sea. It resonated deep inside her, and she knew she could lose herself in its passionate embrace.

But that was why the king and Ryland had cursed her with *sylveth*. She knew it without a doubt. This was the thing that would allow her to forge it, if it could be called forging. She doubted she'd need an anvil or hammers or any of the tools of the metalsmithing trade to work the *sylveth*. Though what she would need she had no idea. Not that she intended to do it.

"Never!" she snarled defiantly in the quiet of her forge.

Something moved out from her with the word. A wave of ... *something* ... powerful. She didn't even let herself think the word *majick* as the paving stones fractured with a sound like snapping twigs. Spiderweb cracks chased up the walls and across the ceiling. Dust clouded the air. Fairlie breathed it in. It filled her nose and her lungs and sank into her blood and her muscles. Her body flushed hot with heat and vigor.

She reveled in the feeling, and then realization washed over her like cold water. She went to a worktable and found a lump of ironstone. She lifted it to her lips and licked it. The flavor was dark and cool and metallic. Her body flared with hunger, with craving deeper than a desire for food, as deep as her hunger for blood. She bit down on the ore. It crunched like a cracker between her teeth. The flavor was delightful, beyond anything she'd ever tasted. Fairlie chewed eagerly and swallowed, gobbling down the rest. More heat and a boundless sense of power and exhilaration exploded in her abdomen and flooded into the rest of her body. And something else.

A hot heaviness spiraled through her. She felt a fullness; a need inside her wanted release. She closed her eyes and searched for it like a blind beggar, feeling carefully along an interior landscape she neither recognized nor understood. She came to a *seething*. It boiled and churned. She thrust against it.

Instantly, heat coalesced in her arm and streaked downward. Her fingers glowed like the inside of a stoked forge and thick liquid condensed beneath her fingertips. She stared as wisps of smoke rose from the top of the workbench.

She jerked away. Cooling inside five blackened divots on top of the wood surface were five thin circles of iron. She looked at her hand and back at the workbench. She'd eaten the ore and pushed it back out as metal. And the rest of it? Where had the rest of the minerals and stone gone?

To feed her body. She knew it the same way she knew she couldn't breathe water. Still couldn't breathe it.

Fairlie's breath caught in her lungs and she pushed a fist against her chest. Her legs went weak and she sagged to the floor. *What was she?* She rolled onto her side, pulling her legs up to her chest and knotting herself into an agonized ball.

She did not know how long she remained so. More stone dust filled the air until it was impossible to see more than a few inches in front of her.

She started when a knock sounded at the outer door. It opened before she could speak. With silent grace she sprang to her feet, hunching low with one hand on the floor, the other raised and ready.

She swiveled her head and sniffed the air, smelling sweat, grease, perfume, and leather. Metal too. She licked the air. She tasted five different men. Four were Crown Shields. The last one—there was something familiar about him. He wore perfume and *sylveth* jewelry. . . . One piece in particular caught her attention. It dangled from a necklace—like every man and woman of royal blood. An unbreakable, unremovable necklace of protection was put around each of their necks at birth. And though not every person who wore a *sylveth* necklace was royal, Fairlie knew in her gut that this one was. Her lips curled back in a snarl. He should never have come here.

Someone sneezed and coughed, swearing at the thick dust. There were other explosive sneezes and harsh coughing. Fairlie tensed herself, her craving for blood intensifying. They'd come hunting her. Now she would hunt them.

There was the sound of stumbling and the clang of falling tools. Fairlie followed the sounds, crab-walking fluidly on her hands and feet. It felt comfortable and right. She didn't let herself think about how right because she thought she might scream.

"Fairlie? I would speak with you."

The king's voice was pitched gently and warmly. Like he was a friend. Her anger roared. The walls rumbled, the stones grumbling together as they vibrated with her new-born majick. More dust filled the air, and there were more sounds of cracking and cries of pain as flagstones shattered and rained upward into the air, spinning like a windstorm.

"Fairlie, stop!" King William's voice was full of command now. If he was afraid, she couldn't hear it.

Fairlie licked the air again. Oh, yes. He was afraid. His sweat had turned sour and sharp. *Good.*

She pulled her majick back. To her surprise it came. Debris continued to rain down through the dust-thickened air. She crawled easily through the wreckage of the room.

Though she could see no better than anyone else through the dust, her new majickal senses and her nose and tongue told her everything. A beam fell from the ceiling and crashed to the floor with a thundering boom, sending wood and stone chips flying in every direction. Something hit Fairlie in the forehead and bounced away. She stopped, examining herself with careful fingers. There was nothing. No cut, no blood, no bruise.

But the Crown Shields were not so lucky. One was unconscious beneath the fallen beam. Another moaned softly in a crumpled heap. The other two shouted for the king, who had taken refuge in the doorway leading into Fairlie's bedchamber.

The noise of their shouts and coughing and sneezing covered any slight sound Fairlie might have made. She came to the first Crown Shield. She lifted her hand, reaching for his throat. It took everything she had to stop herself from crushing his neck.

She had a right! she told herself. *They had come here to hurt her. Again. Why should she not defend herself?* But then the terrible question prodded at her again. *What sort of monster was she?* She did not need to kill.

Her fingers curled and she slammed the back of his head with her fist. Fairlie stepped over him and went after the other Crown Shield. She dropped him in his tracks as well. Neither moved. She thought they still lived. But she didn't really care if they didn't.

"Ross? Drake? Gavin? Andrews?"

King William's voice was worried. Fairlie's teeth itched. Damn him to the black depths. Had he worried for her? Had he even hesitated when he ordered her to be cursed? Had he regretted it at all? He'd always been so kind to her. Ryland had come by his coldhearted treachery honestly.

She closed on him. She breathed in the stone dust. It filled her with heat and power.

"Fairlie? Are you here?"

He was only a few feet away. One arm was extended, searching blindly. He held a dagger in his other hand. It

might have done him some good against the old Fairlie,
but what she was now could not be harmed by a blade.
She doubted she could be harmed by anything that was
born of Chayos. Or Meris, for that matter. King William
had meant to make himself a pet compass-majicar; she
would never be anyone's pet anything.

She dropped low and edged closer. She was mere
inches away now, standing just behind his right shoulder.
She stood slowly, knowing he still could not see her. The
dust was too thick, and there was no light.

Gently she closed her hand around his throat. "I am
here," she crooned.

The king went rigid. "I want to talk to you and explain."

"But Ryland did explain."

"I wanted to tell you myself. How much Crosspointe
needs you . . . to make compasses."

Her fingers clenched, and it was all she could do to
stop herself from crushing his throat. He coughed and
choked. She let go, then grabbed him by his arm and
shoved him over to her bed, making him sit. She didn't
try to take away his paltry dagger.

She reached out, calling the dust out of the air and
pushing it away. Suddenly a small island cleared. King
William stared. The dagger twitched in his fingers. He
looked old, Fairlie realized. His thin hair was mostly
white. He was coated in dust, looking very much like a
corpse, with haunted red-rimmed eyes. He was gaunt,
like something was eating him from the inside out. She
hoped it hurt.

"You look surprised. What exactly were you expecting?"

He licked his lips. "I need you to understand," he said
gravely. "I would not have done this to you if Crosspointe
wasn't at stake. I had to sacrifice you to save the rest of
the country. It was not an easy decision, and Ryland is
devastated. But there were no other options."

Fairlie stepped back, so angry she almost clawed
his eyes out of their sockets. She could smell his blood

pounding in his veins. He was frightened. She licked her lips. She would like to taste his fear, hot and red on her tongue. She could let him see exactly what he'd turned her into; she could show him just how frightening she could be. She smiled, letting him see her pointed teeth.

"I have Shaye," he grated, flinching back.

Instantly the room started to rumble, the floor bucking.

"If I don't come out of here, if you do not cooperate, I'll have him killed. Stop this now."

The last three words were sharp as a whip crack. He'd come to his feet, his chin jutting. He was no coward. He was a king and he had Shaye.

Desperately Fairlie tried to reel in the majick so that the ceiling and walls did not collapse. At last she succeeded, though the floor continued to vibrate, showing just how on edge she was.

"I will give you some time to think," the king said, walking around her. He stopped in the doorway. "I am sorry that it had to be done this way, and I am sorry for what you suffer, but I am determined in this. I need ships' compasses, and you must make them for me. If you do not, the cost will be Shaye Weverton's life. And if after that you are still reluctant to work for me, then I will put you in a knacker box and let the majicars have you." The corner of his mouth twitched. "Do not make the mistake of thinking the majicars will treat you any more kindly. They know what to do with spawn. They will bring you to your knees and Shaye will be dead for nothing. Consider well. I will visit again soon. I shall send guards to retrieve my men."

Fairlie could only watch him go. She wanted to cry; she wanted to scream; she wanted to level the castle. Everything in her told her she could. But Shaye. King William had taken Shaye. She was certain he would make good on his promise to murder him.

There was more pain in that knowledge than she knew what to do with. She sank to the floor, holding in her fury and anguish. All around her the stone floor powdered. She sank through the floor, finding herself on hard dirt. She didn't know how long she sat so before flickering movement caught her attention.

Between her feet a pale green shoot rose and unfurled. It grew taller and thickened. Fairlie backed away to give it room. The little tree had smooth gray bark and small oval leaves, seven or eight leaflets paired on a fire-colored stem. Bunches of tiny white flowers opened, and then the petals dropped. In their place were orange berries. She knew this tree. She had seen it only that morning in the Maida of Chayos. It was a Lius tree.

Fairlie ran her fingers down the bark. It felt warm and full of life.

She was not alone.

She had to think; she had to plan. She would bide and she would save Shaye. He was her heart. And she would not let King William or Ryland take anything else from her.

Chapter 19

The sun was just rising. William stood at the window, watching the first blush of pink and gold tint the sky over Blackwater Bay. The wind ruffled whitecaps across the water. A handful of ships stood at anchor or in the docks. Out beyond the pearly green lights of the Pale, Merstone Island lumped up out of the water, its tall peak hidden inside a curtain of creeping mist.

Everything looked peaceful and quiet. A perfect morning. But the truth was that beneath that serene aspect ran rivers of treachery, unrest, and fear. Like dry wood waiting for a tiny spark to explode into a conflagration. And there was no shortage of sparks. The merchants and majicars were striking their flints like madmen, and the people—good, hardworking, and gods-fearing—they would be the kindling.

William rubbed a hand over his mouth. Sylmont and Crosspointe would burn to the ground if he didn't find a way to douse the situation. At least until he could completely implement the first stage of his plan. Once Chance hit and ships with unregistered compasses and nomad Pilots sailed inside the Pale for safety, there would be no stopping the fires. But by then it would be too late. Crosspointe would no longer have a choice; it would have to change the way it did business. But most importantly, it would finally have allies on the water in a war against the Jutras. And a war was coming. Crosspointe was too tempting a prize for the Jutras, and the fact that they'd failed once would only whet their appetite. That was the only argument that would smother the flames of panic when they erupted. With the promise of allies, he could persuade his people of the wisdom of this strategy. Even if the Jutras ended up with a handful of compasses through the black market or theft, the number of allied ships would greatly outnumber them. The Jutras had no friends among the Freelands. They'd be slaughtered on sight.

He took a deep breath and let it out slowly. His people would never give him permission to do this, but he was certain he could obtain forgiveness when he showed them what they'd gained. If things went according to his plan. Which meant he had to have a compass-majicar. That was the key to everything.

He looked down at the crumpled message in his hand. His fist tightened. It contained news that turned his plans for Fairlie upside down. William shook his head, still unable to believe the words written there. Somehow Shaye Weverton had managed the impossible and locked himself inside the smother cell. There was no way in, short of a battering ram, and William wasn't convinced even that would work.

He threw the paper with a violent movement and scraped his fingers through his thinning hair. Shaye had been his trump card to force Fairlie to make compasses for him. He didn't have another. If only he had more time. He'd been forced to make too many quick decisions and had no contingency plans prepared in case things went awry, which they inevitably would. He'd sent men to Stanton to bring back Fairlie's mother, but they wouldn't return for at least a sennight. Even if she cared what he might do to her mother, he didn't think he had that long. She was too full of rage and too powerful. A chill ran down his spine. She could level the castle, perhaps even all of Sylmont. If only she would use that power to make compasses!

Having Ryland anchor Fairlie's transformation had been a mistake, one that William was still kicking himself for. It wasn't that Ryland was still sulking in his quarters. Every man needed a chance to lick his wounds in private, and this act had torn a hole in his son's soul. No, the mistake had been not holding his son in reserve. If he had, Ryland might be able to reach Fairlie now. She might still consider him a friend. But Nya had been so sure that Fairlie needed an anchor, and William had overestimated the strength of their relationship. Or overestimated Fairlie's willingness to forgive.

Compounding the problem was Fallon's report that Fairlie had injured Nya deep inside her mind. Though Fallon indicated that she was recovering, William had not been allowed to see her to know for certain. Fallon was guarding Nya like a bear protecting her cubs. The man was besotted. William shook his head. Gods save him from men in love. They were all maggot-brained.

Not that he hadn't been that way himself once. A pain struck him, slicing down deep to a place of unimaginable pain. *Naren.* He missed her so much. He kept her quarters just as they had been before she died. He often went into her closet and closed the door so that he could just smell her again. Fairlie had given him an immeasurable gift with her sculpture of Naren's face. And he'd repaid her with dreadful betrayal.

And he would do it again. Because as much as he missed his beloved Naren, Crosspointe meant more. It always had.

He sighed, guilt aching in his stomach. Naren had always known she came second to Crosspointe. He could never hide it. He could never make her pain of knowing that go away.

A soft knock on his door pulled him from the morass of his thoughts and made him stiffen. What, more bad news? He grimaced, then smoothed his expression into a mask of pleasant interest before turning around and linking his hands behind his back.

"Come in," he called.

Niall entered, bowing low. "Sire, your breakfast is served."

William followed his steward without a word. He wasn't hungry; he hadn't been hungry since Naren had been killed. He ate every day, because not doing so would endanger his health and make his subjects doubt his strength and mental acuity.

He cut his food precisely, counting how many times he chewed each bite—always ten—and drank his juice and tea. He tasted nothing. He might as well have been eating paper or dishrags. As he slogged his way through his meal, he read through the newspapers. They were full of anger and resentment, and more often wrong than not, but bits of real truth shone through here and there, even if the writers didn't understand their import. William had an extensive network of spies and informants, but he was no fool, nor was he too full of pride to examine every possible source for new information. Knowledge was power.

When he had finished his meal, he folded his papers in a careful bundle. Niall, who'd been waiting quietly, now stepped forward. He held a sheet of parchment covered in tiny, spidery writing. William took it, a sick feeling like being punched in the gut hollowing his insides. It was the same feeling he got every morning since he'd embarked on this dangerous course. He was always waiting for an ax to fall that he hadn't prepared for. The feeling had worsened with his recent snap decisions. Seldom was there positive news in his morning brief; mostly it contained wildfires that had to be stamped out and plots against him and Rampling rule.

"Anything urgent?" William asked as he began to scan the sheet.

"If I may be so bold, sire, it has been two days since Shaye Weverton's disappearance, and it's starting to raise questions among the Majicars' Guild and the Wevertons."

William glanced up. "Does anyone suspect crown involvement?"

"Not yet. Master Plentop has had his people spreading tales of seeing young Weverton in the Riddles passionately occupied by a woman. Thus far his friends and family are willing to believe that he has found a new lover who has enthralled him. But they will not swallow that story much longer. He is not wont to disappear for so long."

William pinched his lip. Imprisoning Shaye may have been another mistake, but an unavoidable one. He would not have kept silent about Fairlie's transformation and he would have fought to protect her. Still, his disappearance created another set of problems.

"Keep me apprised."

"Of course, sire. Do you have instructions for handling young Weverton?"

"There is little to be done at the moment. We cannot break inside his cell without a great deal of trouble and attention, and that would expose us to far more questions. Nor do I think I want to call on the guild for any favors at the moment."

Niall's brows rose. "Certainly a family majicar would be discreet."

William's lips quirked in something very nearly like humor. "I expect so. But family majicars have never had to choose between the guild and the crown before. With the merchants stirring things up and the guild in a fury over the new service requirements, the family majicars may find their loyalties strained. And if they do remain loyal, this is not sufficient reason for them to expose such flaws to the guild. The time will come for that, and when it does, I will make sure the favors I ask for count for something."

He turned back to his briefing sheet, then tossed it onto the table. "I had better go deal with Fairlie." He tapped his fingers thoughtfully. "Before I do that, I want to see Nya."

"That may be difficult," Niall cautioned.

"Take a note to her quarters. Tell her I'll be there in the next quarter glass. Do make it clear I won't be deterred. Not if they want my help on the Root."

Niall bowed. "Right away, sire."

His steward left without another word. William went
to sit at his desk and began making notations in the mar-
gins of the brief. He shoved aside the two diplomatic
pouches sitting prominently in the middle of his desk.
One was from Azaire and the other from Glacerie. It
was the second from Azaire in as many days. William
had little doubt that it contained exactly the same message. Azaire had learned of Glacerie's new compasses
and wanted some for themselves. He also knew exactly
what the Glacerie message said. They wanted more.
And Pilots. Neither of which William could provide.
He'd sold Glacerie eleven of the twelve compasses that
had been scavenged from downed ships. The last one
he'd installed on a black ship, the *Eidolon*, one that was
completely at his bidding and outside the knowledge of
anyone on Crosspointe.

Glacerie had been given the responsibility of finding
their own Pilots. William could well imagine how they'd
found them. He'd given them the key—*sylveth*. But
without time and someone like Fallon to point out the
likely candidates, he was betting they'd have begun hauling people in droves to the sea and dumping them into
sylveth tides until they had Pilots. And majicars. They
would have made some of those too. Though for now,
their majicars would be little enough threat. They had
no training, nor did they have much power in Glacerie.
They were too far from the source of their majick—the
Inland Sea and its arteries of *sylveth*.

Azaire was a different story. It perched on the shores
of the Inland Sea, tickling its toes in her waters. Azaire
had long ago discovered the making of majicars and Pilots, though they protected the secret as fanatically as
Crosspointe did. Most of the coastal countries were the
same. But none had ever found the secret to making
compasses. That belonged only to Crosspointe.

William continued reading the brief, noting the Til-
man mayor's request for more majicars to deal with a
growing rat infestation and a report of three murders
in Cheapside, all apparently related to one Randall

Turvey's inability to keep his cods tied tightly. Apparently his wife had killed him and his mistress and their bastard child, poisoning them all. Turvey had been a reliable and discreet crown spy inside the Merchants' Commission. Other than that, his death required no punishments, as no one who was legally entitled suffered financially from his loss. Likewise for the mistress, who was unmarried and worked as a laundress. Such employees were easy enough to replace. William scratched a note to keep eyes on Mistress Turvey until it was established whether she knew of her husband's connection to the crown and to evaluate her as a potential replacement spy. If nothing else, she clearly had a strong stomach for dirty work.

Next there was a list of Jutras sightings. Twenty reports since yesterday of ships on the seas and warriors on the beaches. There had been seventeen similar sightings yesterday and twenty-four the day before. Since the Jutras had managed to attack the mainland, people were seeing them everywhere. And every report had to be followed up. Beneath the list of sightings was a request for more personnel and additional funds. William rubbed his fingers against his lips thoughtfully. He had more than enough money in his coffers—selling the compasses had given him a great deal of liquidity.

A small smile curved his lips. Yes, and the timing was perfect, too. Taking a blank page from his drawer, he penned a few lines in bold black letters and signed in a broad scrawl. He blotted, then melted a blob of blue wax on the bottom and pressed his seal into it.

Just then Niall returned. He approached William and bowed. "Majicar Fallon sends his regards and indicates that Nya is too unwell for visitors, but that he shall be willing to meet with you."

"We shall see about that," William said. He stood and handed Niall the parchment. "Take that to Poole and authorize him to draw down the required funds from the compass account. Send word to George and Margaret that I want to meet with them this afternoon. Invite

Abelard as well. He'll want to know that the ranks and duties of the Crown Shields are expanding."

Niall read the parchment, his eyebrows rising slowly. Then his forehead smoothed into careful neutrality once again. "Quite," he said dryly. "He'll not like interference from George or Margaret."

"No, but this is the beginning of the army he's been nagging me about. And I've a good excuse for creating it. We'll establish forts strategically along the coast and keep standing troops there—all in the name of protecting Crosspointe from the Jutras. They'll answer only to the crown and they'll be trained in the arts of war. With the money from the compass funds, no one will be able to cry foul, though I've no doubt the populace will be loud in their support. It also wouldn't hurt for our Freeland allies to know that we are prepared to defend ourselves, in case they decide Crosspointe is too tasty a fruit to leave hanging unmolested on the tree, once they have their own compasses."

"Abelard will be positively giddy."

"Won't he, though? I'd better see Nya now."

William rose and allowed Niall to help him on with his long, sleeveless robe of office. It was made of crimson velvet embroidered with obsidian *sylveth* thread. He ran his fingers over the soft black fur that edged the robe as Niall fastened it at his throat. No one now knew what kind of animal had worn the fur. The robe was as old as Crosspointe. It had graced the shoulders of every ruling king or queen since the founding. It never tattered or got dirty, thanks to the spells layered thickly onto it. It also protected against majickal and some physical attacks. William straightened and followed Niall to the door. Outside, a squad of ten Crown Shields in crimson and black waited, standing at alert. Niall held the door wide and William marched out.

"Sire, where may we escort you?"

A square-shouldered man blocked the passage. His thick dark hair was speckled gray, and the expression in his blue eyes was obdurate. William stifled his annoyance. Hiring family meant that too many of his people were unimpressed by his being king. Lofton was a cousin three times removed. They'd fostered together as children. Even then Lofton had made a habit of getting underfoot and making things difficult for William. Like the time William had tried climbing up the outside of the bell tower at Baridon Manor in order to recover his mother's keyhole pin that he had taken from her jewelry box in order to show it to his fellow fosterlings.

The keyhole pin was a remnant of the times before the settlement of Crosspointe; it was a window into the mysterious past of those who fled torture and hatred and ventured across the Inland Sea to find Crosspointe, guided by the first William Rampling, the majicar Errol Cipher, and Trevor Culpepper. Before William could return the priceless piece of jewelry to his mother, Hugh Chessmill had taken it and hidden it at the top of the bell tower and locked all the doors. To get it back before his mother discovered it missing, William had to climb up the outside of the tower to the top. There had been a late late ice storm just the night before, making the climb a dangerous proposition at best. But William had been desperate. He started up, only to be grabbed by Lofton and yanked to the ground before he'd gone fifteen feet.

Lofton had torn a strip off him and then climbed up himself and retrieved the pin. From that day on, he'd made himself William's personal bodyguard, and nothing William said could dissuade him. Years later, when he asked Lofton why, his bodyguard cousin had told him, "You were marked to be king. We could all tell. Wasn't going to let you kill yourself before you could get elected."

Lofton was William's best armsman, and after the last couple of assassination attempts had come so close, he'd not let William walk alone anywhere in the castle except his own private quarters, and then only because they were so tightly warded that no assassin could get inside to lay a trap. Anywhere else he caged William inside a box of well-armed Crown Shields. William trusted Lofton as much as he trusted anyone. But he didn't have to like the mothering.

"I shall attend the lady Nya this morning," William said curtly.

"Very well, sire."

Niall fell in behind William and around the pair formed up a box of six men—two before and two aft and one on either side. Two more walked ten paces ahead and another pair trailed ten paces behind. Each was armed to the teeth, six of them with nocked crossbows. All were alert for danger.

Together, they marched off into the guest wing. As they did, William couldn't help but wonder if he'd need the aid of his escort to pry his way in to see Nya. Fallon wasn't entirely rational when it came to her. William grimaced, glancing at the men and women making up his escort. They had been chosen both because of their skills and because they knew how to be discreet. But he doubted they could be discreet enough if Fallon dropped his disguise and showed what he really was. At least he'd already established that Lofton was not allowed to accompany him inside Fallon and Nya's apartments. Lofton was steady, but William wasn't ready to trust him with what Fallon and Nya truly were, or what they were here for. Hatred for *sylveth* spawn ran too deep.

But as it turned out that was the least of his worries. They had paraded down several corridors and were crossing the marble gallery between the royal residence and one of the diplomatic wings when the assassins attacked for the third time in as many months, though never so overtly.

Suddenly slender crossbolts launched from miniature crossbows filled the air. They clacked and rattled as they battered the beautiful marble statuary and dropped to the floor. William was thrust instantly to the ground, Niall crouching over him, a knee hard in his back to keep him from moving.

There were sodden thumps as several bolts struck flesh. William struggled to free himself.

"Damn you, stay where you are put before you get a bolt in the eye," Niall growled, grabbing William's shoulder and pinning him more tightly to the ground.

It was humiliating, lying there prostrate while men and women fought a battle over him, and though he knew it was the right thing, William continued to struggle, grappling for his sword. Niall straddled him, hunching across his back, his forearm an iron bar against the back of William's neck.

William could see little. His guards had their backs to him as they faced outward. Those with crossbows shot carefully and steadily, reloading from quivers strapped to their thighs. Another hail of the small bolts fell, and there were more sodden thumps and more rattling clatter.

"Exit through the north corridor," Lofton brayed over the noise. "Winsome and Butle cover the left, Doris and Effley cover the right. Close ranks and slow—leave no windows to the king. Let's go. March!"

Niall slid off William, gripping him under the arm and pulling him to his feet. As William started to draw his sword, Niall gripped his elbow hard with one hand and shoved his head low with the other.

"Stop trying to get yourself killed. Or stab your escort in the back. Now keep your head down and start moving. Neither your robe nor your necklace will cure a crossbolt through your skull."

Another arm was flung over William's neck from the other side as his escort clustered around him and hustled him across the floor and out through the chosen exit. They met no resistance in the passage, their attackers fleeing ahead of them.

William and Niall were thrust against a wall with four Crown Shields in a semicircle in front of them. An eerie hush fell as Lofton and three Shields returned to the gallery. A few grains later, they returned, their faces grim. Through the picket of his guards, William could see the crossbolt protruding from Lofton's shoulder. The woman on Lofton's left sagged, her eyes rolling into her head. Lofton caught her before her head cracked against the floor and laid her down gently. A bolt had penetrated deep into her thigh and was bleeding profusely. Lofton didn't try to bind the wound, but thrust himself back to his feet.

"They've pulled back, but we can't take any chances they'll be lying in wait. They'll expect us to return to the residence. We'll take him to the throne room instead."

"No," William said. "I have business that cannot wait. We proceed."

Lofton's upper lip lifted as his teeth bit hard into his lower lip. "Sire, this wing is not secure."

"But that in no way discounts the urgency of the business that brings me here. If anything, it increases it. So let us proceed."

"It's your hide, Highness," Loften said dourly.

Once again the escort formed up; there were only seven of them now. Two Crown Shields lay dead or dying in the marble gallery, and the fallen woman was now unconscious on the floor of the corridor. They left them there. The king had to be secured; no one could be spared to treat wounds or send for help.

In a matter of ten more minutes they arrived outside Nya's apartment. Niall knocked and the door swung open quickly. Fallon scowled at them. William didn't wait for an invitation but thrust past, Niall hard on his heels. He turned before Lofton could follow them in.

"I'll be here half a glass. Until then I do not want to be disturbed." He shut the door before there could be any argument—from Lofton or Fallon.

"What trouble did you bring down on us now?" Fallon demanded, blocking the way. His covering illusion melted away.

William met the creature's strange yellow gaze steadily.

"I want to see Nya."

"She can't see anyone. She's ill, thanks to you." Fallon's three-fingered hands clenched, the ropy muscles on his four arms flexing.

"Do not play at innocence," William retorted sharply.

"You came to me; you sold your services to me. You were quite eager, if I recall correctly. Do not cry foul now because you are unhappy with your bargain. You knew the risks far better than I."

Fallon's lipless mouth pulled tight, revealing his sharply pointed, snaggled teeth. He stroked a finger across his chin, his head tipping back and forth as he watched both men. A chill ran down William's spine all the way to his heels. His toes curled and his heart clenched. Fallon was a majicar and his mind was truly alien. When he turned spawn, he had shed the guise of civilization with no backward glances. He was very, very dangerous.

Before Fallon could respond, Nya spoke. "Your Highness. Welcome. Please come in."

She stood braced against the archway. She wore a loose burgundy silk robe. Her voice was low and scratchy, as if she was just getting over a cold. Her eyes were half shut and her fur looked drab. Fallon whirled, leaping to her side. Without looking at him, she lifted a taloned hand, palm out, halting him in his tracks.

The sleeve of her robe fell to her elbow. She was not wearing her gloves. A two-inch-wide woven metal cuff circled her wrist. Tiny ruby, emerald, and sapphire beads were woven into the fine gold, copper, silver, and black wires that made up the fluid pattern. Fluid because they moved, William realized. He frowned. Her hand dropped as Fallon stopped short of her. She turned, leading the way into her salon. As William followed, he knew there was something about that bracelet he should remember. He'd seen it before. Or one very like it. But where?

Chapter 20

Nya sank into a wingback chair, curling her feet beneath her. Though she was clearly weak and unsteady, she still moved with a startling liquid grace. William sat opposite, with Niall standing silently behind his chair. Fallon paced restlessly.

"You have had an adventure this morning," Nya said. "What happened?"

"Assassins," William said. "They are of no import." He bent forward, his elbows on his knees. "Tell me about Fairlie. Tell me what happened."

"I already told you," Fallon snapped.

"I want to hear it from you," William said to Nya.

She laced her fingers together, leaning back against her chair and watching him from beneath her heavy eyelids.

"We were losing her. I couldn't hold her. Her mind was ... wild. She attacked me." Nya paused, a ripple of pain flickering across her expression. "I did not expect her to reach me. This is not common for those who have been kissed by *sylveth*. She cut me deeply. I ... lost my way for some while. I do not know what else happened except for what Fallon has told me."

William rubbed a hand across his jaw. "She's angry. She has a strong majick. I thought she was going to turn the castle walls to sand."

Nya nodded. "It is not surprising that her majick is over stones. She is a metal master. Such would matter in what she's become."

"How do I control her?"

If Nya had had eyebrows, they would have risen into her hairline. "There is no saying."

"Because you don't know? Or because you won't?"

She shrugged. "Does it matter? I am Warden. She is mine to guard now. You understood this when we made our bargain. She may choose to help you, but if she chooses not, I will guard her. As will Fallon."

She looked at her companion then and something flashed between them. Something hot and angry. William noted the look and tucked it away. These two were not as united in purpose as they wanted him to believe. Nya faced him again.

"Surely you can tell me something about what she's become," he prodded

Nya shook her head, speaking slowly and deliberately, as if she considered each word. "I can tell you only that she is different from any Kin I have yet encountered. That may be the root of her compass-making ability."

William looked at Fallon, not allowing the disappointment that stormed through him to show on his face. Without Shaye, without some insight or help, he wasn't going to convince her to make compasses for him. "Have you discovered anyone else with the talent for compass making?"

"I have not," Fallon said, crossing both sets of arms, bracing his legs defiantly. "But I have been busy." His strange gaze flicked to Nya and stayed there.

"I ask that you begin to look."

Nya bent forward in a very catlike way, her talons biting into the fabric of her chair. Her robe fell open, revealing that she was naked beneath. Short buff-colored fur covered her stomach and breasts like velvet. Her nipples were dark like the black stripes on the rest of her body. William swallowed and averted his gaze. There was something powerfully sensual about her, despite the strangeness of her appearance. Or perhaps because of it. He clenched his stomach and thought of his dead queen.

"We only promised you one," she said.

"I have to have a compass-majicar," William said. "Fairlie may be of no use to me."

"You should have asked her."

"I'll not make the same mistake twice." Not that he'd ask for volunteers. But he would prepare better. "Will you help me find a candidate? Help him make the transformation?"

"She won't," Fallon said, striding forward and standing between Nya and William. "The risk is too great."

"Does that mean you are no longer interested in your own Pale on the Root?" William asked, sitting back and folding his hands in his lap.

"We had a bargain," Nya said, her head tipping to the side. She did not sound angry. "We find you one person to be a compass-majicar and help with the transformation. That is all. Are you reneging on your word?"

"It seems so," William said heavily. It was a bad choice. He couldn't keep allies if he couldn't keep his word. But he didn't have any other options.

Nya looked at Fallon. His fury rolled off him in palpable waves.

"I should kill you," he said to William.

"That will not get you your Pale, either."

"And if we help you find another compass-majicar? What then? What more will you demand before you decide to honor your word?"

William gave a humorless smile. "Nothing I can say will mean much. I know that. But Crosspointe's future depends on my having a compass-majicar who will work for me. There is a great deal I will sacrifice to protect my people. But I will do this much. Along with the Pale you need, I will help you build a city and I will agree to negotiate favorable trade with you."

"Your word is worthless."

"Under ordinary circumstances it is as true as steel. But circumstances are not ordinary; I need what I need, and only you can help me."

"We will not do it," Fallon declared. "It is too dangerous for Nya. Should something happen to her, a Pale will do us little good. The answer is no."

"You know who will have what talent. Find another Speaker," William suggested.

Fallon's arms were a blur as he leaped forward. The air in front of William's face stirred as Fallon's three-fingered hands slashed through it. Then the spawn majicar was yanked backward. He smashed onto his back, crushing a low table beneath him. Nya stood in his place. Her robe had opened entirely and William couldn't keep himself from looking at her. Again he felt a surge of desire for her. He averted his eyes. But he didn't think he'd forget. His fingers itched to pet her, to discover her softness and her hidden secrets. He gritted his teeth. Was this majick? He had never felt such lust before—and for *spawn*. It had to be majick. He swallowed hard.

Nya sat again, pulling her robe closed and tying it. "Gladly would I like finding another Speaker. I hope for it. But they are more difficult to find than compass-majicars," she said, eyeing Fallon as he flung himself back to his feet.

He went to stand behind her, glowering over her head at William. His lower pair of hands rested on the back of the chair, the fingers of the left tapping slowly. His other two hands were raised and ready.

"Fallon's words are true. As Warden, I cannot risk myself without a very good reason," Nya said.

"And do you consider a Pale a good reason?"

She stared at him, her orange eyes unblinking. He could read nothing of what she thought of his proposal. As last she nodded. "I will think on it."

William stood. "I would like your answer by sundown."

"You will have it."

She held out a hand. He took it, feeling the strength in her fingers as she closed them around his. *She could crush my bones*. A shiver threatened him. He smothered it. Was it fear or want? He bent and kissed the back of her hand, astonishing himself. His lips pressed against silky fur. As he straightened, his gaze hooked on her bracelet. As he watched, the patterns moved. Before he could ask about it, she pulled away and drew her sleeve down. *There was something so familiar about it. . . .*

It would come to him in time. And when it did, perhaps he'd have another carrot with which to lure her cooperation.

"Would you dine with me in my private quarters?" He surprised himself. He hadn't intended to ask. But her touch lingered, fanning the heat of his unexpected desire.

She seemed equally startled. She eyed him for a moment. "We are honored. But I may be feeling unwell. I will send word later."

William nodded. "Of course." He glanced at the glowering Fallon. There was no good reason to exclude the spawn majicar from the invitation, and he didn't know if she would come without him. He looked at her again. "I look forward to tonight."

She frowned, an uncharacteristic expression of emotion. William bowed to her and then to Fallon and withdrew.

Once again their escort formed up around him. This time there were two dozen Crown Shields, every one of them carrying crossbows and wearing chain mail beneath their tunics. Lofton was pale, but his wound had been healed.

"The forge wing," William told him softly.

Lofton started to argue, but William gave a short shake of his head, his expression forbidding.

"As you command," Lofton said, bowing sharply and clicking his heels together, and they set off.

This time there were no ambushes. William considered the matter as they traversed the castle. Who had done it? Too many had access to the castle grounds with the endless comings and goings of servants and petitioners and guests and laborers and people with twenty dozen other legitimate reasons for being there. The castle had always been a place of welcome for those who wished to enter.

"The Ramplings rule at the indulgence of the people. They should have the right to inspect us at their leisure." William had heard it all his life. It might as well be embroidered on the nappies of every Rampling ever born. Adding Crown Shields and restricting the castle would only further damage his standing among his people, and his enemies would make much of it.

Perhaps that, more than anything, was the reason for the attempts on his life. If anyone learned that the king might be in danger in his own home, there would be a panic comparable only to the terror sparked by the Jutras. Whether they killed him or not, his enemies won.

He set the questions aside when they came to the entrance of the forge wing.

"Wait here," he told his escort.

Lofton immediately started to object. William held up his hand.

"Wait. You too, Niall."

He stepped from his escort and strode up the corridor. The *sylveth* lamps were dark. They'd been robbed of their majick by Fairlie, he was certain. How, he couldn't begin to contemplate. The wood floor was cracked and rippled. The stone walls were tilting, and rubble littered the walkway, making him stumble and trip. He twisted his ankle but continued on, running his fingers along the broken wall to steady himself. Dust filled the air and he coughed.

He came to the end of the hall and felt his way in the darkness until he found the door. He kicked over a tray of food, the sound reverberating in the silence. Since her transformation, Fairlie had not opened the door; she had eaten and drunk nothing that was brought to her. He rapped sharply on the door before turning the handle. It did not give. He knocked again. Nothing.

"Fairlie, let me in," he called, knocking again and wondering if he was going to have to send for men to chop through the door. Not an auspicious beginning to this meeting.

Then suddenly the handle softened and turned to liquid, melting from his grasp. William snatched his fingers back, expecting the searing heat of a burn. But there was no injury. The door opened silently.

The only light came from the bank of grimy windows set at head height along the left wall. William stepped inside and then stopped dead in surprise.

What had been a cavernous three-room workspace was no longer. It was now one large room. The only thing still identifiable as what it used to be was the forge. Where Fairlie's bedchamber had been was a Lius tree. It looked like it was a hundred years old, its crown brushing the rafters of the tall roof. A bezel of emerald moss surrounded the tree, and inside it danced a ring of flames. Behind it was a wardrobe and a bedstand, giving evidence that the space had once been a bedchamber.

The rest of the room was crowded with trees and bushes made of metal, stone, and jewels. Gone were the workbenches and the bins and tools. If not for the cold forge on the far wall, William would not have known this had ever been anything else.

He found himself wandering forward, staring about in awe and dawning hope. Fairlie had created a majickal forest. The leaves were tissue thin and delicate. Roots crawled across the floor like tentacles. Birds and animals that existed only in Fairlie's imagination populated her forest, perched in the branches and clinging to the trunks. One looked down on him, seeming almost alive. It was about three feet tall with a reptilian tail and long curved teeth. There was a crimson sheen along its snarling lips and claws. The forest was full of teeth and eyes and claws. Hunger surrounded him.

Then suddenly one of the statues moved.

William gasped and jerked back. He caught himself and stood firm.

Fairlie.

She lay on her stomach along a limb. Her eyes burned like embers in the dim light. She wore only a vest and a pair of trousers cropped short. Her glistening metal mane pooled like liquid on her back. She let a hand drift down, then she followed, sliding gracefully to the floor and dropping into a crouch. Black and blue ridges circled her neck like two loops of a well-grown snake. He hadn't noticed that before. But then his gaze jerked up to her eyes. She watched him. Her upper lip pulled back in a snarl, exposing her sharply pointed teeth. His hair prickled over his body and ice filled his belly.

"I came for your answer," William said abruptly. He immediately wished the words back. He'd meant to be diplomatic and persuasive.

"Where is Shaye?"

"Exactly where I put him."

"I want to see him."

"No. I won't let you near him until you have made me the compasses that I need."

Her lips pulled from her teeth. "Then I'll find him myself." Her voice turned guttural.

"I'll have him killed before you lay eyes on him."

Flames flared in her eyes, turning them smoky orange. "Then I will have nothing left to lose and I will raze this castle."

William stared at her, thinking quickly. He had not handled this negotiation well. Was there any way to salvage it?

"You have a right to be angry, Fairlie. I know I have not treated you well. Toff would have had my head for it."

He linked his hands together behind his back, pacing back and forth. He felt her watching him. At least he had her attention.

"I *am* sorry for my methods, but it does not change why I did what I did, nor does it change the fact that Crosspointe needs you. I did not make this decision lightly. But I am sworn to protect and serve the people of Crosspointe, and I will do that, whatever unsavory things I might have to do."

"Unsavory?" she repeated. "I would call what you have done to me evil—dishonorable. Do you forget I am one of the people you are sworn to protect?"

"The good of the one does not outweigh the good of all. Perhaps it *was* evil. But there is only one compass-majicar left on Crosspointe—that in itself would be enough cause to do what I have done. But I need compasses to give to our allies. The Freelands have to unite against the Jutras, and the only strength we will have together is on the Inland Sea."

"Some would call what you do treason."

"My grandchildren will call me a patriot," he said. "If we are to survive, we have to change."

"And why should I care what happens to Crosspointe?" she demanded. "If I walk out on the streets I will be hunted down and put in a knacker box. I'll be sent to Merstone Island. Or I can make compasses for you. You will make me your slave. You have taken everything from me and you can never give it back. Not that you would even try."

The leaves on the trees began to rustle on the invisible wind of her anger. The ground vibrated.

"I could do nothing else," he said softly.

"You could have asked me," she snarled.

"Would you have said yes?"

"I should have had the chance."

Then she smiled and William's blood turned to ice. She lifted a hand and crooked a finger at him. It was an elegant, graceful gesture, and terrifying.

"Come."

She turned and wound through her forest. William followed; he had no choice. They did not go far—perhaps twenty paces. Before them was a thicket of shining thorns. A narrow path opened as the branches pulled apart. Fairlie stood aside and motioned him to go before her. William hesitated, then squeezed through the opening. Despite his care, he sliced his hand and cheek. Blood ran freely from the wounds—the thorns were sharp as knives.

As Fairlie pushed through behind him, the path closed again. He was trapped within the metal thornbush. William looked at her, pressing his handkerchief to his cheek, refusing to let his rising fear show. Her nostrils flared and he knew she could smell it.

"Your heart is racing," she said.

He didn't answer. He became aware of another sound, soft and sibilant. He couldn't place it. He started to step forward. Fairlie caught his arm.

"Look down."

His gaze dropped. At his feet was a blue basin made of worked *sylveth*. Inside it, silvery raw *sylveth* swirled and lapped. It was making the noise he'd been hearing.

"I had no idea there was so much *sylveth* here—in the lamps and all those chips and bits I used for my work. It wanted to return to liquid. It's very hungry. I wonder what sort of spawn you'd make," Fairlie said. She no longer sounded angry; she sounded merely curious. And icy cold.

Something clenched in William's chest. Fear. Not for himself, but for the mess he would leave the next king or queen if he was suddenly gone. The lord chancellor would be made regent, and he was certainly in bed with the Merchants' Commission and the Majicars' Guild. The damage they could do— And if the Jutras chose to attack— The devastation would be terrible.

"Don't do this," he said. Pleaded. "Crosspointe needs a king right now. Surely you must see that."

She lifted his bleeding hand. Her tongue slid across his wound. It was hot against his skin. He shivered.

"Bring me Shaye."

William nodded and lied to her. "It will be at least a few days. He's angry and he's a majicar—I can't just let him walk free. I'll have to contain him so that I can safely bring him here."

"Tomorrow," she said. "By sundown. Or I will go find him myself. And if I do, I will return every *sylveth* lamp and ornament in this castle to its raw form. There will be spawn everywhere. After that, I'll go down into Sylmont and do the same."

William bit his tongue before he could accuse her of heartlessly transforming innocent people; it was an argument guaranteed to fail. Instead he nodded again. "It seems I have no choice. And when you have Shaye—what then?"

"I don't know." Her voice softened, sounding lost and even confused. "Go now," she said suddenly. "I don't want you."

The thorny thicket flattened outward with a sound of metal bending and protesting. William walked across it and headed for the door.

"Tomorrow by sundown," Fairlie called after him. He waved acknowledgment and stepped out. In the darkness of the hallway he stopped and took several deep breaths. His legs were shaking and his heart continued to race. Sweat made his shirt clammy.

He dabbed again at his cheek and then tucked his bloody handkerchief into his pocket and marched away. His escort formed up around him as he came to where they waited. No one asked any questions, though Lofton's eyes glittered and his jaw thrust furiously.

"The royal residence," he told Lofton and they set off.

Once again there were no assassins. Outside the door of his apartments, William keyed open the wards and turned to Lofton.

"I shall not need you for a while. I'll expect a report on the assassination attempt in two glasses."

Lofton bowed stiffly. "Yes, sire."

William went inside, followed by Niall.

"Sir, a message arrived while you were attending Miss Norwich," Niall said. "Prince Vaughn has come to visit Prince Ryland. He was apparently agitated."

"Let's go," he said, heading for the secret door in the unused bedchamber. They traveled quickly through the warren of passages to Ryland's quarters. When they arrived, the door was locked. Niall tried it, then stood back. William stepped forward and pressed his hand flat against the door. The wards flared and the door swung silently open. There were no ward-locks in the castle that would refuse his touch. As he stepped into Ryland's closet, he heard the murmur of voices.

He walked quietly, following the voices to the sitting room. He halted outside, listening.

"As much as I don't care to see him right now, the fact is he needs to hear this directly from you. This is too big and too dangerous to miss any important details," Ryland said, his voice gravelly with too little sleep and too much liquor.

"And when he *does* need to see you?" Vaughn challenged.

William waited to hear the answer. He shouldn't have. Ryland had proven himself and his loyalty. Still, he wanted to see what his son would say.

"I serve the crown in whatever capacity is necessary. Whatever capacity. Father can rely on me."

The words sounded bloody and jagged, like shards of glass torn from his throat. William drew a heavy breath, feeling like he'd been punched. He deserved it. For everything he'd asked of his sons and what he was still going to ask.

He stepped into the room. "That is good to hear, though I did not doubt it." But he had. He quashed the thought.

Ryland and Vaughn leaped out of their chairs. Ryland looked haggard. His eyes were red-rimmed. He smelled like he'd been soaking in a vat of alcohol. His clothes were wrinkled and stained as if he hadn't changed them in days. He probably hadn't. His hands trembled, and he looked like he'd rather be anywhere else than in the same room as his father.

William embraced Vaughn, who hugged him back fiercely. He reluctantly let his elder son go. With effort he held himself to a nodded greeting to Ryland. William doubted his younger son would welcome his touch. Not now, perhaps not ever. He pushed the hurt of that aside.

"I heard Vaughn had arrived and you let him in. I thought I had better come see how things are."

"The door into the passage was locked," Ryland said in surprise, and then he flushed.

"It was. It is not now," William replied and then pulled a chair up to the table and sat down.

Niall retreated unobtrusively to a corner.

"Now, tell me what is going on. What are my subjects up to?"

He looked at Vaughn, letting Ryland collect himself. Vaughn explained what he'd learned.

"The Merchants' Commission and the Majicars' Guild are strongly committed to each other. It's going to get ugly. The merchants don't like the new taxes and fees you've implemented—no surprise there. And the majicars don't like the added service requirements. Again, not unexpected. But what is unsettling is that they have made an alliance of mutual benefit. The majicars plan to refuse service to the crown outright, though they will continue to engage in normal majickal commerce otherwise, as well as offering charitable majicks to those in need. In the meantime, merchants will raise prices on goods and services to offset their losses. The Sennet will issue a declaration for the support of the merchants and decrying the crown's policies. They are certain they can arouse a strong public outcry against you. Once that happens, the majicars will demand you reduce the service requirement to half what it is now, and the merchants will demand all sorts of subsidies and repeals of more than just the recent fees and taxes. It's a major step in giving the Majicars' Guild independence, not to mention making the crown impotent."

"What about family majicars?" Ryland asked.

His voice was cool and thoughtful, belying his ravaged appearance. William allowed himself a small smile. His younger son was made of stern stuff. He wasn't going to break.

Vaughn gave a little shrug. "The guild seems confident of their support," he said, looking a question at his father.

William ignored it. The truth was he wasn't sure which way the family majicars would fall. They'd never before been pushed to choose between the guild and blood, and though many would certainly choose family, he couldn't say how many wouldn't. Vaughn's news wasn't all that surprising. He'd expected an alliance between the merchants and majicars, sooner or later, and had already heard inklings of it.

"That isn't all. They plan to announce their intentions at the beginning of next sennight. Should the crown not bow to their demands within three days, they will proceed with a plan to destroy the grain supplies. It will be a mold or an infestation—perfectly natural and nothing to blame the majicars for, but it will be discovered too late to save anything. If they get the support of the Water Guild and the Pilots as they intend, then ships won't put in here again until Chance. People will starve and there will be riots."

"The Water Guild and the Pilots?" Ryland repeated. "Surely it can't happen."

"Weverton succeeded in bringing the Naladei here to force my hand with a regency. He can do much that seems impossible." William steepled his hands, considering. As surprised as Vaughn and Ryland were, he'd known it was possible that something like this could happen. With the family majicars who remained loyal and Vaughn's warning, he could save the grain stores. So long as there was no danger of starvation, it would be difficult to rouse people to riot. Instead, their anger would turn on the merchants and majicars who raised prices and denied Crosspointe their services.

He nodded thoughtfully. He was ready for this. His mind roved swiftly over his many plans and the problem of Fairlie and Shaye. A new idea bloomed in his mind. His mouth tightened. Ryland was not going to like this. But William needed the time and turmoil the distraction might buy. And whether or not he could get at Shaye, having him safely locked away would give Nicholas Weverton pause in this business. In the meantime, William would have to make sure that Nya and Fallon agreed to find him another compass-majicar. And other majicars, as well. He would build his own cadre of loyal majicars to

fight the guild. He wasn't unduly worried. He had more
things to sweeten the deal; he could convince them.

William glanced at Niall. "Send word to Keros. Get
him back now. We may need him. And the *Eidolon*. Have
it put in at Narramore Bay."

"I believe the captain accompanied Keros on his journey, sir," Niall said. "They left several days ago."

"Then send word for them to divert to the *Eidolon*
and bring her around."

"The *Eidolon*?" Vaughn asked.

"A black ship. My ship."

Vaughn frowned thoughtfully. William could see the
wheels of his mind spinning as he pieced things together.
He was going to make a good king. William's enemies
were already currying him for it. If only they knew.

He looked at Niall. "Go now."

"Yes, sir." The steward disappeared through the secret
passage.

"I'll need something to take back today if they are not
to get suspicious of me," Vaughn said.

"I know. Very well," William said, making up his mind.
"Tell them that I have a compass-majicar. I can't make
her make compasses for me and I plan to put her in a
knacker box and hide her in the forge wing so that they
can't get to her."

"But . . . why would you do that? They'll come for
her."

"I know."

"Why?" William heard the rest of the question that
Ryland didn't voice. *Why did you make me do this if
there was no point?*

"I'm sorry, Ryland, but she won't budge for me and I
have no way to force her. That's my fault. I thought she'd
be easier to convince, and I didn't prepare sufficiently for
someone of her power. Next time I won't make the same
mistakes. But the fact is that her power is extraordinary
and she's threatened to destroy Sylmont. I believe she
has the ability to do so. I have no choice. The guild is
desperate for compass-majicars. They'll come steal her

from me and whatever they have to do, they *will* succeed where I have failed. In this, they know what they are doing better than I. Crosspointe will have another compass-majicar, which we both know is desperately needed. Additionally, this will distract them, hopefully long enough for me to find another compass-majicar."

"But ... they'll learn your plans," he protested. "Fairlie will tell them."

"Fairlie? You're talking about Fairlie?" Vaughn asked. The other two men ignored him.

"I have no choice," William told Ryland. "She's too dangerous to keep here, and locking her in a knacker box would be a waste when Crosspointe is so desperate for compass-majicars. With any luck the guild will assume I was merely trying to find a way to undermine their majickal monopoly on shipping. It's a logical conclusion. But even if Fairlie tells them everything, the guild won't publicly reveal it. If they did, they'll have to acknowledge that they are spawn and they would no more do that than the sun will stop shining."

Ryland looked unconvinced and Vaughn looked staggered. William pushed himself away from the table and stood.

"Sooner or later the guild is going to figure out what I'm doing. Making them aware now allows me to benefit from it. This distraction may divert them enough to allow me to outmaneuver them on this other business. Now, I've got to get back. Oh, Vaughn. You can tell your new friends that there have been Jutras sightings on the Inland Sea and I'm doing everything I can to keep that a secret. See what they make of that."

"Is that true?" Vaughn asked, blinking at the change of subject.

William shrugged. "There have been plenty of sightings, though none have proved true. They don't need to know the latter, however." He turned away, feeling exhausted. He felt like a mountain had settled onto his shoulders. He stiffened his back, not wanting his sons to see. He nodded farewell to Vaughn and squeezed Ryland's shoulder. He pulled his hand away before his son could shake him off.

He took a step. Another thought struck him and he stopped. He considered, closing his eyes as he shuffled through the possibilities. Yes. It could work, and if he was going to do it, now was the time. Slowly he turned, knowing neither of his sons was going to like this. He looked at Vaughn. "One more thing. Tell them that Ryland has turned against me. Tell them he's furious that I cursed Fairlie Norwich with *sylveth*, that he thinks I've gone mad."

Vaughn gasped.

"I will always be loyal," Ryland protested, looking sick.

"As will Vaughn. But it might be useful for them to think there's a wedge between us. Maybe they'll think Vaughn can turn you entirely and help them to destroy the crown. Between this and the news of the Jutras and Fairlie, they will be slavering over you." William looked sternly at them both. "I need time to find a new compass-majicar and put my plans in motion. I need you to buy it for me. Keep them distracted, and keep them from getting in my way. Ryland, move down to Sylmont with Vaughn and explain everything to him. I've no doubt the wolves will quickly be nipping at your toes. Let them see how angry and disgusted you are with me." His lips twisted with self-derision "I'm sure you'll be convincing. If anything comes up, get word to me any way you can."

He left them without another word. He returned to his quarters, his mind scrambling. The game was changing up again. He had to start moving his pieces around the board.

Chapter 21

Fairlie watched King William go. She licked her lips, tasting his blood again. It was . . . delicious. She knew she ought to be revolted at herself. *Only monsters drink blood*. But the thought was distant, like the roll of thunder on a sunny day. She ignored it. Her attention narrowed. There was something in the way the king had spoken, something in the rapid pace of his heart and the sour-sweet tang of his sudden sweat. It tasted like . . . lies. But that was no surprise. Not after what he'd done to her.

She paced uneasily beneath the spreading boughs of her forest. She'd spent the last two days playing with her new majick. It didn't give her the same satisfaction that heating the metal and beating, bending, and chiseling it into shape had always given her. There had always been such joy in the heat and the sparks and the heavy swing of the hammer; she'd loved the tightening of her muscles, the long draw of her breath, the sweat rolling from her skin. There was such accomplishment in the work of joining two pieces of metal, or casting a shape, or simply putting an edge on a blade. Now it was all too easy.

Unless she tried to join metal and *sylveth*.

She had tried but once, a day and a half ago. The result was that both melted in her hands and she found herself suddenly confronted by three small *sylveth* spawn. All were mindlessly hungry. One had been the size of a cockroach. It was a brilliant green with pink horns curving upward in pairs along its back and tiny legs all around its narrow barrel. It had launched itself at her, trying to burrow beneath her skin. She'd caught it in the air and crushed it in her fingers. The second had been the size of a mouse. It had been soft, moist and pale like a mushroom, with brown patches and fine white hairs that unraveled like spiderweb around Fairlie's hand. They leached out a yellow liquid—poison, Fairlie presumed, though she was unaffected. It had then opened a maw and sucked her fingers inside where a tiny tunnel of teeth tried to chew her flesh from her bones. She'd killed it too, coming away none the worse for wear. Her skin was impervious to its attacks.

The third was larger, the size of a well-grown rat. Fluffy black and blue–striped feathers ran the length of its head and body, each one edged with tiny grains of *sylveth*. Pushing out of its back were two delicate, leathery wings of cobalt blue. It stood on four tiny hands that looked bizarrely human. A long, snaky tail the same brilliant blue as its wings curled over its back. Its eyes were black gleams inside the thick feathers on its head, and its mouth was a wide blue streak just below.

This one had intelligence. It chewed on its dead brethren, stuffing them whole into a mouth that opened like a gaping purse. It crunched them loudly and swallowed, then hunched down as if to spring, its wings flaring wide. Fairlie stared back at it. She had no fear of the creature. She sniffed. She smelled its hunger, like an oily smoke. It also smelled faintly spicy, like cinnamon and hot pepper.

It opened its mouth and made a low humming sound that rippled through Fairlie's flesh. She shook herself. Its mouth gaped and the hum came again. It stared expectantly. Suddenly she knew it was waiting for her to feed it. She shook her head.

"I have nothing for you to eat. Just metal and stone and a little cloth here and there."

Another humming sound, higher-pitched this time. It sounded pained. Fairlie crouched before it, her hands lacing together beneath her chin. She eyed the little beast. Then she reached out, palm up. It leaped onto her hand, its wings flapping to steady itself. Fairlie stood and carried it to the Lius tree. It was heavy with clusters of mealy orange berries. Fairlie picked a spray and offered it to the feathered spawn in her hand. It grabbed the berries and shoved them in its mouth. A grain later it popped its mouth open and made a trilling hum.

Fairlie picked more berries and the little creature ate them. She lifted it up so that it could crawl into the tree and fetch its own meal, but it clung to her hand with surprising strength and hummed an imperious demand. Fairlie shrugged and continued to pick the berries and feed the beast.

It took nearly a half a glass to satisfy its hunger. Its belly was distended and its breathing sounded faintly labored. Fairlie bent to set it on the moss and it clutched her hand again, its tail wrapping tightly around her forearm. She lifted it up level to her eyes.

"I am not your mother."

Except that maybe she was. It was thanks to her that the copper-and-brass alloy she'd been working with had come in contact with the *sylveth*. If not its mother, what was she?

She sat down on the moss, frowning at it. It continued to grip her tightly. "What do you want me to do with you?"

As if in answer, it opened its mouth. Its entire body vibrated with a sound so deep Fairlie could barely hear it. It rolled through her flesh and ached in her bones. The patterns on her body seared hot. The Lius tree trembled, and for a moment Fairlie felt everything in her body stop: her heart, her lungs, her blood. Something flashed in her mind, almost too quick to see. Almost. It was a brilliant, shining spark, the kind that leaped from hot steel when she was grinding it. It streaked across her vision like a miniature star and was gone.

Fairlie looked down at the little beast clinging to her hand. "Spark."

A trill sounded. Happy.

"It's your name?"

Another trill. Longer. A nuzzling against her palm. Fairlie combed her fingers through her metallic hair, hearing the musical sound as it slid together. The little creature had a name. But then so did she. Did she think she was the only spawn that could think? She thought of Shaye. Majicars were spawn too. She flinched at the thought. She wasn't ready to think about that, about the fact that she was in love with a man who'd kept such a secret. It wasn't that she blamed him really. She didn't like to think what she probably would have done if he had told her. But it made her wonder what other secrets he was hiding.

She stared down at Spark. Its eyes gleamed up at her, and then suddenly the little creature clambered up her arm to her shoulder, coiling its tail twice around her neck. It wasn't so tight that it felt like a threat, merely a firm decision to stay. Then Spark burrowed under her hair and made another happy trilling sound.

Fairlie brushed her fingers across the two loops of tail banding her throat, which had become tighter as Spark burrowed. She could tear the little creature loose. She could destroy it with her majick, dissolving the metal and *sylveth* from its flesh. There was a sharp yank on her hair as she thought the last.

"Ouch! What was that?"

A low, troubled hum answered and her vision went entirely black. Panic surged through her at the sudden loss. She spun around, staggering as she tripped over a root of the Lius tree. She fell, catching herself blindly on her hands. Her fingers clawed deep into the moss and earth. She flung herself onto her back and grappled at the tail around her throat. It tightened. She could not breathe. Her body spasmed with mindless fear. She scrabbled at her neck, gouging away flesh as she tried to get a grip on the tail. When she couldn't, she reached under her hair to grab Spark's small feathered body. *Spawn. She would kill it.*

Almost without thought her magic flowed through her. It wrapped the bleak place that had abscessed inside her since her transformation and sent coiling wires of molten heat corkscrewing through her. Her entire body went incandescent hot. The heat flowed into the hand holding Spark.

For a moment the little creature did not respond. Then it screamed as Fairlie found the minerals and *sylveth* that made it what it was. The sound drove spikes through Fairlie's skull. Her hand clamped tighter and she poured majick into Spark.

A fleeting image flashed across her mindscape, the brilliant spark shrinking, turning blue, and then fading altogether.

Then suddenly Fairlie could see. She was lying on the ground on her right side, one hand on the tail strangling her, the other clenched around Spark at the back of her neck. In front of her the flames of the Lius tree danced. Suddenly the tail on her neck loosened and fell away. Startled, Fairlie lunged to her feet in one powerful movement. Something slithered over her shoulder. She looked down. Spark was knotted in her hand, its tail dangling limply.

"Chayos, no!" she whispered.

She cupped both hands around the broken creature. She pushed the hot wires of her majick out. They burrowed into Spark. Fairlie could feel the wrongness instantly. There was an imbalance in the alloy of blood, feathers, *sylveth* and minerals. There was a stillness inside, a heaviness here, a settling there, a loosening all around. Everything was melting together as in a crucible. Spark was disappearing into a puddle of sameness.

She couldn't let it happen.

Fairlie reached for more majick. She felt it rising up out of the ground and drifting in the air. The Lius tree flared like a pillar of pure flame. Fairlie gathered the majick and poured it into Spark. But what to do?

But somehow she knew. Just as a sunflower knows how to follow the sun or a spider knows how to make its web.

It was what she was born to do. She remade Spark, molding and bending, twisting and melding. In her mind's eye, she saw hammers and tongs and anvils and wedges and punches and swages. In imagining killing the creature, she'd thoughtlessly taken its measure. She knew what fit where, what shape each part should be, the balance and the tension of blood, bone, and flesh, the weight and alloy of each feather, each vein, each tiny finger.

Carefully she separated what had melted and fused together, hardening and softening and tempering. She worked with her eyes shut, her majick flooding through her in a torrent. Again she was faced with marrying *sylveth* with something else. She hesitated. She held the *sylveth* separate in a cocoon of power. She had to put it back where it belonged or Spark would die.

The idea wrenched her, twisting her stomach. It wasn't that she cared much for the little creature but rather that she didn't like thinking it was so disposable. It had a name. It could feel and it could fight to survive. There was too much about Spark that reminded her of herself. She could not bear that she could take the part Ryland had played in her betrayal—that she could callously transform Spark without a care for its being alive and thinking and fearing.

She began by pulling the *sylveth* inside her. It burned, a fire so bright and sharp that she felt like she was being carved from the inside out. She pulled it closer, deeper inside to the core of herself where she'd harbored her pain and the infection of Ryland's betrayal, made more virulent by King William's visit. But the *sylveth* was cleansing. It carved away the pus and the rot and burned it bright with a clean flame.

Fairlie caressed it with spectral fingers. Shock made her go completely still. Her mind went blank. The *sylveth* wreathed her touch, reaching out to her.

It *understood*.

It was not cold, dull, and lifeless. It *hurt*. It yearned to return to the sea. It wanted her help.

~*Take we home*~

Desperation. Hope. Desire. Love. Fear. Need. Hate. All roiled inside Fairlie, matching her own feelings. Who should she choose to save?

Spark.

"I cannot," she whispered aloud. "I cannot choose."

But she already had.

It was betrayal. Neither Spark nor the *sylveth* merited better than the other. But she shared more in common with Spark than she did with the whirling, bright majick inside her.

I am sorry. She could not speak the words aloud. They felt hollow after learning of the desperation and pain. She was only going to add to it. *I would do it differently if I could.* Ryland might have said the same if she had given him the chance. It was a pitifully weak excuse.

But if she did not help Spark? The little spawn would die and she would have murdered it. That was the thing she couldn't live with. No one had forced the *sylveth* to make Spark. It owed the little creature. Hard, unrelenting anger flared inside her. It had done this to her. If it had mind and feelings enough to think, then it could have stopped itself. It deserved no sympathy.

She felt a weary ache of acquiescence permeate her heart and spread through her body. It didn't belong to her. It came from the *sylveth*. It could not stop its nature; it had made Spark and Fairlie and it would make many more things if allowed. But it longed to go home to the sea all the same.

~Hurt we here~

"I know," she said with grudging pity, her anger thawing slightly. She had also been ripped from her home, from her very self, and she could never go back. That was the one thing she knew for certain. What she would be, what she was, what was left of herself, she still didn't know. She grimaced. Too bad. Whatever she was she was. Now she had to get on with it.

She felt a *relinquishing* from the *sylveth*, a bowing to a fate unearned. After all, it had not come from the sea on its own.

As gently as she could, she gathered the *sylveth* and began the process of melding it back to Spark. With every rivet of majick and every weld she made, she said a mental thank-you for the unwilling sacrifice the *sylveth* made. For a fleeting moment she wondered if King William would do the same if she ever consented to make him compasses, or if he'd said it when he ordered her transformation. She shoved the thought aside along with the fury it called up. There was little enough point in either.

Instead she focused on completing her healing of Spark.

She layered the *sylveth* back in where it belonged. She beaded it along the edges of each feather and filigreed it along the insides of Spark's bones and skin. Time stopped. It could have taken the space of a heartbeat or a dozen seasons.

She finished and in the same breath she felt a pulse ripple through the little creature's body. Spark stirred and went rigid. Hardly daring to breathe, Fairlie stooped and set it on the ground and backed away. She knelt. It fluffed itself, making a whiffling noise. It nuzzled under its feathers and then sat up on its haunches. It looked at Fairlie. Its mouth opened and it made a cautious hum. An image of a dull spark fluttered weakly across Fairlie's mindscape. She blinked, her stomach knotting.

"I'm sorry. You scared me."

A flash of light. Surprise.

"Yes. Your tail around my neck. And then I couldn't see. I was . . . scared," she repeated. Mindless with terror. "I didn't mean to attack you. That's not me."

But it was. Because she *had* attacked.

Another hum. A flash of green, too quick to understand what it was. But Fairlie understood the message. "You won't hurt me," she said. Another green flash. She shook her head, feeling a headache starting behind her eyes. "Slower. I am expecting it now. I won't hurt you again."

A grayness followed. Fairlie recognized it for hesitation. Then an image of Spark on her shoulder slowly faded into being. It was watery, as if the small spawn didn't quite trust Fairlie's promise.

"Are you sure?" she asked, surprised.

Bright flames erupted across her mindscape and a spark fell down into them. Fairlie was the flames and Spark wanted to come home. She reached down and Spark leaped onto her arm and nimbly climbed up to her shoulder. The tail looped her neck once and then twice. The coil settled loosely against her collarbone.

A field of gray nothingness, the edges tinged purple and yellow, floated against Fairlie's mind's eye. It rippled like a flag. It was a picture of uncertainty. This time, instead of speaking, Fairlie reached out with her mind, stroking a mental hand over the silken gray flag. Her entire body jerked when she felt it physically. Slowly she brushed the gray again. She concentrated on answering that uncertainty with a promise of trust. More than trust—she offered welcome. *Misery loves company, and so does the newly spawned*, she thought sardonically. Her touch trailed brilliant color, uncurling and spreading like jewel-bright watercolors.

She felt Spark tense, and then a small hand ran lightly across her cheek. Once again the little animal burrowed under her hair, its tail tightening until it circled her neck firmly.

Now, a day and a half later, Fairlie sat beside the small pool of *sylveth*. Anger made her blood race and her heart pound. King William spoke of need and patriotism, offering excuses and lies to mitigate his betrayal. He'd say anything to convince her to make compasses for him. Her fist clenched. Was she even capable? She turned raw balls of it over in her fingers. Spark leaped down to sit on her lap, wrapping its tail around her waist. Could she?

She'd never know. She wasn't going to try. And not only because she'd never consent to help the men who had betrayed her. No. She refused to hurt the *sylveth*.

"I won't do that," she murmured to the ball of *sylveth* cupped in her palm.

Then it did the impossible. On its own, it flattened, wrapping around her hand and sliding up her arm like a long glove. Fairlie started to shake it off, then stopped herself. If it fell, it would transform whatever it touched. She didn't want to have to kill anything.

Spark made a threatening sound and licked the *sylveth*. Fairlie was astonished to see a strip of it disappear into Spark's mouth. The empty spot filled in as the *sylveth* sealed itself. Spark started to lick again.

"Wait."

The little spawn stopped. It trembled with tension, making a worried humming noise.

"I'll be all right. It can't hurt me any more than it can hurt you."

Spark glanced up at her, and then settled to watch, puffing its feathers and reminding Fairlie of a nervous cat. Fairlie turned her attention back to the *sylveth*. It was thinning as it sheathed her arm and spread over her shoulder and up her neck. She forced herself to hold still as it slipped up over her face, covering her mouth, nose, and eyes. She held her breath. Then realized she didn't need to. She pulled air in through her skin, the same way she pulled in majick or pushed out metal.

Then the *sylveth* sank inside her.

It felt both hot and cold and not uncomfortable. She felt it spread a thin layer between muscle and skin, nestling into crevices and folds. She resisted the urge to push it back out of herself. Instead she reached out to it.

What are you doing?

~Go with you we do~

Fairlie frowned.

"Where? Why?" Startled, she said it aloud.

~Hurt we here . . . carry with you~

She felt its struggle to make words. Sliding through its emotions was a bitter alloy of despair and hope, and she found she couldn't deny it. It would be safe enough. It couldn't hurt her and she could keep it from escaping and making spawn. And maybe she could help it get out to the sea and beyond the Pale.

"All right," she said. The pool around her feet seeped inside her. She released the majick on the basin and absorbed that too.

Spark made a sour sound and then leaped up on her shoulder and twined its tail around her neck twice. It gave a sharp yank of her hair. She glanced sideways, letting her hair twine around its body.

"It can't hurt either of us. It doesn't belong here—it wants to go home. Maybe I can do that much for it."

Spark made a sound suspiciously like a sigh and stroked her cheek again before disappearing under her hair. Fairlie smiled. What had she become that her friends were *sylveth* and *sylveth* spawn? Slowly her smile faded. And Shaye. She had to plan. Either the king would bring Shaye to her tomorrow or he wouldn't—either way, she had to be ready.

Chapter 22

"I will go to dinner in the king's chambers alone."

"No. This man cannot be trusted. He may try to imprison you."

Nya winced as Fallon battered at her mind, trying to force himself past her barriers and make her yield. He never stopped. She wasn't even sure he could. It was his nature. But the assault made her entire body throb, and she shook with the effort of keeping him out. She was weak. Fairlie had slashed the fabric of her mind, shredding open great wounds. Slowly Nya was repairing herself, but it would take time to be strong again. Time to build her defenses. She felt fragmented, her mind a whirling kaleidoscope, constantly spinning in new patterns that often made little sense. She felt madness swirling around her. Fallon's constant barrage did not help.

"He may. But there is no choice. We must make him think we will do as he asks."

"Of course we will. We have to have the Pale and he knows it," Fallon said furiously.

Let me in. Let me protect you. Let me in let me in let me in let me in.

"Then I can be in no danger. As long as we cooperate, he has no reason to try to harm me."

"He wants you. I could smell it on him."

Want. Want. Want. Want.

Nya's stomach curled. Yes. Something else unexpected. The king desired her. As did Fallon. Since arriving on this island, every male seemed to hunger for her, every day more and more strongly. It wasn't natural desire. Her body was sending out seductive invitations on tendrils of majick that Nya could do nothing to stop, and they seemed to be growing increasingly powerful. Fallon paced around her as if he could hardly keep from leaping on her. His mind confirmed his hunger, and his control was fraying. Their close quarters did not help. Soon he would climb on top of her regardless of what she wanted. It terrified her. Why was this happening? But she knew. It was an elemental, animal drive to reproduce. *She had a husband.* A voice inside jeered. *He'll call you spawn and try to kill you.* She didn't want to believe it. But it didn't matter. Her body didn't care. It wanted to be seeded and didn't care who took up its invitation.

"He will not touch me. I will not let him." Being with the king without Fallon would be a respite.

"I will go with you and wait."

She looked at him, mustering all her strength to thrust his mind from hers. She needed distance from him. "No."

He started to argue. She growled. She could get no rest here. "First I will go to Fairlie. Alone. I do not wish to be seen."

With that she transformed into her other self, the same one that had allowed her to explore the castle unseen when they'd first arrived. It came easily, thank the shadows. She padded to the door and opened it, sliding through. She half expected Fallon to follow her. She broke into a sprint and fled down the corridor, following a twisting route, not caring if she got lost. As she went, she felt the pressure of his demands fading.

She wound through the castle on four feet, invisible. There were few minds here that she could touch and none that knew to touch hers. The silence against her mind was a balm. At last she found her way to Fairlie's forge. She smelled majick long before she entered the destroyed wing. The floors were buckled and the walls sagged. Beams from the roof had collapsed and the air was full of dust. Nya passed a dozen guards, leaving footprints in the dust. They did not notice.

When she reached the door, there was no handle. She pushed against it and it opened easily. Inside was a gleaming forest of metal. Nya went in and closed the door before transforming back to herself.

"Fairlie?" she called, not moving to search. She carefully reached out, finding the other woman. She *seethed*. There was another Kin with her. Nya stroked across the small one's mind, a whisper of friendship. Its mind was careful and thoughtful, rather than bristling and wild. She hadn't expected that.

Fairlie reacted to Nya's intrusion with all the speed of her new heritage. In an instant she stood before Nya. Her eyes were on fire. Her head tipped sideways. "Did you come here to die?"

"No."

"Then you made a mistake."

"I came because you are mine now, mine to protect. You are Kin."

Fairlie snarled and a growl rumbled low in her chest. Her fingers flexed into claws. "You make me a monster and then want to protect me? Are you maggoty?"

Nya shrugged, a graceful ripple of her shoulders. "It is what I am. In exchange for changing you, the Kin on the Root were to receive a Pale of their own to protect their homes and land."

"I don't care."

"Yes. But I must. It is what the *sylveth* made of me. I have no choice. I am called Nya. I am called Warden—guardian of Kin. I am called Speaker—I can touch the minds of Kin. I must guard."

Fairlie was quiet a moment. "You are saying that majick made you transform me?"

"Yes. Because majick made me what I am and I cannot be anything else, even if I wish to be."

"Do you wish it?"

Nya nodded slowly. She had no interest in lying to

Fairlie and like the other woman, Nya still clung to that life she had before. "Yes." She hesitated. "Sometimes."

"And what does it mean that you'll protect me now. Will you help me escape?"

Another slow nod. "Yes."

Fairlie made a strangled sound, half sob, half laugh. "The king has Shaye. I can't go anywhere without him." She broke off, then tensed. "He is spawn—Kin. Are you obligated to guard him too?"

Nya gave a slow shake of her head. "I can touch the minds of Crosspointe's majicars and Pilots, but they are not mine. They are different somehow from what we are. I am not compelled to ward them."

"Of course not," Fairlie said caustically. Her hair stirred on invisible currents, and her eyes burned orange and red.

"That does not mean I cannot choose to."

"Will you?" Fairlie demanded.

Would she? Nya rubbed a hand over her forehead in a way she had only done before her transformation. She caught herself, slowly lowering her arm. Suddenly Fairlie snatched it, her hand clamping tight. Nya stiffened, starting to struggle, but then stilled when she realized Fairlie's gaze was fastened on the bracelet circling her wrist. Her marriage bracelet, the last remnant of her life before *sylveth* had claimed her. It could not be removed, its majick too strong to be overcome by even *sylveth*. Fairlie stroked the band with one finger, the pattern shifting and rearranging.

"I've seen one of these before," she said. Her face lifted. "You are Captain Plusby's wife."

Nya didn't expect the wave of emotion that crashed over her. She went boneless, sliding to the floor, Fairlie still holding her arm. "You know him? You've seen him?" she gasped, her breath thickening in her throat.

Fairlie nodded. "Just before—" Her hand tightened and the bones in Nya's arm compressed painfully. "That day, when you did this to me." There was less bitterness in her voice now, as if she didn't hate Nya so strongly.

So close. "He was . . . well?"

"Losing you broke him. He went mad and lost his captain's ticket. He is on an even keel now, but he's not given up on you."

"Nor I him," Nya said softly.

"Why haven't you told him you're alive?"

"Like this?" Nya said quickly, looking disparagingly at herself. She shook her head. "I cannot. Not yet. I have duties to the Kin."

"Won't you always?"

Nya didn't answer. She couldn't. She loved her husband still, but even more she feared the hate and disgust that would suffuse his face when he saw her again—and saw what he had bound his life and soul to.

"He might surprise you," Fairlie said.

Nya wanted to believe it. "Your people hate and fear spawn," she argued weakly. But he wouldn't. Not now while her body was sending alluring invitations. But it would be a hollow reunion if that was the only reason he accepted her.

Fairlie sat back on her heels, letting go of Nya's arm. "What do you gain if you stay silent?" She pushed to her feet. "Will you help me free Shaye?"

Nya stood, feeling like the ground was spinning. "I will. I will return soon."

She started to leave, but Fairlie called her back. "Are you going to do this again? To someone else?"

Nya did not hesitate. "If I have to. Your king desires it."

"And what will he give you this time?" Harsh words, sharp as knives.

Nya bared her teeth in a silent snarl. "He may very well give us nothing. He is not to be trusted."

"So I have learned."

"I *will* help you."

"So you say. Just find Shaye. That's all I want from you."

The anger remained. Nya had not expected forgiveness, or even civility. But neither had she expected that Fairlie would know her husband and respond to her grief with kindness.

As if reading her mind, Fairlie said, "You should find Captain Plusby. He may surprise you."

"I will." Nya was surprised that she truly meant it. But first she had to dine with the king and then she had to search for Shaye.

"Why me?" Fairlie asked suddenly. "Why did you pick me?"

"Because you were the first one we found who could be a compass-majicar. You are rare."

"And what makes me so special?"

"I do not know. But there are very few who can be a compass-majicar. Perhaps you have been kissed by the gods. Perhaps this was always your destiny."

"And was this *your* destiny?" Fairlie asked mockingly.

Nya went still. "I hope not." And with that she left.

Chapter 23

The next day Fairlie waited for King William to return with Shaye as he'd promised. She alternately paced and sat like stone, pulling stillness around her like a cloak against the cold. The sun inched up into the sky and then slid slowly down beyond the mountains. When every last ray had faded and her room was dark as ink, Fairlie knew exactly what King William had been lying about.

But she did not know what she was going to do about it.

Was she willing to do as she'd threatened? Turn all the worked *sylveth* in the castle back into its raw form and unleash a horde of spawn on Crosspointe?

The answer was an instantaneous and resounding no. She could no more turn innocent strangers into spawn than she could not try to save Spark. Nor could she turn a horde of hungry spawn loose on the castle and the city. And even if she would, she could not use the *sylveth* so selfishly.

King William must have known it. He'd lied about Shaye so that he could get safely away from Fairlie, betting all along that her threat was empty.

The knowledge left her with a feeling of helplessness and frustrated rage. And with a question: What was she going to do now? Should she wait for Nya? But time was her enemy and she didn't know how long it would take Nya to return, if she did return. Now that she knew William had no intention of living up to his side of the bargain, Fairlie had to go look for Shaye herself. But she had no idea where to start.

The castle was as much a maze as the Riddles, and certainly King William had posted guards around her forge to keep her from wandering off. They wouldn't hesitate to hurt her or kill her if they had to, if that was what the king ordered—and she was certain he had. He couldn't chance that her threat had been real. She wasn't invulnerable. A crossbolt would likely penetrate her armored skin. A heavy blow to the head would likely crush her skull, and as strong as she was, enough men could truss her up in ropes, especially knacker ropes. They'd have an easy enough time of it if they were dressed in knacker gear. They'd toss her in a knacker box and send her off to the majicars on Merstone Island, or maybe bury her in a pit and forget all about her. She stiffened, glancing over her shoulder. Was a knacker gang waiting outside for her even now?

She had to believe there was.

Fairlie sank down beneath the Lius tree and stared at nothing, trying to come up with a plan. A glass went by. Then she roused herself from her stillness. She could not just sit idly and wait for something to happen. She'd been waiting too long already. It was time she did something. She had to move while it was still dark, when the castle was less busy and there were more shadows to disguise her.

Her entire attention closed on finding Shaye. She had nowhere to go and no one else who would truly miss her. Shaye was all that mattered. He loved her. And she . . . loved him. Still. That had not changed. Maybe it had even grown stronger, despite the secret of what he was.

She remembered him sitting at her feet, poison running through his body, pleading with her to hold tight to herself, to stay with him. She remembered his kisses and his terrible uncertainty as he confessed his feelings. He had not lied about those things. He'd risked all that truly mattered for her.

She felt the hard knot release and she drew a breath.

He'd lied about nothing important. Not really. And now she had to figure out how to find him.

She reached out to the stones of the castle, but they told her nothing but their own mineral secrets. She considered what to do. She came to a plan. She would make a hole in her wall and climb up to the castle roof, gouging foot- and handholds in the stone. It was dark—no one would see her make the climb. From there she would search. If she turned up nothing, she would go into the castle and search every room and cellar until she found him.

Fairlie wasted no more time. She went to the wall beside her forge and pushed her fingers through the stone. It crumbled and she scooped the powder away until she'd made an opening large enough to crawl through. If there was a knacker gang waiting for her outside, they'd be watching the doors and windows.

She emerged in a flower bed, the dirt still packed and hard from winter. The outside air was cool and humid. She turned and began climbing, wedging herself in the sable shadows made by the chimney. She was halfway to the roof, crawling easily up the sheer wall, when something hit her.

At first it felt like a splash of warm water. The liquid drenched her clothing and dribbled down her arms and legs. She felt herself stiffening and tried to hurry faster up the wall. But suddenly she couldn't move. Numbness spread in thickening clots through her body. Beneath her hair Spark made an angry sound and squirmed.

"Don't!" Fairlie rasped through the hardening tunnel of her throat. She couldn't feel her back at all anymore and only splotchy patches on her arms and legs.

She sucked in a breath, reaching for another handhold. Another splash of warm wetness splattered her. One hand slipped. Her arm fell limply down beside her. Both feet dropped uselessly. She hung by one hand. Her last thought as she lost her grip entirely was for Spark. A black field and a bright ember fading to a pinpoint. *Hide.*

And then she was falling.

She didn't feel the rush of the wind as she plummeted thirty feet into the fallow flower bed. She felt herself bounce on the turf. Her vision jerked and clouded black and the air rushed out of her with a guttural noise. She couldn't move. Fear filled her, but it rode on billowing waves of gauze. She could not blink. Even the tears that burned in her eyes refused to fall. There was no pain; there was simply no feeling at all. She tried to leap to her feet and fight. But she was frozen and helpless.

They closed in on her. She heard the crackle of twigs and winter-brittle grass and the swish of cloth. A hand gripped her hair and her head was twisted. A face came into focus. A man with ginger hair scraped back from his face and a closely trimmed beard crouched beside her. His skin was pale and sprinkled liberally with freckles. His eyes were silvery gray and rimmed with crimson. When he spoke to her, Fairlie could see that one of his front teeth was chipped.

"We're taking you to Merstone with us. We're going to put you in a knacker sack and then a box." He looked across from her at someone else. "Ready?"

Fairlie was lifted and a sack was drawn up over her and tied at the top of her skull. Then she was lifted into a knacker box. She heard the lid settle and then there were little knocking sounds as her captors secured it shut. Then it lurched as it was lifted into the air. For a while, the journey was smooth, almost as if she were floating. There was another lurch and a clunking sound as the box came to rest. Then she heard wheels and they started to roll forward. She was in the back of a wagon. They were keeping a brisk pace too. She could hear the rapid clop of trotting hooves, the box bouncing and jouncing on the rough cobbles.

Eventually she was transferred to a boat, the knacker box swooping up and down on the swells. Her captors remained imperviously silent through the entire journey.

Fairlie had never been beyond the protective ring of the Pale, the fence of tide and storm wards that protected Crosspointe from *sylveth*. In fact she'd forgotten

that Merstone lay beyond the Pale. Thus she was caught
completely unawares when they crossed.

Despite the knacker box, majick slammed into her,
beating against her mind with heavy clubs. With repeated
crossings, a person could grow accustomed to the pum-
meling majick, suffering few ill effects. First-timers often
fainted, sometimes remaining unconscious for days. Despite the strength and armoring of her new body, Fairlie's
mind was unable to defy the clobbering majick. Black-
ness swallowed her and she knew no more.

She opened her eyes. She was no longer in a sack or a
box. She looked down at herself. She was naked. Even the
pendant Shaye had given her was gone. Anger twisted in
a thorny knot. She stiffened with realization—she could
move again. Fairlie touched the tail tightly circling her
neck. Spark was still with her. Slowly she sat up and then
froze in shock.

She wasn't sitting *on* anything. She was suspended in
air. All around her was woven a black web of majick. She
felt the *sylveth* in it and tried to reach out to it. Something stopped her, something as solid as a wall. Then
she realized the black color came from the impervious
knacker cloth that wrapped every inch of the web.

"You cannot escape." The voice came from below
her and just beyond the web. A woman stood there, her
head covered in black bristles. She was dressed in a long
gray robe and her hands were folded together inside the
bell sleeves.

"You will not be permitted to leave this web, to
have food or drink, unless you agree to become a guild
compass-majicar," she continued in a clear, deliberate
voice. "If you agree, you will be given comfortable quarters and a spacious workplace. You will wear shackles
that will permit us to destroy you if you attempt an escape
or an attack, and you will be watched closely throughout
each day and night. Do you have an answer?"

Fairlie bit back the caustic crude words she knew
Shaye would have flung at the majicar. Words she dearly

wanted to say. Instead she dissembled, glancing nervously about herself and shivering, covering herself as if embarrassed.

"Where am I?" she asked. "What did you do to me? Where are my clothes?"

The majicar made a *humph* sound but did not answer. Fairlie scrunched into a ball, decorously crossing her legs and shaking her hair about herself. It was not easy—she floated in the air like a drunken cloud, tipping and waving her arms for balance until she stabilized.

"What's happening?"

The majicar stared, then shook her head, a look of derision on her face.

"We know the king cursed you with *sylveth* in order to make you a compass-majicar, and we've verified your talent with our people. You can't pretend."

"But I don't know how!" Fairlie said in a shrill voice that was nothing like her own. She wanted the majicar to think she was stupid and helpless and totally unaware of what she was capable of. In the meantime, the anger in her belly coalesced into a hate deeper than anything she'd ever felt before. King William had given her to the majicars. He couldn't control her and he wouldn't give her Shaye, so he'd betrayed her a second time. *She would kill him.*

Somehow she would do it, no matter the cost.

"The knowledge lies within you. Every compass-majicar is different; each knows the craft instinctively. If you do not know now, it will come to you. I ask again, do you agree to the terms?"

"I want to see Shaye," Fairlie said, covering her eyes. Real emotion leached through into the words and she sounded as desperate as she felt. If only to see him free and well— She clenched her hands. "He'll tell me what I need to do. I trust him."

That caught the other woman up short. She stared, her mouth falling open. "Shaye? Weverton?"

Fairlie nodded eagerly. "Yes! That's him. I've known him since we were children. He'll tell me what to do. Can

I see him?" Then she hesitated and let her shoulders wilt, her head dropping. She wished she could call up tears, but she was too angry. "But the king has taken Shaye. He told me. He said he'd kill Shaye if I didn't make compasses. But I don't know how," she said again, staring beseechingly at her captor. "What will the king do to him?"

For a moment the majicar was silent, her mouth flat and tight. She nodded. "I will speak to the Sennet." With that she spun on her heel and left in an angry swirl of gray robes.

Fairlie clenched her teeth, hiding her face against her knees, hiding the hard smile that curved her lips. There were majicars still watching her. She felt their eyes on her. She didn't want to expose her charade to them. But triumph rolled through her. Now King William had a new problem. The Majicars' Guild would not suffer him to imprison one of their own, and neither would Nicholas Weverton. Soon they'd be battering the castle doors, demanding to see Shaye. It was all she could do to help him, if he was still alive to be helped.

The pain that followed that thought skewered her with a white-hot knife. She gasped, hardly able to breathe. No. She would not believe he was dead. She would not believe it was possible.

She gathered herself tightly, grinding her teeth. Her muscles bunched and strained as she clutched herself. She pressed her forehead against her knees, counting as she breathed slowly and deeply. In a while, she felt herself steady. Bit by bit she unknotted her muscles. She couldn't think about Shaye or King William. She eyed the web containing her. She had to concentrate on breaking free of her new prison before she starved or died of thirst. Because she certainly was not going to give in.

An entire day passed before anyone came to speak to Fairlie again. This time the woman majicar was accompanied by the ginger-haired majicar. He wore green robes with intricate embroidery and spangles of glittering gems. The high collar looked painful.

Fairlie eyed them both with all the earnestness and tremulous fear she could muster. She opened her mouth as if to speak and then shut it, putting her hand over her lips as if to hide the trembling.

"We have come to ask your answer. The Sennet requires it," the woman said, once again hiding her laced hands inside the sleeves of her gray robe. This time crimson embroidery uncurled across it, making her look like she was splattered in blood.

Fairlie sniffed, rubbing her nose with the back of her hand. "Did you ... did you find Shaye?" she whispered.

In the past day, she'd done all she knew how to do to test the walls of her prison, only to find that she was well and truly trapped. The thickened air holding her suspended also prevented her from touching the spell web. The knacker cloth kept her from reaching out to the *sylveth* and melting it. She felt it, just beyond her reach, throbbing like the pulse of blood through a body. As promised, she had been given no food or water, which meant there was no chance to escape when they opened the spell. Surprisingly, she did not yet feel hungry or thirsty, though she pretended, asking repeatedly for something to eat and drink. Her guards never answered; they never spoke at all. New ones entered to relieve old ones every five glasses.

"Shaye Weverton is not your concern," the woman declared. "What is your answer?"

Fairlie bit her lower lip and looked as beseeching as she could manage. "You're going to help him—aren't you?"

"We have come to hear your answer," the woman said, her lip curling in obvious disgust at Fairlie's frailty.

Fairlie hugged herself tightly and turned her shoulder as if to hide her nakedness. "Where are my clothes? Why have you taken them away?" A note of anger crept into her voice, and she quickly tempered it, sharpening it into affronted modesty. She was getting really tired of the majicar bitch.

The word startled her, as did her attitude. The old Fairlie had always been deferential and forgiving of people.

She rarely took offense and always overlooked insults. She did not know how to hold a grudge. But this new Fairlie was impatient and angry and she didn't overlook anything. As for grudges—she would hold them until she finished them. Permanently.

"You will be provided clothing when you agree," the woman said.

"Why are you treating me like this?" Fairlie asked, summoning a little sob.

"You are precious to us," the ginger-haired man answered. He smiled. His freckles and chipped tooth made him look boyish and friendly.

Just like King William. Just like Ryland. Fairlie smothered a snarl, watching him.

"But you are a breed apart and you are also dangerous." His voice was soft and gentle, as if he were trying to calm a wild animal. Maybe he was. "We must take precautions. And"—he gave a little shrug—"you must be made to agree to our terms. Your discomfort may help you come to that decision more quickly."

"Is that why you won't give me anything to eat?" Fairlie asked plaintively.

"It is."

She was silent, thinking. She would not be able to free herself. And she was not going to bow down to their demands. They could watch her starve to death.

"What do you say? The faster you agree, the faster you will have food and clothing and comfort," the ginger-haired man said.

Fairlie looked at him again, her eyes narrowing. "What are you called?"

"I am Amberdel and this is Gliessithe."

A mouthful. Majicars chose their own names, usually pretentious ones. Amberdel wasn't too bad, but Gliessithe? Fairlie snorted softly. Then she smiled, lifting her head and straightening her shoulders, dropping her pretense of embarrassment. Her voice rang out, unwavering and undaunted.

"I will tell you the same thing I told the king. If you

bring me Shaye—if I see that he is safe and well—only then will I consider what you wish."

Neither spoke. Gliessithe looked taken aback. Amberdel stared measuringly back at Fairlie, his brows furrowing.

"The Sennet is taking steps," he said finally.

"Good. Let me know when they succeed. Until then, I don't want to see you. Either of you."

Every day, either Gliessithe or Amberdel returned to ask her for her answer, despite her declaration that she didn't want to see them. At first Fairlie responded with, "Come back when Shaye is with you." Then she ceased replying at all. She sat with her knees bent so she could rest her chin on them, her arms wrapped around her legs. Awake or asleep, she did not change position. She became used to balancing on the air, and discovered that it thickened just inches away, acting as a support when she eased herself out of the center of the spell web.

In the days she'd been imprisoned in her workshop, she'd realized she had no use for a chamber pot, and the definition of what was food had changed. She ate nearly anything—metal, wood, stone, meat ... her body used it all. What happened to those things inside her was a question, but all of it seemed useful to her majick or to the crafting of things. She had no waste to purge. Perhaps that was the way of it for all who had the capacity for compass majick. Otherwise, wouldn't they have given her a slop jar? Or maybe not. They'd stripped her. Maybe the lack of the jar was just another way they thought to make her uncomfortable so she'd agree to their terms.

But it bothered her a great deal that she did not thirst. All living things wanted water. It made her feel more inhuman than anything else had done, even looking in the mirror the first time.

As the days passed and she sat in stillness, she had little to do but think. She found herself trying to come to terms with herself. But more often than not, she returned to King William and Ryland and the fact that the Maji-cars' Guild was holding her prisoner. The heat of her anger increased with every passing glass as she stewed. Her skin grew hot with it. Her hair twisted around on it-self, revealing her growing tension to anyone who cared to look. She did not know if they did.

If Fairlie was not hungry, Spark was ravenous. And thirsty. She did not know how long the little creature would survive without sustenance. The images from Spark had dwindled to intermittent flashes of ulcerating yellow and orange. The creature clutched her hair, pull-ing and releasing it like a nervously kneading cat. Fairlie could do nothing to soothe it, though occasionally she chanced to comb her hands through her hair and stroke along Spark's feathers. The result was always a tremu-lous croon, more felt than heard.

She felt Spark's energy dimming and thinning as each day passed. It wasn't going to last much longer without food. She could save it. All she had to do was agree to become a guild compass-majicar and Spark could be fed. She would never be free—there was no hope for her. Could she not do this thing for Spark?

But Shaye.

So long as she held out, they had to keep trying to find him. But wouldn't they do it anyway? He was one of theirs. They wouldn't let King William have him. They could never allow it.

The questions kept chasing each other round and round, and she didn't know which path to choose. More days passed and Spark grew weaker yet. Finally Fair-lie nipped the end of her finger, her teeth cutting eas-ily through her flesh. The pain was sharp, but hardly unbearable. Blood that was not blood oozed from the tip. It was dark blue-black and thick as syrup. She lifted both hands behind her neck as if stretching and reached under her hair to find Spark. Its mouth fastened on her finger almost instantly, two hands gripping the barrel of her finger. Its sharp teeth gnawed as it licked and sucked. Fairlie stared off into nothingness, knowing the guards were used to her sitting still for long periods. They would not be suspicious.

It was a long time before Spark was satisfied. She let it feed until it stopped on its own. Only then did she lower her arms. She was surprised at the tremor that shook her hands. She looked at the finger where the little spawn had fed. The wound closed swiftly. The tip of her finger was a sickly pink and she could not feel it. She put her head on her knees, feeling slightly dizzy. A churn of anger flared through her. She jerked in surprise. The emotion didn't belong to her. Suddenly there was a creeping under her skin and the sensation of liquid flowing down the inside of her arm. The *sylveth*.

It trickled down through her hand, filling her wounded finger. The unhealthy pink faded again to black, and as it did, Fairlie felt a surrendering, a dying.

"No!" she whispered in horror. "Don't."

~No go home we if die you~

Fairlie frowned. *I'm not dying. And you will survive even if I don't.*

~Die you and captured we~

The accusation in the words was strong. Fairlie grimaced and rubbed her hands over her face. Spark and the *sylveth* were relying on her. How in the black depths had this happened? What would she do when she could not feed Spark anymore? Knowing what she knew of the *sylveth*, that it could speak, that it could feel, how could she even think about making compasses for the king or the guild or anyone else? It was her only trump card—that they needed her to make compasses. And now she didn't know if she could bring herself to play it. Not that she knew how. Just at the moment, she was glad of it.

~Show you, can we~

Shock made Fairlie freeze. "What?" she said loudly.

She heard the stir of her guards.

Why would you? How strange was it that she could speak mind to mind and not find it remotely exceptional?

There was a slight hesitation, and then suddenly Fairlie was spinning away on a maelstrom of sensation.

She felt herself spread out over miles and miles. Currents tugged at her. She slid through depthless waters, felt joyous exuberance as she ribboned through the cold black liquid, caressing deadly knucklebones, coiling around toothy Koreions, dipping down into the blackest depths to tickle the eggs of vescies and vada-eels. She felt the wash of waves slipping up on the sands of Normengas and crashing against the stone walls of the Bites.

It was . . . mesmerizing.

As the sensations rode her, a part of Fairlie realized for the first time just *where* she was. Merstone Island was beyond the tame confines of the Pale where *sylveth* ran wild.

~Home we almost are~

Threading through the words was a dreadful, rapt hope, a hope pinned entirely on Fairlie. The *sylveth* would teach her to make compasses so that at least some of it could go home.

For the first time since Shaye had left her alone, Fairlie wept.

Chapter 24

Shaye awoke, a sense of danger thrilling through him. It brought him instantly alert.

He was not alone.

He opened his eyes. That is, he *tried* to open them, but they were stuck shut. He rolled onto his side, rubbing at them. Thick crustiness glued his lashes together. He scraped the seam of his eyelids, clawing them open. He blinked, his vision blurry. All he could see was a dancing orange light flickering through the room.

He turned onto his back and sat up. The light did not dim. And the floor—it had changed to lush grass. He looked about in wonder. The walls were twined with climbing vines heavy with clusters of purple and black grapes. The ceiling was a rustling canopy of leaves. The small space was redolent with smells of sunlight and summer. He even heard the twitter of birds. At the center of the room was a gnarled oak tree with majestic spreading branches, its squat bole broad and knobby. A small spring gurgled up in a misshapen basin made of silver and obsidian. On top of it danced orange flames. Sitting beside it was a young and beautiful woman.

She sat with crossed legs, her night-colored hair parted in the middle and hanging loose to her waist. She was neither young nor old. Her eyes were green as spring grass, her skin the color of walnuts.

Shaye could only stare. He heard nothing but the

sound of his own breathing. He knew very well who she must be.

"I must apologize," he said hoarsely. "I would greet you properly on my knees, but I am rather unsteady at the moment."

"I am not interested in airs or obeisance from such as yourself," the Kalimei said, tartness lending a snap to her voice.

"And just what *are* you interested in?" he asked, too tired for even basic courtesy.

"You called on Chayos for aid. No majicar has ever done so."

"I apologize if I have offended," Shaye said acerbically, but was cut off by the Kalimei's laughter before he could point out that desperate men *will do* desperate things.

"She is curious. She wishes to know why you who were born of Her, whose cardinal affinities are rooted in Her bones and Her blood, who has turned your face from Her to Meris—she wonders why you would call Her in your time of need." The tartness was sharper.

"Don't you know?" Shaye demanded bitterly. "The Naladei surely knew what was going to happen. She could have protected Fairlie—" He broke off, a mixture of rage and tears burning in his eyes.

"My sister?" Her voice hardened. "What has my sister done?"

"Don't play games," Shaye said accusingly, then started to cough raggedly.

"Tell me."

"She knew they were going to curse Fairlie with *sylveth*. The Naladei said she couldn't stop it, but that's bilge. She could have. She wanted it to happen, and she wanted Fairlie to come out a compass-majicar. That's the only reason she sent the leaf. But she should have given her sanctuary in the Maida."

Silence met his words. The Kalimei's expression did not change, but something altered, something dreadful. Fear uncurled inside Shaye, digging roots deep into his bowels. He was speaking to a priestess of Chayos, not just an ordinary woman. And the Kalimei was angry. More than angry. Enraged.

"Mother Sun—she gave them one of Chayos's own children?" she asked softly, her gentle tone belying the waves of heat he could feel rolling off her.

Shaye didn't think she was talking to him. Her attention was inward as she considered his words. She remained still and unspeaking for several minutes. He only waited, hope flickering alive inside him despite his fear. The Naladei had betrayed Fairlie; maybe the Kalimei would help her.

At last the priestess looked at him again. "I can do nothing for her," she said, dashing Shaye's frail hopes. "She belongs to Hurn now."

"Hurn? I don't understand." Shaye's head reeled. What did the stranger god have to do with this?

"Come. Drink. I will tell you what you need to know." She reached down and a wooden cup appeared in her hand. She dipped it into the flaming water and handed it to Shaye. Cold, clear water filled it. He drank deeply, the cold sending a shaft of aching pain through his chest. Again he coughed. When he had gained control, she filled the cup again and now a heap of grapes, apricots, and starberries sat before him. Slowly he began to eat. With the first taste, his stomach twisted inside out with hunger. He shuddered, shoving fruit into his mouth.

The Kalimei watched him, then began again to speak. "All born on Crosspointe are born of Chayos. But some Meris lays claim to. They hear the song of her blood in the sea and reach out to her. Those who belong solely to her are majicars. Those whom she shares with Braken are Pilots. Both majicars and Pilots completely give themselves up—they turn their back on Chayos and stand in the circle of Meris and Braken. Chayos understands. It is necessary for them to become what they are, and they are necessary for the safety and survival of Crosspointe.

"But many who are cursed by *sylveth* do not turn away

from Chayos. They are half-formed creatures, a melding of Meris's power and Chayos's, with neither claiming them. These belong to Hurn, son of Chayos, secret lover of Meris. These belong to the wild nature of the one you call the stranger god."

"Spawn," Shaye breathed, spearing his hands through his tangled hair. He'd always known he and every other majicar and Pilot were spawn, but it was an academic definition. He was nothing like the creatures that wriggled and swam out of the waves, mindless in their hunger; he was nothing like *real* spawn.

"Yes," the Kalimei said. "But Fairlie is special. There are those few who are true children of Chayos—they carry a fragment of the goddess inside them. They are bound to this land more deeply than the trees or the bones of the mountains. And because of this, when touched by the blood of Meris, they may become compass-majicars. It is difficult for Chayos to part with her children for this purpose, and she does so only with great pain and reluctance. But from time to time it must be done for Crosspointe." She paused, again looking inside, her green eyes hard as winter ice. "But only Chayos can make this gift. To do so without Her blessing is—"

"And do you think I did not have Her blessing?"

Shaye lunged to his feet, spinning around. Standing behind him was the Naladei. She ignored him, staring past him at her sister priestess. Her gaze was measuring, her lips curved with cold anticipation.

"I think you take too much on yourself," was the Kalimei's adamantine reply.

Something crackled between them. Shaye recognized it. It was a bubbling brew of long-standing enmity, driving ambition, and fury. He eased slowly back, stopping only when he bumped against the foliage-covered wall.

"It is as well that your opinion matters little. You matter little."

"Don't I?"

"You do nothing. You are nothing but a weak worm, a poorly chosen vessel for Chayos. But that can be remedied," the Naladei said with soft venom. "Chayos deserves better than you."

Shaye did not see her move. But suddenly light whirled around her like shards of shattered glass. It spun through the air like spinning knives, aimed directly at the Kalimei. The dark priestess laughed, and fire rose to surround her in a flickering shield. The Naladei's shining attack flared and sizzled. Shaye closed his eyes. Heat licked across his skin. When the brilliance passed, he opened his eyes again, his stomach curling in fear.

"You dare to strike out at me?"

"How dare I not? You stand obdurately in my way at every turn. I can no longer allow you to keep poisoning the heart of Crosspointe with your stupidity and blindness. I know what must be done and I will do it, and if that requires choosing a new Kalimei better suited for the task of serving Chayos in a time of war, then I will certainly make that happen."

"You overstep. It is not up to you to choose."

"I am the Voice, Hands, and Heart of Chayos. It is my responsibility." The Naladei spat the words, shaking with purpose, her eyes beginning to glow soft green in the gloom.

"As it is mine," the Kalimei replied, each word a sliver of sharpened ice.

"We shall see."

Again the Naladei struck, this time with lashes of lightning. They coiled through the air, snapping like thunder where the Kalimei had been standing, but she'd disappeared behind a whirling column of oily black smoke. It surrounded her like a mass of seething vipers and the Naladei's majick had no discernible effect. Then suddenly the snakes streamed out and cocooned the Naladei.

The Kalimei ignored her, turning to Shaye. Her cheeks were flushed, her lips tight with rage. "There is not much time before my sister frees herself. You must retrieve Fairlie from wherever they have taken her. Chayos is angry. She will not allow anyone to profit from crossing

Her and using Her child so. Her fury will be dreadful
and Crosspointe will suffer. It may be lessened by re-
trieving Fairlie. Such is my hope."

Shaye stared. Chayos angry? He swallowed jerkily,
his mouth dry as ash. By the depths, such a thing had
happened only once in Crosspointe's history. There had
been earthquakes and drought and blight on every crop.
It had lasted three entire seasons and it had been another twenty or more before Crosspointe recovered.

"But it was the Naladei," he said in a parchment-thin
voice. "She did this. Chayos's own priestess."

"Yes, and my sister will answer to Chayos for her
crime. But she was not alone. It was also King William.
And Hurn's children. These she will not easily forgive."
She turned her head as if listening. "My sister will be free
soon. You must go. But before you do, I have a gift."

She lifted her hand, the palm flat. Shaye's breath hardened in his lungs. She held a silver pyramid—his spell.

"It worked," he said incredulously.

"You have wrought a terrible majick," she said. "I did
not intend to let you keep it, but it will help you. I cannot
feel Fairlie anywhere on Crosspointe. Even my sister
could not hide her from me here. That means that they
could only have taken her to Merstone, and to rescue
her you will have to battle your guild. Will you do that
for her?"

"I would battle the gods themselves," Shaye said
fiercely, even as his gut clenched. The guild would have
taken her into the bowels of Merstone Island. Finding her
would be nearly impossible. Getting her out—he'd need
an army of majicars. He had only himself. He thought of
a dozen plans and discarded them just as quickly.

The Kalimei nodded at his reply as if expecting it, her
mouth softening. "Then you must have weapons. The
first is this." She ran a finger down one edge of the pyramid. "Do you know what you have done?" she asked,
then continued without waiting for him to answer. "This
spell contains the power of six majicars—those who
made the spells on the smother room, and yourself. And

it is very hungry. It will steal majick and hoard it for you. With this, you will be a very powerful majicar indeed. Your guild will want this spell, more perhaps than they want a compass-majicar. It is the answer many have long sought—a way to gain more power. It could destroy the guild, setting majicar against majicar. You—your knowledge of this spell—will be a prize beyond anything. You will be a key to opening up vast secrets of majick."

Shaye could only stare. She was wrong. She had to be. He wasn't capable. . . .

But then hope flickered alive. If she was right, this spell would be the army of majicars he needed to free Fairlie.

"This is not the sort of majick a mortal was meant to possess. But I have no choice. I fear what Chayos will do if Fairlie is not freed."

She paused, then met Shaye's gaze. It felt as if she peeled back his skin and saw every one of his private thoughts. He had no secrets from her. At last she withdrew with a sensation of snakes wriggling through his skin.

"There are gifts that can be given that will lead to terrible conclusions. I hope you are worthy of my trust, for this majick you have made and the knowledge you have learned could unleash such horrors that make all else seem nothing."

She held the pyramid high. Shaye watched it, unable to drag his gaze away. It began to gleam yellow, the light growing brighter and brighter until Shaye was forced to look away or go blind. It was as if she held a sliver of the sun in her hand. Then suddenly he felt a sharp blow to his chest and the light went out. He looked down and instantly his stomach revolted. Her hand was buried in his chest. The light had disappeared because the pyramid spell was inside him. Slowly she withdrew. He felt his flesh give way, felt her hand sliding through the opening. There was no wound, no tear in his clothing. He gasped and fell to his knees, clutching his chest. Searing heat washed through him and then was gone. He panted, feeling an ache near his heart.

"No one will know you have the spell. You cannot lose it. Its power will be forever in your grasp. Use it wisely," the Kalimei said. "My second gift is this advice—do not try to do this alone. Even someone as powerful as you cannot watch all directions at once. You will want help. Take the prince, and the children of Hurn with you. It may go some way toward redeeming what they have done and appeasing Chayos."

He drew back. "Not Ryland. And sure as the holy black depths not that bitch spawn and her majicar partner."

"Do you wish to rescue Fairlie?" The priestess asked, her voice turning to ice. "Will you refuse to use the weapons you have because you don't like what they are? Do you think you have that luxury?"

He glowered at her. He was entirely uncowed by the flash of annoyance that flitted over her face. "I don't need their help," he snapped.

"Perhaps not. But you will not know until it is too late. Will you take that chance?"

"But why would they help? They did this to her."

The Kalimei smiled. It was a dangerous, predatory expression. "They should regret what they have done. If they do not, convince them."

He looked away. It was true. Though he possessed this new majick, he was facing an army of majicars in their stronghold. Ryland had one of the best sword arms around, and the other two—they had majick as well as teeth and claws. As much as he despised them all, the fact was their help could make all the difference—if they could be made to give it.

Shaye rubbed the palm of his hand over his chest. He could feel the spell ready inside him. It pulsed with power and hunger. He nodded. "Very well." He looked up at the priestess, then bowed his head deliberately. "Thank you."

"So you do have manners then," she said acerbically. Then her hand touched his head, stroking his hair. "Do not fail. Much depends on you. In this you belong to Chayos."

"I'll get her back."

"Be careful. My sister will not easily give up her claim to Fairlie. Crosspointe will not be safe."

"Then we'll go somewhere else."

"Chayos protect you. Go now."

He glanced at the Naladei. The horde of snakes had begun to turn translucent. He then turned to follow the Kalimei's gesture. At the base of the great oak was a hole. Dirt steps led away into stygian darkness. He started down without hesitation. Ahead of him a spark of light brightened. Then another farther ahead.

"Do not fail," the Kalimei called after him as he descended. Then, "If ever I may help you, call on me."

Shaye followed the sparks like a trail of bread crumbs. How long had the guild held Fairlie? Even an hour was too long. He knew she'd fight them. They would not kill her, but they wouldn't have to. They had endless methods to coerce the unwilling. They had never yet failed to achieve the cooperation of a compass-majicar. But Fairlie would rather die than give in.

Shaye started to run.

He ran as quickly as the darkness allowed, stumbling on the soft, uneven ground. The sparks of light that guided him danced impatiently. They flittered away, leading him on. His legs ached and his lungs bellowed. The tunnel sloped downward, sometimes dipping in a sharp hill. Finally it occurred to him that he'd left the castle far behind.

He glanced behind and was confounded to find that the tunnel ended just feet away. He grimaced. The Kalimei was making sure he went where she wanted. His gut tightened, jagged shafts of white-hot fury impaling him. He knew exactly where the tunnel would take him.

To Ryland.

He surged forward, his hands digging gouts of dirt from the walls as he thrust himself along. The sooner he got there, the sooner he could put his hands around the bastard's lying throat.

On and on he went, pausing momentarily here and there to brace his hands on his knees and suck deep breaths. Hunger and thirst made his body shake. Still he didn't stop. There was no time for rest. He hardly noticed when the slope of the ground steepened. He climbed, hoping he was nearing the end.

His journey came to an abrupt conclusion against a stone wall. Shaye was boxed in a narrow grave between stone and dirt. Before he could think to do anything, a rectangle of green light coruscated across the surface. Shaye raised a hand and hesitated. As much as he wanted to, he couldn't kill Ryland. It took all Shaye's will to leash his hatred. *Not yet. Not until Fairlie is safe.* Then he would flay the meat from the prince's bones.

Slowly he reached out and stabbed his fingers into the green light. It flared at his touch. Then the green sank into the stone, wavering like sunlight on emerald water. The wall vanished. In its place was a translucent green curtain. On the other side, Shaye could see a well-appointed bedchamber. Beyond was a door leading into a spacious sitting room. Inside it, Shaye could see Ryland. His back was to Shaye. He sat on the edge of a desk as he talked earnestly to someone who was out of sight.

"I don't like this. It's a mistake."

"It's what Father wants. It's what he demands. This is not for you to decide."

Shaye's lip curled as he recognized the voice. Vaughn. Not a traitor after all. Another lie.

He didn't wait to hear more. He pushed through the green curtain. It poured over him like warm sunlight. He smelled the sweet scent of spring grass and wildflowers. It soothed his lungs and filled him with strength.

Then he was on the other side. A quick glance around the bedchamber showed him that Ryland was living there. No doubt he was pretending to be estranged from his father, like Vaughn. Shaye's mouth twisted and his fingers flexed. He strode through to the sitting room, stopping on the threshold with his legs splayed, his jaw thrusting.

"Look what I've found. Rats in the grain. And what pitiful sod are you planning to *bless* with *sylveth* today, Prince Ryland? You've run through your few friends. Who's left for you to bend over and ram your prick into?"

Chapter 25

Ryland had been drunk for more than a sennight. It didn't help. His guilt was as acute now as it had been when he'd ordered Fairlie's transformation. Worse since she'd been taken to Merstone.

He slouched in his chair, sloshing liquor into his glass and gulping it down. He tasted nothing. He didn't even know what he was drinking. He'd not bathed, eaten, or left his apartments for five days—since he'd moved into the Gilded Lily, Sylmont's finest inn.

He'd ignored the regular knocks of Vaughn, maids, and a dozen other visitors. He couldn't stomach seeing anyone.

All he could see was Fairlie. He could hear her begging him for help. Then the uncertainty when she realized he was responsible for holding her captive. He saw the confusion and agony when he told her he was going to curse her with *sylveth*. . . . He saw the fear and desperation when Shaye was poisoned.

Shaye. Ryland's empty hand clenched. Where in the holy black depths was he? He ought to have been battering down Ryland's door. Ryland had been waiting for it. *Why hadn't Shaye come to take justice for Fairlie?*

But he knew why. There was only one thing that would have kept Shaye from coming here to cut out Ryland's heart. He'd been imprisoned. Ryland's father hadn't wanted Shaye to know what was done to Fairlie and he certainly didn't want Shaye running to tell the Majicars' Guild or Nicholas Weverton about it.

Ryland drained his glass and refilled it, emptying the bottle. Without a thought, he threw it, shattering it against the opposite wall. The shards rattled down to join the thick semicircle of glass carpeting the floor.

Ryland closed his eyes. In the darkness, Fairlie's spawn face haunted him. He couldn't seem to remember what she had looked like before. Tears rolled down his cheeks and he opened his eyes again, taking another slug from his glass. He stared straight ahead.

He'd cursed her with *sylveth*.

He'd made himself watch as she transformed. Thank the gods for Shaye. If not for him and that leaf, Fairlie would have been lost forever. He was sure of it. It had been a relief to hear her speak, to know that she knew who she was. She also knew who he was and what he'd done. She hated him. That hurt him in places he didn't know he could hurt. But what had he expected? That she would pat him on the head and say it was all right? How could she? He'd betrayed her in the worst possible way.

She would never forgive him. Not that she'd ever have the chance. She belonged to the majicars now; he'd never see her again.

There was a sudden pounding on his door. He ignored it. Then he heard Vaughn's voice.

"Damn you to the depths, Ryland! I'll break down the door if I have to. You have to stop this nonsense. There's work to be done and you're needed."

Ryland shut his eyes. The game was on again. He swallowed the rest of his drink and stood to go to the door. His head spun, as much from lack of food and sleep as too much drink. Vaughn pounded again. Slowly Ryland keyed the wards and opened the door.

Vaughn filled the doorway, a leather case under his arm. "You look like shit," he said, sympathy softening the worry on his face. "And you stink." He shoved inside, shutting the door with a booted foot. He set his case down and turned to face his brother, hands on his hips as he eyed him from head to foot. "This has to stop.

You're going to kill yourself. Father needs you and so do I. It's time to clean up and get to work."

Ryland stared, his hands hanging loose at his sides. Silent tears rolled down his cheeks. "What have I done?" he whispered. "I'm a fiend."

Vaughn said nothing; he simply wrapped his arms around his brother and pulled him against his chest. Ryland sagged, then began to sob.

He cried until he had no breath. Snot ran from his nose and his eyes were swollen. Vaughn just held him, stroking his back. When at last the storm of weeping eased, Vaughn pushed Ryland away, holding his shoulders.

"You are a prince, and a Rampling, and you have been called upon to serve the crown. We do what we have to, no matter how unpalatable." He punctuated his words with a shake.

"Unpalatable?" Ryland repeated derisively.

Vaughn shrugged. "What word do you want? Awful? Dreadful? Appalling? There are no words that can convey the truth. One serves as well as another."

Ryland nodded. It was true enough.

"I've ordered food. Go bathe and dress."

Ryland obeyed like a child, grateful to have someone directing him. He'd cried himself hollow, but pain and sorrow continued to thrust spears through his soul. He undressed, leaving his filthy clothing in a heap on the floor at the foot of his bed. He ran a bath in the garderobe. The tile was cool and smooth against his feet. Moonlight gleamed through the beveled glass windows. He sank into the blistering hot water, grateful for the pain. He took the rough scrub cloth and smeared soap on it. He rubbed himself hard, like he could grate away his skin and his guilt with it. Half a glass later, he got out and wrapped a towel around his waist. He went into his room and put on clothing, choosing black. It bagged loosely; he'd lost weight. He combed his hair and scraped the bristles from his jaw with a straight razor. Each time he put it to his face to carve away the hair, he thought of pushing just a little harder, just a little lower. It would take little to cut his own throat and put himself out of his misery.

Coward.

He deserved to live with what he'd done. He deserved far worse than that.

He finished shaving and then reluctantly returned to the sitting room. Vaughn had set it to rights and was standing by the window, looking out over Sylmont. He turned when Ryland entered.

"You still look half dead," he said.

"I'll have to work on getting the rest of the way there, then," Ryland said, his glance going to the liquor cabinet. Astonishingly enough there were still a few bottles left.

"Drink isn't going to solve it," Vaughn said dryly. "Trust me. I walked that road myself."

"It doesn't hurt," Ryland answered, but he didn't let himself indulge any further. The alcohol had not helped him forget. He couldn't seem to get drunk enough. Perhaps that was a curse from Chayos, so that he couldn't avoid facing what he'd done.

"Do you want to talk about it?"

Did he? What could he say? "No."

Vaughn nodded as if that was the answer he expected. Before he could say anything else, there was a knock at the door. Ryland went to answer it, letting in four servants carrying steaming trays. They set the food on the table and withdrew, their expressions full of avid curiosity. He locked the door again behind them.

They dined in silence. The food was good and Ryland found himself enjoying the flavors. He'd thought it would all taste like sawdust. He pushed back abruptly, the food in his stomach lurching sourly. He clenched his hands on his knees and stared down at his feet. How could he just sit and eat? What was happening to Fairlie right now? Was she hungry or thirsty? Was she terrified?

Had they hurt her? The questions chewed at him like a herd of Koreion. Except the sea dragons would be more merciful.

"Stop dwelling on it. There's nothing to be done. Eat. You need your strength. Father needs your strength, not to mention your wits," Vaughn said from across the table.

Ryland scowled at his brother, then forced himself to scoot back to the table and eat. Now the food was as tasteless as he could wish for. He ate until his stomach was distended and aching. He thought he would puke.

"Do I need to send for more? Or do you plan to eat the table next?"

"I've got a bellyful, thank you."

Vaughn chuckled and stood, going to sit on a chaise. Ryland followed him, leaning against the edge of the desk. He felt unsettled and uneasy.

"There's news. The Merchants' Commission and Sennet are going forward with their plan—you *do* remember, don't you?"

"Much as I'd like to forget, it's been impossible," Ryland said.

"Tomorrow they will begin the destruction of the grain supplies. The majicars will declare their independence from the crown and will walk through Sylmont, giving aid to anyone who asks without charge. They plan to continue such a practice indefinitely."

"Which will win them a great deal of public support, while making Father and his demands seem ridiculous and unnecessary. Then when the grain discovery is made, the people will turn to the Merchants' Commission and Sennet for help, effectively castrating the crown."

"That sums it up," Vaughn agreed.

"And what is Father doing?"

"I am uncertain."

"So now the question is, what are we to do?"

Vaughn shrugged. "Act like the lapdogs we are supposed to be, exactly as ordered."

Ryland's lips twisted. "I don't like this. It's a mistake."

"It's what Father wants. It's what he demands. This is not for you to decide."

Vaughn dug his fingers through his hair almost violently. He was not as tranquil as he seemed. For that Ryland was grateful. He felt like someone was carving out his innards with a spoon. Before he could speak, before he could think of anything to say, an almost guttural voice yanked him around. In the doorway was a haggard Shaye. And he was very, very angry.

"Look what I've found. Rats in the grain. And what pitiful sod are you planning to *bless* with *sylveth* today, Prince Ryland? You've run through your few friends. Who's left for you to bend over and ram your prick into?"

Chapter 26

Shaye didn't even glance at Vaughn, but he heard the sound of him rising out of his chair and the chime of his sword clearing its sheath. Shaye reached for the spells in his *illidre*, but paused when he realized that through the pyramid lodged in his chest, he could draw on the power of the many wards protecting Ryland's quarters. He smiled and yanked all the majick out of them. There was a flash of rainbow light and a distortion in the air as the majick sucked into the pyramid spell. With a thought, he drew on the reservoir, forming it into a quick, brutal spell. He hurled it at Vaughn. The elder prince flew through the air, smashing against the wall and sliding senselessly to the floor.

Ryland gaped and then rushed to his brother's side. He pulled him into his lap, bending to listen to his chest. Blood ran freely from Vaughn's nose and trickled from the corners of his mouth and ears.

"He's alive," Ryland rasped.

"That's too bad. Maybe I ought to finish him." Shaye glanced at the *sylveth* wall sconce. It was astonishing how comfortable the people of Crosspointe were with worked *sylveth*, when many majicars could return it to its raw form in a matter of moments. He reached up and stroked it lightly. "Or better yet, I could drip a little *sylveth* on his head. What do you think? Could he be your next compass-majicar?"

Ryland looked up. His expression was agonized. He'd

lost weight, and his red-rimmed eyes were sunken and ringed with black bruises. *Good*.

"You wouldn't," Ryland said, but he couldn't hide his terror. He knew Shaye didn't make idle threats.

"Wouldn't I? Why ever not?" Shaye drawled, tasting bile. In his mind's eye he saw Fairlie, saw her body drifting into smoke and then solidifying again. He'd almost lost her. He very well still might. *No*. He couldn't let himself think it. His hand clenched on the sconce.

"Where did you come from? How did you—" Ryland broke off, swallowing hard.

"How did I get out of your father's prison? That is my business. As for where did I come from—I walked through the wall. I am here because as you no doubt already know, Fairlie has been taken to Merstone. We are going to get her back—you, me, and your two friends. So get up off your treacherous ass and let's go before I peel the skin off you and your brother."

Ryland stared a moment as if he hadn't quite heard, then looked back down at the bleeding Vaughn. Shaye wanted to grab him by the neck and shake him. He was half ready to simply go to the Merstone by himself, but the more he thought about it, the more reckless and stupid it seemed. With the pyramid he was strong, but he doubted he was strong enough to take on the guild. His body was still vulnerable to physical attack—a well-placed dagger and he'd be dead.

"I can't leave Vaughn like this. He needs a healing."

"Crack Vaughn," Shaye spat. "He can rot."

"What are you expecting me to do?"

That was a problem. Shaye hadn't had time to think of anything beyond storming Merstone Island. "I'll figure it out on the way."

Ryland shook his head. "Merstone is a fortress. With so few compass-majicars, they'll defend Fairlie with everything they've got. Or they'll kill her to keep us from taking her."

"Don't pretend you actually care what happens to her. Or are you worried about your own precious skin?"

"I care."

"Sure you do. So much that you turned her to spawn."

Ryland was silent. Then he slipped his arms under Vaughn and lunged to his feet. He staggered and carried the unconscious man into the bedchamber and laid him on the bed. Shaye followed him.

Ryland took a cloth from his washstand and dipped it into the water pitcher. He dabbed away the blood on his brother's face, not looking at Shaye. "I can't help you. Crosspointe needs her."

Shaye's fury boiled up and for a moment it burned so bright he couldn't see. He felt power rolling away from him and heard glass shattering. With all his might, he grappled himself under control.

"Help me, or you can watch your brother be cursed by *sylveth*."

"What? You wouldn't—" But by the expression on his face, Ryland knew damned well Shaye would. "He's hurt badly. I can't just leave him."

"Why not? You seem pretty good at abandoning the people you're supposed to care about."

The prince's shoulders stiffened and he bowed his head. "I didn't want to do it. But it was necessary. For Crosspointe."

"For Crosspointe," Shaye repeated. "And so long as it's 'for Crosspointe,' it doesn't matter how unspeakable the act, is that it? The end justifies the means? Even if you destroy your best friend?"

Ryland dashed tears from his cheeks with his left hand, sniffing thickly as he continued to clean Vaughn. "My king ordered it. I had to obey."

"Braken's brass balls. You could have refused. *You* should have."

"If it had to be done, better by me than someone else."

"You could have told me. We could have spirited her away where no one could find her."

Ryland shook his head. "No. I could not betray my father; I could not betray my king."

"But you didn't mind turning on Fairlie." Shaye's loathing was palpable.

"No!" Ryland choked. "I can't tell you—" He stopped, his eyes closing. He rubbed his shaking hands over his face. "I despise myself for what I had to do to her. I deserve to burn for it. But it was necessary. My king ordered it. I could not refuse."

Fury clutched in Shaye's gut, and he lunged forward, snatching Ryland by the collar and smashing his face with his fist. Ryland didn't fight back. He merely stood there. Shaye pulled back to hit him again and then thrust him violently away, stalking to the other side of the room to put distance between them. He needed Ryland; Fairlie needed him. The knowledge burned like acid, but he had no choice.

The prince wiped his mouth with the back of his hand, his lip already puffed and turning purple.

"I deserve that," he said.

"You deserve a whole lot more than that." Shaye ground out. "But now is not the time to pay. We have to get Fairlie. Or I can curse him with *sylveth*, and then I will go up to the castle and do the same to every Rampling I find." It wasn't a threat; it was a vow.

Ryland went even more pale than he already was. "Heal him first. Please."

"Do you really want me to put hands on him?" Shaye asked. He smiled venomously. "Do you think he'll survive?"

Ryland stiffened. "You would kill him?"

Shaye just looked at him.

"Let's go then." Ryland pressed a hand to his brother's forehead, then grabbed his coat from the chair where he'd flung it. Wordlessly he buckled on his sword belt and then donned his cloak. He spared a glance for the fuming Shaye and then strode to the door. Shaye didn't follow. He stared down at Vaughn. Once they got to Merstone, what was to stop Ryland from raising the alarm? Shaye couldn't risk it; he needed a guarantee.

He reached for a dagger on the bureau.

"What are you doing?" Ryland demanded.

"Making sure you don't get any stupid ideas," Shaye said, then plunged the knife into Vaughn's neck, severing his jugular vein. At the same moment, he wrapped a spell around the wounded prince. He stepped back, examining his handiwork. The dagger protruded from Vaughn's flesh, but no blood flowed, nor did he breathe. Instead he lay as still as a waxen figure.

"What have you done?" Ryland shouted, shoving Shaye aside. He reached out to touch his brother, but majick held him back.

"If you do anything to betray me or Fairlie again, I'll release the spell and Vaughn will die. Don't think that I can't. Even from Merstone, I have the power to heal him or kill him. Now let's go. We are running out of time."

"And what happens if you die? If we don't get Fairlie out?"

Shaye shrugged. "He'll die. Chalk it up to the cost of what you did to Fairlie. Come on."

When they both stood in the hallway, Ryland shut the door firmly and brushed his hand at heart-height on the wall to activate the wards. Nothing happened. Ryland tried again.

"Best use a key to lock it. Your wards are gone."

Ryland glanced at him in shock. "How?"

"Bad majick," Shaye said without the slightest smile.

Ryland's brow furrowed, but he said nothing, returning to the room to get the key. Then the two unfriendly companions started for the castle, to fetch the spawn majicars.

The inn was located in Tideswell, just south of the Burn and Salford Terrace and northeast of the city center. The royal docks were a stone's throw away. It was late—past midnight. The Gilded Lily's tavern held only a few sleepy souls and the streets were largely deserted but for a few footspiders in their distinctive green and white uniforms, trotting tiredly along, hauling their fares. Ryland started to lift his hand to hail an empty one. Shaye caught his arm.

"We'll walk. We don't want to be remembered."

Ryland offered no objection and so they walked along the streets together in silence. Shaye concentrated on ideas for rescuing Fairlie from Merstone. He didn't think about what would happen after. It wouldn't matter if he didn't succeed, and that was going to be a nearly impossible task. Though the island of Merstone was not warded—the Chance storms would demolish any wards—the interior fortress of the guild was. The Kalpestrine was a massive complex, carved deep into the bowels of the island. It was more than thirty-six levels from top to bottom. Inside were housed majicars, their workrooms and training rooms, the Sennet chambers, the guildhall, as well as dining rooms, kitchens, servants' quarters, storerooms, washrooms, laundry rooms, wine cellars, and a myriad other rooms necessary for making Merstone habitable. Shaye's primary residence was there, though he kept another in Sylmont that he'd used more and more frequently these last months while he'd helped Fairlie with her sculpture.

The inside of the Kalpestrine was safe from the Chance storms, the mountain's walls protecting it. Some spawn inevitably crawled up onto the island, posing a temporary danger, but for a team of majicars, the creatures were easy enough to collect. The lowest levels of the Kalpestrine were reserved for the compass-majicars. Getting down to them required going through the entire complex, much of it off limits to everyone but the Sennet. There was no way to get there without notice.

As if reading his mind, Ryland asked, "What is your plan?"

His voice was wooden but businesslike, as if he'd realized there was no way to save Vaughn without saving Fairlie first. A life for a life. It would be poetic, except that even if they got Fairlie off Merstone, she would still be spawn; her life would still have been destroyed. Shaye decided to take a page from Ryland's book and concentrate on the rescue. Otherwise he might go insane.

"I can get us inside the Kalpestrine. But it will be difficult to avoid attention. I can cast an illusion on the spawn woman—"

"Nya," Ryland interjected.

"I can create an illusion to disguise Nya, but while majicars are as susceptible to the effects of majick as anyone else, they are also more likely to see through it. Particularly if they maintain protective spells."

"So once inside we can expect to fight?"

"Yes."

"That's suicidal. We'll be cut down in moments."

"We might get farther than you think," Shaye said, thinking of the pyramid spell inside him.

"You should know that the guild and your uncle have been searching for you. They got word you were a prisoner of my father in the castle."

Shaye stopped in his tracks. That wasn't good. So much for entering the Kalpestrine unnoticed. Then a thought wriggled up.

"How did they hear?"

Ryland glanced at Shaye. "I don't know."

He was lying. Not that it mattered how the word had gotten out, only that it had.

But suddenly Shaye found himself whirling on Ryland, gripping his neck with one hand as he shoved him against the wall. "If you do anything to keep me from rescuing Fairlie . . . If you even think about betraying her again, I warn you: I will not only kill you and Vaughn, but I will unleash the bonds of all the *sylveth* in Crosspointe. Then there will be nothing but a land of spawn left for your father or the majicars or the Jutras to care about. Don't make the mistake of thinking I can't do it. I'm stronger than I was. Do you understand?"

Ryland nodded and Shaye dropped his hand, spinning away and striding up the cobbled street. The prince caught up with him, panting heavily.

"There is something that might be useful," he said after a while, his voice hesitant.

"What?"

"Tomorrow the majicars and merchants plan to announce an alliance. They oppose the crown's new service measures and taxes. The guild will go on strike—they will not answer any of their service obligations to the crown. The merchants will announce price hikes on all goods, including a twenty-five percent increase in staple grains, meats, and vegetables. They will say it is because of the new taxes and tariffs and these increases merely offset the costs the crown has forced upon them. In two sennights they plan to destroy all grain stores to increase their leverage. Many majicars will come and perform charity majick for any who ask. I expect it will largely empty Merstone."

Shaye nodded, recalling Brithe's and Maesonril's warning the night of the fete to celebrate Fairlie's sculpture of Queen Naren. "What about Rampling majicars? Where do they fall?"

Ryland lifted one shoulder, looking away as he answered. "I don't know. It's possible some will follow the guild."

"Or will they merely pretend?"

"I don't know. I hope to the gods that Father does."

"Careful. You almost sounded like you were telling the truth there," Shaye drawled. "But you and I both know how good a liar you can be. Nevertheless, the announcement will create the diversion we need."

Ryland nodded. "I do want to help her, you know," he said in a low voice. "I owe her that much."

"You can't pay her what you owe her," Shaye said.

Chapter 27

The walk back to the castle wore on Ryland. He was swiftly out of breath, his body complaining. He'd thought he'd finally lost his mind when Shaye had appeared from nowhere inside his chambers. His nightmares were filled with Shaye and Fairlie. He'd tried to drink himself insensible to the fact that Shaye might remain locked up for the rest of his life. Or that he might be quietly dispatched and his silence guaranteed forever. He'd truly never thought he'd see him again.

Ryland glanced at the other man. Shaye looked nearly as bad as he did. His face was gaunt, his eyes like dark pits. But a crackling energy suffused him.

They'd been uncertain friends since they were children. Born into families that were opposed on nearly every issue, it was a miracle they'd been able to be civil. But Ryland had always liked Shaye's mordant humor and blunt honesty. What bound them together was the same thing that divided them—their birthrights. Each had duties and loyalties to family that took precedence over everything else, including friendships.

Guilt dragged steel hooks through him. He hated what he'd done to Fairlie. He hated that he'd do it again. And worse if he had to. He was his father's hound. And Shaye? Ryland didn't have to ask to know the answer. Shaye had chosen Fairlie. He had not done his duty and warned his uncle and the Majicars' Guild before coming to Ryland. He was intent on rescuing Fairlie. Nothing else mattered to him.

As he looked at Shaye, Ryland couldn't help but wonder if his father had made a terrible mistake. With the transformation of Fairlie, the unique and delicate bridge of friendship between Rampling and Weverton had been destroyed. Such a friendship could have turned into an alliance in time, one that might have proven far more valuable to the crown than a compass-majicar. Nicholas Weverton owned the Merchants' Commission. With his goodwill, much could have been accomplished. Ryland's father could have pushed Fallon to find another candidate to transform, protecting the friendship between Ryland and Shaye. But now things were going to get much uglier. Nicholas Weverton had personal reasons to defy the crown now, and he was known to be rabid when it came to attacks on his family.

Ryland shook his head. None of that mattered now. Only getting Fairlie back and saving Vaughn. A small voice inside him wondered whether his father would agree that saving Vaughn was worth losing a compass-majicar. Ryland quashed the voice violently. He'd ask when Vaughn was safe again.

"When we get her free—what then?" he asked finally, breaking the stony silence.

Shaye snorted. "Why would I tell you that? So that you can try to capture her again?"

"Whatever you think, I don't like knowing she's in the hands of the majicars."

"Even though your father gave her to them?" Shaye narrowed his eyes, thinking. "Or maybe he regrets his decision. He gave Fairlie to the guild because he couldn't force her to make compasses and he thought they could, but now he needs leverage to bend them to his will. Maybe you think you'll get her back for him and he can trade her for their cooperation. If he succeeds, Crosspointe will have gained another compass-majicar and the alliance between the majicars and the merchants will be broken. A clever ruse. But he's not going to get Fairlie back. Remember what will become of Vaughn."

Ryland's lips clamped together. He'd not thought of those things, but he should have. His choice to save Vaughn should be balanced against what his father needed, what Crosspointe needed. But he didn't care. Vaughn was the only thing that mattered to him. He couldn't lose his brother.

"And you say you don't like politics," he murmured mordantly.

"I don't. But I know damned well how the game is played."

They reached the top of Harbottle Hill, following Glamley Street up toward the castle. It would be easy enough to get inside. The main gates had closed only once in four hundred years, and that was when the Jutras had landed their ship on Crosspointe.

Just out of sight of the gates, Shaye pulled Ryland off the road beneath the trees. He glanced around to be sure they were alone, then put his hand on Ryland's head.

"This will feel more than a bit uncomfortable, I hope. From this point on, you will be able to speak to no one but me. I can't have you alerting anyone of our presence."

Ryland felt the spell wrap around him like wet rags. It was smothering. He struggled against it, but it only clung tighter.

"Do fight. It only makes it harder on you and so much more enjoyable for me," Shaye said.

"Knob off," Ryland muttered.

He made himself stand still as the spell closed tighter. It hardened. He felt as if he was encased in stone. He lifted his hand. It felt heavy but looked just the same as always. He looked at Shaye, his question dying in his mouth. In Shaye's place was a short, paunchy man dressed in baggy brown trousers with muddy cuffs, a brown vest stained with food and ink and topped by a rusty black frock coat decorated with frayed embroidery.

His shoes were high heeled with tarnished buckles—one hanging loosely to the side. His face was rosy, his pate covered with a slouched hat. Muddy blond hair hung in greasy strings about his round, florid face. When he spoke, Shaye's voice emerged.

"You look like you are going to faint. Am I such a fright, then? Trust me, you're no vision of beauty."

"Who are we supposed to be, coming in so late?"

"Guests from Dagfrith. We are consulting the royal records over disputed timber rights. We've been out enjoying a few drinks and some light skirts."

He gestured for Ryland to precede him onto the road, reaching for the prince's arm and slinging it over his neck.

"Remember, they can't hear you. You should look as if you are so pissed you can't see straight. Lean on me. Let yourself drag."

Ryland did as he was told, slumping against Shaye, letting his head dangle and shuffling his feet. Shaye clamped his arm around Ryland's waist.

"One more thing," Shaye said against his ear.

A sharp pain speared along Ryland's neck just above his collarbone. He felt a trickle of blood and then the chill of healing majick closing the wound.

"That's a shard of *sylveth*. If you do anything to call attention to us, if you do anything to keep me from rescuing Fairlie, I'll not only let Vaughn die, I'll curse you too. So choose your path carefully."

He started walking and Ryland shuffled along beside him. Horror spread through him on slow, chill currents. His fingers itched to touch his neck, to feel the hardness lumping under his skin. His stomach twisted and his mouth filled with bile. He swallowed the bitterness down, but he could not quell his fear. *It served him right.*

As Shaye predicted, there was nearly no interest in the two men as they passed through the gates. Ryland noted to himself that he would have to report that. The Jutras had skilled majicars. They could no doubt cast an illusion spell as easily as Shaye and walk right into the castle unchallenged. His father was right. Even after the Jutras attack, the people of Crosspointe were still complacent; they still believed they were safe and always would be. It appeared his father and the Crown Shields might be the worst offenders.

Once inside the castle walls, Ryland led the way through the gardens and park until he came to the entrance he wanted on the western side. It was locked, but Shaye easily opened it with majick.

"You didn't used to be able to do that. Or destroy powerful wards," Ryland noted, more than a little curious.

"You didn't used to turn your friends into spawn. Things apparently change," Shaye said coldly.

For the first time it occurred to Ryland to wonder just *how* Shaye had escaped. He'd been in a smother room, of course—it was the only place to imprison majicars where they could not use their majick. Asking was a fool's errand, but he did it anyway.

"How did you escape?"

"With difficulty" was Shaye's unhelpful response.

He had to have had help. There was no way to simply walk out—the interior of the smother rooms lacked door handles or windows, and majick simply didn't function inside. The only way in or out was for someone outside to open the door.

"How long before someone knows you're gone?"

"Long enough, I hope."

Ryland had to be content with that.

The door they entered led into a vestibule filled with couches and an array of marble sculptures and opulent oil paintings. Ryland pointed to a small door hidden in a curtained corner.

"Let's take the servants' passage."

The door was not warded and opened easily. The passage was narrow, the walls and floor paneled with rough-hewn pine. *Sylveth* sconces every forty feet dimly lit the way. A smooth streak was worn down the middle of the floor from regular use.

There were no servants wandering about and they made quick time. Ryland pulled Shaye to a stop just before they reached the corridor that ran behind Fallon and Nya's suite of rooms.

"They are guarded," he said in a low whisper, before remembering that the illusion spell made it impossible for the Crown Shields in the passage to hear him.

Shaye nodded, rubbing his fingers lightly over his chest. It was a habit of his to stroke his *illidre* when he thought. But now Ryland realized that Shaye no longer wore it outside his clothing. It was hidden beneath. Why?

"Wait here," Shaye said, then stepped around the corner.

Ryland did as told for several grains, then pressed himself close to the wall and inched forward until he could peer around the corner.

Shaye ambled along, muttering as he curved this way and that as if too drunk to walk a straight line. The four Crown Shields standing in mirrored pairs around the door stiffened at his approach, and two stepped in front of him to block his passage.

"Who are you?" one demanded sharply.

Shaye stumbled to a surprised halt, scratching his paunchy belly with both hands.

"Name's Figg," he declared boomingly. "Charles Norman Figg from Dagfrith."

"You don't belong here. This is a servants' hallway."

Shaye turned about, making a show of looking around. "I'll be damned to the depths! Where am I?"

He completed his rotation, but before the irritated guards could answer, he brought up his hands flat on either side of himself and pushed gently at the air. Instantly the four guards crumpled to the ground.

Ryland stared and then came around the corner. A quick scan of the three men and one woman showed that they still breathed. He gave a quiet sigh of relief.

"Impressive. Had I known you could do that so easily, I would have convinced you to try it out on some rather boring dignitaries," he said, his mouth dry. Shaye had grown much, much stronger since he'd been inside the smother room. How was that possible? "How long before they wake?"

"A glass or more," Shaye said curtly.

Then he put his hand on Ryland's head. The prince felt the illusion spell loosening and spinning away. For a moment he stood in the eye of a majickal whirlwind. He rolled his shoulders and took a deep breath, watching Shaye's disguise melt away as well.

The lean majicar put his bony fingers over the door. There was a *bending* in the air and a flash of crimson light that billowed outward and then faded, blotching Ryland's vision. The air pulled out of his lungs and he felt a tugging at his insides. Then the sensation vanished with the light. Without a word or a knock, Shaye opened the door and walked inside. Stunned at the show of power, Ryland followed close on his heels.

Chapter 28

Shaye felt the majick from the wards flow into him, filling him with crimson energy. It felt glorious, like standing in the halo of the sun. But it knuckled hard at his insides, swelling and twisting. The majick soaked into his muscle and bone and erupted like a wildfire in his blood. It was nearly too much for him to hold. It wanted release and was going to burn him to a cinder to escape. He didn't understand. He'd made the pyramid spell to hoard energy. Why wasn't it working? He didn't have time to consider it. Instead he reached into his *illidre* and fed some of the majickal overflow into a shield spell. It hardened instantly around him.

For a fraction of an instant he could only marvel at the strength of the spell. And not just that one—he should have had to be in constant physical contact with Ryland to maintain the illusion spell. He had become a far stronger majicar than he had ever been before.

Casting the spell took the edge off the majick inside him so that it began to settle enough to allow him to hold it without splintering apart. But he didn't know what would happen if he had to take more in.

Shaye stopped just inside the room, Ryland just behind. They were in a salon decorated in pale teal and cream. Priceless artwork covered the walls and occupied every shelf and niche. The small space was crowded with furniture. The entire room seemed to be evidence of someone in the castle looking to put to use all the bits and oddments that had been collecting dust in the basement storerooms.

A set of double doors on the left indicated the entrance to the main sitting room. An archway on the right led into the rest of the suite. From that side came the noise of a loud argument.

"Do you mean to go to his bed then? Do you think it will win you his favor? To him you are merely an exotic curiosity, an animal he can ride to vent his lusts."

Ryland and Shaye exchanged a startled look.

"If I went to his bed, the concern would be mine," came a rich feminine voice. It was sharp with anger. "But you forget I have a husband and I remain faithful to him."

"Then why isn't he here with you? The king wants you and he means to have you. Do you think you can stop him?" the jealous masculine voice demanded.

At the mention of his father, Ryland jerked, his mouth dropping open, hard spots of red rising in his cheeks. Shaye couldn't suppress his bitter grin at his former friend's discomfort.

"Fallon, do not forget yourself. I am Warden and Speaker. You step over the line."

There was a snarl in the words, like a mountain lion. It raised the hair on Shaye's arms, despite himself.

"I am responsible for your safety!" Fallon insisted. "You cannot trust him. He is treacherous. He could lock you in one of his prison rooms and do whatever he wanted to you. I would not be able to find you."

"*I* am Warden. I will keep myself safe." Her voice had gone quiet and flat.

"And if you can't? To him you are nothing but spawn. If he will force his own people to be transformed, you can be certain he will have no mercy on you."

Shaye didn't wait to hear her response but strode forward through the archway. On the other side was a larger room with a formal dining alcove on the right and an uncomfortable-looking sitting area on the left. The spawn woman—Nya—sat in one of the window seats.

For the first time, Shaye got a really good look at her and knew well enough why the king was interested in her. She exuded exotic sensuality. She wore a green silk blouse and loose trousers, but every curve of her body, every supple movement of her limbs, every ripple of her fur, each and all invited petting and stroking. An unwilling hunger stirred in the pit of Shaye's stomach. He brutally quelled it, disgust at himself churning in his chest. He wanted Fairlie—*only* Fairlie. How could this bitch raise lust in him? He wondered if it was majick that made her so desirable or some attraction peculiar to her nature. No doubt Ryland would be relieved to learn his father's lust was unnatural. Shaye didn't intend to enlighten him.

Nya's companion was pacing uneasily along the bank of windows, his four arms raised as if he wanted to hit something, his head lowered and tilted, like a bull about to charge. He pivoted and began marching purposefully back toward his companion.

"Am I interrupting anything important?" Shaye drawled, stopping the spawn majicar in his tracks.

Fallon whirled even as Nya rolled into a crouch, ready to spring.

"How did you get in here?" Fallon demanded, his vertical yellow eyes narrowing to slits.

"The servants' entrance," Shaye said mildly as he gestured dismissively.

"Impossible. I warded it." Fallon's wide, lipless mouth was expressive and his serrated teeth chopped through the words.

"I broke them."

That caught the other majicar up short. He stiffened and glanced quickly at Nya before stepping between her and Shaye.

"What do you want?"

"You two are going to help me retrieve Fairlie from Merstone Island."

Fallon's mouth curved in a vicious smile. Then he hit Shaye's shields with a bolt of majick. The force drove

Shaye back a step, but the shields diverted the majick harmlessly around him, and then the pyramid spell absorbed it. Shaye staggered from the sudden influx. He had to get rid of it quickly. He reached into his *illidre* and meshed forms together in a simple spell. He thrust it out at Fallon. The other majicar was swept up and slammed against the wall. He hung a foot off the ground. His eyes widened as he struggled to breathe.

"Stop this," Nya said. She stood up and crossed the room to stand in front of Shaye.

Her closeness stoked the heat of hunger and Shaye snarled at her and stepped back.

"If you can control that, you should. Or I'll do it for you," Shaye grated.

She only eased closer. She reached out and gripped his hand—his shields could prevent only majick attacks. He started to jerk away, but then went still. There was a prickling along the outer edges of his mind, then a cool sliding as something penetrated. It circled curiously and then wriggled down deep into the core of his thoughts. It wandered through his memories and nosed through dark doors and down bleak corridors.

Shaye tried to yank himself away, but her grip was tenacious, and now he felt a numbing as she touched something inside him. He could no longer move. He still held Fallon against the wall, but it was growing harder to maintain the spell.

Do you understand? I am Speaker. Let Fallon go.

Her voice sounded inside Shaye's skull. It was intimate in a way that did more to fan Shaye's fury than anything else she could have done. He fought the touch of her mind. Instinctively he reached for the power stored inside the pyramid spell. He drew on it recklessly. He focused it, turning it into a spear. He drove it at her with all his might.

He felt a tearing. She screamed as she flew back to smash into a high-backed couch. The force of the majickal blow sent her somersaulting over the back of it.

Fallon made an inarticulate gurgling sound of fury or fear as he strained against his bonds.

Shaye dropped to his knees, panting. He felt like someone had stirred his brain with a dagger. His stomach heaved.

"What in the holy black depths just happened?" Ryland demanded, one hand on Shaye's shoulder.

Shaye shook him off, clambering jerkily to his feet. He leaned his hands on his knees as the room spun around him. His chest throbbed with the release of the majick from the pyramid spell. He sucked in a breath and straightened.

He walked around the back of the couch, Ryland close on his heels. Nya had sat up and was clutching her head in her hands, her forehead bent to her knees. After a glance at Shaye, Ryland knelt beside her.

"Are you all right?"

She made a sound that could have been a laugh and looked up. Her eyes were narrowed and blood trickled from her nose. She gazed at Shaye, who stood over her with his arms crossed, his legs splayed. It was all he could do not to back away from her.

"I have been surprised here," she murmured, letting Ryland help her to her feet. Her hand lingered on his arm a moment as she balanced, and then she eased away into a chair. There was a cloudiness to her eyes that had not been there before. Shaye didn't know if he should be glad of it or not—he needed her and Fallon to rescue Fairlie. But he sure as the black depths didn't need her in his head.

"What happened?" Ryland demanded.

"I Spoke in Shaye's mind," she said breathlessly. "He did not care well for it."

She knew his name. Suddenly he needed distance. He put the couch and a low table between them. It wasn't enough. He still felt that disturbing lust. He was disgusted with himself.

He turned back to Nya and found her watching him, her head resting weakly against the back of her chair.

"You have more strength in you than I believed," she said ruefully.

He nodded, but said nothing. His anger and resentment for what she and her companion had done to Fairlie were grappling with his need for their help. He was choking on it. And mixing into all of it was this tawdry desire for a creature he'd rather kill than bed. And yet his body was telling him to touch her, to lick her, to stroke her fur and make her purr.

"I cannot stop it," she said as if she was in his mind again. "I don't know why the attraction started. It began several sennights passing."

She sounded not just honest, but worried and annoyed. It was that which convinced Shaye she was speaking the truth. He nodded. It helped to know she wasn't trying to manipulate him. He glanced at Ryland, who now looked half green and was beginning to make his own retreat.

"Every day it grows stronger." Her voice fell and she looked away. The laces at her throat had pulled loose, and she drew her blouse back up on her shoulder and tied the neck securely. "I do not understand," she muttered. Then she collected herself. "You have come here for help for your Fairlie." She glanced to where Fallon continued to hang helpless against the wall, then back at Shaye. "Much more strength," she murmured, staring speculatively.

Shaye didn't look away, letting the pull of her wash around him and away. Now that he knew it was majick, it was easier to ignore.

"Let Fallon be released, please," she asked, rubbing the sides of her head with taloned fingers. Shaye's eyes narrowed as he considered her request. His shields were gone. He'd used the power to break her hold on him. Still, any majickal attack Fallon made on him could be sapped of its energy and turned back on him. It was a risk, if Shaye was too slow or if Fallon used brute strength. But if he wanted their cooperation, he had to bend a little.

"Very well."

He pulled the spell apart, letting the remnants of the

majick flow back into him. Fallon crashed to the floor, choking and gagging as he struggled to breathe. Shaye looked back at Nya.

"Will you help me?"

She nodded. "I must. I told Fairlie I would find you and then help her escape, but then she was taken away and I could find neither of you. So whatever it requires, I will do."

"No!" Fallon said raggedly, and then began coughing again.

"There is no choice. I am Warden. She is mine. I must. You may choose not."

"Warden? What does that mean? When did you see her?" Shaye demanded. His anger was kindling hotter again. There was something going on here that he needed to understand.

"I am guardian for my people on the Root. We who are all changelings—Kin. I must protect them. Fairlie is mine. I went to her days ago. She was angry with me, even as you are. But she accepted my help—she had no other choice."

Fury flared so hot in Shaye that he couldn't speak. He clenched his hands, his entire body shaking with the force of it. "You *changed* her. She would not be *yours*, as you call her, if not for you."

"Yes," Nya agreed. "Before she was Kin, I was not bound. Now I am."

"You cracking bitch!" Shaye spat.

Fallon made a warning sound and leaped to his feet. Nya raised a quelling hand.

"No, Fallon. He can have this right. He is Kin also. Though he belongs to Meris."

"I am nothing like you."

She tipped her head, her hands falling into her lap. "No?"

"I don't turn people into spawn against their will. You're bilge scum." But he would do just that. He'd meant every threat he'd made to Ryland. There was nothing at all he wouldn't do for Fairlie.

Nya touched the bracelet on her wrist, slowly spinning it. "Much that is required of me does not bring happiness."

"Balls," Shaye retorted.

"We are promised a Pale on the Root. It is worth more than your woman," Fallon declared, having regained his feet.

"Why her? How did you know to pick her? Why didn't you pick someone else?"

Nya gave a bare shrug. "Fallon knows what majick Kin will have once changed. He sees who will be compass-majicar, majicar, or Pilot. Sometimes he can tell even more."

Shaye could only stare at Fallon, who had come to stand beside Nya's chair. The spawn majicar's skin had an ashen quality to it. His fury was palpable.

"Is that true?" Shaye asked, feeling as if he'd been struck. Someone like that—the guild would do a great deal more than kill to have someone with that talent in its control. And so would the king, for that matter. Shaye wondered that there was not an entire army of Crown Shields standing guard over Fallon. He looked back at Nya. "So—you help get Fairlie out of Merstone, then what? You take her back to the Root with you?"

"Where else can she go?"

That was a question Shaye had no answer to. He had no idea where he and Fairlie would go. They could not stay in Crosspointe. He couldn't even trust his uncle Nicholas—the temptation of having his own compass-majicar would be too great.

"You're lucky she didn't rip your throat out," Shaye said.

"Risk is necessary."

"You risk too much," Fallon said harshly.

She ignored him, concentrating on Shaye. "There are no other Speakers. I guide lost ones back to what is real. I help new Kin keep their minds."

"That's what you were trying to do with Fairlie. But

she did something to you—she hurt you, pushed you out, didn't she?"

Ryland stepped forward as if eager for the answer. Shaye had nearly forgotten he was there.

"Yes. She is not an ordinary Kin. It's possible that compass majick is mind majick also. I was almost lost."

"I guess you won't try that twice with her," Shaye said, pride for Fairlie swelling in his voice.

"No," she said with a slight tip of her head. She rubbed a fist between her breasts as if trying to ease a knot. "Nor with you."

"Good. Then maybe we should get to business. We have to go get Fairlie." And pray that the guild had not harmed her. But she was valuable and the guild would be both careful and patient. He told himself this and knew it was true, but all the same, he couldn't help but fear what they might already have done to her. "We have to go now while it's dark and before anyone knows I've escaped. We'll land on Merstone and wait until morning when most of the majicars will cross the strait to Sylmont. Then we'll go inside."

"And can you unlock the wards where they will keep her? I do not think you are so powerful. It is death to go, for you and for us," Fallon said.

Shaye's mouth twisted. "I can handle the wards." He spoke confidently, though doubt spread thorny roots through him. The pyramid spell wasn't working properly. He'd quickly be overwhelmed, even killed, if he wasn't careful. He doubted he could afford to be careful. He was going to have to try to fix it, or figure out a way to release the majick as it boiled over.

"And the majicars? They will not simply let us take her."

"We'll do our best to sneak in. We'll use illusion, and when that fails, we'll fight."

"That is not a plan," Fallon said disparagingly. "That is stupidity. We will die."

"We might," Shaye agreed. "But she's one of yours,

right? You have to try, don't you?" He looked at Nya, who nodded.

"Yes. If you will wait, I will prepare."

"What about the king and your deal with him?" Shaye asked as she stood.

For the first time she smiled. It was a dangerous expression, reminding Shaye of a coiled cobra. "He needs us. He will forgive, or he will not get what he wants. Time is his enemy. We need a Root, but we will survive without if necessary." With that, she withdrew, followed by a fuming Fallon.

Shaye blew out a quiet breath. One step closer to getting Fairlie back. Fallon was right. It was a stupid, reckless plan, if it could even be called that. More like a wishful prayer. But he could do no better. And brass balls had won more than one war.

Ryland went to a window and lifted the curtain with one finger. "We don't have much time. It will be dawn within a few glasses."

"It will be enough."

His former friend turned, sitting in the window seat. He rubbed the back of his hand across his mouth. "We may not get a chance to talk again if this goes badly."

"Then there is a silver lining," Shaye said, slumping in a chair. He was tired. The majick had sapped his strength and suddenly he felt lethargic.

"I just wanted to say, in case, I *am* sorry."

"Keep it," Shaye snapped. "It's too late and you'd do it again."

Ryland nodded. "Yes. But I truly believed then and I still believe it will save Crosspointe. And Shaye, Crosspointe does need saving. *Someone* has to make compasses."

Shaye tipped his head back, staring up at the ceiling. "Gods rescue me from fanatics and fools." He looked at Ryland. "You are both. And worse, you are a traitor and a bastard without any honor. You had better pray we get Fairlie out safely. Remember Vaughn, and remember that *sylveth* in your neck. If I die, Vaughn's dead too. Betray me and I'll make you spawn."

"And if we do get out alive?" Ryland asked. "Will you keep your word?"

"I'll heal Vaughn. And I won't transform you. And then maybe, just maybe, if you're really helpful, I'll give you a head start before I put my dagger through your throat."

Chapter 29

William jerked awake to the desperate howling of the wind and the angry rattling of sleet pebbling against his shutters. Niall was shaking his shoulder.

"Sire, I have news."

William sat up, swinging his legs over the side of his bed and running his fingers through his thinning hair. "What is it?"

Niall looked grave, his thin lips pinched together. He didn't speak right away but knotted his hands together in agitation. William frowned.

"Out with it. It can't be that bad." But of course it could be. His body clenched.

"I had George send two of his people to check on Prince Ryland. They found Prince Vaughn in his quarters, a knife in his neck. He is not dead; a spell keeps him from bleeding to death. But it also prevents anyone from healing him. Of Prince Ryland there was no sign. No one saw him leave."

"Has a majicar seen Vaughn? Can he speak?" William kept his voice steady with effort, though his entire body was seized with black fear, the kind he'd not felt since the Jutras had invaded and his wife, Naren, had fallen insensible. He had watched her die, unable to help her. He would not let that happen to his sons.

"Prince Vaughn is not awake. Hedriod was sent for, but he hasn't the means to break the spell. It is very powerful."

"Send for more family majicars," William ordered. What one could not do, perhaps several could.

"There is something else, sire."

"What?"

"The smother room doors have opened. It has ... changed. Young Shaye was not inside."

"Changed? Where did he go? How did he get out?"

"We do not know by what means he left. The room is now ... Perhaps it is best that you see for yourself."

William looked sharply at his steward. Suddenly it all came together. "Where would Shaye take Ryland?" he asked, his mind racing over the dreadful possibilities. For it had to be Shaye. But how had he escaped? He pushed the question from his mind. It didn't matter right now. Ryland did. Ordinarily Shaye was a darkly brooding man and vicious with his tongue, though not particularly given to physical violence. But after being poisoned and being forced to watch Fairlie's transformation, and then being imprisoned in a smother room, he was likely insane with rage and hungry for revenge. If he'd taken Ryland, it wouldn't be long before he went after Nya and Fallon.

"Send a squad of Crown Shields to Nya and Fallon," he ordered harshly. "Now."

Niall stiffened a bare second, and then he nodded and withdrew. Once alone, William covered his face with his hands. "By the gods," he whispered.

William thrust to his feet. He was dressed and pacing when Niall returned. His steward's expression was uneasy.

"Majicar Fallon and Lady Nya are not in their quarters," he reported. "The Crown Shields in the servants' passage were overcome with majick. They were attacked by two men, neither of whom fit the description of Shaye Weverton. I have sent for Princess Margaret and Master Plentop. They will see to the investigation."

William seethed. Shaye must have been using an illusion spell. Was the second man Ryland? He would not have accompanied Shaye willingly, but with Vaughn ly-

ing on his bed with a knife in his throat, Ryland would
do nearly anything to save him. But now where would
they go? Would Shaye send demands—try to trade his
hostages for Fairlie? William had to get Nya and Fallon back, but he was fettered by secrecy. He could make
no public search without betraying what they were and
what he'd been doing.

"Tell George and Margaret that I want everyone they
can spare on this. Everyone, do you understand? Whatever it takes, Nya and Fallon must be recovered."

"And Prince Ryland, of course," Niall added with
raised brows.

The hand gripping William's heart twitched, sending
shafts of pain down his arms and up his neck. He couldn't
let his emotions rule him. Of the three, Ryland was most
expendable. His jaw hardened. "You have your orders.
Go now. I will meet you at the smother room when you
are finished. Tell them I want a report in one glass."

His steward gave a small bow. "As you wish, sire."
Then once again he departed, silent as a shadow and
just as cold.

After Niall left, William didn't move for a long moment. He would never admit it out loud, but he also
feared what might happen to Nya. It was absurd, the way
he was pursuing her. But she made him feel alive with
the heat and green strength of youth. And now Shaye
Weverton had taken her away from him.

Grimly he collected himself, donning his robes and
settling his crown on his head. He stopped before the
outer door of his quarters, schooling his expression.
He glanced at the windows. It was just becoming light.
He had precious little time before the merchants and
majicars made their announcement. It very well could
be the first feint in a civil war. But there was nothing
to be done now. He'd made all the preparations that he
could. All there was to do was wait. And go see what
Niall had been unable to tell him.

He deactivated the wards and swung the doors wide.
An alert Lofton waited outside as usual. The number of

Crown Shields guarding the royal residence had tripled. Guards lined the outer gallery, each alternately carrying a crossbow or a halberd. Lofton nodded when William announced his destination, then called his squad to formation and escorted William down into the bowels of the castle where the smother rooms were housed.

There were ten smother rooms total, each threaded like a bead along a long corridor that looped back around on itself, with yards of stone and dirt separating each room. There was only one entrance to the level. It was guarded by four Crown Shields. Two stood watch at the entrance while the other two patrolled the circular corridor.

When William arrived, all four stood at the entrance, each looking tense. The door into the smother room passage was shut and barred as if they feared that something might escape. William frowned.

As he approached, they stood sharply at attention.

"Open it up," Lofton ordered.

They hesitated, then obeyed. Just as they opened the door, Niall arrived. He bent close to William's ear, speaking quietly.

"Sire—I suggest leaving your escort out here."

William glanced at him in surprise and then nodded. "Lofton, leave your people outside," he ordered, knowing that Lofton would not be left behind.

The passage inside was dimly lit by *sylveth* sconces along the wall. A brighter glow emanated from around the curve of the loop. William glanced in surprise at Niall, who only nodded.

"That way, sire."

William followed after Lofton. They passed three silver-inlaid knackerstone doors. There was no one being held behind any of them. Shaye had been the only occupant of the loop.

A prickling ran down William's spine as the scent of flowers and green meadows eroded the musty, damp smell of stone and dirt.

"What is this?" he asked, brows drawing together.

Niall only shook his head wordlessly, then pointed.
"There."

William stopped dead, his mouth falling open. All
along the walls and ceiling, vines crawled along the
stone. Grapes and berries hung heavy and ripe from the
greenery. Thick roots roped across the floor, prying up
the flagstone and burrowing into the dirt. The only areas that remained free of the greenery were the smother
room doors.

"It began two glasses ago," Niall said, sounding shaken.
"It has expanded considerably since it was reported
to me."

Even as they watched, the roots on the floor rippled
and lengthened, stretching farther. There was a cracking
sound and a flagstone pushed upward as the tip of a root
worked its way beneath it.

"You need to see the smother room itself," Niall said.

Together they picked their way through the writh-
ing greenery. Lofton put a hand under William's arm to
steady him over the broken, uncertain footing. William
wanted to shake him off, but it would be more embar-
rassing to fall flat on his back.

An impossible bright green glow illuminated the thick
foliage ahead and cast a heat like summer. There was a
rustling and a sound like birds twittering. Impossible.
Not here. Not buried twenty yards in dirt. But then William caught a glimpse of brown and white wings and a
patch of scarlet. It looked like a royal finch.

They pushed beneath low-hanging limbs and tall grass
emerging outside Shaye's smother room. Where the
room had been was now an emerald sanctuary. Thick
trees circled the perimeter and vines twined through
them, heavy with fruit. The only ceiling was a canopy of
leaves. Shining through them were golden beams of sunlight that dappled a carpet of thick grass sprinkled with
colorful wildflowers. At the center of the space was an
ancient oak tree. Its squat red-brown bole was gnarled
and knotted. Branches larger than William could close
his arms around jutted outward in every direction like

yardarms on a ship. At its foot, a silvery spring bubbled merrily into a shallow basin made of silver and obsidian. Flames flickered on its surface. William stared at it. The basin was all that remained from the smother room. He looked up.

"This is the work of Chayos," he murmured in astonishment. There could be no doubt of it.

Slowly he stepped inside. Warmth closed around him and a breeze cooled the sweat on his face. He walked around the tiny glade, turning in circles as he gazed about himself in awe.

He returned to the spring. Majicars avoided anything to do with Chayos. They worshipped only Meris. What did it mean that Chayos had made this place—here where he had imprisoned Shaye—a sacred place?

His chest hollowed as doubt crept inside him. Was it a message? Had he been wrong to transform Fairlie? Wrong to imprison Fairlie? Wrong to sell compasses?

He glanced around again.

No.

Whatever the message was, if he'd been so wrong, Chayos would never have offered such a blessing as this. This was a benison, not a chastisement.

He turned to the tree and knelt on one knee, bowing his head. "Chayos, give me guidance. What is it you mean for me to do?"

As usual, there was no answer. He'd never had an answer from the goddess his entire life, though he knew she appeared to many through the medium of her two priestesses.

And if she did answer? He might not like what she had to say. He shook his head and slowly stood, feeling every season of his age.

"Thank you," he said to the greenery. "It is a wondrous place and I thank you for your blessing on this castle and Crosspointe. I will endeavor to be worthy of it."

With that, he retreated to where Lofton and Niall waited. Both remained uneasy. William reached up and picked a heavy cluster of purple grapes. He ate one, sweetness bursting in his mouth. Suddenly he felt a rush of strength and warmth. In a moment, all his aches and pains were gone, as was the headache that had been throbbing at the base of his neck. He offered one to Lofton and one to Niall.

"Blessing of Chayos on you both," he said.

They put the purple fruit in their mouths and blinked in surprise and awe at the effect. William glanced back at the grotto, his gaze lingering on the silver and obsidian basin. Then he turned and the three returned to where they'd entered the smother room loop.

William glanced at the unsettled Crown Shields, then held up the cluster of grapes, an idea striking him. The merchants and the majicars thought that they'd have the biggest news of the day. They thought they'd win the hearts and minds of Crosspointe with fear and bribery. But thank Chayos, he now had a more powerful weapon than they could ever expect. One that would sweep the populace to his side.

"Today Chayos has blessed Crosspointe and Rampling rule." His voice rang down the narrow confines of the corridor. "She has given us a sanctuary inside the castle so that we will never be hungry or thirsty, so that our enemies will ever know She holds us close in Her embrace. She has raised Her golden hands and laid them on my head so that you all may know She has chosen me above all others to lead Crosspointe. Soon storm winds will blow and many may doubt, but She who knows and sees all tells you today that She believes I will lead Crosspointe through the darkness to the light."

He began to pick grapes from the cluster and handed one to each of the guards as he walked down through them.

"Eat now of Her bounty. Go inside and see what She has wrought. Tell everyone you know what has happened here. Let anyone who wishes to come and offer thanks for Her blessing. Have no fear. Chayos is watching over us."

His words had exactly the effect he was hoping for.

The nervousness turned to wonder and beatific joy. The Crown Shields ate their grapes and then began to crowd inside.

William looked at Niall. "Arrange to have the rest of the smother room doors covered to hide what they are. No need to make it public that we might keep majicar prisoners here. Have it done right away."

"Yes, sire."

William started to walk up the corridor, but found Lofton blocking the way.

"A moment, sire, if you will. Until your escort returns."

"And if I won't?"

Lofton did not look away from William's scowl, only crossing his arms over his chest and jutting his chin resolutely. William ignored him, turning instead to Niall.

"Be sure to send word to the papers so that the news will be in the afternoon editions," he said. "And declare the day a holiday. Also, let us plan a feast for a sennight hence. We'll hold it on the castle grounds and invite anyone who wishes to attend."

"It will be done, sire," Niall said.

"One more thing," he said. But before he could speak another word, sharp twangs of multiple crossbow strings being released echoed in the passage. There were muted popping sounds. Lofton jerked and went rigid, his arms thrusting out to shove William behind him.

"Get inside!" he gasped, fumbling at his hip for his sword. Then his eyes rolled up in his head and he dropped suddenly to the floor. A bare moment later came more twangs, and pain exploded in William's chest, arms, and neck.

He opened his mouth. Blood gurgled in his throat. He could not breathe or shout for his guards. He heard a thump as Niall fell. Fire roared through his body, followed by a wave of cold as healing majick rushed from his royal pendant to his wounds. It numbed the pain. It should have protected him more from the bolts. More crossbolts pounded into him, sending him in stumbling jerks back against the wall. He slid slowly to his knees. He was dizzy, and black shadow creatures gnawed at the edges of his vision.

He looked down at himself. The bolts that sprouted from his flesh were obsidian and silver sheathed in *sylveth*. His pendant would not save him from such a devastating majickal and physical attack. He fell forward onto his hands. He coughed, deep wet spasms. Blood sprayed from his mouth and trickled from his nose.

William struggled to push himself up, but his strength was gone. His body seized. He collapsed, falling flat on the floor. His head cracked on the flagstones. His weight pushed the deadly bolts deeper into his flesh. William's last thought before he could think no more was a prayer: *Please, Chayos . . . guard Crosspointe.*

Chapter 30

The storm that had begun to move over Crosspointe during the dark hours before dawn continued to build as the sun slowly climbed up the sky. Black clouds hung low, obliterating much of the light. Sleet fell in punishing curtains, driven by a scouring wind. Whitecapped waves rose in ten-foot swells, and the black sea boiled with treacherous currents.

Ryland, Shaye, Nya, and Fallon had taken refuge in a shallow cave just above the waterline on the north side of Merstone Island, halfway between the Thumb and the west docks. It had taken them almost three hours to sail so far on the cutter Shaye had quietly 'borrowed' from the Weverton docks. They'd beached it, tying it off to a pair of hemlock trees. Shaye had cast an illusion to hide it. If a *sylveth* tide didn't roll in, it should be there when they returned. If they returned.

Ryland sat at the entrance of the cave, staring across the sound at Crosspointe. He was soaked to the skin, despite the majickal protections on his cloak. The wind and waves had forced themselves underneath. The skin on his face was raw from the beating sleet and his hair was crusty with ice. His head still pounded from coming through the Pale, and his body ached with cold, not to mention the throb of his lip from where Shaye had punched him.

But the chill went far deeper than mere temperature and weather. Against his back he felt Shaye's hatred like ice off the White Sea—it was just as obdurate and endless. Ryland swallowed. He could no longer drown his guilt and self-repulsion in drink. He had to face what he had done and accept the consequences. He had made these choices and he must take responsibility.

He was his father's son. He was a Rampling. He had chosen his country over his personal feelings. He had committed the worst act possible and done it to his best friend. He would do it again. No matter the cost—and that cost cut him more deeply than he had imagined. All his life he'd planned and trained to be a diplomat and a man worthy of his father's trust. Until now, he had not truly understood the burden of rule, or how dirty a king's hands might have to get in the process.

"What now?" Fallon asked.

He was stone dry, as were Shaye and Nya. Majick had its uses. Neither Shaye nor Fallon offered to help Ryland. Not that he expected it.

"We'll climb up along the ridge there," Shaye said, pointing. "There are entrances all over the mountain. We're not far from my quarters. Once inside, we'll work our way down into the Well—the bottom levels of the Kalpestrine, where I believe the guild keeps compass-majicars. We should be able to go a fair way inside without encountering too much trouble."

"What is too much trouble?" Fallon asked.

"The fatal kind," Shaye said, just as caustically. "We should go. They'll be starting across to the mainland soon. Between the storm and the trees, no one will notice us, and the trail may be difficult. We should not wait."

Ryland started to his feet, exhaustion weighing on him. Something caught his attention. He tipped his head, trying to a capture a sound. The wind howled across the waves, drowning all other noises. He walked outside. He heard it again. It sounded like bells. A lot of them. As if every bell in Crosspointe was tolling. His heart seized. His gaze went to the blur that was the castle. He traced his way to the carillon standing high on a steep hill just behind the castle. He closed his eyes, listening with all his body, praying he was wrong. He heard it then—a low, somber tolling that rippled through his bones and his blood, summoning him home. Every Rampling in Crosspointe would feel it and come.

He let out a sob, and then scrabbled for the chain around his neck. He tore away his cloak, and clutched at the front of his shirt, ripping the buttons off until he could reach his royal pendant on its unbreakable chain. The pendant was shaped like a compass, a drop of clear *sylveth* filling its heart. At least it had been clear. Now the *sylveth* had turned black as the waters of the Inland Sea. It meant death and rebirth: the king was dead, long live the new king.

His father was dead.

The air went out of Ryland. He fisted the pendant, feeling the points cut through the flesh of his palm. He no longer felt the whip of the sleet or the bite of the wind. He felt only a vast emptiness. He'd lost his mother only a few months ago. He had loved her dearly and still felt an abiding ache that nothing could assuage. But to lose his father—

It was beyond his ability to comprehend. An avalanche was crushing him beneath an infinite weight of smothering ice and stone. Every bone ached. Razor pain spread through his chest and out his arms and down to his legs. His father was the moon and the sun of his life. Ryland didn't know who he was without him.

His mind splintered to pieces.

He came back to himself slowly. Someone had struck him across the face. He felt the shock of it, but nothing of the pain.

Hands gripped him beneath the arms and lifted him. He had fallen on the ground. He was set on his feet. Instantly his legs sagged. He was caught again. Someone grabbed his collar and shook him hard. His teeth rattled and his eyes hurt.

"Get ahold of yourself. The old bastard is dead, but Fairlie's not and you're going to help me get her back. Now. Do you understand?" Shaye's voice was searing.

He shook Ryland violently. "Damn you! Stop your sniveling. Don't forget Vaughn. He can still be saved, but you have to do your part."

Ryland shoved him away weakly. "Get off me."

He shook off Fallon's hands, still holding him from behind. The bells from the mainland continued to toll. There was nothing he could do—and Vaughn still had a knife in his neck. Ryland swallowed his maelstrom of grief and pain, pushing it down deep into the bottomless chasm that had opened up inside him.

"I'm ready," he said hoarsely, bending to pick up his cloak. He slung it around his shoulders. The pin he used to fasten it was gone. He tied it instead.

Shaye had already walked away. Nya hesitated, then followed, Fallon close on her heels. Ryland trailed behind, listening to the bells as they continued to ring his father's death knell, the wind shrieking the grief that he could not. He kept his gaze on his footing, allowing himself to think only of the next step and then the next.

His legs began to burn with exertion and his body grew hot, despite the wind and sleet. He slid and slipped on the rocky path, grabbing for branches and bushes to steady himself. After a long trek, Shaye turned, following a manicured path of crushed black granite. It ribboned along the mountainside, more paths branching away here and there. They took one of these. It tunneled upward through the trees and rhododendron bracken, leveling out for a bit before rising again. At the top the path ended in a flat terrace of rough, smoky quartz. It was bordered by stone pots full of skeletal plants. On the opposite side of the path was a door. It was made of craggy granite, like the rest of the mountain, and blended well enough that anyone not standing on the terrace could be forgiven for not realizing it was a door at all.

Shaye crossed to it and pressed his hand to the center. Threads of white light ran up his arm, weaving a glove of ghostly lace around his skin. He shoved and the door pivoted in the center. He waved his companions to enter.

Ryland stopped just inside and glanced about. They might have been in any manor house. The walls were paneled with linen-fold maple. The floors were covered with elegant rugs. Everywhere were bits and pieces that Fairlie had crafted over the years. Mixed in with them were a few paintings and tapestries and several marble sculptures. A band of skylights let in the dim light. The place was warm though there was no obvious fireplace.

Shaye touched the wards on the inner wall and light bloomed from dozens of golden globes made of *sylveth*. He disappeared through another door and returned with an armful of blankets and towels. He dropped them into an armchair.

"There's nothing to eat in the larder, I'm afraid," he said curtly. "But there is drink. Help yourself."

He went to the sideboard and poured out a generous measure of brandy and drank it down. He filled the glass again and strode across the room, thrusting the glass into Ryland's cold hand.

"Drink it before you faint," he ordered before turning away. "Make yourselves comfortable. I must make myself presentable."

Ryland didn't move from his position, drinking slowly from the glass before setting it aside, still three-quarters full. He didn't like the way the warmth trickled down inside him. He was numb and if he was going to be of any use, he had to remain that way.

He flinched from thinking about how his father might have died. He wasn't sick, which left an accident or assassination. The latter was far more likely. Ryland shook himself, trying to think of anything else. He picked up a towel and scrubbed his hair before dabbing ineffectually at his soaked clothing.

Fallon dried Nya and himself with majick, then tried to wrap a blanket around her shoulders. She rebuffed him, walking around the room to examine the many examples of Fairlie's metalwork. Ryland watched her. The lust he'd felt for her in her chambers and since was growing stronger. He wanted to shove her against a wall and

tear her clothes off. His fingers tightened on his towel.
His hunger bore a wild edge that was hard to explain
or resist. He adored women and spent many a pleasant
hour enjoying their wares. But this was different. This
was primal and raw. He turned away, putting more distance between them. He didn't trust himself.

He turned around to find Fallon staring at him. The
spawn majicar was seething. In that moment, Ryland
realized that the majicar was walking the same ragged
edge of violent lust for Nya as Ryland. His frustration
and jealousy throbbed, and his muscles twitched and
bulged, straining against his obviously fraying control.

Ryland silently raised his hands, palms out, in a uni-
versal sign of surrender. He backed away another step
and was rewarded with a slight relaxing of Fallon's ag-
gressive stance. Ryland carefully did not look again at
Nya. He remembered her conversation with Shaye in
her quarters. She could not control this thing she was
doing that made men go mad for her. Ryland licked his
dry lips. If she didn't do something soon, she'd find herself mobbed by strangers and raped. Though perhaps it
wouldn't be strangers.

They waited thus, the silence thick, until Shaye returned, ten minutes later. He'd changed clothes, combed
his hair, and shaved off the scraggly beard he'd grown
during his imprisonment. He wore a long, sleeveless surcoat of heavy burgundy brocade over his black dosken
suit, and he'd buckled a sword on his hip.

Shaye stopped in the doorway, surveying his companions. Then he wordlessly strode over to Ryland and
splayed a bony hand hard against his chest. Power unraveled from his hand. It spread over Ryland like tentacles. Then Shaye pulled away sharply, snapping his
fingers closed. The majick yanked away from Ryland,
carrying with it the wet. He staggered at the force and
caught himself. Shaye turned away.

"From here, we will descend through the west tower.
That will take us to the main level. I doubt we'll encounter many people until then. To get into the Well, we will

have to navigate through the public areas that take up the next four levels. After that, the passages are warded and lower still, they are guarded."

Ryland looked hard at Shaye. "We can't afford any witnesses."

"I'll provide our illusions. But if we come up against a strong majicar, he'll be able to rip them away without much trouble."

"I can help with that," Nya said. "I can fog inside their minds." She hesitated. "One time, possibly two. Strong majicars are more difficult and I am not entirely well."

Shaye tapped the fingers of one hand against his thigh, his pale face turning to marble. Then he nodded. He turned to Nya. "I'll begin with you."

She shook her head. "No need."

She pulled away her cloak and laid it over a chair. She looked very much the way she had when Ryland had first seen her. She was wearing a leather vest laced tight with no shirt beneath and leather pants. She wore no shoes. Once again she had on fingerless gloves laced up to her elbows. She removed them and set them on her cloak.

Then she drew a deep breath and bent her head so that her chin touched her chest. She let the breath out slowly. As she did, the bottom half of her body blurred, shimmering like a heat mirage. Then she seemed to shrink, falling forward onto her hands. The distortion ran upward over her shoulders and swallowed her head. Then slowly it cleared. Ryland could only stare.

Nya stood on all fours like a large cat. She still wore the vest and the pants, but her legs and arms had *changed*. Her legs now angled forward and then backward like the hind end of a mountain lion. Her upper arms had shortened and her forearms had lengthened. Her spine had stretched and become more supple. Though she was still recognizable as Nya, she'd become something else entirely. She turned her head to look at her companions and then as they continued to watch, she faded from sight.

"Is it . . . illusion?" Ryland whispered.

"No. She is much like a chameleon," Fallon said. "She can be seen if she moves too quickly."

"Can she protect herself?" Shaye asked.

"I can," Nya said, her voice a deep rumble.

She flickered back into sight. She snarled and now Ryland could see that her sharp, curved teeth had also grown longer. Her upper canines protruded nearly two inches along her bottom jaw. She lifted a hand—or rather, a paw. The palms had toughened, the talons had thickened, and her fingers had shortened slightly. Then, without warning, sharp, hooked spikes sprang up along her forearms. They were a milky white, the points a glistening orange.

"Touch those not," Fallon warned. "A drop on the skin kills in moments."

"Good. Nya is taken care of. Fallon can make his own disguise. And I . . ."

Shaye's voice trailed away. The air around his body shivered and softened. A moment later he was no longer Shaye. In his place was a spare-looking man with a shock of loose white hair, the ends yellowed. He was clean-shaven, with a flat, crooked nose and a round face. His cheeks and nose were rosy. His eyes were the majicar silver ringed in red. His *illidre* was a Koreion knotted around itself. Ryland recognized him, searching his memories for a name. "Meet Arcolithe," Shaye said. "He happens to be away from Crosspointe at the moment— or he was a month ago. Hopefully no one will question his presence. Which leaves just you," Shaye said, turning speculatively to Ryland. "I thought to give you the face of one of the majicars, but it will be impossible for you to back it up with any substance. You'll have to be a servant. Few are allowed in the Well. But we have little choice."

"So we'll make it up as we go and hope we don't get killed?" Ryland knew as well as Shaye that they didn't have time to plan this any better. Too much was unknown. All he could do was keep his sword loose in his scabbard and be ready for whatever came.

"In your case, I can hope you will get killed," Shaye said with a curl of his lip, then splayed a hand on Ryland's forehead. Once again Ryland felt the illusion spell wrap him. This time he was prepared and didn't struggle against the smothering feel of it. It tightened around him, squeezing his ribs and pressing on his lungs. It felt like he was trapped in stone.

Shaye stood back, examining his work with a critical eye, and then nodded. "Let's go. Keep your wits about you," he said to his companions and then headed for the door.

Ryland trailed behind, rolling his shoulders and trying to adjust to the stiff weight of the spell. Fallon had adopted his usual disguise, mimicking the fashion of the majicars, with the high-necked robes and long, sweeping sleeves. Like Shaye, he had created a false *illidre* for himself. It was shaped like a bull thistle, the colors brilliant amethyst and emerald. Ryland caught flickers of Nya from the corners of his eyes as her coloring adjusted to the background. But even if he hadn't seen her, he'd have known she was there. His prick throbbed uncomfortably. He dropped back farther to give himself relief.

As they had hoped, they encountered no one as they went down the corridor to the west tower stairwell. The corridor arced in a long curve following the contour of the mountain. There were no carpets or decorations. It was bone-dry, without any of the moisture that Ryland associated with caves or cellars, nor was there any chill. The temperature was actually quite warm. *Sylveth* lights recessed in the roof provided golden illumination. Doors and passages branched off on either side.

It was the first time Ryland had ever been inside the Kalpestrine, and probably his last. As far as he knew, his father had never been within its walls.

His father was dead. It changed everything and noth-

ing. Vaughn was still a breath away from death. Should it
matter? His father would never have let it.

What exactly was he doing here?

Rescuing Fairlie wasn't the answer. It was the question. Because once she was free, he'd have to choose
between her and Vaughn. Fairlie was still a compass-
majicar; Crosspointe still needed her. His father's death
didn't kill his plans, and Ryland had a responsibility as
a Rampling, as his father's son, and as prelate. He had
to carry forward his father's plans for Crosspointe. That
meant he'd have to kill Shaye before his former friend
could curse him with *sylveth*. The question was, who was
more important? Vaughn, who would surely be elected
king next? Or Fairlie, who could make compasses? Ryland didn't know. What would he do?

Chapter 31

Nya's skin twitched and rolled as if she were being attacked by a swarm of biting flies. The majick here was thick as smoke. Her entire body felt tense. Fallon's mind battered at hers and it was all she could do to wall it off.

But something else was here. More than the sift of majicar minds—those few who still remained inside the Kalpestrine. She brushed against them, tasting, hating. Beneath them whispered faint, blurred voices of hopelessness and desperation. They sounded like death.

Her flesh crawled and her entire body tensed with readiness. Something dreadful was here. It was waiting.

Chapter 32

Shaye marched along, trying not to look conspicuous. The prod of the sexual invitation rolling off Nya put him on edge, and he found himself jumping at every noise. He ground his teeth together. *Fairlie*. He imagined her, not as she had been, but as she had become. She filled his mind, her eyes mysterious and wonderful, her body supple and fluid. Her skin was like one of her own sculptures. He ached to hold her and explore her body. He wanted to hear her laugh again with real happiness. He wondered if she could ever feel happy again. He would do everything in his power to make her so.

The hunger for Nya faded. Fairlie filled Shaye entirely, leaving no room for anyone else. As it should be.

He glanced behind him. Fallon looked sleepy, as if he'd been awakened too early. He yawned hugely. Just ahead of him Shaye could see where Nya walked. Now that he knew what he was looking for, he could see the slight distortion at the edges of her body. If she stood still, he doubted he'd be able to find her. Farther back, Ryland scuffed along. Shaye's jaw tightened. He hated that he'd felt pity for the prince when the bells had started tolling. Ryland deserved all he got. Even now he was no doubt plotting how he could convince Fairlie to build compasses for the new king, whoever that was going to be. Or else he was thinking up ways to capture her again. Would he sacrifice Vaughn and risk himself? Once Shaye would have been certain the answer to both questions was no. But now he had no idea of what Ryland was capable.

He turned around again, his body rigid. Ryland could make the difference in this rescue. He had a good sword arm and he was smart. But he could just as well betray them all.

They reached the west tower. It was one of four enormous stairwells that spiraled from the top of the mountain to sea level. Ten men could stand abreast on a step. The stairs were attached to the wall, and a hole five feet across ran down the middle. Colored lights twinkled like fairy gems, chasing along the inner and outer rims of the steps. Like the corridors, the steps and the tower seemed to have been carved from the bedrock of the mountain. The entrance was an arched opening. There was no door.

Inside, Shaye could hear the echo of voices and footsteps. He could not tell if they were above or below.

"Quickly now," he hissed and started down.

Several times on their way down, the four companions were forced to hurry or slow their steps to avoid people, once taking refuge on a storage level. Shaye's stomach tightened the farther they descended into the Kalpestrine. Sea Level contained meeting rooms, salons, and an array of dining rooms, some small and intimate, others large and sprawling. It was almost never empty, and he could not expect that it would be now, even if most majicars had gone to Crosspointe as he suspected.

The next level housed the kitchens, bathing rooms, laundries, the servants' dining hall, and an assortment of small businesses, including milliners, cobblers, two taprooms, and an apothecary. They had been founded by family members of those who worked in the Kalpestrine. The rest of the level was given over to the storage of food and other supplies needed for the day-to-day running of the mountain fortress.

Beneath it was an extensive library and a variety of salons and party rooms. Then came the guildhall and Sennet offices. Below them was the Well: a warren of

workrooms and smother rooms where majicars practiced
their craft. The upper levels were reserved for apprentices. The next were for journeymen, and finally lowest
of all were for masters, with the bottommost rooms belonging to the members of the Sennet. Beneath them
was where captured spawn were taken for study. And
below them was where it was rumored that the compass-majicars were kept. Shaye didn't know for certain.
They might be elsewhere, in secret rooms hollowed out
of parts of the mountain. But he had to hope they were
keeping Fairlie in the bottom of the Well; otherwise he
didn't know where to begin to look.

There was no bottom to the fear that swamped him at
that thought. No. She *had* to be there. He couldn't bear
it if she wasn't.

The western tower ended in a grand balcony made
of translucent black *sylveth* that circled the entire Sea
Level. Wide windows were strewn periodically along the
balcony. Outside, the storm continued to blow furiously.
Shaye estimated it was nearing midday.

Broad, sweeping stairways dropped down to the
main floor at regular intervals around the entire vast
space—it was nearly a quarter of a league in diameter.
The center of the Sea Level was a tall monolith of obsidian that stretched from the high ceiling to the floor like
an enormous tree trunk. Inside it were private salons,
dining areas, and meeting rooms. A waterfall dropped
from its zenith, falling into a deep pool. Spreading from
it was a network of fountains and streams that artfully
spiderwebbed through the vast space. In between grew a
fairy forest of trees, bushes, trailing vines, and flowers, all
made of rainbow-hued *sylveth* lit with sparks of majick.
They twisted and reached, forming walls and hedges,
and creating cozy bowers and nooks filled with couches
and tables. Above it all hung a constellation of white *sylveth* lights. Against the black granite of the ceiling, they
were like stars in the night.

"It's lovely," Nya whispered as they stood at the bal-
ustrade.

"There's an entrance to a spiral stair at the base of the monolith," Shaye said softly, his lips hardly moving. "That's where we're going if we get separated. If you are forced to go down the stairs, do not go past the next level. There are wards. Fallon, walk with me."

He didn't give the others a chance to ask questions, but began down the sweeping black steps with Fallon beside him. He set a brisk pace, as if in a hurry.

No one accosted them as they made their way across the Sea Level to the center. What few majicars Shaye saw had their heads together, talking furiously in low voices. Still, he held his breath most of the way. Though he tried to steer far from everyone, twice they passed close enough to hear what the speakers were saying.

"It's a mistake now—a new king will be more reasonable."

A snorting laugh. "Ramplings are never reasonable."

"Careful. There are Ramplings in the guild."

"Let's put one of them on the throne, then."

"The bylaws and Charter declare it impossible."

"Do we even trust them? They *are* Ramplings. If it comes down to the guild or the crown, they'll choose blood."

"*Sylveth* is in their blood now. Most of them supported the alliance with the merchants."

"All I am saying is that they bear watching."

"The merchants say that Prince Vaughn will be reasonable once he's king."

"Once? There might be challengers."

"With the backing of the Merchants' Commission and the guild, we can put whoever we want on the throne."

The rest was lost as Shaye passed out of hearing. He glanced back at Ryland, wondering how much he'd heard. But the prince's disguise gave nothing away. He walked with his head tipped down, looking humble. The conversation withered suddenly as Nya walked by. The men shifted and looked about uneasily. The women didn't notice at all.

The next conversation was between a pair of women

majicars, both white-haired and wrinkled with age. He knew them—Leandoras and Vengeeta. Both were master majicars and both were members of the Sennet. Shaye nearly stopped when he heard Vengeeta say his name in a quiet voice.

". . . word about Shaye Weverton?"

"Nothing. I think the king's death must have something to do with it, though."

"You think King William was assassinated?"

"Nicholas Weverton is ruthless and he would not just sit still while the king held his nephew prisoner. Mark my words, the papers will say the king was murdered. If I was a betting woman, I'd put my money on Nicholas Weverton as the man behind it."

"King William has made a lot of enemies, though," Leandoras said doubtfully.

"But the timing—and Weverton has the means too."

Shaye hurried on. All he needed right now was for the prince to start thinking about getting revenge. He bit the tip of his tongue, tasting blood. Vengeeta was right, though. If his uncle had learned of Shaye's imprisonment, he might have taken steps against King William. It could not be overstated how much his uncle Nicholas despised the crown—King William in particular—and how protective he was of his family.

They reached the monolith and the main stair. Shaye plunged downward. His fingers curled into his palms. The next wards he could open easily enough—he held the keys all the way down to the master workshops. Then he'd have to use the pyramid spell to break them. He just didn't know how he was going to get rid of the majick fast enough to keep from incinerating himself. Though he'd emptied himself in fighting off Nya on the mainland, the pyramid would fill to overflowing quickly once he attacked the wards.

The servants' halls were bustling. With so many majicars away from the Kalpestrine, many servants had a holiday. Nobody paid attention to Shaye's small party as they descended past the library and then to the guild-hall. Shaye keyed the wards for each level as they went down. The library was empty but for the librarian, and the guildhall was busy with clerks scribbling in account books and making copies of documents.

As they reached the first workshop level, Shaye glanced back at his companions. "These are the apprentice rooms. They shouldn't pay much attention to us."

The apprentice levels were as busy as the servants' hall. There was loud chattering, and very little work of any kind getting done. With their masters gone to the mainland, most were engaged in avoiding their studies.

By contrast, the journeyman levels were nearly empty. They heard voices murmuring several times but saw no one. Shaye felt a trickle of sweat rolling down his back. They were nearly there. One more level down to the masters' workshops. That was where things were going to get ugly. On the landing above, he stopped and turned to his companions.

"Wait here."

Both Ryland and Fallon started to speak, but Shaye cut them off with a sharp shake of his head. "Wait."

Swiftly he ran down the stairs. They were made of obsidian and circled around an obsidian root. There was only one way in and one way out of the Well. Shaye had an ominous feeling that leaving was going to be much harder than going in.

He came around the last curve to the landing, where the first exit leading into the master workrooms arched to the right and the stairwell continued downward, protected by wards. The doorway was guarded by a majicar. She was tall, her hair hanging in a blue-black curtain to her waist. She wore orange high-necked robes over a dark blue dress. She wasn't much older than Shaye. She was sitting in a comfortably appointed alcove, reading from a large tome and making notes on a parchment. He didn't recognize her, but she smiled when she saw him, leaping to her feet.

"Arcolithe! When did you return? I thought you weren't coming back until Fury or Loyalty."

She put her arms around his neck, standing on tiptoe to kiss him. It was a quick, friendly kiss. Shaye smiled with his false face. No witnesses. He had killed once in his life, and the man had deserved it. But to murder her because she was unlucky enough to be standing watch today made his stomach heave. He pushed her back gently.

She looked curiously at him. He didn't know what to say. He scrabbled for something.

"The king is dead. Did you hear?"

She nodded soberly. "A messenger came down earlier. It is awful. I know how much the Sennet doesn't like his policies on service, but first to lose Queen Naren and now King William? It isn't good for Crosspointe. And he meant well. He loved his people."

"Yes, he did," Shaye said. He was out of time. He gathered himself. He knew how to strike with his majick. He could stun or kill with it. Most majicars were not trained in combat—there was no need. But his uncle Nicholas had insisted that Shaye know how to employ his majick for something "useful," just as he'd insisted Shaye learn to use his sword and his fists. Because you never knew when you might be attacked.

Suddenly Nya's voice trickled into his mind.

If she is not awake, I can make her forget you. She will come to no harm.

Profound relief flooded Shaye. Quickly he summoned his majick and drove it out at the other woman. She was unshielded. Her legs buckled and she fell. Shaye caught her around the waist and picked her up, settling her on a couch in the alcove. Nya shimmered into being and settled a paw on the unconscious woman's forehead.

"Tired. Fell asleep. Dreaming Arcolithe was home. Missing him. Dream now of summer and when he will be coming home." The words were whispered. She lifted

her hand before bending to lick the unconscious majicar's cheek. Nya's tongue was pink and long.

She settled back on her haunches, looking at Shaye.

"I'll get the wards. Fetch the others. From here we
need to shield ourselves."

She stood and leaped up the stairs. He didn't wait.
He snatched the majick of the wards and drained it into
himself. There was a flash of crimson and green as the
wards broke. He pressed a hand against his chest, feeling
the majick pulsing and ready. The pyramid spell could
take more than that. He grimaced. It would have to take
a lot more.

Fallon and Ryland trotted down the stairs behind
Nya.

"Can you shield?" Shaye asked the spawn majicar.

Fallon frowned and nodded.

"How good are they?"

"On the Root, shields are necessary. Especially working with young spawn," Fallon said loftily.

Shaye nodded and turned to Ryland. "I'll shield you.
But you need to stay close." He glanced at Nya. "What
about you?"

She shook her head, then rubbed her face against her
foreleg. "I am unable. But I will not be seen."

"I'll shield you too," Shaye said, silencing Fallon before he could bluster at her, as he clearly wanted to do.

He closed his eyes, reaching inside his *illidre*. Shields
were easy enough to make and maintain, especially
given his affinities for stone and fire. He snapped together what he wanted—another old habit established
by Uncle Nicholas. "You need shields most when you
are unprepared. They should require no thought. Practice!" And he had practiced. Now he shoved them out to
Ryland and Nya and wrapped them around himself. He
fed them with the majick from the pyramid.

"Did you do it? I don't feel anything," Ryland said,
looking at his hands.

"It's done. As long as I feed the spells, both of you

will be protected from majickal attacks. Physical attacks are another thing. You'll have to protect yourself. Also, shields can be broken. I will try to warn you if that happens. Now if you all are ready, let's go."

"The wards?" Fallon asked.

"Taken care of."

Shaye did not elucidate, but started down the stairs again. The next few levels were not warded except at the entrances into the workrooms. On the landing of level thirty-three he stopped again.

"Things are about to get trickier. There will be more guards—all Sennet master majicars."

"I will go ahead," Nya said, shimmering into sight. Before Fallon could object, she glared at him. "Do not. This I must do."

Nya started away, fading as she went. Shaye followed, Fallon hard on his heels. Ryland hurried after. By the time they came around the corner, the majicar guard was sprawled across his desk. There was no sign of blood or violence.

"He will die soon," Nya said in an expressionless voice. She remained camouflaged.

Shaye went to look at the fallen man. He was Moroflagin, a majicar of good humor and practical jokes. Shaye's mouth pinched together as the other man struggled to breathe. Then he shook with an uncontrollable palsy, spittle bubbling from his mouth. A moment later his body loosened and went soft as the life went out of him. There was a gut-churning stink as his bowels let go. Shaye backed away, his stomach lurching. He took a hard hold of himself, swallowing back the bile that filled his mouth. His face felt like stone.

"You poisoned him?" he asked, his voice strained.

"Yes."

"We should hide the body," Fallon said.

Shaye shook his head, recoiling from the thought of touching the dead man. "There is no time. Besides, with the wards down, anybody who wanders by will know something is wrong, body or no."

"You're going to take the wards *down*? How?"

Shaye's mouth twisted. He rolled his neck on his shoulders. "Like this." He reached for the power of the wards. They were old and complex and very powerful. Majick surged and there was a sound like far-off thunder. Majick slammed into Shaye, sending him sprawling. His head bounced against the stone floor and the air exploded from his chest. His head spun. Light wrapped him—scarlet, green, blue, purple—a wildfire of majick. The pyramid spell drank in the power, filling and overflowing. Shaye's body spasmed as majick soaked into his muscles and rushed through his blood.

He pushed some of it out, feeding the three shield spells. It helped only slightly. He had to release more. No. He needed this power. He was about to go to war, and this was his weapon. He needed it all. So he did the only thing he could think of. He pulled his shields tight, reversing them so that they would not let the majick get away.

He melted in fire.

The pain was infinite and unbearable. He thought he screamed. He tried to stop. He didn't want to bring the guards down on them. But he had no control. His body trembled and convulsed. His feet kicked and his hands flopped. He felt himself floating free of his flesh. No. He would not give in to death. He clutched at himself. The pyramid spell was a hard anchor in the sea of lava. He grappled it with all his strength.

Something happened. The sides of the pyramid opened, spreading apart like the petals of a flower. Inside was the heart—his heart. *Bliss* and *Blood* and *Fire* and *Stone*. Instinct drove him. He poured himself into the opening. The moment he touched the drop of scarlet *Bliss* in the center, his world exploded. Waves of power swept away and rushed back in the space of a heartbeat. A ball of majick coalesced around the opened spell. Slowly the pyramid started to close—reversing itself so that it was inside out. The heart of it—the structure of *Blood*, *Bliss*, *Fire*, and *Stone*—had grown too large for the pyramid. It pushed out through the *sylveth* and silver walls, half inside and half out. The surrounding ball of majick shrank and hardened into a protective shield around the inside-out spell. As it did, it sucked the remaining wild majick into itself, settling into a steady pulse and waiting for Shaye to tap its power.

He lay still a moment. Relief trickled through him. He'd come close to dying—to abandoning Fairlie. But he was all right, he told himself. And the pyramid spell was working. It would draw majick without killing him. He could feel its rightness. He let go a shaky breath and opened his eyes.

Ryland stood by Shaye's feet. His face was pale and he looked worried and helpless. Fallon was beside him, frowning, as if he was trying to figure out what had happened. Shaye turned his head. Nya stood beside him. She lowered her head so that her nose nearly touched his. Her breath mingled with his. She sat down.

"What happened?" Ryland asked.

Shaye sat up. His bones felt uncomfortably soft and pliable. He scrubbed both hands over his face, then pushed to his knees and then upright. He staggered, but waved off Ryland's helping hand.

"Swallowing that kind of majick gives me indigestion," he said as he dusted his clothes off.

"Swallowing . . . ?" Fallon repeated in a strangled voice. "That isn't possible."

"I must be mistaken then."

"You sounded like you were being ripped apart," Ryland said, his voice hardly audible.

Shaye lifted his shoulder in a half shrug. "Close enough. Come on. Be ready."

As he started down the stairs again, he checked the shields on Nya and Ryland. They were steady.

The silence in the stairwell was eerie. Had no one heard his screams? Or was there an ambush waiting? The hairs on Shaye's neck prickled. Nya rubbed his leg as she passed by to scout ahead.

He stepped slowly. His ears strained for any sound.

A squall like an enraged cat ripped through the silence. It bounced off the walls, flying upward. If Shaye's screams had gone unnoticed, that would certainly remedy the situation. Every available majicar would be pouring into the Well, and with the wards broken there was nothing to slow them down.

Fallon leaped past Shaye, who was already running. They hit the landing at the same time, neither making any attempt at stealth or caution. They found one majicar on the floor. She was convulsing, her tongue protruding from her mouth. Two other majicars were facing off against Nya. She crouched on the floor, snarling. They were flinging majick bolts at her. They were loose, gauzy things, unsure and unpracticed. But they were masters and Shaye could see that their technique was improving with every blast. Shaye's shields around Nya were holding, but she could not move.

Fallon yelled and threw a blast at the brown-haired man on the right. His name was Rostiene. The shorter man on the left was Evergerithe. Both had come into the guild just after Shaye, though they had proved far more dedicated and brilliant in their studies and had recently been voted into the Sennet.

Shaye hesitated only an instant as he met Evergerithe's stunned gaze.

"Arcolithe?"

"Afraid not."

He sent a weak blast at the other majicar. Evergerithe stumbled back, then sent a return bolt. It was what Shaye had wanted. He reached out and grabbed the majick before it finished leaving Evergerithe. He pulled it into the spell inside him. This time there was no pain. Evergerithe fell to his knees with a sobbing scream, horror twisting his face. Shaye felt the burn of tears in his eyes, but he was relentless and merciless. He kept drawing the majick until he emptied Evergerithe. The other man fell senseless to the floor.

Without hesitating, Shaye spun toward Rostiene, who

was exchanging thrusts of majick with Fallon. He sent another blast and Shaye snatched it from its path. In only a handful of grains, Rostiene had slumped to the floor. Stolen majick warmed Shaye. He felt exhilarated and boundlessly powerful. He went to the two fallen majicars, kneeling beside them. Both still breathed. But they were majicars no longer. Shaye had stolen all their majick.

Disgust rolled through him, even as his blood bubbled with euphoria. *It was war. It was to save Fairlie.* He stroked his fingers over Evergerithe's brow. He had been a pleasant companion in those times Shaye had had occasion to visit with him. When he woke, he'd almost certainly go hunting for raw *sylveth* to restore himself. So would Rostiene. Would it work? Or would it turn them into the kind of spawn that Nya and Fallon called Kin?

Stiffly Shaye rose. This was not the kind of power any man should have. His mouth hardened. But for Fairlie, he'd do it again, and worse.

He turned around. Ryland, Fallon, and Nya were all staring at him. There was fear in their expressions.

"What did you do?" Ryland asked in a shaken voice.

"He stole their majick. That isn't even possible," Fallon said. "How . . . ? What are you?"

Shaye ran his tongue along the inside of his lip. "I am what you all made me," he said finally, bitterness turning his voice to ice. "Now let's go get Fairlie."

They said nothing as he reached for the wards. Breaking them and collecting the wild power was easy now—no harder than breathing. And still no pain. He wondered if there was any limit to how much the spell inside him could now hold.

He continued down. Nya faded from sight and again brushed past him. So he would know she'd gone ahead? Or to offer him reassurance of some kind? But he was too cold for reassurance. Too cold to feel even the slightest tug of lust for her. He could empty her. And Fallon.

There was no majick that could hold him or stop him. If it helped him rescue Fairlie, he was happy for it. But dread curved a skeletal hand around his throat.

When Fairlie learned what he could do—what he *had* done—would she run in fear?

Chapter 33

What in the holy black depths had Shaye turned into?

Ryland paced behind Fallon, his mouth parched, his legs shaking. Something had happened to Shaye in that smother room—something miraculous and horrible. Maybe even evil. Shaye had the ability to steal majick—from spells and from majicars. He had drained those two dry.

How had he done it? Was it intrinsic to him or a spell? If it was a spell, then it could pit majicar against majicar. They were as corruptible as anyone else. If just a few obtained such a spell, it could allow one majicar to become so powerful that no one could stand against him. He'd be a god. The ramifications of that were endless. If that majicar was loyal, it would mean Crosspointe would never be unguarded; it would never be at the mercy of the Jutras. But if Shaye had been loyal, he was no longer. Nor was he a paragon of virtue. Ryland wondered . . . With such power at his fingertips, what revenge would Shaye take for what had been done to Fairlie?

A shiver rippled down his spine. The possibilities were horrifying. What could he do? But there was nothing. All that was left was to help Fairlie get out of the Kalpestrine safely. And then let her go and hope that would be enough for Shaye. Her talents would be lost to Crosspointe, but there was no choice. Not with what Shaye could do now.

Ryland went cold, sweat springing up all over his body as sudden realization struck him. Was it possible Shaye could absorb the majick out of the Pale? He staggered, leaning one hand against the wall. It was all he could do not to throw up.

By the gods . . .

He was standing at a bloody, bleak crossroads again. Wisdom decreed that Shaye had to be stopped—he had to be killed. He was too great a threat to Crosspointe to let live. Even if he was not eager for vengeance now, the chance that he could change his mind would always loom.

Ryland dragged his fingers through his hair. He could almost hear his father's laying out his reasoning. *It wouldn't be murder; it would be a preventive strike. We are sworn to protect Crosspointe; we cannot abide such a threat.* It was so rational. There was simply no other honorable choice for a Rampling—for the trusted son of the king—to make.

He recoiled from the idea. Shaye was too strong to kill. *Unless he was caught by surprise*, the echoes of his father's voice argued. It was true. Majicars were as susceptible to physical violence as anyone else. Or maybe Shaye would die rescuing Fairlie. *Maybe Ryland could make sure of it.*

Every muscle twisted tight. Could he do it? Could he make himself? He'd done worse to Fairlie. If he didn't at least try to kill Shaye, he would be a traitor. Even without orders from his king, even without anyone else knowing about Shaye, he knew what was right to do. He *knew*. But how could he bring himself to do it? He'd hardly survived transforming Fairlie. And that wasn't the worst of it; killing Shaye meant letting Vaughn die.

He felt a nudge against his leg and looked down. Nya stood beside him, half-visible, like a wraith.

"Do you come now?"

He nodded and followed. Fallon and Shaye were waiting on the next level. Shaye lifted his eyebrows, his dark eyes knowing. Heat filled Ryland's cheeks and he looked away. Before either could speak, Nya growled. The sound lifted the hair on Ryland's neck.

"What is it?" Fallon asked, looking about for her.

She remained invisible. Her voice, when she spoke, was bitter and angry. "Can you not smell them? Kindred. Your brothers and sisters. They are here."

She shivered into sight. She was standing at the archway leading into the workrooms beyond. Her skin twitched as if she was being stung by a swarm of wasps. Ryland looked past her. There was little to see. A wall rose just inside as if designed to block anyone from looking in. Or out. It was only fifteen or twenty feet long, but to go within, a person would have to go around it. It was the only floor thus far with such a screening wall.

Shouts sounded from far above. Then more from below.

Shaye didn't hesitate. He broke the wards with a flash of orange light and stepped inside the room. "Hide. Be quiet."

They did as told. Ryland watched Shaye from the end of the screen wall. The majicar set his fingertips against the stone just outside the entryway. There was a ballooning of black, darker than obsidian. Shaye turned around and saw Ryland. The disguise he wore melted away to nothing.

"There's no point in wearing these anymore. Even Arcolithe shouldn't be down here. If they notice the change to the wards, we'll be trapped," he said, walking around the wall. "We'll have to fight our way out."

There was no answer to be made to that. Ryland turned around the corner after Shaye with a last glance at the doorway, feeling the weight of the disguising spell melt away. With any luck, the searchers would pass by without noticing the new wards.

Ryland stopped short and stared at the room spreading out before him. It was a long cavern. Overhead the ceiling was rough-hewn. The floor was flat and polished to a brilliant shine. Along the outer walls was a series of doors spaced widely apart. At the center was a broad, flat oval of knackerstone inlaid with lacy tracings of silver. Sitting in the middle was a barn-sized knackerstone building with broad double doors at one end. Nya was standing outside them on her hind legs, her hands and face pressed flat against the doors as if listening to something within. Her eyes were closed. Fallon stood behind her. His disguise was gone, stolen by the knackerstone oval he was standing on.

Shaye leaned back against the wall, his arms crossed, his eyes half closed in that sleepy manner of his. Ryland was not fooled. Shaye was fully alert. Nya thrust herself away from the doors. She fell to all fours again. Her body-shifting majick was unaffected by the knackerstone oval. Her haunches bunched and she bounded across the distance separating her from Shaye. Her taloned hands slammed against his chest as she stood up again, thrusting him hard against the wall.

"Free them," she snarled. Black tears streaked the fur of her face. "They scream. The majicars . . . they *hurt* them."

"If I free them, won't they try to eat us?" Shaye asked, making no effort to push her away.

"I can Speak to them."

"All of them? There must be a hundred or more in there. You said yourself that you are unwell."

Her mouth opened and she gave a guttural hissing sound. Suddenly Shaye reached up and closed his hand on her muzzle-like mouth.

"Hush, now. They are coming," he whispered.

She twisted away, landing on all fours. But she made no sound. Black and tan coruscated down her body, then she flickered and faded from sight. Ryland was certain she'd gone around the wall to watch.

The majicars from below reached the landing first. They hesitated only a moment before dashing upward. Ryland didn't know how many there were, but it sounded like at least six and probably more.

"We have to hurry. It won't be long before they figure out where we must be," Shaye said.

He levered himself away from the wall and keyed off the wards at the door. The small group passed through.

All except Nya. She stood in front of the wall, her head dipped low, her lips curling into a snarl. Her curved fangs gleamed white.

"We must free the Kindred."

"Not now. We came for Fairlie," Shaye said.

"Will you leave the Kin behind to be tortured? You have the power to free them."

"And if I do? What will happen to them? They will be captured again, or killed. They have nowhere to go. The only escape is up into the arms of the guild."

He paused. Ryland could almost hear the whir of his mind as he thought.

"On second thought, if I release them, they might occupy our pursuers for a while."

"Might make getting out a little more complicated for us, though," Ryland pointed out.

Shaye's shoulders twitched in a dismissive shrug. "Getting out is going to be difficult no matter what. Maybe the spawn will create enough confusion and carnage to do us some good."

With Shaye's majick, it was a better bet than it seemed. "Then do it."

The corner of Shaye's mouth lifted as if amused that Ryland should tell him to do anything. He wordlessly snapped the ward into the stairwell leading down. He jerked his chin at his companions to urge them on their way. Ryland started down, halting when Nya didn't move, and though Fallon shifted his feet uneasily, he remained close to her side.

"Wait below. You'll be safer there," Shaye said.

"I cannot leave them," Nya said.

"Yes, you can," Shaye said implacably as he turned back to face her. "I'm going to let the spawn loose, and then I'm going to reset the wards to keep them from following us. If you want to stay here and face the guild with them, then do it. Likely you'll end up in a knacker box or dead. Your choice. Now get out my way. We don't have much time."

He strode past her out of sight. A few minutes later,

Shaye broke the knackerstone barn's containment majick. The air rippled violently and thrust Ryland back against the wall. The breath exploded out of him and his vision darkened and spun, the back of his head cracking hard against stone. He slumped to the steps, hardly aware of the rumbling fury of sound that rolled up and down the Well. An eerie wind raised every hair on his body as it swept back inside the room where Shaye was. His entire body quivered with the force of it.

Then suddenly it was gone. Ryland pushed himself up, staggering, his head and ribs throbbing. Blood trickled from his nose. He wiped it away on his sleeve.

Shaye appeared on the landing above. His face was flushed with ruddy health, and the tarnished silver disks of his eyes were nearly white, the red circle surrounding each and the pupils glowing like a sinking sun. He looked uncanny. Evil. Cold prickled along Ryland's arms and legs as he again considered whether Shaye could snap the Pale as easily as he had the wards.

Shaye surveyed his companions, his gaze riveting on Nya. "Are you coming?"

Nya glanced behind her, her body straining toward the opening. The moment stretched. Then she bounded forward past Ryland with a shrieking cry that echoed loudly, fading from sight as she went. Fallon trotted after her. Shaye said nothing more to either of them. He reached out and pressed his fingertips to the wall. White smoke wreathed his hand before sinking into the stone. Suddenly the stairwell above was filled with a black curtain of majick. It swirled like liquid, glinting with blue and green. Shaye stood back and nodded.

He spun and slipped quietly down the stairs. He looked ... deadly. His face was set, and everything about him was relentless. He would not stop. He would not hesitate to do anything at all to rescue Fairlie. Fear squirmed through Ryland's innards. The problem was, Shaye actually had the power to do just about anything at all.

The stairs spiraled downward into the depths of the

island without offering an end or a place to rest. After
a while, Ryland began to feel the weight of the island
above pressing down on him. His lungs tightened and
his heart thumped. Cold sweat dampened his shirt so
that it clung to his skin.

Then, without warning, the stair simply stopped.

Ryland turned around the last curve and stopped
dead just behind Fallon and Shaye, who were gazing in
slack-jawed awe. Ahead was yet another archway. Beyond was a vast cavern. Ryland marveled at it. It was . . .
there were no words for it. *Astonishing* was a poor description.

The ceiling and walls were hidden in shadow, too high
and too far away to be lit by the bright white *sylveth*
lights that illuminated a broad avenue leading away into
the shadows. The avenue was a ribbon mosaic of polished tile, each of which were no larger than the tip of
a thumb, many smaller than that. The detail was astonishing. The images were of an endless variety of spawn,
twisting and cavorting, lurid and ghastly, and each and
every one altogether terrifying. The creatures were
separated and connected by rippling bands of black and
silver flowing like rivulets direct from the sea. Scattered
throughout were various incarnations of the moon.

Ryland's gaze followed the avenue until it disappeared, and then he began to notice what else the vast
cavern contained. Shock held him rigid. Enormous
buildings, like strange castles, lined the avenue. The
smallest stood easily a hundred feet tall, with the largest
more than twice that, its rooftop disappearing into inky
shadow. Each of the castles was built of knackerstone inlaid with silver. The plazas around them were also paved
in silver-scrolled knackerstone. But only two contained
lights inside. The rest were dark. Ryland couldn't help but
feel it was a dead land. Understanding dawned. Two compass-majicars and two lit castles in the deepest depths of
Merstone Island. One of them must contain Fairlie. And
the rest? The empty ones? Who had lived in them? Had

this place once been full of compass-majicars? And if it had, what had become of them all?

There was no sign of any guards, but Ryland knew they must be there somewhere, watching and lying in wait to stop the invaders.

As if reading his mind, Shaye spoke quietly. "The majicars waiting for us will be some of the most powerful in the guild. With the events of the day on the mainland, I hope we won't be facing many. But know that they will each have a great deal of experience battling spawn. That means they'll know how to fight."

Fallon bared his teeth. "They aren't the only ones."

For the first time since coming to Merstone, Ryland paid real attention to the spawn majicar. His massive body bristled with weapons. On his left hip was an ordinary straight one-and-a-half hand sword. On the other was a kriss, its blade curving back and forth like a wriggling snake. On his back was a vicious-looking weapon that Ryland had never seen before. It had a long, flat blade ending in a split tip, with one side rounding to a spike, the other curving in a wicked hook. On the back of the blade were two more spikes. It was a weapon designed to maim and kill.

Fallon pulled a pair of spiked bars from a loop on his thigh. On the underside of each was a loop of metal. He slid his upper-right three-fingered hand through both loops and flexed. The four-inch metal claws raked the air. Next he bent and pulled a knife from its sheath on his thigh with his lower-left hand. It had a straight handle with a ten-inch blade that hooked like a sickle. He switched it to his upper-left hand and then drew the kriss. With his steel-clawed upper-right hand, Fallon reached behind his head and yanked the weapon free from his back, switching it to his lower-right hand. Now each of his four hands was armed with a deadly weapon. Ryland had no doubt the Root majicar knew how to use them. Except for Shaye, he was going to be the deadliest thing in the room.

Fallon glanced back at Ryland, who drew his own sword in readiness. The Root majicar smiled. It seemed to cut his face in half.

"I thought you'd use majick against them," Ryland said carefully.

Fallon's eyes narrowed to thin, vertical yellow slits. "So I will. But shields can defeat majick. Steel is helpful."

Majick could defeat steel too. Ryland didn't say it aloud. Instead he followed the hulking four-armed majicar, feeling about as useful as a babe armed with a wooden spoon.

Shaye settled his hands on the wards inside the wall. The flash and concussion that accompanied the breaking of the wards sent him sprawling into Fallon, who grunted and staggered from the blow. Ryland stumbled back and caught himself on the wall. Sound and majick vibrated through him, making every bone in his body ache and then burn. The ground grumbled and the walls shook. Before Ryland could even so much as moan, a hot wind blew sharply down through the stairwell. It spun in a tornado around Shaye. It tore the breath out of Ryland's mouth and lungs. He gasped and coughed. Then suddenly the air was absolutely calm and he tasted sweet fresh air. He sucked in deeply. Fallon did the same, and somewhere close, Nya made strangled growling sounds.

Shaye was on his hands and knees. His ribs worked like bellows. Slowly he pushed himself upright, wiping a fist across his mouth. Crimson smeared his pale skin. His eyes glowed bright in the shadows. Ryland swallowed hard. Fallon took a step away and Ryland thought he saw a tinge of nervousness on his strange face.

"They will have felt the effects of that all the way to the mainland," Shaye said in a gravelly voice. "We need to hurry."

"Which one do we start with?" Ryland asked.

The two buildings that were lit stood adjacent to each other on the left side of the mosaic avenue.

"That one," Shaye said, pointing at the second, which was octagonal, with ornate decorations. .

"How do you know?" Fallon asked.

Shaye turned, giving the Root majicar a bitter smile. "The wards are new—the majick still stirs in them. I can feel it."

He turned back and left the stairwell, starting up the avenue with slow, deliberate steps. Fallon strode to the left, a step behind. Ryland bracketed him on the other side. There was no sign of Nya, except for the constant prodding of lust in his groin.

Ryland's neck prickled. They were being watched. He could not see from where. His hand tightened on his sword, and he nearly laughed at the silliness of carrying nothing but a sharp piece of steel into a majickal war.

Outside the first building Shaye paused. He looked at it. It must house Crosspointe's only other compass-majicar. Then he smiled and Ryland felt a rush of fear that chilled him to the soles of his feet. He knew what Shaye was going to do. That the other man *could* do it was beyond frightening.

"Wait here," Shaye said.

Crosspointe has only one compass-majicar besides Fairlie.

"Shaye—don't do this."

"Why not?"

"Crosspointe will die without a compass-majicar."

"I don't care," Shaye said, sneering.

Ryland put his hand on the majicar's arm. "You should. Without a compass-majicar, the guild will only want Fairlie more desperately. Not to mention the new king." He was proud that he managed the last without his voice cracking.

Shaye jerked away. "Or it could distract them. They'll try to round up the compass-majicar they *know* can produce compasses. We can escape while they are busy."

Ryland licked his dry lips. He couldn't let Shaye do this.

"Think, Shaye. Crosspointe depends on compasses.

Without them we'd starve. Think of your family—think what this would do to them. Your uncle Nicholas would be ruined."

Shaye snarled. "You don't give a tinker's damn about my family. The Ramplings would be a whole lot better off without the Wevertons nipping at your heels."

"But *you* care about them. You know I'm right. Think of all the innocent people, including your family, who will suffer."

Shaye's mouth tightened, his jaw flexing as he looked at the building before him.

"It is right that you free him," came Nya's voice from between Ryland and Shaye. "He is a prisoner. He is unhappy. I hear him."

The majicar shook his head. "You are right. But so is Ryland. I can't."

He turned to look at Ryland. His eyes were sunken and his face was tormented. For a moment Ryland thought he read a faint trace of tortured understanding there, as if Shaye recognized how difficult it was to walk the line of friendship and loyalty. And then it was gone. Shaye's expression turned austere and he looked away.

He started walking up the avenue again. Ryland's relief evaporated almost instantly. He looked at the darkened buildings. At any moment the majicars could strike.

"There are seven," Nya said. "I hear them."

If anything, Ryland tensed more as they kept walking as if Nya had not spoken. But nothing happened.

Two minutes later they approached the front of the second building. Ryland marveled at the artistry of its exterior. Every square inch was covered with carvings in colored rock. Stone vines traced all over the building, spawn faces peering through the foliage. Niches provided homes for spawn statuary, each of them baretoothed and furious. Compass points radiated from around the octagonal windows and doors. Beneath all the ornate decorations was the smooth black surface of knackerstone.

Shaye stopped in front of the low wall surrounding the

building. His nostrils flared and the corners of his mouth twisted down, his chin jutting. Ryland could almost feel his fury. Shaye's hands curled into fists and he lurched as if to step forward. But before he could cross over the low wall, a majicar stepped into the road from a darkened building just beyond. He was lanky with pale yellow hair and wore a severely cut high-necked blue robe.

"Shaye. What do you do here? You are not of the Sennet. You are not even a master."

He was talking to Shaye but watching Fallon. Clearly he thought the Root majicar was responsible for breaking the wards.

Shaye turned slowly. "Brithe. I came for Fairlie."

The other majicar tipped his head quizzically. "You know what she is. She is ours." He frowned. "We have been looking for you. She said the king was holding you prisoner."

"He was."

"He let you go?"

"No."

"Your uncle helped you, then?"

"No."

Brithe stepped forward slowly, and Ryland had a sense that he was trying to keep Shaye talking. Ryland glanced at the other buildings and saw no one else. But he was certain more majicars were lying in wait.

"What happened? How did you escape?"

"I left."

Brithe frowned, starting to pay more attention to Shaye now. "How? They must have had you in a smother room. I suppose someone opened the door wishing a reward from your family or the guild."

Shaye didn't respond.

"But that doesn't answer how you managed to get all the way to the bottom of the Well," Brithe said. "Perhaps the spawn with you might have an answer. And Prince Ryland, let me welcome you. Unfortunately, you are not supposed to have seen all that you have seen. You will not be permitted to leave. None of you will."

Ryland said nothing. Fallon did not so much as twitch a muscle. Brithe turned his attention back to Shaye.

"When we spoke last, you indicated your first loyalty was to the guild. But you have broken many of our laws. I am disappointed." His voice turned cold and condemning.

"Fairlie is my soul," Shaye said, sounding like he was discussing nothing more important than a stain on his clothing. "If you let her go, I will leave here without harming anyone."

Brithe snorted. "An empty threat."

"For the loyalty I owe the guild, I will warn you this once. I have power that you cannot match—that the entire guild united cannot match. If I have to raze Merstone and kill every single one of you, then that is what I will do," Shaye said, still in that same dispassionate voice.

Brithe laughed, the sound echoing.

Ice trickled through Ryland's veins. "He escaped the smother room on his own," he said urgently. Crosspointe could no more afford the loss of its majicars than it could afford to lose its one remaining compass-majicar. He didn't think Shaye would actually destroy the island, but he also didn't doubt that he was capable of it. If that was what was necessary to rescue Fairlie, he would do it. "He is a master now, and far more. Do not underestimate him."

Brithe glanced at the prince and smiled. "Do you suppose me so stupid? It is obvious that you helped him escape. It is no secret that you and he are close friends."

Ryland shook his head sharply. "Not anymore. I am the one who cursed Fairlie. Shaye would as soon kill me as look at me."

"And yet here you are together."

"Because he's holding my brother hostage and because he's threatened to curse me with *sylveth*." Ryland told the truth flatly.

"Really?" Brithe wagged a finger at Ryland. "You should be ashamed. I had heard you were a much better politician than this. Your lies are thin indeed."

Ryland bit his tongue. Nothing he could say would

convince Brithe. Only a demonstration by Shaye would do it, but then it would be too late.

"Well then," Brithe said after several grains passed, "I suppose we should get on with it, shouldn't we?"

He raised his hands and turquoise majick billowed from his palms. It boiled in an uncertain cloud for a moment before snaking at Shaye in a thick vine. Shaye watched it without moving. At first the majick moved slowly, like a blind worm. Then it drew into itself, firming and hardening. It hesitated, rearing back like a cobra. Then it darted forward, streaking through the last twenty feet like lightning.

Shaye didn't flinch. The head of the turquoise snake enveloped him, pushing down and twining about his body until Ryland could no longer see him through the majick.

For a long moment nothing happened. Brithe began to walk forward, his face set with concentration as he continued to feed the spell. Ryland watched him, waiting for his calm focus to turn to anxiety and then panic. His stomach churned, knowing it would not be long now.

From the corner of his eye he saw the turquoise start to thin, like mist evaporating in the sunlight. Brithe's face paled and sweat trickled down his forehead as he sought to strengthen his spell. He stopped, then struggled to back away. But he was caught. His arms jerked forward. Majick was dragged out of him, sending him sprawling on his belly. He made an agonized sound and then slumped unconscious.

There was no time to take a single breath. In another moment, six bolts of majick streaked toward Shaye, exploding on him at nearly the same moment. The concussion sent Ryland reeling, the heat singeing his hair. He leaped over the low wall and ran for the safety of the doorway. The majicars would be stuck using ordinary weapons once they stood on the knackerstone courtyard. At least then Ryland might be useful. Right now, this was Shaye's battle, and he was more than equipped to handle it.

From the door he turned to watch the battle. The bolts of majick pummeled Shaye, but while he absorbed their majick with little effort, he could not snatch them to uproot them at their source. The guild majicars were too careful for that.

Beside Ryland, Nya rippled into sight. "We should not wait," she said. "Four majicars are inside. Fairlie also. And the little one."

So Shaye had chosen right; Fairlie *was* here. Then he caught the last bit. "Little one?"

"Kin. One Fairlie made."

Spawn? That Fairlie made? Ryland could hardly comprehend the idea. But it wasn't important right now. "What about Shaye and Fallon?"

"Fallon comes now."

As she spoke, Fallon twitched and jerked his head to look at Nya. She had no doubt spoken in his mind. He bounded over the low wall and ran across the courtyard, his myriad weapons flashing in the light.

More bolts hit Shaye. How long would he do nothing? Ryland didn't know if it was a plan to exhaust his opponents or—

He recalled that fleeting look of torment on Shaye's face when he'd decided not to free the other compass-majicars, and before that, the horror in his eyes as he knelt beside the fallen majicars in the stairwell after sucking them dry of majick. These men and women were his brethren and possibly his friends. Maybe he could not bring himself to attack them.

An ache filled Ryland's chest. So much was broken that could not be mended; so much was lost that could never be regained. He pitied Shaye. But what could he do to help him?

"Could you sneak out there and poison the other majicars?" he asked Nya.

"Yes. But he does not need my help." She sounded bitter. "Are you coming?" she demanded. "Fairlie is waiting for our help. He will follow when he is done."

Ryland hesitated. If the majicars decided to use ordinary weapons like bows or swords, Shaye would be vulnerable. But with all the majick he could command, he would certainly be able to defend himself. Slowly Ryland turned and followed Nya and Fallon inside.

It was time to face Fairlie. He wasn't looking forward to it.

Chapter 34

It had been four days since Spark had fed on Fairlie's blood. It was getting hungry. The images it sent her were growing thin again. She'd hoped it would last longer. She surreptitiously reached up and scratched it. Warm wetness stroked her hand. A lick. Was Spark tasting her? Or offering comfort?

Fairlie preferred to believe the latter.

There were four guards in the room with her. She could tell nothing about them, what little of them she could see. They never spoke to her. Neither Gliessithe nor Amberdel had come to see her yet this day. If it was day. She could no longer tell. She counted the glasses by the changes of her guard.

She was getting very tired of sitting still inside her web. And yet— She was not going to back down; she would not let them so easily beat her. It was a matter of pride. And too, she didn't know if she could bring herself to make compasses. Except to help Spark, there was no good reason to do so.

She missed Shaye. She *ached* for him, more so every day. She'd never been so long alone and without his company. She knew he was locked up in a smother room in the castle, helpless. She imagined his agony. He'd beat his fists bloody on the walls. She bowed her head, anger boiling inside her. How she'd like to wrap her hands around the king's throat. Or Ryland's. The hatred she felt for them was as black and deep as the Inland Sea.

Time passed and her guards changed again. She sniffed. Two women and two men. They had watched her before. By the scent of it, the two men were lovers, and had become so recently. She smelled sex, their musky odors entwined like they'd just rolled out of each other's arms. It could have been her and Shaye—it should have been. Her back stiffened and her lips curled in a snarl. She heard herself give a low growl, the sound unfurling from a sere, bleak place deep in the pit of her soul.

There was a sudden silence as her four guards came alert.

After a while, the door opened and Amberdel appeared. He stood outside her webbed cage and looked up at her.

"Do you agree to our terms?"

Fairlie looked at him without speaking. He waited a long minute and then looked down, blowing out an irritated breath. Then he met her gaze again.

"You must. Don't you see you have no choice?"

"Did you find Shaye?" she countered.

"No luck yet," he said, after a pause.

Her eyes widened. They had ignored all her questions to this point. Perhaps he would answer more. "You have looked?"

"We have. But King William has many secrets and if he has smother rooms in the castle—"

"He does," Fairlie said. There was no other explanation for why Shaye had not returned to her when she'd sent him away. *Unless . . .*

She could not bear to finish the thought. She would not.

"If he has smother rooms, we do not know their location. We continue to search. We will continue no matter what you do. We won't tolerate the king administering justice or punishments to any members of the guild."

"So I should just comply and get it over with?"

"I should think you would at least be tired of your accommodations, if not hungry and thirsty."

The last words were inflected up in a question.

"I am," she said vaguely.

"Then won't you consider agreeing? It is inevitable."

She cocked her head at him. He looked like he cared. But so had Ryland. Amberdel was bound to the guild as tightly as Ryland was bound to his father. Even if Amberdel pitied her, the guild came first.

"Why should I?" she asked. "You have caged me; you have taken my clothing to humiliate me. You have never treated me like anything but an animal. Perhaps not even as well as that. Do you think I will just offer my throat to your dagger without fighting?" Her hair rose, twisting on invisible currents, and her anger flared hotly.

He shook his head. "It will not be so bad. You will be made more than comfortable. Anything you ask for we will bring you. You will be treated very well."

Her voice dropped to a throaty whisper as she rocked forward, thrusting her face at him as far as the thickened air around her would allow.

"I. Want. Shaye."

Amberdel nodded as if expecting nothing else. "I will see you tomorrow," he said and turned to leave.

Before he went three steps, the door was flung open. Gliessithe stood there.

"Come quickly!" she said. "The Well has been breached."

"That's not possible—"

The door slammed shut behind them and Fairlie could hear no more. She strained her ears but heard only the speeding hearts of her guards and the quick rasping as they breathed. She twisted, lurching awkwardly on the pillow of air. There was nothing to see, nothing to hear. What was happening? Spark gripped her hair tightly and made a soft, high-pitched sound of concern.

Grains trickled past. Nothing happened. She had just settled back to watch the door when it was flung open again. Amberdel and Gliessithe strode in with two other majicars. Amberdel glanced up at Fairlie and then looked at the four majicars who'd been standing guard over her.

"There is trouble. Go below and get instructions from Brithe. The four of us will remain here."

Fairlie's four guards hurried out without a single question. Gliessithe followed them to the door. She swung it shut and then settled her hands on either side of the jamb. Black light twisted with thin red flared from her fingers and unraveled across the door, walls, ceiling, and floor. It traced shapes and patterns like flames crawling along oil, igniting other colors in rainbow flashes as it traveled around the room. In a moment the room was flooded with jewel light that pulsed and then steadied.

"What is happening?" Fairlie asked.

Gliessithe glanced at her and then away, ignoring her. Fairlie's teeth bared. She did not say anything more—she would not beg from these people.

"Remain alert If they get as far as us, they will likely be worn down, if not depleted. They may only perform majick inside this room—if they can get past the wards. The rest of the house is smothered. You must time your strikes for the moment they enter, before they have time to gather their majick. Do not hold back. They strike at the heart of the guild and the heart of Crosspointe. The sentence is death," Gliessithe instructed her companions, taking a position with a clear line of sight to the door.

"It is possible they will not come here at all," Amberdel added, taking his own position.

"They are coming here," Gliessithe retorted. She flexed her hands together, her knuckles cracking.

"It is likely," Amberdel conceded. His touched the hilt of his sword and the dagger in his belt as if to reassure himself that they were within easy reach.

Fairlie waited for them to say more, but they fell silent. She squirmed uneasily. *They?* Who was coming for her? *Shaye.* Her heart pounded and her chest clenched like a fist. But no. He was locked in a secret smother room in the castle. Unless—had he been freed? Maybe his uncle had helped him. It was possible. More possible than the alternative—that King William had sent his pet family majicars to retrieve her. That made little sense. After all, he'd gifted her to the guild on a silver platter. There was no one else who knew she was here.

She waited, her body rigid with fear. If it was Shaye— It was too dangerous. They would kill him. Fear made her struggle. She threw herself against the invisible bonds of her prison. She clawed and kicked. Her teeth snapped together and she shrieked her fury and a warning to those who were coming. None of her guards tried to stop her. Amberdel's expression was pitying. Gliessithe smiled smugly, and Fairlie knew that no sound could escape the wards.

At last she subsided. She huddled in the middle of her prison. Her hair stood out around her head. Spark chirped and climbed out on her shoulder.

"What is *that*?" Gliessithe demanded shrilly. She was pointing. "How did it get in there?"

"It's spawn," said another majicar. She was small with a cap of graying black hair and a fiery orange robe heavy with beading.

"How did it get in there?" Gliessithe repeated.

"You must not have checked her thoroughly enough," Amberdel said.

"I was thorough. I took everything."

"Apparently not," was the black-haired majicar's tart response.

Gliessithe glared at her and then back at Fairlie. "We have to get it out of there."

"Not now," Amberdel said.

"It's helping her. Sustaining her somehow. That's why she's remained so strong."

"Not now," Amberdel repeated with more force.

Gliessithe's mouth pinched together as if she'd just eaten something very sour. She gave a little nod. "When this is done, then," she said petulantly.

"When this is done," he agreed.

He looked up at Fairlie, and she thought she saw a hint of sorrow in his red-rimmed silver eyes. She turned her head away. His eyes—all their eyes—were too much like Shaye's. The eyes of spawn. Her heart twisted. So many lies and deceptions. She hardly knew what was true anymore.

Time passed with agonizing slowness. She could hear nothing beyond the walls of her prison. The quiet grated her nerves until she thought she'd go into a frenzy again. Spark nuzzled her cheek and stroked a hand over her ear. She leaned into the caress. Warm beams of sunshine yellow fluttered through her mindscape.

"Thanks, Spark," she said aloud.

Gliessithe looked sharply at her. Fairlie bared her teeth at the other woman, daring her to open her cage. Just a crack was all she needed. She was not going to let Spark go easily.

"I have a cage just the right size for the beast," the majicar said with a malicious smile.

"I'll gut you first," Fairlie snarled.

"You can try. But we know well enough how to handle spawn like you."

"You're just as much spawn as I am."

Gliessithe shook her head. "No. I am perfect. You are . . . sloppy, third-rate work. A mistake."

"And yet you cannot make a compass, can you?" Fairlie taunted, her fingers curling into claws.

"Neither can you."

"Have done, Gliessithe," Amberdel said sharply. "You are not worth her spit. Do not forget it."

"*I* am not worth her spit? And what about you? You're no better than I am. Or maybe you want a bite of her pie? She'd rip you in half."

Amberdel's jaw tightened. He walked over to Gliessithe, standing so that his nose nearly touched hers. "I said—*Have done*. If you are the reason she holds out her agreement, the rest of the Sennet will know it. I will have you ousted."

Her face whitened. She did not speak again. Amberdel nodded once and returned to his position.

The first sign they had that the outer defenders had failed was a scratching noise at the door.

Gliessithe started. "What is that?"

"We have guests," the black-haired majicar replied tensely.

There were hard thumps on the door, but it did not open. Fairlie rocked unsteadily as she came to her knees, watching the door as avidly as her guards did. More thumps and then silence. Every muscle in her body tensed as she waited, but nothing happened. Grains dribbled past, turning into minutes.

"What's happening?" the fourth guard asked. He was older than the others, with a bulbous forehead and fleshy lips. His robe was yellow, making him look jaundiced.

"The wards hold," Amberdel said, his eyes narrowed as he watched the door. "But how did they get past Brithe and the others?"

He exchanged a worried glance with the black-haired majicar, whose lips pinched together.

Then things changed.

The wards flared incandescently, and then they started to silently untie themselves and flow in tangles toward the door, disappearing through it. Her guards gasped.

"That's impossible," the black-haired majicar murmured, her eyes wide with horror and a stirring of fear.

"Apparently not," Amberdel said in a voice devoid of emotion.

Fairlie glanced at him. Though he revealed no outward tension, his heart galloped and there was a vinegary smell of sweat rising from him. And not just him. All of them. Gliessethe had gone completely white, and the older majicar was biting his lips hard enough that Fairlie thought he would draw blood.

She felt the *gather* of majick as they prepared themselves. Spark fluffed its feathers and made a humming sound. Spiraling pink light on her mindscape asked a question.

"I hope they are friends," she told it softly. "But I don't know."

That earned her a swift look from Amberdel, and then he turned away, focusing his attention back on majick spells draining away through the door.

It seemed to take forever for the last of the wards to vanish and the door to open. It started to crack apart, upon which the black-haired majicar and Gliessithe let loose with powerful bolts. Stone and wood shattered. Shards spun wildly through the air. They slammed against the web holding Fairlie and ricocheted away. A hail fell on the majicar defenders, but most of the rubble and debris fell on Fairlie's rescuers. Dust plumed into a fog. Fairlie could see nothing.

Something tickled her mind. It was tentative, and it was familiar.

Fairlie?

"Nya?"

We are coming to help. Shaye is with us.

That took Fairlie aback. "How? The king had him."

He escaped.

"That's impossible."

But true it is. I cannot lie to you. Not when our minds touch. You should be able to know that.

Fairlie frowned, not answering. How should she be able to know? But she knew how. She could almost see the connection between them. If she wanted, she could follow it and be inside Nya's mind. She'd done it before, when she'd been transformed. She'd reached deep inside the spawn woman's head and torn at her moorings. Fairlie squinted, trying to see through the fog of dust. The only sounds she could hear were the rattle of stones slipping over each other, the scrape and crunch of boots, and the rustle of clothing.

"Shaye?" She couldn't help herself. She needed to hear his voice. But there was no answer. Her stomach twisted. "Shaye?" Her voice echoed.

"He's hurt."

Ryland. Her face contorted. She threw herself at the walls of her invisible prison. She clawed and a scream of hate tore from her throat. But her frenzied struggles did nothing. The wards of the room had vanished, but the web holding her was fully intact. At last she quieted, crouching in her web, tensed and ready.

Where are the majicars? Can you find them? Now—in the confusion—we can hunt them!

Nya's voice was eager in Fairlie's mind. She scanned the scene below her, ignoring the interfering screen of her prison. The dust remained thick. It confused her. This was her element. She ought to be able to see better. She eyed the prison web angrily. It suppressed her abilities. Still, she had the advantage of height, and the majicars had dressed themselves brightly.

She hunched down, searching the rubble. Half of the room's walls remained somewhat intact, though large chunks of stone had fallen from above. She spotted the yellow robe of the fleshy-lipped majicar mashed beneath one. She sniffed and smelled blood.

One is dead, she said silently, pushing the words back along the invisible thread connecting her to Nya. Gliessithe and the black-haired majicar had been closest to the door. Gliessethe had been wearing dove gray robes and the black-haired majicar's had been fire orange. Fairlie saw the second one first. She was crouched next to a stub of the wall, her robes so dust-covered that Fairlie only saw a flash of orange. It was enough.

She reached out to Nya and grabbed her mind. She drew the other woman inside her to let her see through her eyes.

There.

I will take care of her. Nya withdrew back to herself, but not before she and Fairlie shared a moment of pure animal fury.

Grains later, Fairlie caught a glimpse of movement. Nya crawled over the rubble on all fours like a cat, sniffing the air. She sneezed, but did not stop. She had an elegant, deadly grace as she stalked her prey. Fairlie frowned. Could *she* change her body?

Just in front of you. Go right. You can come up from behind. Fairlie gave the instructions dispassionately. She didn't have the slightest pity for the majicar, though on some level she recognized that the woman must have family and lovers or a husband. People would miss her.

But she was also Fairlie's enemy, and in this war there could be no prisoners.

The majicar never knew she was under attack. Nya skulked around behind her, never making a sound. Then she bounded forward. She struck down with her fists, driving the spikes that protruded from her forearms into the majicar's back. The woman was dead before she hit the ground.

A brilliant green light flashed and then a flare of dark blood red. The two collided and the air sizzled and popped. Fairlie swung around and found Amberdel dueling with a four-armed spawn. Fallon. He had poisoned Shaye, and he had turned the splinters of worked *sylveth* under her skin to raw form.

Now he stood in front of Shaye and Ryland, protecting them. Now that the dust had begun to thin, she could see them on the ground behind him. The bottom half of Shaye's body lay crushed beneath a pile of rubble. He was gasping, blood streaming from his mouth. Ryland knelt by his head, speaking quickly. Fairlie flung herself at her cage again in a frenzy of fear.

"Shaye!" she screamed in an agony of bitter helplessness.

Suddenly another bolt struck at Fallon. Gliessethe appeared directly below Fairlie's cage. She swayed, her robe dusty and torn. Blood trickled down both her pale cheeks. Her bristle-cut hair was gray with dust. She limped forward, driving bolt after bolt of yellow majick at Fallon. Amberdel redoubled his efforts, ratcheting Fallon with hard-hitting bursts of green majick. The Root majicar stumbled back. He tripped and fell to one knee.

Stop them! Fairlie shrieked at Nya.

And suddenly Nya was there. She gave a roaring cry as she leaped up onto Gliessithe's back and bore her to the floor. Then she bent, her toothy mouth opening wide. She ripped the majicar's throat out. Blood fountained and Gliessithe's scream died in a gurgle.

Fairlie watched, grimly satisfied. Blood pooled on the

ground below her and she licked her lips. Then there was another cry. She looked at Fallon and then Amberdel. The guild majicar had fallen to his knees, sagging down so that he was sitting on his heels. His hands braced against the floor. Blood ran from the wound in his chest where a dagger protruded.

Fallon picked himself up off the ground and stalked forward, brandishing two swords in his upper hands.

"Stop!" Fairlie cried, when Fallon lifted one arm high over Amberdel's head.

He hesitated, looking up. His expression was pitiless. "He needs to die."

Part of Fairlie wanted to agree. Anger churned like acid, corroding and burning. But Amberdel was only doing what he thought right. And he had been as kind as he could. He had pitied her.

"No," she said, unable to explain.

"Leave him, Fallon," Nya said aloud. "It is her right to say."

The Root majicar hesitated and then lowered his arm and set the tip against the guild majicar's throat. "Twitch a muscle and I will skewer you."

Amberdel did not move. The dagger in his chest lifted with every breath, blood splotching his clothing. His breath rattled in his chest. He would die soon anyway, with or without Fallon's help. It sorrowed Fairlie. But then she looked at Ryland and Shaye and forgot about Amberdel.

"You need to help Shaye," she said to Fallon.

He glanced at her. There was no friendship in the look.

"He needs *sylveth*. It will heal him."

He looked at Nya. The two exchanged more than a look, Fairlie was certain of it. She wished she could follow the thread back to Nya's mind and eavesdrop.

"What is it? Help him."

"We cannot open the cage without him," Nya told Fallon aloud. She sounded unhappy.

They didn't *want* to help him, Fairlie realized. They

were afraid of him. She could smell it. And more. She could feel Nya's anger at him. It filled her like a putrefying cancer.

"Watch him then," Fallon said.

He waited until Nya came to stand over Amberdel, one clawed hand on his shoulder, the points of her poisoned arm spikes a breath from his face.

"Move and you die," she whispered. The words were drenched in the same rage she had directed at Shaye. Fairlie wondered at its cause.

Fallon went to stand by Shaye. He lay too still. His arms were outflung, his head gray with dust. He was hardly breathing.

"I need something made of *sylveth*," Fallon said to no one.

Ryland glanced down at himself, patting himself down and then pulling the royal compass pendant from his shirt. "I have this. Will it work?"

"Something else would be better. There is much majick in the pendant. It will be difficult to contain."

"Even with—?"

Ryland broke off the question, gesturing with his chin toward Shaye. Fairlie could have ripped his tongue out when he stopped. What was going on? Fallon shook his head, evidently understanding the question better than she did.

"I don't know how that works. He is unconscious and cannot control it. It is too great a risk."

"What about his *illidre*?" Ryland asked.

The Root majicar slowly shook his horned head. "I— His majick is something I do not understand. Releasing his *illidre* could destroy us all."

"Hurry!" Fairlie almost screamed. She could hear Shaye's heart slowing. His and Amberdel's. They would die together. "There's not much time. You have to hurry," she urged, once again struggling ineffectually against the air that held her. She forced herself to stop, her mind snagging on another idea.

"Amberdel. Free me. Let me go. Let me help him."

"How?" Fallon demanded.

Fairlie ignored him. "Amberdel. I can save him. And you. This is part of what I am now. Trust me. Let me try."

The guild majicar eased his head around. Nya let him move, her bloodstained muzzle close against his ear.

"Careful," she whispered.

"Please," Fairlie begged. "Please. I will stay. I will be a compass-majicar for you. Just let me help him."

The words tumbled from her. She meant every one.

He gave a faint nod.

"Let him go," Fairlie ordered.

The Root woman hesitated. Then she slowly stepped back. Amberdel closed his eyes. He drew a breath. He moaned, his face tightening with pain. Then he brought up a hand. It shook. With an effort he steadied it. He thrust out his fingers. Nothing happened. There was no green light. Then his body convulsed and he fell over on his side. Fairlie howled with fury and frustration.

Before the sound of it died away, something *changed*. She felt a softening in the air below her. She began to sink down. She felt the breaking of the web more than she saw it. There was a high-pitched sound, like a shrieking wind. And then suddenly the web cracked apart and fell with a thunderous clatter. Fairlie fell with it. She landed on her hands and feet. In an instant she thrust herself up and leaped across the rubble to Shaye's side.

He still breathed.

Her heart clenched tight, she put her hand on his chest. She felt the *sylveth* inside her.

Please?

There was a sense of acquiescence. Then she felt the *sylveth* sliding beneath her skin to her fingers. She pushed it into Shaye. He shuddered as if struck. Fairlie looked at the blocks of stone covering his lower body.

"Get that off him." Without waiting to see if she was obeyed, she fixed her eyes back on Shaye's face. She knew the *sylveth* could cure him. She knew it because it told her so. But she didn't know if there was time.

She bent close, resting her forehead against his, pressing her hands to either side of his face. He felt hot, like a fire roared inside him. His breathing was stertorous.

"I am here. Come back. Don't let them win."

She murmured the words over and over. She hardly heard the sounds of shifting rubble as Ryland, Nya, and Fallon worked to clear the debris from his legs. All she could hear was the uneven beat of Shaye's heart and his labored breathing.

Then she heard nothing.

Shaye spasmed, his back arching. He did not breathe. His heart froze. Fairlie clutched his head.

"Shaye!"

Then suddenly he gave a great gasp and his eyes opened. He dragged in a jagged breath and began to cough. He rolled onto his side, his coughs deep and tearing. Then he pushed to his feet, spinning around. His eyes were wild.

Then he began to register his surroundings. His gaze skidded over Ryland, Nya, and Fallon, and then shot behind to the broken room. His eyes widened and he started forward. He stumbled and fell into Fairlie. She steadied him.

His gaze bored into her as if he couldn't quite believe she was there. Then he pulled her to him. Spark chittered and slapped his cheek with its small blue hand. Shaye jerked back.

"What is that?"

"This is Spark."

Shaye looked at the little creature a long moment. "A pleasure, Spark," he said at last, and then pulled Fairlie back against him, wrapping his arms around her, ignoring Spark's uneasy chirping.

Fairlie clung to him, pressing her face into the crook of his neck. He was going to live. And then she remembered Amberdel. Slowly she pushed herself away, her face hardening. She'd made a promise. Shaye followed her to her feet.

"We should leave. It may be a battle to get out," he said.

Fairlie shook her head. "No."

She turned and went to Amberdel's side. Shaye followed after.

"What are you doing?" he demanded. "We have to go. Leave him. He's better dead."

Blood seeped from the guild majicar's wound. His heart fluttered erratically. In a minute or two he'd be dead and her promise to him wouldn't matter. But she couldn't do it. She put her hand to his chest, and once again the *sylveth* answered her. She ached with the hurt she caused it, and more for what she was going to have to say to Shaye. She pulled the dagger from Amberdel and flung it aside. It clattered loudly in the silence.

She stood, watching as the majicar's body seized and his wound closed. Shaye grasped her arm, spinning her around.

"What are you doing?" he demanded.

His face was twisted. He looked furious. But Fairlie knew him better than that. Dread drove him.

"I promised him. He freed me to save you," she said, not letting herself look away. "For that I will stay and make compasses for the guild."

Shaye's mouth opened and his throat worked. No sound emerged. He grabbed her, his fingers gouging her arms. She felt no pain. Her spawn body was too strong for his grip to hurt.

"I can't lose you," he rasped. "I can't. Do not do this. Please. How can he expect you to keep a promise made while you were a prisoner, when I was lying there dying? You were right to do whatever you needed to do and to the depths with promises. They *kidnapped* you and held you prisoner. They have no right to expect anything at all." He shook her. "Please," he whispered.

She stroked her fingers down his face. Her glance flitted to Ryland, who stood behind him. Something congealed inside her. She looked back at Shaye. "I promised. I knew what I was doing and I was willing to do anything." He started to speak, and she pressed her fingers to his lips. "I am so tired of broken promises and betrayal. Of course I can find a reason not to do it. Just like— Just like Ryland and King William. But I won't. *I won't*. Can you understand?"

"No. I don't." His mouth tightened. He stepped back. "All right, then. I'll stay with you."

"You can't," Ryland said. "Think, Shaye. After what you've done? With all that you can do? They'll never let you stay. They'll kill you as soon as they can manage."

"As if you care," Shaye snapped. "You just don't want the guild to get their hands on me."

Fairlie stiffened. "What? Why? What's going on?"

Both men looked past her. She turned. Amberdel was sitting up, watching the exchange. He stood slowly, pain creasing his face.

"I would like to know that as well," he said. "How did you get down here? You aren't even a master. I thought it was him." He gestured at the silent Fallon. "But it wasn't, was it? You managed to bring them into the Kalpestrine and down into the Well. And outside— there were seven Sennet majicars waiting for you. You shouldn't have been able to get past them. And yet you did." He paused, his brow furrowing deeply. "*You* took down the wards in here. But—how?"

Shaye stepped around Fairlie, putting her behind him. "What will you give me if I tell you?"

"He won't give you anything. He'll have to keep you here or kill you. You know it. You cannot trust him."

Shaye ignored Ryland. "Let Fairlie go. I'll tell you what you want to know."

"Shaye—"

The look he turned on Fairlie was hard and cold. She flinched from it. Then a wave of raw desperation flickered across his countenance. He reached out to cup her cheek and then dropped his hand before he touched her. "You made your choice. Let me make mine. I can't leave you here with them. I won't."

Amberdel watched the exchange, his expression unreadable. "I can make no agreement for the Sennet."

"I'm not asking you to. It's just you and me."

"What happened to everyone outside?"

"They are incapacitated."

"What did you do to them?'

Shaye glanced again at Fairlie and back. "I stole their majick. They are no longer majicars."

Amberdel's face went white and his mouth went slack. Fairlie knew how he felt. She looked at Ryland, Nya, and Fallon. None of them looked surprised. Ryland was grim. She thought of the way the wards had unraveled and knew that Shaye had done the same thing—stolen the majick right out of them.

"You're Pale-blasted. That isn't possible," Amberdel rasped out at last.

"So I am told. Perhaps you want to ask Brithe. He was still alive, last I checked. Though I don't think he qualifies to stand in the Sennet any longer." Shaye paused, then spoke slowly. "I crafted a spell that allows me to steal the majick from any source."

"And you want to trade the knowledge of it for Fairlie."

"No. I do not *want* to. This is not the kind of majick any of us was intended to have. It would pit majicar against majicar and destroy the guild. But I will give it to you if you will release her."

Amberdel stared at Shaye. After a moment he turned around and stared at the wall, his hands knotted behind him. A minute passed, and then another. At last he faced them again.

"I don't want to know. It's better if you go, now. Far away. Leave Crosspointe and take her with you. Hide well. The guild will hunt you for eternity to learn the secret of that spell. But you are right—it will destroy us."

Fairlie stared, stunned. She'd meant what she said. She would stay. Amberdel looked at her, the corners of his mouth lifting in a ghost of a smile.

"If it had been me, I would have let you die. Shaye is correct. You owed me nothing. I thank you for my life." His smile faded. "I was left here today because of this." He fished in the neckline of his shirt and pulled out a pendant. It was identical to Ryland's. A royal pendant. "I was not entirely trusted to carry out today's events on the mainland."

"But you aren't family," Ryland declared in surprise.

"Actually, I am. From the wrong side of the sheets. And as far as the Sennet knows, I am quite bitter about the whole matter." He grinned at the prince and then looked at Fairlie. "Shaye can't stay and he won't leave without you," he said. "Crosspointe is better off without you both, right now. I think my cousin agrees with me," he said, raising his brows at Ryland.

The prince nodded slowly, looking bemused.

"Then you must leave as quickly as possible. There is a secret passage I can show you. I can't key the wards, but I suspect Shaye will have no difficulties."

He began to walk away, and then a faint blush colored his cheeks. He slid out of his blue robe and offered it to Fairlie. She glanced down at herself. She was still naked, her skin streaked with dust. It didn't bother her, but she appreciated the gesture. It was a kindness. She took the robe and donned it, buttoning it down the front.

"Quickly now," Amberdel said, starting across the rubble.

Ryland, Fallon, and Nya fell in behind. Shaye and Fairlie didn't move. She stared at him. She couldn't find the words for what she felt. She wanted to apologize—he would have given everything up for her. Everything. But she hadn't. She'd clung to an elusive pride and honor, intent on keeping a promise that no one but she expected her to keep. *Sorry* seemed paltry in the face of his sacrifice.

He stepped closer to her, sliding his hands along her shoulders and around the back of her head. He pressed his forehead to hers, the warmth of his breath whispering over her skin. Spark fluffed its feathers and made an indignant sound.

In a voice thick with emotion, Shaye said, "*Do not* try to let go of me again. I won't survive."

Fairlie swallowed the lump that lodged in her throat. "Never again."

He closed his eyes. Then he brushed his lips against her in a feather-soft caress. "Good. Now can we go before I have to hurt someone else?"

There was real pain in the question. Fairlie realized that coming after her had cost him dearly. Her jaw tightened. He was done paying. Not for her, never again.

Shaye pulled away, frowning. "What is wrong? Your eyes are like wildfire."

"I love you. I won't let go of you again." She paused. "I promise."

He grabbed her hand and started after the others. "I'll hold you to it."

Chapter 35

They picked their way out of the rubble. In the undamaged rooms below, Fairlie discovered that Amberdel had not lied when he told her she would have been comfortable. The furnishings and decor were as luxurious as any of the royal rooms in the castle. Fairlie eyed it all disparagingly. She preferred the narrow bed in her forge.

A tremor ran through her. Her hand tightened on Shaye's. She would have another forge, she promised herself. Just because she didn't require one didn't mean she couldn't use one if she wanted. Spark chittered softly and patted her cheek. She reached up and scratched its chest.

"Where did you come by Spark?" Shaye asked.

"I made it accidentally," she said. "After you didn't come back to me."

His expression tightened. "I should never have left. I'm sorry I took so long to come get you."

"How did you get free?"

"I couldn't let them hurt you anymore," he said softly. "I had to get back to you."

He paused and Fairlie waited for him to say more. The love he felt for her was something she could not quite grasp. It was so vast, so deep—how could she be worthy of such a thing?

"There are things I need to tell you. But now is not the time." He glanced meaningfully ahead at their companions.

Fairlie nodded and fell silent again.

They stepped out onto the courtyard and she gazed about her in wonder. They crossed the majick-deadening courtyard. Before she stepped off it, she crouched, running her fingers over the silver-inlaid knackerstone. She closed her eyes. There was no time for this. But she was driven by the hopeless silence of the *sylveth* inside her. It had sacrificed itself—themselves—for Amberdel and Shaye. She could have forced it—she *would have*—if it had not given itself willingly.

Beneath her fingertips she felt the *sylveth* inside the knackerstone. It resonated with pain. She could not leave it. She looked around at all the buildings along the corridor. She could not take it all. There was no time, even if she could physically manage it. But she could do a little.

She pressed her hand flat on the stone. She pushed down into it. Then she reached outward through the stone, calling the *sylveth* to her. The gold lace patterns on her arm swirled and writhed.

Sylveth collected around her fingers and slid beneath her skin. As it had before, it insinuated itself into crevices and between folds, filling every empty space inside her. More wormed inside. She felt heavy and full. Her insides were being squeezed uncomfortably. But she could not stop, not until she had pulled it all in. She groaned.

"Fairlie?"

Shaye's hands settled on her shoulders. "I am here. Take whatever you need."

The generosity and blind trust of that offer boggled her. It shouldn't have, not after all he'd done, after all he'd been willing to do. The *sylveth* would not hurt him. He was a majicar. She felt him stiffen, his fingers clenching as she allowed the raw *sylveth* to flow into him. She traced its touch, making sure it did no harm.

She was not prepared to find *sylveth* already inside him. It was hardened, shaped like an upside-down pyramid. The *sylveth* flowed around it as if it didn't exist.

It was a spell. It had to be. It had something to do with

his ability to steal majick. She caressed it with a phantom touch and felt him shudder, his knees buckling so that he fell to the ground behind her. His hands clutched her shoulders.

"Don't," he gasped.

Fairlie froze, her stomach clenching. What had she done? "Did I hurt you?"

"No. That was— Just don't do it . . . again. I can't— Not here. Not now."

His thick, disjointed words made little sense, but Fairlie understood well enough to leave the thing alone.

She continued to let the *sylveth* flow into him.

"Tell me if it's too much," she said.

But he did not speak and eventually the *sylveth* from the courtyard was gone, leaving behind only a lumpy plane of obsidian and a tangle of silver wire.

Carefully Fairlie pushed to her feet. She felt heavy and unwieldy. Shaye rose and staggered. She caught him around the waist, bracing against him. Together they found balance.

"It doesn't hurt," he said in dazed surprise.

"Should it?" But then Fairlie remembered the first time that she had taken *sylveth* inside herself. Unwilling, it could and had hurt her. But how did Shaye know?

She started to turn them around and found Amberdel standing beside her, his gaze fixed on the destroyed courtyard. He shook his head slowly.

"There have been a few compass-majicars who could do that. That's why the spell web was wrapped in knackercloth." He looked at her. "Why?"

Fairlie lifted her head, her eyelids sagging. "Because it wants to return to the sea."

He frowned. "What wants—? You mean the *sylveth*?"

"Yes."

"It *wants*?" he repeated, incredulous.

She nodded.

"But it's not . . ." He trailed off in consternation.

"It is. It can speak. To me, anyhow."

"It speaks?" His voice rose in a squeak. Then he pulled himself together. "We can't stay here any longer. Someone will come soon."

"They may be busy," Shaye said. "I loosed the spawn on the floor above and I warded the stairwell."

"I don't know how long it will hold. Let's hurry."

But Fairlie and Shaye could not hurry. The *sylveth* nestled inside them, but the weight was dreadful. Every bit of Fairlie's insides felt squeezed. Her lungs would not expand, and her heart ached with the pressure against it. Amberdel paused beside the body of a blond maji-car sprawled on the intricate mosaic avenue running through the vast cavern of buildings. He turned the unconscious man onto his back.

Amberdel's face pinched tight. He looked at Shaye. "His majick is gone?"

Shaye nodded.

"Can he get it back? If he touches *sylveth*?"

"I don't know."

Amberdel dragged a hand through his ginger hair. "By the gods. This is—" He broke off with a grimace.

Fairlie wondered what he had been about to say. *Evil? Dreadful? Amazing? Astonishing?* Any and all of those things? Shaye's face was shuttered, but she could feel the pain enveloping him. He had not wanted to hurt anyone this way, and stripping a majicar of his power was a torture beyond reckoning. Like transforming a friend into spawn.

She scowled at Ryland. He'd come to help her escape the majicars, but she wasn't sure how much that mattered. Could he ever make up for what he'd done? *Never*. Her grip on Shaye tightened. He looked at her, following her gaze to Ryland.

"King William is dead."

"What?" Shock and angry satisfaction rolled through Fairlie. "Did you—?"

Shaye shook his head. "No. It happened just after we came to Merstone. Ryland's helping us because I put a blade in Vaughn's neck and bespelled him. If he betrays us, Vaughn dies. And I'll curse Ryland with *sylveth*."

"Good," she said, loud enough for Ryland to hear.

The prince flushed, his mouth clamping so hard it was ringed with white. Fairlie stared at him, her lip curled. She had not forgiven him. Nor would she pity him the loss of his father or his fear for his brother. The old Fairlie would have. But Ryland had murdered her. Now he had to deal with the Fairlie he'd created.

They left Brithe where he lay and started off down the long avenue. As they walked, the *sylveth* began to feel less alien and Fairlie found herself able to walk more easily. It took her a while to realize that Nya no longer walked on all fours. She paced along just ahead. Fallon walked abreast of her, though he kept his distance. Likewise, Ryland walked well ahead, with Amberdel.

Her gaze slid to the bracelet circling Nya's wrist. As she watched, the patterns changed She groped in her mind for the thread that had connected them and found it, like a deserted road. She pressed outward along it, slipping inside Nya's mind.

Thank you. For coming for me.

I told you I would help you. Nya stopped short, turning to look at Fairlie. *Your lover is dangerous.*

Fairlie grimaced. *So am I. So are you and Fallon. We are all dangerous. But he is not evil.*

What is evil? The question was heavy and bitter.

I suppose it depends on whether you're inside the cage or outside, Fairlie said grimly.

"Is something wrong?" Amberdel asked. He'd retraced his steps and come to stand beside Nya. A strange look swept his face. His cheeks flushed scarlet. Fairlie heard his heart begin to race and heat pulse in his body. He looked hungrily at Nya as if swept by a sudden lust. Fairlie frowned. Amberdel put out his hand and stroked Nya's shoulder. She cringed from his touch, snapping her teeth at him. Fallon leaped forward and yanked the majicar away, shoving him back.

Amberdel blinked dazedly. He swayed, shuffling toward Nya.

"It's getting worse," she said, backing away toward Fairlie and Shaye. "Why now?"

"What is?" Fairlie demanded as Fallon caught Amberdel by the waist and dragged him farther up the road. Ryland's face was turning red as well, and he began backing away, following the two majicars.

Nya hung her head, her body shuddering. "It is getting harder to resist," she murmured.

"You didn't say anything about that before," Shaye said. "That you felt anything."

"I should be stronger than this. I have want for no one but—" Her teeth clicked together. "But my body is wishing something different. You are not affected now," she said. It was as much an accusation as a question.

Shaye shook his head. "No. Fairlie is all I want."

Warmth rushed through Fairlie at his words, at the way he spoke them as if he could imagine nothing else. "What is going on?" she asked, looking at them both.

"She's putting off some sort of majickal come-hither. Any man caught in it starts lusting after her."

I do not want of any of them. How can he resist me, but I cannot resist them? I love Leighton as much as he loves you. The words were anguished. Beneath them wriggled a worm of fear. Nya's body was struggling against her mind, and she did not know if she would win.

How could you? You have abandoned him. She felt the other woman recoil and withdraw like a wounded animal.

Fairlie found herself pitying Nya. She was still angry with her for helping the king and Ryland turn her into spawn, but she could not ignore Nya's obvious pain. No more than she could bear Spark's or that of the *sylveth* inside her. Without letting herself think about it, she reached out with her mind, offering comfort. She felt Nya's startlement, and then gratitude as the other woman leaned on the strength that Fairlie offered.

They began walking again. This time Nya paced along

beside Fairlie and Shaye, with the other three men ranging far ahead.

He pines for you still, Fairlie said after a while.

I am not what he married. Bitter, bitter words.

Then let Fallon have you and be done with it, Fairlie said harshly.

Nya withdrew again as Amberdel turned off the mosaic avenue and led them on a winding path toward the wall of the cavern. In the distance behind them, they heard a sound like a thunderclap. The earth grumbled and pebbles battered down in a hail from above.

"They've broken through my wards," Shaye said, looking up. "We should hurry. There will be a backlash soon—we've manipulated a lot of majick. It could get ugly."

Amberdel nodded and walked faster. They ran into a dead end, and he turned and walked along the cavern wall. He found a narrow track that led upward into the darkness. It was so small that it would have been easy to overlook. Ryland and Fallon followed after him. The prince stumbled and skidded, unable to see well in the murk. Fallon, like Fairlie, seemed to have no difficulties.

Nya, Fairlie, and Shaye waited as the others went ahead, wanting to allow some distance between them and the three men susceptible to Nya's lure.

Fairlie began to think about Nya's explanation for why she'd cursed Fairlie with *sylveth*. She'd said it was in trade for a Pale on the Root. But what would spawn need with a Pale? They were immune to *sylveth*, after they'd been cursed once. She snorted softly at her stupidity. Their clothes were vulnerable, not to mention their houses, tools, livestock or anything at all—a Pale would protect those things from the Chance storms. It would allow them to have homes and live like . . . *people*. The word troubled her. Was she not a person? Or Nya? Or Fallon? But even majicars kept the fact that they were spawn secret. As far as the rest of the world was concerned, spawn were vermin.

The ball of anger and hatred that Fairlie carried in her chest loosened. Nya had wanted to protect her people. Just like Ryland. Fairlie could understand it, even if she could not forgive. At least Nya had not been her friend. Nor had she had a choice, not if she was driven by majick. Not like Ryland.

When their three companions had climbed well away, Nya started up. At the top was a narrow cave. Fairlie had to turn sideways and duck her head to squeeze through. It went on for fifty feet before opening into a small chamber. Both Amberdel and Ryland were staring hungrily at Nya, who was pressed up against the wall as far from them as possible. Fallon held the two men with his muscular arms, but he also could not tear his gaze from Nya.

"What now?" Fairlie said. Then she noticed an opening behind the three men.

Shaye pushed inside the chamber behind her and went to the opening. Fairlie stepped protectively in front of Nya, though she doubted anything she did would deter the men. A glazed look had swept over both Amberdel and Ryland, and they were beginning to struggle against Fallon's grip.

A thunderclap and a flash of yellow and green light marked the death of the wards. Majick slammed against them and dug gouts of sand up in a stinging whirlwind. A moment later it was gone. Fairlie coughed, rubbing the grit from her eyes and nose. She glanced at Shaye. He was looking at her. There was expectation in his expression, and a bracing, as if he was waiting for a blow. But why? Then he was pushed aside as Fallon grasped Amberdel and Ryland and thrust the men into the passage ahead of him. Nya sagged against the wall, her heart thundering.

"Soon even Fallon will not be able to stop himself," she whispered.

Maybe it's time you find your Captain Plusby.

I do not want him to want me because of majick, Nya said fiercely.

*Then choose the man you will take instead. Or soon
you won't have any choice.*

Nya did not answer. She stalked down the passage,
her mind roiling. Fairlie followed, with Shaye close behind. He caught her hand, pulling her to face him.

"Are you afraid of me?" he demanded.

"What?" Fairlie asked stupidly.

"Are you afraid of me?" He ran his fingers through
his hair. His hand shook. "I can steal the majick out of a
majicar. I don't know who or what is strong enough to
stop me. You should be afraid of me."

"Have you gone maggoty? Of course I'm not afraid of
you. There's no one I trust more."

His hand gripped hers. "Are you sure?"

"The question is, are you sure? I'm not exactly the
woman you fell in love with."

"Yes, you are," he said fiercely. He swallowed. "Where
are we going to go? If we stay in Crosspointe, I think we
can hide for a while. I can disguise you, but the guild will
come hunting for us. And sooner or later they will find
us. I—" He swallowed hard. "I would rather not face
them. I will win, I think."

"We'll go to the Root," Fairlie said as if she'd planned
it. "For a while at least. But what about your family?
Your uncle? He is powerful and influential. Surely he
could hide you."

Shaye's voice was glacial. His hand clenched on her arm.
"You promised you would not try to let go of me again."

"That's not what I'm doing."

"No? I won't be separated from you again."

"But your family—"

"Why are you arguing with me?"

Fairlie didn't really know. She wanted to grab him and
never let him go. But Shaye had a lot of reasons to stay
in Crosspointe. And going to the Root— It was an un-
civilized place. There was absolutely nothing there, not
one town, not even a port. They'd have to carve a life
from nothing. It wasn't the life he was meant to lead.
How could she let him follow her there?

"All right. If you are certain that's what you want."

Shaye snorted. "I want you. That's it. However I can get you. Don't you understand that yet?"

"I'm beginning to."

"Good. Let's get going before the guild catches up with us and I have to fight again."

He pushed her ahead of him, following closely on her heels. She smelled the others ahead, and the scent of the sea. Reaching behind her, she grasped Shaye's hand firmly. His fingers convulsed on hers. She stopped and slid her arms around him. He clutched her close. Neither spoke.

"Shaye? Fairlie?" Ryland's voice echoed down the tunnel.

Fairlie stepped back and followed his voice, still holding tightly to Shaye's hand.

Outside, Nya perched on a tall boulder. Waves splashed around her, drenching her in spume. The night sky was cloudy and the leaves dripped from a recent storm. Fallon paced along the strand, and Amberdel and Ryland waited by the mouth of the tunnel. Far across the sound, bells tolled. *The king is dead.* Fairlie smiled tightly. Then she turned her face to the moon. The breeze was chilly and brisk, but something in it was sharp and foreboding.

"There are boats up around that spur," Amberdel said, pointing. "Be careful. The dock is small and discreet but well used."

"You're going back? Won't they suspect you?" Fairlie asked.

Shaye was looking up at the mountain. "We have to go. All of us," he said suddenly.

"A backlash?" Amberdel asked.

"The Well was not protected with smother spells." Shaye's head tipped as if he was trying to listen very hard. "So much majick was released—the backlash will be terrible. I can feel it. Spells are twisting—distorting. It's spreading through the entire Kalpestrine. It's not safe for you to go back inside."

"The stones are crumbling," Fairlie added suddenly. Her hand was pressed to the side of the mountain, her eyes closed. They popped open. "It's coming down! We've got to get out of here now!"

Shaye didn't wait to hear more. He grabbed Fairlie's hand and began pelting along the strand. The others followed hard on their heels.

They were panting when they came around the spur and found the small harbor. There were lights on two ketches.

"We'll take the one on the near side in the second slip," Shaye said.

"Where will you go?" Amberdel asked breathlessly.

"Off Merstone to start. After that—we'll see."

"Good luck. I'll take the second ketch. It might be that I can help when—" Amberdel broke off as a grinding, echoing noise filled the night. The ground shook, the trees creaked and waved.

"Let's go!"

Fairlie saw Shaye mouth the words but heard nothing. The noise was deafening. Fear flooded through her, but she was frozen in place. Shaye yanked her, waving at the others to get to the boat. Fallon grappled Nya's arm and dragged her forward. She looked terrified. Ryland followed, with Shaye and Fairlie close behind.

They leaped on deck and cast off. As quickly as possible, they hoisted sail and began slicing trimly through the chop. The wind was picking up and the edge of it was cutting. Despite the protection of her new spawn body, Fairlie felt it. Its touch stroked fingers of pain over her skin and deeper, into her flesh. Her companions were no better off. Nya was crouching against the deck, huddling tight into herself. The noise of the collapsing mountain had only grown louder. It sounded like the sky itself was falling. Shaye pointed at Fairlie and Nya and then to the cabin of the ketch. Quickly Fairlie picked Nya up and carried her inside. The other woman was shuddering violently. The sharp spikes on her arms had extended and liquid beaded on the ends. Fairlie had seen her use those spikes against the majicars in her prison; the liquid was a potent poison.

Fairlie dug inside a locker and found a stack of wool blankets. She pulled them out and wrapped Nya carefully before laying her on a narrow cot. She sat beside her, rubbing a hand soothingly over her back. Inside the cabin the wind could no longer touch them. It was a relief. Unable to be heard, Fairlie pushed out along the thread connecting them, but Nya's mind whirled chaotically and Fairlie could not reach her. She withdrew, continuing to stroke the other woman's back.

Once again, there was no warning when they crossed the Pale. Fairlie fell unconscious, waking later to profound silence. She sat up. Nya remained unconscious, but her body was quiet and she slept peacefully enough.

Fairlie went out on deck. The wind had died and the night was as cold as a midwinter day. Her breath plumed in the air and ice sheathed the rails and deck. Fallon remained passed out, a blanket keeping him warm. Shaye and Ryland stood at the rail and stared east over the water. Both looked shaken. Shaye turned the moment Fairlie emerged from the cabin and pulled her close against him.

"What's happened?"

"Merstone is gone," he said.

"Gone?"

"The Kalpestrine collapsed into itself and the sea flooded it. No one could have survived."

"But—" Words failed Fairlie. She couldn't grasp the magnitude of such a disaster. "How? Why?"

"Using majick always creates a backlash. It can distort, twist, or break other spells. A majicar has to be very careful so the majick he casts doesn't tear apart nearby spells. That is why we use smother rooms for our workshops. But the Well was unprotected. I loosed a great deal of majick and then collected it again. It was enough to affect the foundations of the mountain. Add in the battles and dismantling the knackerstone, and I am surprised that we got out before it fell."

Pain etched his face, though his voice was remote. "So

many people inside," he said softly. "So many innocent people."

"What now?" Ryland said in an exhausted voice.

"Fairlie and I leave Crosspointe."

"My father has a ship. A black ship. It should be anchored in Narramore Bay. It will take you where you want to go."

"What will it cost us?" Shaye asked, his lip curling.

"Nothing. No—Vaughn. Give me back Vaughn. Please."

"You plan to just let us go—Fairlie, who can make compasses; Fallon, who can predict the nature of a majicar's talent; Nya, who can speak in the minds of spawn; and me, who can break any spell and steal any majick? The last compass-majicar is buried in the rubble of the Kalpestrine. You need another more than ever. You'll pardon me if I am skeptical, especially given your record of duplicity."

"I don't have much of a choice, do I? I dread to think what you would do to Crosspointe if I tried to force you. But you know it can't end there. Crosspointe needs all of you, especially now. Imagine what you alone could do for Crosspointe if you were willing, Shaye. Sooner or later I'll have to come for you. I won't have a choice. When I do, I will be asking for your help. I will crawl on my knees. I will do whatever you want, whatever it takes. You know that I will."

Fairlie's throat closed. Was it a threat? But no. It was a promise. That he would come, and he would pay whatever price they demanded for his betrayal. Not that he was saying he was sorry. He wasn't. He didn't like having transformed Fairlie, but he would do it again. What he was saying was that Fairlie deserved compensation for what he'd cost her. He would give it. And then he would ask for more. For what he would get, he would pay more. That was his price and his bargain.

She looked at Shaye. He nodded. He didn't fear Ryland. The prince had done the worst he could do already. Now they simply needed to get to the Root.

At dawn they slid into Narramore Bay. A single ship

sat at anchor. Fairlie watched it with trepidation as they coasted closer. It was a three-masted clipper with a sharply raked hull and fast lines. It was painted black from stem to stern. A handful of lights glimmered from lanterns hung on the yards and up on the poop deck. Even as they watched, the lights were doused as the morning sun lightened the sky.

Fairlie went to the bow for a better look.

Nya was already there, leaning on the rail and twisting her bracelet around her wrist. She had regained a facade of calmness, though through their connection Fairlie could feel the other woman's agitation. Fallon and Ryland remained in the stern, as far from Nya as was possible on the small ketch. The two spawn women watched together in companionable silence, and then Fairlie returned to Shaye.

"How long do I have to carry this *sylveth* inside me?" he asked.

"We'll let it go in open waters. I can ask it to avoid the ship."

"Ask it?"

"It talks to me." She shrugged. "It's part of what I've become."

"Compass-majicar."

"Maybe. I don't know. I don't want to hurt it. It doesn't like being made into things."

Shaye eyed her askance.

"Are you afraid of *me*?" she asked.

"Never," he said quickly. And then, "What about Spark?"

She looked up on her shoulder, where Spark perched. The little creature had flown off during their journey, returning later with a fat belly. Now it dozed, its tail wrapped firmly around Fairlie's neck, its leather wings tucked tightly against its body.

"It talks to me too. In its way."

"As long as it doesn't bite me." He paused. "I'll have to put an illusion on you to go aboard. On me too. We can't let anyone recognize us."

Fairlie nodded. She'd thought of that already. "I know."

"Have you thought about her?" He jerked his chin toward Nya. "She'll drive the men insane with lust, even if she hides. It could get ugly."

"I know that too. I suppose we'll deal with that when it happens. Now we just have to get away."

There was nothing else to say. Shaye settled a hand on her, and she felt majick wrap around her in thick, sticky folds. She looked at him. He was nondescript, with sun-bleached hair and a boyish face. She would not have recognized him if she didn't already know who he was, and if she didn't know his smell.

"What about Spark?"

"So long as it stays close to your neck, no one will see it."

"Do you hear that, Spark? Maybe you should crawl around under my hair again."

The little creature hummed low and then curled up at the nape of her neck to sleep.

Grains later, they dropped anchor and Ryland shouted up to the watch. "Ahoy the *Eidolon*!"

A round-faced sailor with weathered skin and wearing a leather skullcap peered over the side.

"Who be ye?"

"I am Prince Ryland. Wake Captain Plusby. I have passengers for him."

At the sound of Captain Plusby's name, Fairlie rocked back against Shaye. "Oh, dear Chayos," she murmured. She turned to look at Nya, but she'd already vanished in preparation for boarding.

"What's the matter?" Shaye asked quietly. "Are we in trouble?"

"Do you remember meeting Leighton Plusby that day?"

He nodded. That day was forever burned in both their memories. It was the day he'd confessed his feelings and the day she'd been transformed. It would always be *that day*.

"Do you remember his story? How his wife was lost at sea and he went mad?"

Again Shaye nodded.

"Her name was Sherenya." When he merely looked confused, she repeated the name, this time emphasizing the last three letters: "Sherenya."

A moment later comprehension hit. He glanced at the bow and back at Fairlie. "What will she do?"

"I don't know. She doesn't know he's the captain of this ship. But with any luck, it could solve the problem of driving the crew mad."

The sailor asked no questions. He withdrew, and several minutes later Captain Plusby appeared at the rail. His blond hair was tousled and he was scowling. Fairlie felt Nya press against her leg. She was trembling. Plusby eyed his guests in surprise. His eyebrows rose.

"Prince Ryland, you're looking the worse for wear. What brings you out at this time of the morning and after such a night? It sounded like the world was falling apart." His breath plumed in the cold, and he coughed and spat over the side.

"Not the world, Captain. But Merstone has fallen." The silence that met his statement was full of disbelief. "I have urgent crown business, Captain. Merstone is gone—you will certainly see for yourself when you set sail. My father is dead, and things are uncertain in Sylmont. I have passengers to take to the Root. I wish you to set sail with the tide."

Plusby looked the prince over from head to foot and then scanned his companions. Fairlie glanced at Fallon, who was now back in his human disguise. The captain rubbed a hand over his mouth. It was clear that King William's death was not news to him.

"How could Merstone fall? What does that mean?"

"Apparently some majick got out of hand. I know nothing else. As for what it means, that remains to be seen."

Plusby considered, then looked over his shoulder and muttered something. With her enhanced hearing, Fairlie could hear it clearly.

"He sent for someone named Keros," she murmured.

"Good," Ryland said.

In another few minutes, a second man joined Captain Plusby at the rail. His long, curly brown hair was tangled and he was unshaven. His clothing was rumpled and stained. He scratched his head and yawned.

"Good morning, Keros," Ryland said.

"Good morning, Prince Ryland."

He didn't look welcoming. Fairlie wondered who he was.

"They say Merstone fell. The Kalpestrine collapsed. That was the noise last night," Plusby said.

Keros went rigid, his fingers clutching the rail. "Fell? That's not possible!"

"It is, because it happened. I don't have time to waste," said Ryland. "I have need of the *Eidolon*. I have passengers who must sail to the Root as soon as possible. Sylmont is not a safe place for them at the moment."

"I take orders only from the king," Plusby said.

Keros rubbed a thumb over his lower lip, then looked at Plusby. He'd gone pale and his hands trembled. But his voice was steady. "I would have thought you would jump at the chance to go back to the Root."

"I have been making an effort to be patient."

Keros gave a fleeting smile that faded as swiftly as it appeared. "King William declared Prince Ryland prelate—equal power to the new regent. His orders are good enough. If you would prefer to wait until we have a king—or queen—you may be here until Chance."

Plusby looked faintly disconcerted and then nodded. "Very well. I'm done arguing. Crabbel—lower the ladder."

Fairlie, Ryland, Shaye, and Fallon clambered up the ladder with some difficulty. It was made of rope with wooden rungs. Even with someone holding the foot it was no easy task to climb up. The ladder twisted and swung. Fairlie relied on sheer brute strength, pulling herself up with her powerful arms. Shaye had gone first, and he steadied her over the rail. Ryland followed, and finally Fallon. Fairlie searched for Nya, but saw no sign of her. Nor did she see signs of sudden lust among the crew. Had she come aboard?

"Captain, this is Orin Walkerbrook," Ryland said, gesturing to Fallon, who bowed. He next introduced Shaye and Fairlie. "This is Robert Prior and his wife Gwyneth." He glanced at Keros, who was staring hard at Fallon, but did not introduce him.

"My condolences on the death of your father," Plusby said gravely to Ryland, after greeting his unexpected passengers. "Would you and your friends be kind enough to join me for breakfast?"

"Thank you," Ryland said stiffly. "I cannot stay. I must be on my way. Keros, may I ask you to join me? There is need of you at the castle."

Keros's mouth tightened. He flicked a glance at Shaye, Fairlie, and Fallon. Then he gave a shallow bow. "Certainly, Your Highness."

"Very good. I would like to be off as quickly as possible."

"I shall collect my things."

Keros went belowdecks. An awkward silence fell. Finally Plusby spoke. "I will leave you to make your farewells. When you are ready, Blot will show you to your quarters. If you would, please join me for breakfast as soon as we cross the Pale." He gestured toward a bulky sailor. The captain then returned to his cabin.

"Did Nya come aboard?" was Fairlie's hushed question.

"I didn't see her," Shaye said.

"Nor I," said Fallon, visibly upset. "I cannot leave her. She is too important."

Suddenly both he and Ryland straightened.

"She's here," Ryland said in a strangled voice. He shifted uncomfortably. He looked at Fairlie and then Shaye. "Remember what I said." He paused. "Whatever you think, I want you to know—I miss you both dreadfully."

Fairlie could only stare. Then abruptly she turned and stalked to the rail, keeping her back to him. She watched him and Keros leave, rejoining Shaye and Fallon only when they were gone. Blot led the three of them belowdecks to a pair of small cabins in the stern below the captain's and Pilot's quarters. The cabins were cramped, but well appointed and comfortable. Deadlights covered the windows.

Fallon retreated alone into his cabin without a word, and Fairlie and Shaye went into theirs. Blot lit a fire in the stove. "I'll send a snottie w' some water once we hoist anchor." He touched his forehead in a careless salute and left.

After the door shut behind him, Fairlie wandered about nervously. Shaye watched her, leaning against the bulkhead.

"They took the pendant you made from me," she said at last when the silence stretched thin.

"I'll make you another."

"That one was special." She wasn't sure she could have worn it anyhow, not knowing what it did to *sylveth*. All the same, she wished she still had it. She scrubbed her hands over her face. "I am filthy. I can't remember the last time I had a bath. I must smell like carrion. And all I have to wear is Amberdel's robe."

"If you want to stay, you can still change your mind. We can slip overboard and swim to shore."

"No. There is nothing for me in Crosspointe." She certainly was never going to go back to Stanton now. Better for her mother to think Fairlie was dead. She was sure that was the story that would be told. The problem was, she wasn't sure if there was anything for her on the Root either. Except Shaye.

"I should have lit Ryland's ass on fire," Shaye muttered.

"What?"

"Don't you remember, the night of your fete? I offered to light Ryland's ass on fire for you. You refused."

Fairlie grinned. "I changed my mind. Do it."

"Bit late now. I've already taken care of Vaughn. He will be well."

But the humor released something in Fairlie. She looked at him. "What will happen now? We've lost everything."

Shaye straightened and crossed the room, letting the illusion that surrounded him fall away. Fairlie felt the release of the majick that disguised her loosen as well. He stopped in front of her, cupping her cheeks in his hands.

"Everything? No. You are the one thing I cannot live without. The rest is . . . unimportant. We'll sort it out. It will be a different life, but you will not be unhappy. Not if I can do anything about it. Just keep your promise. Don't try to leave me again."

A knot rose in her throat. She remembered what the Naladei had said to her in the Maida. She was on a road with no fork and must follow it wherever it would take her. *All life is change. This is the one truth.* Her entire craft as a metalsmith was devoted to change. She could rail at her misfortune or she could embrace the gifts she'd been given. If she was honest, she was intrigued with the possibilities of what her new body could do, of the new ways she could craft metal and stone.

She pressed her hands over his. "I promise. And I promise this too—I am done with regret. What has been done cannot be undone. I am still a master metalsmith and I am still myself. The rest is just . . . decoration."

Shaye grinned. "You always did know how to find a silver lining."

Just then, there was a sound at the door. A scratching.

Let me in.

"It's Nya."

Shaye wrapped himself in illusion in the blink of an eye and went to the door. Grains later Nya shimmered into sight, standing on all fours. She tensed and crouched to the floor when the whir of the capstan and the rattle of the anchor chain sounded loud. Captain Plusby had wasted no time getting under way.

Slowly she straightened and padded farther into

the cabin. She went to Fairlie and sat beside her, close against her leg. Fairlie could feel the other woman trembling. She squatted down and put her arm over Nya's shaking shoulders.

"I need some air," Shaye said and quietly took himself out of the cabin, shutting the door firmly behind him. There was a flare of black light as he warded it. No one would disturb them.

Fairlie sat on the floor cross-legged, facing Nya. "You and I are a lot alike. Neither of us wanted this change, but we are what we are and we cannot go back. We have to live with it. Not just live with it—we have to embrace what we have become. I have decided to do that, starting now.

"The question is, what are you going to do? You can tell Captain Plusby who you are or not, but I wonder, will you forever regret not telling him and not knowing? I saw him after your ship went down. He was utterly destroyed. You most certainly still love him. I can't see that you have anything to lose."

Nya said nothing. Fairlie could feel the struggle going on inside the other woman. "Don't waste any more time. It's too precious." She hesitated. Then spoke carefully, taking the first step in embracing her new self and building a new life. "You and I are going to have to be friends, though why in the black depths I can forgive you and not Ryland, I don't know."

She brushed her fingers over the tail wrapping her neck. Spark remained asleep, oblivious. Then she extended her hand, palm up. Slowly Nya covered it with hers. Her hand was hot.

Friends, she said in Fairlie's mind. There was wonder in the word, and a deep loneliness. There was also uncertainty. Fairlie could easily read the reason why. She couldn't believe Fairlie could forgive.

But I do. Because I choose to. See for yourself.

And then she did something she thought she'd never do. She opened herself to Nya. The other woman hesitated, then slipped into Fairlie's mind. Her touch was whisper soft and delicate. Her eyes opened wide as she found the truth of Fairlie's words.

Friends. This time the word was more sure. The trembling of her body eased. Her back straightened.

Fairlie's hand tightened on Nya's. Whatever was to come, none of them—Nya, Fallon, Shaye, Spark, or herself—would be alone.

A new forging had begun.

Chapter 36

It was night. The ship rose and fell on rough swells, and a blizzard filled the air with snow. Nya slipped through the whirling white, intent on the captain's cabin. Her heart pounded. It was all she could do to keep from turning back, but Fairlie was right—she had little to lose.

Though it was late, well past midnight, a light still burned in his cabin. Outside the door, Nya paused and returned to her normal shape. She didn't give herself time to think. She twisted the handle and pushed inside, closing it behind her and locking it.

Leighton sat at his desk, writing in a ledger. A glass of whiskey sat at his left and a fire burned warmly in the woodstove. As the door opened, he looked up and then went still as death.

Slowly Nya walked closer, letting the light of his writing lamp reveal the shape of her Kin face and body. Leighton rubbed a hand over his eyes and slowly stood, but remained behind the desk as if he didn't want to move and frighten her. His eyes focused on her bracelet as it glinted in the candlelight.

"Sherenya?" His voice was raw, almost guttural. "By the gods! At last!" Tears made shining tracks down his cheeks. He started around the desk. Nya took a step back. He halted. "What's wrong?"

His fear was palpable. His hands curled into fists. Pain streaked through Nya. It was inextricably twisted up with longing and need. She quivered, torn between running away and running into his arms. "I am not Sherenya anymore," she said hoarsely. "I am called Nya now."

He ran his fingers through his hair, clearly not seeing the importance of the variation in her name. He could not see that what she was now was just a fragment of the woman she had been. She was less than she was and so much more. The changes were far more than in body alone. She was shackled to the Kin with bonds of majick. She might as well have another lover—another husband. Even if Leighton accepted the physical changes she'd undergone, Nya did not think he could accept what it meant for her to be Warden and Speaker. Her ties to the Kin were as permanent as her marriage bracelet.

"But you've come back to me," he said uncertainly, as if he wasn't sure it was true. "That's why you're here on the *Eidolon*."

Slowly she shook her head. She could not lie to him. Not now that she had come to him at last. It mattered too much. She rocked forward on the balls of her feet, her claws digging into the floor. "I did not know you were captain."

Hurt rippled across his expression and he flushed and then paled. He looked away. "What a bastard you must think me, that what you look like now would matter at all," he said. "So instead you pretend to be dead. I've been bleeding to death since the sea took you. Do you know that?"

Nya's heart spasmed and tears burned in her eyes. She shook her head. "I could not. I am bound elsewhere."

"You're *my* wife!" he said loudly, then glanced quickly at the door. But the snow and the wind made it impossible for anyone outside to overhear. His jaw flexed. "I love you. I never stopped." He looked away, his mouth flattening as if he wished he hadn't spoken. He crossed his arms. "All right. If you're not here for me, if you are *bound* to someone else, then why are you here? What do you want?" His voice was hard and cold.

"I have to return to the Root." Nya shifted her weight uneasily. She didn't know what to say or how to act with him. Every day since she had become spawn, she had ached to see him. When she had dared dream of this moment, she had imagined only repulsion on his face. But the unbelievable truth was that he wasn't repulsed. Instead he was angry and even jealous. He thought she had found another lover. It almost made her laugh hysterically. She had to explain. But how?

"And then what? You'll vanish again? Did I mean anything to you?"

"I'm *spawn*," she said hoarsely.

His chair went flying against the bulkhead as he rounded his desk and gripped her shoulders hard.

"You're my wife," he said again. He grabbed her wrist and held it up. Their marriage bracelets gleamed in the lamplight. "You're *my wife*. I don't care what else you've become. I just want you."

"You don't know it all," she began, but his hand pressed against her mouth.

"So tell me. But it won't change the way I feel. Unless—" He broke off, his face twisting with an alloy of pain, desperation, and fury. "Unless this other man you've bound yourself to means more to you than I?"

She pushed his hand away. "I am bound to no other man," she corrected disdainfully. "I have never wanted anyone but you." The look of doubt and hope that bloomed on his face made the throbbing in her chest flare hot and wild. "If you can want me when you learn what I have become—all that I have become—then I will believe you."

"Tell me."

He led her to the chaise, holding her hand. He did not let go as they sat.

She talked for a full glass, telling him of being Warden and Speaker, of the Kin on the Root, and of her responsibilities to them. She told him of Fallon and Fairlie and why she'd come to Crosspointe. She told him of the fall of the Kalpestrine. At the end she changed form while he watched. And though she searched for the faintest fear or horror in his expression, she saw none. At last she stood before him like a supplicant.

"That's it? Everything? Good and bad?" he asked.

"Yes."

"Fine."

Then he kissed her. It was a passionate kiss, full of hunger and need. His hands ran eagerly over her. Nya pressed against him, just as desperate. She gave a soft gasp of distress when he pulled away, his hands cupping her face.

"It will kill me if you leave me again. If it comes to that, have mercy and cut my throat. It would be kinder."

And then he began kissing her again with a desperation that could not be assuaged.

Chapter 37

Keros helped Ryland rig sails on the ketch and then took the rudder. Soon they were skimming away from the *Eidolon* and out of Narramore Bay.

They each worked in stiff silence. It was a full glass before a stewing Keros broke it.

"Merstone fell truly?"

"Yes."

"How?"

Ryland shook his head. "I can't say."

"This will cripple Crosspointe."

"As it happens, most of the guild were on the mainland at the time. We are without a compass-majicar, however." Ryland said it without a hint of the fear that knotted in his gut. He couldn't let his emotions show. He needed to be strong, now and in the future.

"Are you seriously going to let them leave Crosspointe? Just like that?"

Ryland affected not to know what he meant. How could Keros have known it was Fairlie? "Who do you mean?"

Keros gave him a disgusted look. "Fairlie Norwich. The Root majicar. And the other majicar, whoever he was. Their illusions were very good—I couldn't penetrate Fairlie's or her companion's, but I knew what it was. And the Root majicar—Fallon—he kept the same disguise he wore when we first met him."

Ryland hesitated. He had to be careful. With his father dead, Merstone gone, no compass-majicar, and the merchants and majicars in revolt, not to mention the Jutras threat, it would take little to ignite a conflagration among the people. But his father had trusted Keros. That meant something.

"It was Fairlie. Fallon and Nya went also. And . . . Fairlie's friend," he confirmed.

Keros kicked his legs out, crossing his ankles. "Why? Why let her go? Why let any of them go?"

"It's a long story." Ryland leaned back on the rail, staring at the coastline.

"Isn't it always? What will you do for compasses now?"

"Me?"

"You are the prelate. You are in charge, along with the lord chancellor, at least until a new king is elected."

Ryland stared, then laughed and shook his head. "We will make quite a pair."

"True," Keros said mockingly. "You both seem willing to do most anything to get what you want. No matter how heinous."

Ryland turned and rested his arms on the rail. "I do not much like me," he murmured.

"Neither do I," Keros said without a trace of humor.

The prince glanced over his shoulder at the majicar. "Then we agree on one thing, at least."

Keros grinned. "Maybe you'll make a better prelate than I thought. Why did you let her go?"

Ryland looked back out over the water. "I'd like to say it was because I was her friend, or because it was right. But I don't know. The fact is, right now Crosspointe is safer without her than not."

"*Safer*? That's an intriguing choice of words. How so?"

Ryland shrugged, then let his head dangle. "I made a mistake. A terrible mistake."

"I know you did. But I wonder, what mistake do *you* think you made?"

Should he tell Keros? No. But he needed to tell someone, someone who wasn't family and who wasn't in the guild and who didn't have a stake in all this. Keros fit the bill. Ryland rubbed his hands over his face, then turned around, folding his arms over his chest.

"There was a journeyman majicar who was in love with Fairlie. He came from a wealthy and influential merchant family. He was there when—" He swallowed, digging his fingers into his crossed arms. "He was there when we cursed her. Father couldn't have him telling anyone, so he locked him in a smother room in the castle."

"And?" Keros prompted when Ryland didn't continue.

"And then he escaped. I don't know how. But when he came out, he had abilities he'd never had before."

"What abilities?" Keros asked softly, prompting Ryland again when the silence stretched.

"Mythical. The kind of myth that majicars have been chasing for centuries. He can steal majick. He can rob majicars of their power and pull the majick from spells. I am reasonably certain he could bring down the Pale without raising a sweat."

Keros could only stare. His hands went slack on the rudder. He shook his head in disbelief. "That's— Are you certain?"

"I saw it for myself. The trouble is that he's very, very angry with me and he's not feeling very loyal to Crosspointe." He rubbed his neck. The shard of *sylveth* that Shaye had shoved under his skin still lumped there. It was a warning and a reminder. "I had to let them go. Can you imagine what he could do if I tried to force Fairlie to stay and make compasses? And yet—what a weapon he would make. His power is nearly limitless. So. There you have it. Nothing altruistic about it. Did I do the right thing?"

"I wouldn't want to walk in your shoes," Keros said, reluctant sympathy washing his voice.

Ryland laughed harshly. "Neither do I."

"So what will you do now?"

"Bury my father. After that—go back to playing the game. Whatever else I am, I am a Rampling and I serve as the crown wills."

"Then maybe you should be the one to pick up the crown. Because at least you've a conscience."

"What good does it do if I ignore it? Besides, my father had a conscience," Ryland said without any heat.

"Maybe. He was smart and he had balls the size of the *Eidolon*, but he was also ruthless."

"That's a good trait in a king."

"So is mercy."

"This may not be the time for mercy," Ryland mused.

"If not now, then when?" Keros countered.

Ryland shrugged. He didn't have a good answer. But he did not want to be king. This last month had taught him just how much he neither wanted it nor deserved it. "Anyway, I'm the prelate. I can't be king."

"No? There's always ways around these things." Keros hesitated. "There's something you should consider, before you make up your mind," he said.

"What's that?"

"The fact is that you may make the best king. You don't want to wear the crown, but that isn't really the point, is it?"

Keros held Ryland's gaze for a long moment. Ryland turned away, his stomach clenching. He'd rather cut off his hand. But Keros's words gnawed at him. Would he be better than Vaughn? If Vaughn was alive. He wouldn't know for sure until he was face-to-face with his brother.

Ryland looked over his shoulder at the majicar. "You're a cracking bastard. You know that, don't you?"

"Aye, Highness. I've been told so often."

"If I go after the crown—or if I don't—can I count on you to keep chewing my guts? In case I happen to be deaf to the shouts of my conscience."

Keros hesitated, then nodded, his grin looking strained. "Aye. Can I ask more of you than I ask of myself?"

"All right then."

Ryland watched the shoreline as they skimmed around South Haven and into Blackwater Bay. He trimmed the sails before turning to watch Sylmont grow closer.

"I want to know everything you know," he said, not looking at Keros. "About my father, about his plans, and whatever else might be useful."

"Useful?"

Ryland nodded. "There are decisions to make. Soon."

About the Author

Diana Pharaoh Francis has been a storyteller for as long as she can remember. She tells broad, sprawling, epic stories, and loves magic and its possibilities. She also loves courage and honor and fear and looking at how one person's actions can impact an entire culture or world. She is interested in the way heroes and villains are created.

Diana is a lover of Victorian literature and nineteenth-century Britain, and consequently the Crosspointe books have a strong Victorian flavor. She also loves chocolate, spiced chai, sharp weapons, spicy food, and sparkly jewelry. Diana teaches English at the University of Montana Western. She was raised on a cattle ranch in northern California and spent most of her childhood on horseback or in a book. She spends much of each day writing, and everything becomes fodder for her books. For more about Diana, visit her Web site at www.dianapfrancis.com.

THE BLACK SHIP
A Novel of Crosspointe
by
DIANA PHARAOH FRANCIS

Thorn is a member of the Pilot's Guild—those who possess the magical ability to navigate Crosspointe's deadly seas. When a malevolent master within the Guild bans him from the sea, it seems his life is over. Then he is kidnapped and forced to serve aboard the rogue ship *Eidolon*—pitch black from bow to stern—and Thorn finds himself battling a mad captain, a mutinous crew, and the terrifying magic of the sea.

But there is a saboteur on board, trying to make sure the *Eidolon* never arrives safely in port. Thorn begins to realize his kidnapping may have been no mere chance—and that the cargo the black ship carries may seal his doom…